NO BRAINER

A Teenage Sleuth Thriller

A. J. LAPE

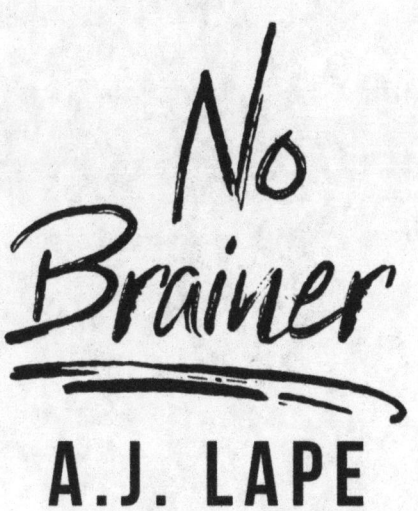

A.J. LAPE

ISBN-13: 978-0-9882641-8-2

Cover by Qamber Designs

This book is dedicated to the little guy who has a dream. You only live once... my wish is that you grab onto the bucking horns of life and hold on until that bull is yours.

Chapter One
COLDBLOODED KILLERS

Dear Darcy,

My cell is cold and damp and the overwhelming taste of mold feels like a man's hands squeezing around my throat. It's hard to breathe sometimes— being alone like this—but the squeaking of the rats in the walls is the only thing that keeps me alive. I had a pet rat once. His name was Reaper. He used to sleep with me and was extremely smart and adaptable. I went away for a week, and my family forgot to feed him. I guess he got hungry because he crawled out of his cage and looked for dinner in my little brother's crib. It wasn't Reaper's fault. He was driven by circumstance...just like me.

*M*y breathing hitched in my chest as I quickly stuffed the letter back inside the Lucasville Prison envelope. It wasn't the time to dissect my fifth correspondence from a cold-blooded killer. But the lunatic, who'd attempted to murder me last spring, had aspirations of making me a jailhouse pen pal. I wasn't sure why I read the letters, but even with several life-in-prison sentences, Wannabe Pen Pal still scared the bejeezus out of me. Why? I'd come to believe the psycho was part cockroach and would survive a nuclear war. Wannabe Pen Pal had been whisked into the back of an ambulance, presumably bound for the graveyard. Some-how, all that crazy survived.

All I knew was I'd always be watching my back...death row or not.

I briefly buried my face in my hands, my breath choking me with the memory. Outrunning a murderer wasn't something a person could file away as the forgettable—you simply prayed your subconscious learned to deal. Unfortunately, I'd just encountered another crime scene that I'd have to process in the recesses of my mind.

The scene looked like any other. Everything remained a clue until proven otherwise. The only items in my room out of place were two dead bodies splayed across the carpet. Rigor mortis had already set in—still, I fumbled helplessly with the body parts and tried to piece them back together. After five heart-pounding minutes, I realized I couldn't resuscitate or sew back together what had been a catastrophic event.

Death was final. I knew that better than anyone.

I'm Darcy Walker, and I fear death will always follow me. I'd been here before—when I was too young to understand—and it sucked like the previous time. I grew up feeling responsible for things that technically weren't my fault, and fate had given me something else I could add to the list.

Never try to outrun fate, I told myself.

The witch had a way of letting you know she had plans you couldn't change.

Last Christmas I received my first pet, a goldfish I'd named after George Washington. It was August, and I'd already endured the deaths of Presidents Washington through Coolidge. Obviously, I lacked in the maternal department. In one of my infamous impulse purchases, I'd bought two hermit crabs the day before I named Frick and Frack. Well, something had happened in the world of Frick and Frack because I just discovered their mutilated corpses in my bedroom, next to the bloody mouth of my BFF, Justice's, black gerbil.

Lesson of the day? Don't gerbil-sit again...ever.

MacArthur (the gerbil, AKA crab murderer), in my meek forensic opinion, was the culprit. Granted, I couldn't justify how two crabs crawled out of a smooth, glass bowl, but MacArthur's two front teeth had no doubt cracked open their shells. I suppose on some level I should be impressed, but the dismembered claws were a grisly visual too hard to erase. Glancing at the blood-splattered gerbil curled peacefully in a ball, I concluded the little bugger was psycho.

While my father and I dropped the crab guts into a Diamond matchbox, I willed my hands to stop shaking as I looked into the round empty fishbowl they'd called home. A crucifix hung above it that was placed there by my nanny when Thomas Jefferson died.

"Help me, Jesus," was all I could mutter.

"Are you okay?" my dad grumbled.

Okay? I had one foot in heck and the other in what-the-freak just happened. "Not really," I answered.

"Did you starve them?"

"No."

"Poison them?"

"No."

"Place them between the pages of a book and jump your godforsaken body all over them?" I gave him a negative nod as I talked myself out of hyperventilating. "Well, I'm tapped out," he grunted, trying futilely to insert humor into an otherwise crappy situation. "Do you have any theories?"

"No, Murphy. I'm theorizing nothing."

My word, if I told him my suspicions about MacArthur, Justice would be looking for a new pet.

My father and I'd been on a first name basis since I'd turned six months old. Murphy stood six foot two with wavy, chestnut brown hair, and deep-set dark, chocolate eyes. His cheekbones were high and chiseled, perched on a flawless angular face except for a scar over his left eye and a crooked nose. To me, they added character. They made him ruggedly real. What didn't make him seem real, however, were his eyes. On a bad day, they looked coldblooded, callous, and uncaring. On good days, they screamed to run to his arms.

For all intents and purposes, he reeked of reformed bad boy...a *fastard*. In Darcyspeak, a fastard was the type to take a woman's heart, rip it out of her chest, and then move onto another girl while she was lying there dying.

Thank God, he'd mellowed and sworn off women.

It was Friday, and I hadn't seen him in two weeks. At sunup, I'd be flying to Florida, and needless to say, happiness was eluding him.

Add the deaths of my hermit crabs, a letter from Wannabe Pen Pal, and he looked like a block of C4 ready to blow.

"I missed you, kid," he grumbled as we made our way downstairs. "And now you're going away again. This will be four weeks total where your father doesn't get to see you. That might be a first."

"After two weeks with Winston, I *need* a vacation."

Murphy gave me his best you're-not-kidding look. Winston sired my father, but let's be real, they loved best from afar. My little sister and I had just returned from our annual vacation at Grandpa Winston's farm in Kentucky. We normally crossed the border the first two weeks in July, but we delayed our trip while he participated in a much-hyped Civil War Reenactment. We all knew how the war ended, but Winston proudly represented a group of men who replayed it for those who failed history class.

After two weeks, I'd hit my limit on his favorite subject too—premarital sex. I'd never had a boyfriend and sixteen was knocking at my door. It was safe to say my virtue remained as intact as the day I popped out of the womb.

I attempted to lighten the mood. "Winston and I talked about boys again. *Soooo*," I said, pausing and laughing naughtily, "guess what I learned?"

Predictably, Murphy bristled up. "This is America, kid, and you have the right to be stupid, but now's not the time for you to exercise your right."

Stupid was my favorite word. It could cover all parts of speech and explain all sorts of behavior. Most might bristle at the word, but according to Murphy (and I had to agree), *Stupid's a frame of mind. It's not an indicator of intelligence.*

Unfortunately, my frame of mind jumped back on the Frick and Frack death wagon as soon as we hit the kitchen. "Maybe they died in some sort of weird copulation ceremony," I muttered. "You know, when they were trying to have baby crabs and things got a little rough." Nothing surprised me anymore, and I didn't know much about the reproductive habits of hermit crabs anyway. All Murphy told me about the opposite sex was that I'd pee the bed if I allowed someone to kiss me before the wedding night.

I longed to pee the bed...I really, really did.

A sigh left his chest. "Can the potty mouth, kid. Your conversations always start in ornery and then nosedive into vulgar."

True.

I didn't use the traditional four-lettered words, but I did have the urge to say things that good breeding claimed was for behind closed doors conversations only. Words like iniquity engineer represented sinners, fastard described the bad boys, habaneros meant the hooters, and the boom boom, hoo-hah was the butt. And to tag a line on all the other sinful behavior I didn't know the meanings of, in the words of Otis Day, I assigned the term shama lama, ding-dong.

Murphy scratched the back of his neck, glanced at the box in his hand, and set the remains on the kitchen countertop with a sigh. He collapsed back onto the brown leather couch in his normal dad attire: white golf shirt, navy shorts, and grass-stained socks. "Give me the 411," he muttered, changing the subject.

Murphy deliberately changed topics—something he always did when relationships, or God forbid, death was on the docket.

I pulled my iPhone out of my back pocket and pitched it on the counter. Kicking off my flip-flops, I crawled onto the sofa, snuggling next to him with the details.

"The usual...sun and fun. Plus, Dylan wants to ride a mechanical bull at a country bar and zip line over gators."

"Country bar?" he grumbled.

"Yeah, it's called Cowboys," I told him. "I figure I'll knock back a few shots of whiskey and then strip on top of the counter."

"Of course," he deadpanned. "Anything less would be a disappointment. What about this gator thing?"

"At Gatorland, you can zip line over breeding gators."

"Make sure to unsnap your harness," he joked.

I burst out laughing and glanced around the four walls, all painted in a neutral shade of khaki. Our house represented your basic single-family unit. Three bedrooms upstairs with a vaulted ceiling and a master bedroom downstairs no one had stepped inside for years. I'd miss it, but it was hardly Norman Rockwell or as exciting as zip lining over gator debauchery.

"I want to see the naughty gators," I said and giggled.

Murphy chuckled, his eyes squinting together. "Kid, your mind is utter filth. You need to work on that."

"I've got a reputation to uphold. I wouldn't want to let my fan club down."

"You put a whole new spin on the term no-brainer," he said, sighing sarcastically. "How much money does gator girl need?"

"Zero."

I vacationed with my best friend, Dylan Taylor, every summer, and his family was loaded. We're talking house-in-Florida kind of loaded. Spring-breaks-in-Maui kind of loaded. Head of the clan, Colton Taylor, worked as a vice president at Go Glam! Cosmetics and made Mark Zuckerberg look dirt poor. Somewhere along the road, I became their stray cat...a privilege that earned an all-expenses paid, annual vacation via their private Learjet. No kidding, a freaking Learjet. If I'd learned anything, you made a major faux pas if you tried to foot the bill for even a pack of gum. Colton had a few rules: the biggest, he paid. The money Murphy sent was reserved for clothing, gifts for my little sister, or a random donation to the destitute or homeless.

Murphy mumbled, "I need to sell eye shadow."

"What's for dinner?" I asked.

Murphy was still stuck in eye shadow. "Dogs and burgers," he finally muttered, "but first on the list is a burial. Sweet Jesus," he prayed, or maybe he was swearing. "I hate burials. Plus, I have to find a murderer."

I had to agree. Even though my mouth watered for a hot dog— my favorite food—dead animal parts took precedence. Especially when the temperature was sweltering like an erupting volcano, and they'd begun to smell.

I live in Valley, a suburb of Cincinnati, OH, and the temperature had topped out at ninety-nine degrees. Half dressed in cut-off jean shorts and a white tank, that small amount of clothing did little to combat a heat index of one hundred and ten. The humidity grabbed me around the throat and squeezed like...

"Holy hell," I finished out loud.

Murphy elbowed me so hard he might've snapped a rib. "Quit cursing, kid. The house is at an acceptable climate of seventy-six degrees," he rattled off. "Watch your mouth, and drink a glass of water." Murphy went ape poopoo when someone messed with the thermostat. Keeping his electric bill low was science, but he wasn't necessarily cheap. He merely liked to beat the system...or gamble.

My little sister, Marjorie, swan dived in between us, her pink dress riding high above her hips. She sang, "Jesus loves me," and I thought of my two dead crabs. Ugh, I didn't want to touch that song any more than I wanted someone to slice my gut open.

"Hey, M," I grunted.

With almond-shaped, brown eyes and fire engine red, wavy hair, we rarely called her Marjorie. I nicknamed her M as a baby, afraid she'd never figure out how to spell her eight-lettered name. She had it mastered by age two.

"Well..." she started.

I heard that song "Killing Me Softly" in my brain. Marjorie tended to be the "wordy" type. Starting a sentence with "well," meant a thirty-minute recap of a thirty-second exchange.

"Well, *what?*" I asked, wincing.

"I'm in love with Bobby Gerber. We're going to get married or maybe live together."

"Oh, God," Murphy prayed. "Live together?"

"You know, combine their resources in this time of economic woe," I said, giggling loudly.

Murphy kneed me in the thigh. "You're messed up ten ways from Sunday, kid."

Marjorie looked confused, assuming he'd addressed her. "I'm not messed up ten ways from Sunday. I don't even know what that means." I didn't either, but Murphy talked in religious-speak when he was beside himself. "I've just found the man I love," she added, smiling big.

Murphy mumbled to the ceiling about going to church more. "Marjorie, that kid is twisted, and you're both too young to have boyfriends."

Murphy made sure of that at the beginning of the summer. There was a guy named Liam Woods who I'd gotten close to at the end of sophomore year...it was inevitable. The psycho student—eh, Wannabe Pen Pal—wanted both of us dead and nearly succeeded with Liam by employing some black belt karate skills. Trouble was, Liam graduated in May, and things fizzled out before they really got started. He visited a few times, but we wound up watching movies or watching Murphy watch *us*. I think it humored Liam, but he moved to Alabama three weeks earlier to attend Auburn University on a swimming scholarship. Let's just say he'd either drowned or found a new girlfriend.

"She said *marry*," I clarified.

Murphy tried, but his patience expired before it reached full maturation. He stared at her, back at me, debated whether to be politically correct, and just blurted out, "He's stupid."

"He's bad?" Marjorie frowned.

Murphy grunted, "A bad apple, kid."

No kidding. Bobby loved to blow crap up. Unfortunately, I was the type that often needed his employ. I'd given him ten bucks for various jobs over the years. In my little corner of the world, I liked to think I'd taught him the value of self-employment. Come to think of it, I wonder if Bobby had paid Frick and Frack a visit.

Murphy smelled under both his arms, slid a glance in my direction, and then narrowed his eyes on Marjorie. "Please tell me you aren't wearing your sister's voodoo cream."

"I am," she beamed. "Claudia said I needed to start early because Darcy's boobies aren't responding."

"Sweet Jesus," Murphy whispered.

Claudia Gonzalez is my Puerto Rican nanny. She practiced what Murphy considered the Dark Arts (ahem, voodoo), and at the top of her list was a potion that promised to provide an ample bosom. She claimed the answer lay in the crescent moon, so during that phase I slathered on a paste concocted by her and her sister. The cream was bogus. I was barely a B-cup and experiencing hot flashes and unnatural chest hair growth.

Marjorie smelled like she'd been dabbling in the goo.

"Claudia said the smell means it's working," she said, grinning big.

"I figured that meant it was rotting," Murphy muttered, "but who am I to judge what is clearly science?"

Murphy did sarcasm better than anyone.

The conversation predictably sailed over her head. "That's right, Daddy, don't judge. But if you must know, it's comprised of witch hazel and island plant life."

Murphy snorted. "Well, you've got the witch part right." Murphy was petrified of the spirit world and even more petrified of anything that had to do with Claudia's sister. Murphy read the part in the Bible over and over about the Antichrist ushering in the end of the world...he believed Claudia's sister might be the vessel delivering it.

He pushed all three of us off the couch and ambled over to the countertop and picked up the Diamond matchbox.

"Make yourself useful, kid," he said to me, opening the back door to scout for a burial plot. He pivoted to Marjorie. "Follow me. We're going to have a little refresher course on appropriate six-year-old behavior." She skipped behind him, not having a clue the two of us together probably warranted a visit from child protective services.

My MacBook Air sat on the countertop. I powered it up and keyed in the webpage for the *Orlando Sentinel*. Each time I left for vacation, I read the community blogs to find out the gossip in town. I scrolled through the main headlines: "Man Arrested for Striking Son with Pizza; Alligator Caught Strolling Upscale Neighborhood; and Five-year-old Boy Still Missing." I read the opening paragraph about the pizza and found my way back to the story on the missing child. That story piqued my curiosity, and even though school records indicated I had a 160 IQ (shocking, I know), it took a lot to hold my interest.

One of the ADHD (Attention Deficit and Hyperactivity Disorder), oftentimes my mind had one idea, and my body had another. People like me wound up trying harder than everyone else or giving up and embracing the inevitable: a life of never really hitting the mark. Tending to have obsessive tendencies, I knew what it felt like to be an outsider, realizing you were different, knowing short of a miracle, not a whole lot ever changed. Did it shape who I was? Absolutely. That was one reason why I interfered when I shouldn't. Why I helped when no one needed it. Why I broke the rules even when forbidden. I sought change and was a sucker for happy endings.

Sometimes it brought hope. Other times it oozed stupidity.

One thing I had going for me was I happened to be a verb. Opening up the refrigerator, I got my verb on and pulled out the condiments, chomped into a pickle spear, and scanned the opening paragraph of the *Orlando Sentinel*.

ORLANDO, FL. Orange County officials are reporting there has been a shift in the case of the disappearance of Cisco Medina. Originally focusing on the thousands of leads that flooded their switchboard, authorities are now of the opinion that Fernando and Guadalupe Medina have not been totally forthcoming in the ongoing investigation of the disappearance of their five-year-old grandson.

Cisco Medina disappeared on his way home from a public park in early February, which launched a nationwide manhunt. No body or ransom ever entered the picture, and an exhaustive search produced no workable leads.

The Medinas, who reported their grandson missing, have thrown another confusion into the investigation by leaving town a month ago and not informing authorities. They had been awarded legal guardianship of their grandson when his mother, Lola Medina, lost him in a high stakes poker game with an undercover policeman when he was two.

In a news release on the sixth month anniversary of his disappearance, authorities reported that his mother, along with his father, are not considered suspects in the case and both have "air tight alibis on the night of his disappearance."

According to the news release, "At the time of his disappearance, the mother was found on video at Walmart off John Young Parkway, and the father, Hank Henry, was seen on television showing his dog in a local dog show."

A trust that finances private investigators was set up in Cisco's name by Elmer Herschel, the landlord of the apartment complex where the Medinas lived. When interviewed by the *Sentinel*, Herschel stated, "I'm shocked the grandparents skipped town. They were a nice couple, but I guess everyone has secrets."

According to the authorities, even if the child surfaces with his grandparents, guardians are required to check in with Child Services and the Medinas are in violation of that agreement. Any information you may have, please contact the Orange County's

I grabbed another pickle and washed it down with a Coke while I wondered where Cisco was. An incorrigible snoop, I could sniff out the biggest stories that professionals couldn't catch a whiff of even if right under their noses. I'd done that with Wannabe Pen Pal. Problem was, going balls-to-the-wall had fallout. The student almost killed our assistant principal whose recovery had been brutal.

But should I get involved with Cisco Medina? For God's sake, it sounded like a job for the Army, Navy, Air Force, or Marines. Still, for some insanely, idiotic reason, I couldn't let it go—although I knew nothing apart from a few paragraphs in an online newspaper and had only two weeks to work with.

A smart person would leave the job to the professionals. A dumb person wouldn't know enough to care. An idiot would contact the newspaper...and lie.

My actions weren't exactly what I'd call a good life-choice, but the longer Cisco was unaccounted for, the colder the trail got. The colder the trail got, the more he'd be relegated to a cold case file. Cold case files were essentially when the authorities folded, or destiny said it was not the time to right your particular wrong.

Been there. Done that. Sucked.

I fired up my email account and typed a few sentences, changed my mind, and decided for a more direct approach. Thumbing the digits for the *Orlando Sentinel* into the house phone, after four rings, an overworked voice answered. "Troy here," he muttered. "Make it front page or go away."

I stood up straight, finding my big-girl voice. "Hello, I have a lead in the Cisco Medina case."

A sweat mustache instantly formed over my lip. "Is that right?" he said chuckling. "Well, sweetie, no one's had a lead on Cisco Medina for months."

"Well, I do," I lied. "And don't call me sweetie."

Rustling paper, amidst sidesplitting laughter. "You don't like sweetie, huh? How about babe?"

"Listen, dude, are you sexist?"

"Who me?" he mocked, his voice innocent. "*Nooooo*, I love women."

"Sure feels like you're sexist to me. Just because I have ovaries, it doesn't mean I can't hang with the boys." My God, I needed to shut up.

"Okay, Miss Ovaries. If you can find Cisco Medina, then you're the Messiah I've been waiting for. My boss just called me 'a frigging dipwad.' Don't make me die a frigging dipwad, babe."

"Well, I'm better than a frigging dip wad," I said confidently. Whatever that was.

My cell phone blasted, I got spooked, and butter-fingered the phone off into never-never land. When I lunged for the receiver, my hand guiltily knocked over the pickle jar. Pawing at the air, I quickly grabbed my laptop and set it off to the side. Unfortunately, I toppled the jar again, and juice splashed me in the face like Orcas attacking a herd of seals. Watching the liquid ripple across the countertop, I snatched the phone from the floor, said "Hello" three more times, realizing we'd disconnected. Whoever had dialed my cell, though, was the persistent type. It had gone to voicemail twice and right then belted out a tune by the late eighties-nineties band Milli Vanilli, my song choice of the month.

Feeling my way to the sound, I grasped the phone and glanced down at the number. It came as no surprise the proverbial good boy in my life was rearing his not-so-ugly head. Dylan had a metaphysical ability to show up at the precise moment I was making a mess out of my day or someone else's.

Dabbing my face with a hand towel, I clicked the speaker with my thumb. "Hullo?"

"Hey, sweetheart," he murmured. "How's my girl?"

Let's think about it...covered in pickle guts. "In a pickle," I mumbled.

Chapter Two

THE BIG MAN

mong Polynesian tribes, there was a big man.

"Big Man Theory" was one of those unspoken things. He wasn't by birth destined to rule, but there was a certain something in his swagger that made him the natural leader. So much so, his mere presence trumped the royal bloodline. As a result, most Big Men were probably forced to watch their backs. My best friend, Dylan Taylor (my Big Man), however, was always busy watching mine.

Everyone wanted a personal bodyguard, and I suppose that was what Dylan was to me. In fact, he fought off the armed student until the unspeakable happened, and the police grounded the shooter like a rabid animal. That, in a nutshell, was Dylan. He didn't care if odds were stacked against him—he understood what needed to be done and hit the play button. It wasn't just the situation with the shooter that made him my hero though. Certain circumstances in my childhood forced me to think of other things—adult things— and before I knew it, my mind was obsessed with so many minutia that I forgot what relaxed looked and felt like. Dylan became my grounding force. He had a quality about his heart that was pure. The weaker you were, the stronger he became to build you back up.

Most never got to experience a love that deep, but we'd been holding hands since we were six years old. Whether through mud pies, backyard baseball, or preschool overnights, we'd always been the other's preferred companion. When someone had that effect on you, it was hard to reconcile those emotions. In some respects, he was a best friend: keeping secrets, talking me through catastrophes, and fighting my battles. In others, he'd been a brother: a ponytail yank, squabbles over meaningless matters, and a kick in the seat of the pants. Still, at times, he parented me: a nurturer, loving disciplinarian, and always accessible.

Every year, I branded him with a new pseudonym, primarily because of the evolving status of those feelings. Right then was the Big Man—not only for reasons of pecking order—for reasons of stature.

We'd always done everything together, even growing inches in sync, but by the end of sophomore year, he'd gone off and left me heightwise. Thankfully, my endocrine system heard my nightly prayer, and I coasted at five foot nine. Dylan, however, rocketed into legendary status. When he jumped, it was five inches higher. When he ran, he clocked two seconds faster. And when he smiled, it grew half an inch wider.

Big Man league in my book.

Mouthwatering, testosterone-in-motion in everyone else's book.

"Wake up, sleepy head. Let's go see Mickey." That deep baritone voice, no doubt, belonged to Dylan. I peeled back an eye, scanned the perimeter, and peeked at the figure squatted within a breath of my face. Yup, it was him: deep voice and sexy as all get out, but on a boy that the Best Friend Rule said was "hands off."

An imposing two hundred and twenty pounds, his muscles were strong, defined, and built like they'd been chiseled from the finest granite. Then there was the hair. All of that package topped itself off with a short, jet-black mane he wore in one of two ways: classic and stylish around his strong brow and cheekbones or modern-messy like he'd just rolled out of bed. Right then, he rocked it messy, and messy looked...oh, my word. I pictured him rolling around in the sheets and almost said, *Mmmm*.

"You're confusing me," I said on an exhale.

Dylan giggled, not having a clue of the filth lurking in my mind. He blinked slowly, snapping me awake with butterscotch eyes that looked taboo.

"Go away," I groaned. "You've got morning breath."

His smile quirked up at one corner. "Crawl on over here and let me taste your mouth, sweetheart. I promise it will be a good experience."

I think I might've died for a second...

Groaning harder, I rolled onto my stomach. I hated him...I hated him and his flirty mouth. Whenever he talked like that, I remembered when the school's supposed dream girl, Brynn Hathaway, suction-cupped his lips right in front of me. Let's just say he wasn't repulsed.

"Come on, Darc," he teased. "Don't make me get rough with you. Murphy said I could if the situation called for it."

Only Murphy would allow Dylan into his sleeping daughter's room. He thought Dylan was perfect. Other boys would have a better chance of remaining suntan-free in the land of hot lava than waking me in the dark. Dylan, however, was given the key to the city.

Dylan, Dylan, Dylan, I thought. If Murphy ever heard, you'd be gumming your meals, tongueless.

"It's too early," I whined.

He tenderly ran the backs of his knuckles down my cheek. "I know five-thirty is early, Darc, but Dad has decreed that we're in the air by eight o'clock sharp." Dylan's family—who I referred to as the Greek god immortals—was chomping at the bit for vacation too. Normally, we traveled to Florida the first two weeks after school released, but apparently, the world of cosmetics had a crisis with their new lip gloss. One thing led to another, and here we were two weeks before school began on our annual trip to their second home in Florida. It was in a neighborhood named Serendipity—the country club of the stars.

"I'm tired, D. Give Mickey my regards, and send me a postcard," I mumbled, and then rolled to my side.

Dylan yanked back the covers, seducing me with what smelled like a cup of java. "Get up. I brought you some black coffee. Evidently, I should've brought a pot." No kidding. Problem was, as a hyperactive person, coffee oftentimes relaxed me. There was a good chance I'd get up. An even greater chance I'd fall into a coma.

"Cookie?" I said, grinning and rising up on my elbows.

"No, a doughnut." Coffee was one of my 3Cs along with a Coke and a cookie. The 3Cs kept my body running in its less than optimal state. A doughnut wasn't a cookie, but it would serve as a close substitute.

"Maybe I should kiss you after all," I said and laughed.

Dylan's deep chuckle traveled all the way to my bones. "We don't have enough time for the kind of kissing I'm interested in, sweetheart. That's going to take a long weekend, handcuffs, and the fire department on-call."

Holy Mother, hose me down. There was no good reason why I reacted that way, but I chalked it up to dumb and blonde...and maybe a little bit of PMS.

Dylan grinned. "I love you," he said.

"Always," I answered. Dylan and I always said we loved one another. Whoever uttered those three words first, the other ended the sentiment with "always."

I fumbled around on the nightstand for my glasses, sliding them on my nose. My glasses were librarian-friendly in a rectangular Burberry black. They made me look studious. Surely that was a capital crime. Once I squinted into focus, Dylan pulled me out of bed as I looped my arms up around his neck. My knee socks hung at my ankles, and Murphy's plaid button-down shirt I'd slept in was rumpled above my boxer shorts. Not head-turning bedroom lingerie by any means, but then again, it was me. Androgynous was kind of my thing.

Dylan ran his hands up and down my back, giving me one heck of a massage.

"You've got great hands," I moaned.

He giggled like a twelve-year-old boy. "Any chance I get to squeeze my hands around you, I'm going to take."

I moaned again. "You say that to all the girls."

"I don't say that to everyone. But seriously, if you don't stop moaning, I'm going to forget you're my best friend."

I wasn't positive, but I was pretty sure one of my legs might've wrapped around his. Dylan growled like a wild animal, sending shivers to places that shouldn't have shivers. "Sweetheart, if you wanted to get up close and personal all you had to do was ask."

I kneed him in the femur, realizing when he talked that way the balance of power shifted. I needed to regain the upper hand, and it didn't help that my involuntary reactions didn't give a flying flip about my dignity. Holy crud, I didn't have any dignity—that was the problem.

"You're ridiculous," I said with a snort. "And you're a flirt."

Dylan shrugged away the comment, knowing it was common knowledge. "Shower and get dressed," he murmured, releasing me with a smile in his voice. "It's going to be a scorcher."

"What should I wear?" Dylan sported black athletic shorts, flip-flops, and a white T-shirt making him appear darker than his normally olive complexion. He looked like a XXX daydream.

"You always look beautiful," he murmured.

Open to criticism. "Uh-huh," I said, laughing in disbelief. "You only say that because you're my best friend."

Dylan's eyes instantly seemed conflicted, like something else clouded his mind taking more energy than he preferred. A protracted silence fell between us, and then he gave me one slow blink, his lips parting a fraction in the process. "No," he said softly. "You're the most beautiful thing I've ever seen."

There were too many levels of weird going on. I mean, what the heck had he been thinking anyway? We were friends—best friends —and the Best Friend Rule declared him as a no-no. I shook off the confusion, wanting to get to Florida ASAP—excited for that slice of Heaven called vacation and even more excited for the deviancy to follow.

"Gimme a sec," I said, grinning and praying those deviant intentions weren't written on my face.

Grabbing some white shorts, a heather gray halter top, and discreetly stuffing underwear between them, I skipped into my bathroom, closed the door, and peered in the mirror. *God help me*. I laughed to myself. I prayed last night for an aesthetic miracle and still looked like a butt crack when I opened my eyes.

I had dirty-blonde hair and puke-green eyes. I'd like to think they were hazel, and maybe on cloudy days they sparkled like emer-alds, but mostly they seemed as dull and washed out as my hair. I had a few curves and muscles, but I didn't possess the attributes that made the girl-next-door memorable. Tall had to be shapely, and blonde had to be beautiful. Sort of blonde on one hundred and thirty pounds didn't say memorable. It basically said, *Get your hand out of the cookie jar.*

I shrugged it away, opting to embrace my deficiencies.

Turning the dial on my antique radio, I scanned the local stations until I landed on WEBN. As I hummed away to "School's Out" by Alice Cooper, I took a two-minute dip in the shower and inserted my contacts. Once I was 20/20, I blew my hair out straight and slapped on some makeup. For me, that included lip gloss and mascara with the occasional trifecta of blush.

Since my brain was back online, details of last night's dream slowly came trickling in. I'd dreamt of Cisco Medina. Holed up in a closet, he cried endlessly to a captor who treated him like a pet, rarely acknowledged. Watching him writhe in mental pain, I woke with a nervous spell and shakes so violent they would've tipped a battleship.

Spying the portable phone I'd left on the sink, all at once I had the burning impulse to call the sexist newspaperman I'd spoken with the day before. I needed a bone...and he was the man to throw it. Turning the faucet on full blast—so Dylan wouldn't hear—I got my verb on and thumbed in the number for the *Orlando Sentinel* that I'd memorized. Hoping he was a workaholic, I almost zapped the call when he finally mumbled, "Make it front page or go away."

"Hey, sexist dude," I greeted.

A moment went by where he processed my words, but then I felt that flirty sarcasm ooze through the receiver. "Well, well, well, if it isn't Miss Ovaries."

"*Ms.*," I corrected him.

"Right," he said and chuckled, "*Ms.* Ovaries. So where'd you go yesterday? Out into the street to burn your bra?"

I imagined myself killing him with a baseball bat. "No, my bra is just fine. I wanted you to know that I'd give you the specifics regarding Cisco Medina later."

"Sounds to me like you're stalling."

"Listen, sexist dude..."

"Call me Troy."

"Okay, sexist dude-slash-Troy. In the words made famous by the movie *Johnny Dangerously*, you sound like a 'fargin icehole.'"

"A fargin' icehole," he said laughing.

"Yeah, that's the Disney version, but I know if I can't handle your verbally offensive remarks that exponentially decreases my odds of getting anywhere."

"Ms. Ovaries, you might actually be smart. What experience do you have?"

"Three people were murdered in my hometown, and I solved those cases in two weeks. Top that, bud."

"I don't believe it."

"Believe it," I bragged, "so bow down. I also survived being abducted by some robotic, confusingly delicious hulk-of-a-man who drove a yellow Dodge Charger."

The day the crazy student wreaked havoc all over my high school, Dodge Charger man showed up, stuffed me in the trunk of his car, and then informed me he'd kept the psycho from killing me on a separate occasion. His advice was to stay close to another man nicknamed Jaws, but I hadn't seen nor heard from either of them since the incident. And it wasn't for a lack of trying.

"Child's play," Troy joked. "I did all of that when I was eight."

"Throw me a bone," I said frowning.

"Here's your bone...read the story."

"Already did, nimrod." He actually laughed.

"Read deeper, but the story is there, Ms. Ovaries. Sniff it out." Then he hung up.

I cocked my head to one side, contemplating the methods I'd use to accomplish what no one else had been able to in six months. Not a clue, but I'd figure it out once my feet hit the Orlando soil. Securing the last of my toiletries, I opened the door and saw that Dylan had made my bed and was wheeling my luggage to the hall, packed and ready to go.

"Thanks," I said, giggling in a throaty sound. I didn't get around to packing, mostly because I was lazy. At least, my clothes had been in piles. Thing was, two weeks of underwear sat right on top— Dylan got a load of my bra size.

Shoving that thought down, I threw my toiletries into a tote bag as Dylan motioned to my chest of drawers that held a Starbucks cup of coffee and a Krispy Kreme doughnut. In my book, Krispy Kreme doughnuts were manna from Heaven dropped from the sky.

Shoveling the doughnut in my mouth, I snagged the coffee and walked out into the hallway when Murphy stumbled toward us with his wallet.

"Have a good time, kids. I'll miss you both." Murphy was shirtless, wearing black sweatpants and a ratty white ballcap, pulled down over his eyes. My theory was he liked to block out the world. He didn't like many people. Dylan was on the short-list.

While he stuffed traveler's checks and a wad of twenties in my hand, his bedroom door swung wide and out marched my little sister—wearing one of my bras and a pair of panties, safety-pinned at the waist.

I fought a laugh. Sad thing was they fit her about as well as they fit me.

She ran forward and latched onto Dylan's leg. He stiffened like he was moments from the death rattles settling in. He then sighed, opened his mouth, and repeated the sequence again.

"You just lost your tan," I mumbled, swallowing the rest of the doughnut. Dylan set the luggage down and reluctantly hugged her with stiff arms. "What's that smell?" he asked wincing.

Oh, Lordy. You couldn't deny the Latin American voodoo.

"Booby cream," Marjorie explained smiling. She put her hands on her hips, spun around, and gave him her best centerfold shot. "Do I look like I have boobies yet?"

Dylan tried to beam himself to Mars. "Not yet," he whispered. "You're killing me," he said even lower.

"Sweet Jesus," Murphy prayed. I likewise turned and struck my best pin-up pose. Arms over my head, butt, and boobs stuck out at awkward angles.

"What about *me*, D?" I said and giggled. "Do *I*..."

Murphy went cuckoo for Cocoa Puffs, slamming both of his hands over my mouth, rattling my teeth. "Shut up, Darcy," he warned. Seriously, it was only for the joke. I still wore a training bra. I trained and I trained. They rebelled and rebelled.

"Keep Darcy on a short leash, son," Murphy groaned. "She's due something bad, and don't let her drag you down with her."

Murphy was right. I usually choked on the chain or tripped the person controlling me. Dylan sucked in a bunch of air, his inner-Boy Scout in danger of getting dirty. Standard SOP. I gave him an evil Cheshire grin...*notsayingaword*.

Chapter Three

GREEK GODS

Colton Taylor is fifty percent Greek, so branding his family the Greek god immortals was like capitalizing on a joke the universe already teed up for you. Truth of the matter, they fit the part. Each possessed flawless skin, and it wouldn't surprise me if they munched on ambrosia and nectar as they flitted from cloud to cloud. Honest to God, I probably ought to rethink our entire relationship. It wasn't easy to hang with the beautiful people when I had the self-esteem of a festering boil.

True to his Greek nature, he'd named his business jet, Pegasus. Pegasus was kept at Lunken Airport near the Ohio River. Flights went in-and-out of Lunken twenty-four hours a day.

Dylan parked his black, fully loaded, large class BMW on the runway next to the airplane. Evidently, he'd been a good boy because his birthday gift was a car whose sticker price represented the average yearly income of people who lived on my street.

If being good was a prerequisite, I'd be lucky to snag a cup of phlegm.

As he retrieved my baggage from the trunk, I stepped out of the car and bounded up the stairs. The Cincinnati air resembled a roasted marshmallow—hot, wrinkly, and full of black gunk. When I had vacation on my mind, I couldn't care less if I were tarred beyond all recognition.

"Excited?" I heard Dylan chuckle from behind. I gave him a

dismissive wave as I scaled up the first six steps, leaping over the last two like a kangaroo. Sounded easy enough, but my flip-flop decided to flip while I was flopping, and I crashed down on one knee landing chin first—and butt last—into the cabin. It was a teeth-jarring thud, and I momentarily wondered if a wheel had fallen off. I army-crawled toward the sounds of happy campers and the smell of fresh fruit, pastries, summer sausage...and big sigh, Dakota "Cody" Wayne.

Cody always smelled *gooood*. A confirmed bachelor, he piloted Pegasus and just might be the first crush I'd ever had. He had thick brown hair and at six feet tall was pure muscle, raging testosterone with a scar down the right side of his face that made him the scary kind of hot. To top it all off, he had Hershey bar eyes. Add "war hero" to his résumé...and he was one big yum.

Dylan's father read an interview after Cody retired from active Army service where he said he didn't want to fly commercial, but he wanted to find a family. Whatever Colton Taylor wanted, Colton Taylor usually got. So he tracked him down and offered him the deal of a lifetime.

My hormones stopped when I made it to Cody's black leather shoes. "Hey Cody," I mumbled, grinning and latching onto those Hershey bar eyes.

"Welcome aboard, Darcy," he murmured, squatting down and tipping my chin upward. "You really know how to make an entrance."

One way to term stupidity.

Pulling me up, Cody greeted me with a warm smile, dressed in black slacks, white shirt, with a gray winged horse monogrammed on the bottom of his black tie.

"Pratfall is sort of my specialty," I said, adding a shrug. No kidding. A thirty-six-inch inseam left you to your own klutzy devices.

After I attempted to straighten my clothes, I extended my hand to shake his, but he tugged me into an embrace. "You're family," he said chuckling. "I only get to see you once a year, and you've grown. You've also had your braces removed. Colton said you were lovely, and I must say the man never lies."

Cody sweet-talked like his tongue had been coated in sugar. Let's be honest, anything was an upgrade. I not only had to work through a gawky body but some goddawful teeth. My canines looked vampiric, my molars were impacted, and my front teeth framed a crossbite so severe the doctor needed graph paper to line them up properly. Since the braces were dunzo, I wasn't sure what I had. I honestly tried not to dwell.

I pulled back, sniffing his breath. "Have you had your head in a beer bong?"

Cody crossed his arms over his chest. "Darcy, there's nothing you won't say."

Oh, yeah, there was. I'd like to ask what was underneath his clothes but opted against it. I glanced back as Dylan boarded the plane, his smile branching wide and unusually delicious.

"Are you flirting with Cody?" he murmured and chuckled. "I prefer when you flirt with *me*."

I frowned, followed by a loud snort. I didn't flirt. Flirting was his department. Darcy Walker was a self-assured verb who had no time for men. "I refuse to flirt with you," I said with little conviction.

Dylan wrapped his arms around my waist, his voice rumbling low in my ear. "Is that right? Your body insinuated something differently this morning."

Yup, my tongue was suddenly mute.

Most people had a fraction of pride, and my minuscule amount demanded it was the time to issue a denial. Thing was, I liked the way his arms felt, and the ravenous feelings he'd given me lately tempted me to go to Badgirlville and never return. But Lord, was it confusing. One minute I wanted to spit on his food. The next I wanted to dance in a red corset and black stockings. Do something really nasty. So the truth was, my mouth said one thing...my body said another.

Schizophrenia at its finest.

Dylan knuckled Cody's hand. "Good morning, Cody."

"Good morning," Cody said. "I was just telling Darcy how she's quite the catch."

Dylan groaned as though someone gutted him but surprisingly remained wordless. Cody's eyes clicked on mine with a wink.

"Cody's had his head in a beer bong, D. You might need to fly the plane."

Dylan's mouth still didn't work.

"I've got Bullet," Cody said and laughed.

"Bullet's not breathing," I said. Bullet Wallace copiloted Pegasus. He wasn't a man of few words. He was a man of no words. Also an Army veteran (rumored Delta Force), he led the unit that rescued Cody from a desert grave when his fighter jet crashed. His light brown hair lay graying at the temples with an unknown eye color hidden behind his shades. As big as a dinosaur, he weighed about two hundred and fifty pounds of I'm-hotter-than-shiz. I'd only seen him stand once but estimated him to be taller than average and like Cody, mid-thirties.

Bullet swiveled in his seat and gave me a two-fingered salute. My tongue stuck to the roof of my mouth. I stared. He stared. The whole dang plane wondered why we were staring. *Gah!* Teenage hormones...I was all over the place and positive I'd just flirted with three males.

Thankfully, Cody clapped both his hands together as if he'd remembered something. Bullet bent down retrieving a white bag, tossing it over. "Bullet and I bought you something," Cody murmured.

He pulled a black ballcap out of the bag for Dylan and a silver-wrapped box, bowed in red for me. *Please be chocolate*, I prayed. *I promise I'll be a good girl.*

I heard a laugh and didn't know if that was Heaven or me.

"You didn't," Dylan whispered. He ran his hand through his jet-black hair and looked at him with sincerity. "Is this legit?"

"Gen-u-*ine*," Cody said in a Southern drawl. My guess was Cody and his accent originated from Georgia, but the further south you went, everyone sounded like fried chicken and black-eyed peas anyway.

Dylan admired his cap that said "Ranger" monogrammed in yellow-gold on the front, turning it end-over-end like a rare artifact he was inspecting. Finally, he gently shoved it on his head and touched his heart. Dylan had two characteristics that were a window to his soul. He'd stroke his heart if something moved him deeply, or he'd run his hand through his hair or rearrange his hat. Right then, he was doing both.

"Open yours, beauty," Cody said to me. Carefully removing the bow, I passed it to Dylan and unwrapped a book entitled *Atlas of the Stars*.

Crap...cue the water works.

Since childhood, I'd been a stargazer. I'd been flying with Cody since age nine, and apparently, he'd remembered our conversations.

"You're welcome," Cody said, smiling and hugging me once more. "You remind me of someone I care about very much." Cody breathed deep, his chest catching some strong emotion that nearly floored him. When it clearly became overwhelming, he gave a quick jerk of his head, gasping twice. *Well, well, well*, I thought. Cody had an unrequited love in his life. Star-crossed lovers? Destiny dictated you crossed paths, but fate said the love was short-lived?

Dylan and Bullet talked about the weather just to ease the moment.

After another round of *thank yous*, I snagged a cup of coffee, two danishes, a spoonful of eggs, and a link sausage for breakfast number two. I skipped over the fruit and whole grain options—unfortunately, that fairy skipped over my bassinet.

Traveling to the middle of the plane, I got a sleepy wave from Dylan's twelve-year-old brother, Zander, as he pulled a navy blanket out from an overhead bin. "I call dibs," he said, grinning and glancing at my legs.

"Hey, Hot Stuff," I muttered, a sausage hanging out of my mouth like a cigarette.

Zander, I'd nicknamed "Hot Stuff," because he was a boiling over hormone in the throes of puberty. Zander loved girls, and at the moment, he loved *me*. Around five foot three, he was built like a scarecrow and still wearing Super Hero pajamas. He was his mother's mirror image, but God love him, his toes curled like a pigeon's, and his knees knocked together when he walked. Evidently, everyone couldn't be a Greek god even if it lay buried in the DNA. We should probably talk about the Super Hero PJs, regardless. He should've chucked those around age eight.

"I'm going back to sleep, Darcy, but I had to say hello to the woman of my dreams."

He tiptoed up, kissing me on the cheek. "Pleasant dreams," I said not able to stop my patented you're-stupid stare.

Zander navigated past Dylan's doppelgänger typing away on his open laptop. Dylan and his father had the same star quality: knockout face, deep-set dimples, and sexy-as-sin mole in the corner of their left eye. The only notable difference lay in the color of the iris. His father's shone as black as the mystery of night.

At six foot three and cut like a body-builder, Colton Taylor had been well on his way to becoming a professional basketball player after college at UCLA. When that dream blew up along with his knee senior year, his backup plan was to follow in his father's footsteps and become an LA police detective. Problem was, his father was legendary for eating more lead than anyone on the force and somehow surviving. When his mother discovered he'd signed up for a life of dodging bullets, she got all Greek, went into seclusion, and he bailed after a few years to find a job in the business world. To say he was successful would be an understatement. Colton Taylor could sell paper to a tree.

Normally dressed to kill, he was ready for the holiday, wearing black board shorts and a matching T-shirt with his left leg bouncing in leather slides.

He pitched his chin to the seat across from him. "Sit, Darcy. I've missed you."

I mumbled behind the sausage. "I called you twice, Mister Taylor."

"Call me, Colton, dear, and you *returned* my calls," he clarified. "There's a difference. I don't like going two weeks without speaking to you." Some people collected stamps. Others cars. Dylan's father collected people. If he cared for you, he'd insert himself into every aspect of your life, wanting to know where you were at all times of the day. Like his son, he had a knack of showing up when I was minutes from disorderly conduct.

You know...*fun*.

He focused on my plate, rolling his eyes with a sigh. "You eat too much sugar. I worry about what you're doing to your body."

No, kidding. My pancreas was probably PO'd.

I collapsed in the seat directly in front of him, separated by a tray table. Most people flew knee-to-knee making nice with the folks sitting next to them. We were flying in a floating living room full of camel-colored leather and dark wood accents.

He stole a glance at his Rolex Submariner, pecking out a few more sentences. "Everything in moderation," he murmured, taking the time to scan my plate. "Eat those eggs, or grab some fruit while we do the crossword. The pineapple slices were nice."

"How about a slice of Dylan Taylor?" Dylan whispered in my ear. "And let me remind you, sweetheart, you can have that slice however you'd like."

Dylan could flirt with the stamina of a Kenyan runner. I couldn't. After thirty seconds, I was ready to smack him or rip off...

I pulled out my mental scrub brush, forking a piece of egg. "How about a flip-flop up your ego?"

Yeah, I'd found my big girl panties.

Dylan's eyes danced like a ballerina. "Darcy Walker, you're a naughty girl, and your best friend was lost without you. Come over here, and let me love on you."

Dylan's idea of "loving on you" by definition wasn't for mixed company. Heck, it didn't qualify for behind closed doors if I wanted to rejoin the rest of the world without a blush and indecent smile plastered on my face.

"I don't want to sit by you," I told him. His father slid over a copy of the morning newspaper and what I recognized as the front page of the *Orlando Sentinel* from a day earlier. My guess was it came with the plane. Once again, I scanned the lead story featuring Cisco Medina. In summary, there'd been a shift in the case. Those assumed innocent were suddenly MIA. Those assumed guilty had been cleared—sort of like the crossword puzzle. Just a bunch of empty boxes until someone came along smart enough to fill them up.

"Darcy doesn't want to sit with you, son," Colton told Dylan. "She and I are doing the crossword puzzle."

"That's right," I said. "I'm doing a crossword puzzle with Colton."

Dylan had a pile of eggs on his plate the size of a newborn baby. He placed them down on a separate tray table and crossed his arms, still considering my reluctance to sit beside him a major act of heresy. "Get up," he demanded.

I held up my palm, giving him a talk-to-the-hand gesture.

When I didn't budge, he 86'd that idea and fisted a large handful of my hair, yanking me out of the seat.

I tried to wrestle away, but sausage lodged in my throat mid-scream. "I just ch-choked on my sausage," I said coughing. Dylan burst into sidesplitting laughter as I picked up my coffee swishing it back down. "Don't make me spill my c-coffee!" I hacked again.

"Ditto on the spilling of the coffee, son." Colton eyeballed his son like he was a sheer and utter idiot.

"Back off, sucker," I said and burst into laughter.

Dylan flinched like I'd just kicked his dog. From out of nowhere, he hoisted me over his shoulder, pivoting toward his chair. I pounded my fists on his back, but it was like striking an anvil. "D!" I said and laughing louder.

"Good Lord, son!" his father gasped. "Quit manhandling Darcy."

Dylan didn't do anything he didn't want to do. Usually he represented the model child, but when it came to me, he didn't understand the terms "invasion of privacy" and "normal boundaries."

"You missed me, sweetheart. Admit it," he flirted.

Glancing down, I realized I was mere inches from the best rear end money could buy. *I longed to smack it.* I laughed to myself. Call me crazy, but I was sure that was frowned upon in the present company. While I continued to bang on his shoulders, I sucked in a big bunch of air when gravity forced my barely digested sausage up into my mouth. I burped loudly and attempted to swallow it back down.

"Come on, sweetheart," Dylan murmured, giggling louder than my burp. "That's so unladylike."

"You gave me acid reflux. Count yourself lucky I didn't puke down your back."

Dylan's I-love-Darcy-on-overdrive had been revving since Thursday morning when he surprised Marjorie and me as our ride home from Grandpa Winston's. As soon as he turned off his engine, he gave me a bone-crushing hug. Not a best friend type of hug—a hug like he'd feared I'd never come home. I received the same hug last night when he took us to see *Invasion of the Body Snatchers* at a late night showing of classic horror films. We borrowed his sister's convertible, held hands, and snacked away doing normal Dylan and Darcy things, except he seemed different. Where he was typically an attentive best friend, he'd appeared even more attentive than usual. Heck, by the end of the show, I had some lasting mental effects.

"Okay, Big Man," I conceded. "I'll sit by you mid-flight to hold your wee-wittle hand when you're scared."

He growled, "Pinky swear."

I threw my head back, bursting into laughter. "Seriously?" Dylan's and my pinkies had been swear-buddies since age eight. It was our way of dragging the truth out of one another, minus the kicking and screaming. With a split candy bar to seal the deal, we swore to tell the other the whole truth, and nothing but the truth, so help us God...God willing that the creek didn't rise.

I honestly didn't need the oath...I was a horrible liar.

"Oh, all right. Pinky swear." I twined my pinky inside his and squeezed away.

Dylan gently released me, dropping a kiss on the top of my head. As I settled back in my seat, I scooted into something slick, hard, and plastic that had lodged between the leather cushion and armrest. Gazing down I discovered a cell phone, concluding it must've tumbled out of his pocket. All at once, something clicked in my head that sounded like the switch on a time bomb. Nosiness took over, and I didn't know why.

Snatching it up, I devoured the text message on the screen:

Midnight tonight. He either talks or he's dead.

Chapter Four

CLIFFHANGER

N ow that was what I'd call a cliffhanger, folks.

Dylan had one foot in Boy Scout. The other in altar boy. Who in the heck had he been trading texts with?

While Dylan chatted with his father and demolished half the food on his plate, I jumped up and acted like Mother Nature's call was seconds from causing me mortal embarrassment. In six strides, I stepped inside the bathroom and slid the lock on the door to "occupied" for an opportunity to sin unencumbered.

Not a fan of restrooms in general, being in an airplane bathroom didn't leave much room for anything. I had about three feet in circumference for whatever the mission, while being deluged with the smell of chemicals and blue dye.

Opting to stand, I curled into myself and began texting. That was wrong—on like a gazillion different planes—but I wanted to know: (A) what my best friend was up to; and (B) why I didn't get an invite.

He deserves it, I texted.

Imagine my shock, when someone typed back: *I can arrange that.*

How so?

Fingers...kneecaps...family jewels...check this video.

Cue the spooky music.

When I clicked on the link, an icy hand gripped my heart and squeezed. If I thought the crazy student stalking me in the spring creeped me out, the person in the video reached a whole other category of psycho that shrinks hadn't encountered. The video seemed amateurish and grainy, but the content remained one hundred percent clear. A body—unidentifiable as male or female—was burned charcoal-black and hanging from a rope in front of a long row of windows. It swung back and forth like the hand on a metronome, hypnotically drawing me into the horror in front of me. After roughly a dozen swings, the head suddenly snapped at the neck with a loud crunch. When the body crashed to the ground, the head bounced twice and rolled across the floor like a bowling ball, landing right at the videographer's black sneakers.

I stammered, soundlessly.

Blinked a few times.

Filed it under *OMG*.

Ambient noise filled what had previously been a silent film. At first, I couldn't place the sounds until I realized the cameraman's heavy breathing and intermittent male laughter were the cause. Like he'd been so amused, he'd worn himself out and needed an oxygen tent. He zoomed in on the head, focusing on what was left of the eyes and the charred, singed hair that had been eyebrows. Then he kicked it with his shoe until it rolled to one side, and I caught the dingy glare of a drop earring in the left lobe in the shape of a star. That practice had no purpose other than to brag to the viewer what he'd just accomplished.

Right when I struck the "play" arrow again to search for clues, the cell phone rang. I jumped, birthing a patch of gray hair on the spot. Shoot...that was bad. Before I sank in deeper, I checked the number and discovered a Los Angeles area prefix attached to it. Oh, Lordy. I'd stepped into deeper-than-crap trouble here. It wasn't Dylan's phone—try his grandfather's—and my guess was the ole switcheroo happened sometime earlier. More than likely I'd just chatted with his partner. Thank God that had been cleared up. I'd begun to wonder if my best friend was the reincarnation of Jekyll & Hyde.

The elder Taylors came to town a few days earlier for Dylan's birthday, and even though his grandfather operated on West Coast time, he never clocked out of his job...a job where he carried a gun and threw bad guys in the slammer. He worked as an undercover detective in the vice unit, so the video, I presume, had to be evidence of some kind. Just my POV, but the person filming didn't need the slammer...they needed a lethal injection.

Once the brevity of the situation settled, an onslaught of nerves slammed into me like waves at spring tide. I fumbled the still ringing cell phone until it landed on the edge of the toilet. I watched in absolute horror as it teetered in slow-mo, seconds from drowning in the blue fluid in the bowl. Quickly plucking it up, I shakily sent the call to voicemail and shoved the phone in my pocket, washing my hands. Drying my palms on my shorts, I counted to sixty doing some imaginary yoga moves in my mind to calm myself. Then I simply stared...stared at myself in the mirror, as reason knocked at my door. Reason told me to show the text to his grandfather. Bow out gracefully. Mind my own business. As usual, I ignored the suggestion.

Sliding the door open, I did my best to swallow down what I'd seen. Charred body. Headless charred body. Insanely crazy videographer. No big deal. I threw my shoulders back and stumbled as confidently as I could back to my seat. I swear Dylan knew I'd dabbled in the forbidden. He'd settled across from me, narrowing his eyes. "What's going on in your pretty, little head?"

I decided to keep it dumb—tossing the phone over, hoping it miraculously erased my texts in transit. "I found Detective Taylor's phone."

Dylan caught it with one hand, panicked, patted himself down, and giggled like a little girl. "I'm dead."

Yeah, dead seemed to be going around.

I slumped down in the seat, drumming my bitten-to-the-quick nails on the armrest. It would absolutely kill me inside until I figured out the subject matter of the video. While the wheels turned in my head, I took a swig of coffee, picked up my second danish, and licked off the lemon ooze. Stuffing half in my mouth, I realized parts of my personality were at severe odds with one another. The part that hated death and the part that was so fascinated by it, I ran for a ringside seat. The blood, guts, and broken dreams didn't faze me. What fazed me was the fact that someone might never right the wrong that was done to the victim.

Knowing a good chance existed that I'd never discover the

details, I cast another gander at the *Orlando Sentinel* and the accompanying photograph of Cisco Medina. He was very Latino looking with dark skin and hair on a round face with intelligent looking eyes. A black mole was under his right eye the size of a baby pea. My gaze settled on the last paragraph.

Any information you may have regarding this case, please contact the Orange County Police Department or **troyoncrime@orlandosentinel.com**.

When I phoned Troy earlier, he implied that the real story lay within the story. If I emailed the next go-around, maybe I'd get a totally different spin and could piece the truth together between the two conversations. That left me in a quandary. I couldn't send information from my normal email account because that would out the liar...the liar being *me*. My only option was to capitalize on the moniker that my good friend, Vinnie Vecchione, bestowed on me when I found a dead body last spring.

When Vinnie and I went to the police station to snoop around, Vinnie introduced us as family of the victim, my name being Jester. The universe broke the mold when it created Vinnie—sometimes he showed genuine smarts, others he embraced his dumb side (you know, illegal substances induced dumb). Whatever the case, the name did the job, and I'd had a hard time letting it go. Jester hailed as my alter ego. *She* got into trouble. Darcy Walker was a good little girl who made straight As and volunteered in a soup kitchen.

Siiiiiinful...that thought had to be a sin.

Someone tapped me on the head. "Hello, trouble," the person said. "It's been awhile."

Sweet Mother of God—he didn't know, did he?

Glancing up with guilt all over my face, I stared into the face of Lincoln Taylor. *Yikes*. If Colton reminded me of Zeus, then Lincoln had to be God Almighty. And like the god of all gods, he held judgment in his hands. Although the three had the same mugs, Lincoln sported brown hair...and was leaner and *meaner*. He met his wife when a thug robbed her family's bakery in downtown Los Angeles. According to urban legend, within three days, he hauled the thief in hogtied and circling the drain, belting out an apology to all Greeks of the world. You had to applaud the man. He let the crook keep his cojones.

To be a good cop, one had to have a level head. Lincoln was polished, adept, and unbelievably personable, but he spent more time watching than talking. Professionally, he had no weakness. Personally, his flaw included females. The older brother to five sisters, when he had Colton first, he and his wife closed the factory and called it a day. But when Colton turned nineteen, an "oops" baby came along named Willow. Willow was Lincoln's greatest passion, but she was wild and free and refused to be tamed. She'd been the face of Go Glam! Cosmetics since age four. Colton acted as her agent, and that became the catalyst that catapulted him into the youngest vice president in the history of the company. In fact, Go Glam! is headquartered in Cincinnati, and that was the reason Colton left his LA roots behind.

Wearing khaki shorts, a plain T, and packing a GLOCK semi-automatic underneath his belt, Lincoln looked like he was on the tail end of the longest twenty-four-hour period on record. His eyes were hooded and a vertical frown line marked the space between them. He kicked Colton's chair in greeting, but Colton grunted and kept typing.

Lincoln didn't appear that anything serious played at his mind (other than staying awake), so I decided not to borrow trouble. Besides, I needed Colton's laptop, and getting my hands on it before takeoff was paramount. I needed to flirt with Troy, and by God Troy needed to flirt with Ms. Ovaries.

Lincoln punched Dylan's shoulder. "Do you have something of mine, boy?"

Dylan grinned, countering, "Do you have something of mine?"

A testosterone-induced stare down began where they both tried to decide who had the bigger gonads. Lincoln raised a brow. Dylan raised two. Lincoln puffed out his chest. Dylan inflated his entire body and poked a finger in Lincoln's sternum. After a few more breaths of king-of-the-mountain, Lincoln threw his head back, laughing. "You're such a cocky little kid, but I love you, son," he murmured. "My presence is required at a party, so we'd better switch devices unless you're prepared to dance with the Devil."

"I want to dance with the Devil," I mumbled, shrugging and smacking my lips.

As usual, they looked at me like I was a buffoon.

Thing was, Lincoln usually brought a party with him. Last year, he talked someone through a hostage situation while sitting on the patio. Some thief said he'd only speak to Lincoln, and while throngs of LA's finest had him cornered in a convenience store, Lincoln promised him everything from no jail time to the secret recipe for Kentucky Fried Chicken. I wasn't certain he had a chance of getting what he wanted, but Lincoln had a distinct voice...a *mesmerizing seduction*...and you found yourself doing things even if your gut told you it wasn't safe.

"Shouldn't you retire soon?" Dylan joked.

"Ten more years or so."

"You'll be past seventy," Dylan murmured and laughed.

"I've always been an overachiever," Lincoln quipped.

When Dylan's grandmother, Alexandra, boarded, Dylan pushed out of his seat to hug her, "Kalimera, Yaya."

"Kalimera, Dylan," she said, showing a porcelain smile. She loved it when he addressed her in Greek, and yaya meant grandma, and kalimera said good morning—the two words I knew...other than the forbidden curse words.

Wearing an emerald green sundress, Alexandra pawed at your senses. She oozed black-eyed passion on a bilingual smart mouth that made her the biggest personality in the room. Her stature, however, was itty-bitty.

"Where are Mom and Sydney?" Dylan asked her.

Her lips curled. "Sydney decided to pack some extra bags."

"Oh, God," Dylan prayed. "The plane will never make it off the ground."

I had to agree. Sydney packing light included two garment bags, a Louis Vuitton trunk, and four pieces of matching luggage. Anything more would land us at the bottom of the Ohio River.

"Plus," she said, reluctantly laughing, "she's breaking up with her boyfriend over the phone."

Dylan rolled his eyes, sitting back down. "Classic Sydney," he groaned, "the love 'em and leave 'em type."

"When's Willow joining us, Alexandra?" Lincoln grumbled.

She touched his arm. "She's wrapping up some business. In a few days, Lincoln."

"I've heard that before," he bit out. Like her brother, Willow was an entrepreneur. She declared herself independent at age sixteen to model in Europe, and as far as I knew, her license picture simply said "Willow." And that made Lincoln very, very...*well??* I really didn't know *what* that made him, but it was safe to say the definition blinked in all-caps, boldfaced, and underscored.

He took his gun out of the waistband of his pants, double-checking the magazine. God only knew whom he thought he needed to shoot on our flight, but the man always liked to be prepared. He'd nicknamed his gun Jackal, the moniker he'd branded his son with during his teen years. A jackal stirred up game for lions. Apparently, Colton occasionally performed that feat for Lincoln before arrests.

An aura of calm fell over Dylan's father as he struck the send key on his last email. If I didn't strike right then, no way would I hit gold. Leaning over, I lightly tugged on his hand, trying to look doe-eyed innocent.

I almost laughed...me and doe-eyed...crazy thought.

"Can I use your laptop for a second to send an email?" I blinked. To *troyoncrime*, I mumbled in my head.

A blissful smile played at his lips. "Keep it dear, I'm done for two weeks. I intend on doing absolutely *nothing*. I want no fires to put out, and frankly, zero excitement."

No excitement for me resembled a forced hunger strike. You couldn't survive on what nature deemed essential. "Sounds great," I lied.

He slid it across the tray table, swiveled around, and pummeled his father.

I quickly logged onto my account and sent an email to Marjorie that said to be good, mind her manners, and that nudity was on an as-needed-basis only. Then I constructed a new email account under Jester. Jester from Jesterville, to be exact. Once I was up and running, I looked at the clock and realized the time said seven fifty-five—only five minutes to unearth potential clues. Troy claimed he loved the ladies, so perhaps it'd be as simple as getting my flirt on

and wowing him with my bad-girlitude. I shot out an email in hopes
we could talk real-time.

DATE: August 10, 07:55 a.m.
TO: Troyoncrime
FROM: Jester from Jesterville
RE: Cisco Medina
Hey, Troy,
Are you there? I have information on Cisco Medina.
Jester

Feeling a set of eyes tunnel through me, my head nervously shot
over to Dylan. His advice was shrewd, careful, and always with a
desired end. In other words, he'd tell me I was headed to sin-city. I
had to watch myself. He had a guiding light, guru, mystic quality
that oftentimes killed my buzz.

He narrowed his eyes suspiciously. "Why all the smiles?"

More teeth, Walker. More teeth...more teeth...more teeth.

"Just excited," I said, smiling sunnily.

"Don't flash those pearly whites at me," Dylan said with a smirk,
pausing to rub his chest. "You know that breaks my heart."

Animated laughter from the front of the cabin alerted me that
Susan and Sydney Taylor had stepped onboard. Colton frowned
deeply, followed by a sharp groan. Several minutes late into his vacation, he acted as though he wanted to skin their hides, hang them
up, and beat them like a piñata. But all it took was a smile of atone-
ment, and his face lit up like a Christmas tree.

Ugh, happily married people.

Sometimes it gave me hope. Sometimes it reminded me what I
didn't have at home.

Dylan's mother glided in with her hair in a smooth ponytail wearing
a white linen skirt, matching sleeveless blouse, and brown leather
strappy heels. The weight of the gold adorning her body might've been
a third of her total weight, but then again, she was born to wear nice
things. An inch shorter than me, she was a debutante sorority girl who
fell for a middle-class boy. Translation? She went gaga for Colton's body.

"Sorry, Colt," she cooed to her husband, bending down to kiss him. "Sydney was tidying up some loose ends."

Dylan called his older sister, Sydney, the black widow. She lured boys into her web and then killed them before they could crawl out of the red hourglass trance. I hadn't met the guy, but it remained just as well. I tried not to get attached to people in her life...neater that way.

I couldn't deny the allure. At five foot seven, she weighed next to nothing, with the delicate face of her mother and dark coloring of her father. Like the black widow, she sported an hourglass shape with a swayback that tipped her derrière out so far it practically hit her in the back of the head. On top of that, she had a morning voice that provided bedroom sultriness 24/7. Trouble was, I think it gave guys ideas.

Poured into a red miniskirt, matching tank and heels, she carried a bag that cost more than Murphy's monthly mortgage. She gently yanked on my hair and then stopped obediently in front of her father.

I stared at the computer screen...zippo. Thumping my nails on the table, I sang the ABC Song twice, rapped the Pledge to Allegiance, debated my cholesterol level, and before I knew it, voilà an email had been returned.

No waaaaaay. That meant my sins were meant-to-be, right?

DATE: August 10, 08:02 a.m.
TO: Jester from Jesterville
FROM: Troyoncrime, Orlando Sentinel
RE: Cisco Medina
Jester,
Are you okay? Is it Lola? Girl, that's where the problem is. Let's get together.
Troy Brown
Man worried about jesters

I gulped, swallowed some gastric juices, and thankfully passed gas as a burp. I'd just struck it rich and barely lifted a finger. Lola Medina —as well as Cisco's father—had been cleared according to the

Orlando Sentinel, but what specifically had transpired in Lola's world that left Troy suspicious? If anything, Troy gave me a starting place. Find Lola Medina, find clue number one.

You're playing with fire, the angel said. *You like the burn*, its evil counterpart countered.

Let me introduce my decision making process. An angel lived on one shoulder, the devil on the other. Unfortunately, that little devil had too big of a say-so—the main reason I traveled the short road to Hades.

I keyboarded a simple, "Yes."

And waited.

Annnd waited.

Annnnnnnnd...waited.

Rapping my fingers on the keyboard, I deliberated what Troy had seen or heard that tipped him off to a less than honest mother. Nervousness? Lack of nervousness? Sketchy story? Rehearsed answers?

Jittery from head to toe, I plucked Colton's ink pen out from his ear, rocked back and forth, and inked the words, "The truth shall set you free" on my left palm. Still nervous, I gnawed off the pinky nail on my right hand. Finally, Colton's laptop chimed again.

DATE: August 10, 08:07 a.m.
TO: Jester from Jesterville
FROM: Troyoncrime, Orlando Sentinel
RE: Cisco Medina
Jester,
Contact me at 407-555-1234 or via email. Be careful.
Troy
Man wondering why Ms. Ovaries is masquerading as Jester

I sucked in a sharp breath...I thought I'd been subtle. Thing was, Ms. Ovaries didn't know whose fist to dodge first. I erased the history of my transgressions and settled in as Cody lifted us to a cruising altitude of thirty-eight thousand feet. Right when I prematurely unbuckled, a big bump sent me slamming chest-first into the tray table.

"Oh, God," Colton prayed, suddenly nervous about the turbulence. "Are you all right, dear?"

"I'm good," I mumbled, but my ribs weren't, and chances were Divine Discipline had come into play. "I just need to relax."

"What do you do to relax at home?" he muttered offhandedly.

"Sometimes I go outside and shoot the squirrels. Just depends."

He attempted a laugh, but I feared he was moments from a complete psychotic episode. For an international businessman, air travel packed some major fear factor for Colton. Evidently, Pegasus almost crashed once, and he hadn't found Xanadu since.

When the twelve-thousand-pound plane jumped forward again, Colton cursed under his breath—clearly needing his mommy. If I had a Marlboro, I'd smoke it. I glanced over to my soulmate. Dylan sat tranquil—reading *Sports Illustrated*—not scared poopless like his lying best friend. "Ah, Darc," he said, sighing and closing up the magazine, "don't be scared."

Don't be scared? I thought. I was doing the doggie paddle down the ditch of desperation. "I-I—"

I couldn't form words.

"What does my girl need?"

A brain transplant. Leaning across the aisle, he gently rubbed his thumb back and forth over the top of my extended hand. Dylan could help me find my stride, and he'd called me "his girl" since eighth grade. As much as I hated to admit it, I wanted to crawl onto his lap and have him promise me I could pull off the impossible... before I died a liar.

———

Toward the end of the flight, the blood born Taylors went to the rear of the plane for their version of the Olympic Games. Grandma Alexandra would speak in her native tongue, and the grandchildren attempted to interpret, Colton being the judge. Since it was "all Greek to me," Lincoln and I settled up front.

"What are you reading, Darcy?" he murmured. I'd pored over the copy of the Cisco Medina story for the past thirty minutes. Honestly, I'm surprised it took him so long to ask. But all I could think was I'd jumped out of the frying pan into the proverbial fire.

Troy was probably giddy with what he expected to be front-page news when I remained thousands of feet in the air...a big, fat lying idiot.

Nudging the paper over, I painted on my concerned citizen face. "The article said he simply vanished. Who do you think did it?"

Pulling reading glasses from his pocket-T, he slid them on his nose and took his finger and speed-read down the page. Lincoln looked scary to the average person. His holster may say he carried a gun, but the bulge of his hands said he'd rather shove an M80 up your fill-in-the-blank.

"Most abduction cases are the other parent," he murmured, "but the article said they were cleared." *Not according to Troy*, I thought. Troy acted like momma might know something she wanted to remain underground. "That leaves psychopaths and predators. It's not a pretty picture."

Recalling that no ransom had ever been paid, I agreed the outlook for the little boy appeared grim. If, in fact, he was living, it wasn't for money that the abductor could collect. A plea would've already been made, and one would think reported on. I twirled a tendril of my hair as I digested what little information I did have, and that was Lola Medina.

"Where would *you* look?" I asked.

"The places I'm sure they already have. When you exhaust yourself on the ground, if it was me, I'd keep plugging away on what didn't feel right. Why the curiosity?"

Honestly? I didn't know. Call me a concerned citizen. Call me an older sibling of a six-year-old nudist. Either way, my laundry list of reasons boiled down to one thing: boredom. Boredom and my hound dog nose sniffed ridiculously along the trail. Did I have the skills to get things done? That remained to be seen. Sure I'd solved who killed three people in Valley, but the difference there was my personal involvement. With the kidnapped little boy, I wasn't even remotely involved. Heck, I wasn't even in the same hometown.

But I would be.

"I guess my heart breaks for little kids," I explained. "If you were coming in blind, where would you start?"

He shaved a hand down over his day-old beard, deep in thought. "I'd start with the people who knew his routine...his neighbors. I'd ask whom he liked to play with, what he liked to play, what he always had in his possession, if he had any enemies. The person who nabbed him might've been someone who had his eye on him for a while or simply might've been an opportunist. I'd retrace his steps."

I briefly wondered why someone would hurt a child. Why do some allow their humanity to drain away? In a perfect world, we were supposed to protect children, clear the obstacles, give them the chances we never had, tell them they could do anything—*be* anything—even if odds and talent were stacked against them.

But it wasn't a perfect world...and that BS slapped me in the face every day.

Chapter Five

PONKEYS

When you're hyper, you have a tendency to feel caged in. It happened to be one of those times, and being in a jet right before landing didn't help matters. Most people feared the liftoff...not me. The landing left me scared-stiff and blowing chunks. What if I never got to my final destination? Talk about disappointing. I went on vacation to have fun. At least, I hoped the dang plane crashed on the way back.

I forced myself to relax, breathe deep, and search for something to occupy my mind.

Lincoln had pushed out of his seat to visit the restroom, leaving four black-and-white surveillance photographs sprawled out on the table between us. First off, you should never leave anything lying around that you didn't want me to look at. Secondly, my guess was they were crooks so looking at them seemed like a social service on my part. And thirdly, I remembered the cryptic text message I'd read earlier:

Midnight tonight. He either talks or he's dead.

A touch on the theatrical, but hey, that's what I lived for.

I couldn't help but ponder what choice the "he" had made. Did his tongue take the hint, or would he meet some untimely demise? In Lincoln's world, that wouldn't necessarily mean a bullet. There's a good chance it could range from a car bomb to an axe to the head.

Thing was, Lincoln and his partner must be referring to a specific threat against someone. Furthermore, did that text even relate to the video I'd viewed? It *did* follow the same conversation thread, but it remained possible it represented a totally different case.

Stealing a quick glance around the cabin, everyone had strapped himself or herself in for landing. Dylan chatted with his mother, Sydney cuddled next to her father, and Zander informed Alexandra why hooters should be a food group.

Status quo. Coast was clear in my book.

Looking without touching tortured my eye sockets. My fingers got all jumpy, but right when I lifted the top photograph to my eyes, Lincoln's cell phone practically jumped out of the seat he'd left it in. That was an FAA no-no, so I grabbed it and thumbed down the volume before anyone could complain.

Pulling it to my eyes, another LA prefixed message lit up the screen:

Making all kinds of weird demands. Told him to kiss my ass.

I was no stranger to the donkey word. My aunt used it at least ten times an hour. It didn't take a genius to deduce it might be the same man that if he didn't talk, death was imminent either. And in my humble opinion, he just might be a donkey if he didn't take the original deal.

I shrugged away his stupidity, leaving Lincoln's phone where I'd found it, but then it vibrated with another message. I snatched it up again, covering the noise with both hands. Clicking the screen, I nearly bit my tongue in two when I scanned the words:

Opened a locker at the subway on a tip and found someone's foot. It was as swollen as a pregnant pig. Sick crap, so I know it was him. Gotta love this job.

I had a horrible habit of biting my nails when nervous. I'd bitten down to three nubs on my right hand, my thumb and forefinger the only two remaining looking normal. How should I respond? Throw up? Pray? Beg for a picture? I erased the history of all my earlier texts, in case Lincoln felt the urge to purge his inbox. If he found out I'd assumed his identity, God only knew the ramifications. The video, however, was evidence. It seemed too important to delete.

When I focused back on the photograph, Lincoln miraculously

appeared out of nowhere like one of those biblical miracles that come just in the nick of time.

'Nuff said...God and I really needed some face-time.

Lincoln's voice grumbled, "You know in the Middle East they'd cut your hand off for what you're doing."

A thwack and a thud pierced the air, and then I figured out it was my conscience banging around in my brain. "Would you believe that photograph jumped into my open hand? I told it not to, but what can I say?" I said and giggled. "It just...would not...listen."

Normally, Lincoln would be proprietary, but he collapsed into his seat, kneading and massaging his temples. All of a sudden I had to know firsthand *what*—or should I say *whom*—caused the tension.

"Who's the weird little guy?"

Lincoln slid his black reading glasses on his forehead, shoving the remaining three photographs over for my appraisal. "Turkey Cardoza. These photographs were taken about six months ago when we started our investigation."

Turkey Cardoza looked like a skunk. A mixed Caucasian, he had coal-black hair and a rattail on his barbershop cut bleached as white as a new fallen snow. His nose had a triangle point, his eyes were beady little peas, and his body resembled an Oompa Loompa. Turkey also carried hips—something I didn't know men were capable of. Couple that with an Italian suit and you were looking at someone trying to be someone that biology didn't intend. Maybe that's what most criminals did...try to hide what lurked on the inside to make their crimes less believable.

"Turkey?" I laughed.

"As in Wild Turkey," he said, adding a frown. "Evidently, he can drink an entire bottle and never lose an ounce of sobriety. Trust me, he needs to be sober judging by the people he's in business with."

"He's bad?"

"I'd rather play with a venomous snake."

Question answered. Lincoln took a long swig of coffee and chowed on the last blueberry danish onboard.

"Career criminal?" I asked.

"Mob," he specified, "and that type are morally ambivalent. You name it...he's done it. He's also got a smart mouth the size of the craters on the moon. "

Cue *The Godfather* theme song.

"Why is he so hard to catch? He sounds like your textbook *ponkey*, and people like that should make anyone's radar beep."

"Ponkey," he repeated.

"You know, when the punk in you makes a donkey out of you're a-s-s. Marry them together and you have a ponkey."

Lincoln burst out laughing. "Dear, I don't know whether to be impressed with your creativity or tell you to gargle with some Listerine."

"I'd prefer it if you were impressed."

He wiped his mouth, appearing pensive and perplexed at the same time. "Fingering him isn't the problem," he muttered. "Getting things to stick is. I have people feeding me information, but when we bring him in for questioning, he's always got an airtight alibi even though we have footage of him in the area." He massaged the space between his eyes, adding a frustrated groan. "I know the answer's in my head. I'm just having trouble piecing it together. Sometimes I think I'm too dumb for this kind of work."

Surely, that had been said in jest. Lincoln's brain ran like the Autobahn—fast, unimpeded, and smooth. My brain moved like the off-road—full of ruts, gutters, and expletives I didn't know I was capable of.

"And you believe your sources?"

I couldn't miss the conviction on his face, while a hard line painted down his jaw. "Wholeheartedly. One gal especially would never steer me wrong."

"Why don't you just bring *her* in?"

Another drink of coffee. "I've offered, but she's not the type to be cloistered away somewhere. So we're being extremely careful in our dealings. If she were ever found out, that would be signing her death warrant, but she's slick. Frankly, she's the first person I've never been able to outsmart."

I questioned who could be so close to Turkey to know firsthand of his dealings? "Do you think she's a friend, enemy, mistress, neighbor?" I rattled off.

He lifted both shoulders in a slow shrug. "I don't have a clear feel of *who* she is. I can't pin down an age, only that my gut says she's good. So she tells me things, and that foists the problem off onto me, but hey, that's my job." Lincoln inhaled and exhaled deeper, loosening up to laugh. "Can I tell you how much I've grown to hate secrets? But in this line of business," he said, pausing to put his index finger to his lips, "mum's the word."

I mimicked the gesture, promising, "I won't say anything."

He gave half a smile. "I've known you since you were six years old, Darcy. You like to talk, but you're not a snitch."

I'd had a lot of experience with keeping secrets. Life oftentimes mandated them, and I wallowed around in the damning truth of it. But that wasn't to say I didn't love, love, love a juicy story. My gossiping, however, stayed primarily between Dylan, me, and the Mrs. Butterworth's syrup bottle. The three of us had ironclad confidentiality.

Lincoln shoved the last bite into his mouth, and when he turned to laugh at something said in the back of the plane, I grabbed the ink pen and drew a circle with a beak and a red wattle on my left palm. He swiveled back around, munching his food. "The thing with Turkey, he's persnickety."

"Excessively over particular," I defined.

His dimples imploded. "Exactly, kiddo, and that's why he's been hard to catch. He's always changing things up in every aspect of his life. Look at this photograph." He pulled the bottom photograph from the stack. It pictured Turkey, a trophy wife under his arm, and two other men in a restaurant corner booth.

"Wife?" I asked. He nodded with a smirk. She was pretty, I guess, in a space cadet sort of way. She appeared around thirty years younger with dark hair, dark lips, and a white form-fitting dress cut down to her pregnant navel. "What's the story with the other guys?"

Both dinner guests were textbook Italian. One man gazed square in the camera, a cigar held in his lips by a hand that had been scarred and twisted by some horrific accident. His hair was slicked back to the scalp, and his face cut into hard lines reminiscent of seeing—and participating in—a life without moral boundaries. The profile of the other male revealed dang little other than a graying military cut. What features resided, however, defined cold-hearted, and a gander at his bulging biceps suggested he worked as someone's heavy.

"Two different mob families," Lincoln responded. "Turkey has run deals for both, but from what we can tell, he's now mostly an envoy for a third party."

I didn't know whether to hire a security detail or ask for an introduction. "And he's alive?" I guffawed. "That's what I'd call some serious talent. What gives?"

Lincoln remained close-mouthed, clicking his jaw a few times before answering, "Both families are concerned this third family is getting too big. Exactly what they're proposing isn't yet clear. The Italian mob is interesting in LA these days. We haven't had a lot of eyes on them for years—the bosses having literally died out—but my snitches are telling me they're trying to make a comeback and some mafia members from the East Coast are moving out West. That can only be interpreted as a sign of aggression."

I held up a black-and-white photograph of two boys and two girls walking up the steps to a private high school. The boys donned dark blazers, khakis, and ties. The girls wore white blouses and plaid skirts with knee socks and penny loafers. They'd just exited a dark limousine with a smiling Turkey waving from a rolled down window. "Children?" I asked.

Lincoln's face took on a paternal protectiveness. "Four out of six. Their mother's alive and well, still cooking dinner, and totally oblivious to wife number two."

Yikes, I shuddered. As they say, the wife was always the last to know.

Lincoln slid over another shot of whom I assumed was the wife the law deemed legitimate. She looked matronly with short dark hair, a plump face and body, but an otherwise sincere smile. Why, oh why, did men look for a younger squeeze when the wife piled on the pounds?

"Butthead," I mumbled.

Thankfully, Lincoln didn't attempt to sanitize my mouth.

Honestly, I understood the confusion with the case. Overall, the family appeared boringly normal, not the family of a career criminal. And for that matter, Turkey seemed normal too, as he waved out the window while his children went to school. His face appeared softer—less like a skunk—and more like a proud father of his progeny. The photograph didn't show how he'd dressed, but my guess was the skunk tail lay hidden away along with his alter ego.

I laid the photograph back down, when a fifth—obviously stuck underneath—fluttered to the table.

Dead man, sunny side up, literally with a heavy chalk outline drawn around him. The side of his face looked like it had been filleted, pulled back like a freaking tuna can. I swallowed hard, convincing my breakfast to stay south.

Lincoln looked like he'd thrown an embolism. "Sorry, kiddo," he gasped, snatching the photograph from my hand. "I'm usually better at hiding my job."

"I don't scare easily."

"You don't," he repeated.

"No, I just catalogue this stuff in my *People Are Evil File*."

He drew the pic up to his eyes. "I need to figure out who he is."

Don't hold your breath on that one, I thought.

I anxiously rapped my fingers on the tray table. "What is it about Turkey that allows him to swim with the sharks without being eaten alive? I mean, his last name is Cardoza. That's Spanish. Yet he's representing a family that's Italian?"

Lincoln chuckled deeply. "I'd forgotten how astute you are."

Awwwww. Astute sounded nice, but it was more like a badger that wouldn't let go of a snake.

He didn't speculate a guess but acted as if he still knew the answer. If anyone could dissect Turkey's particular idiosyncrasies, it would be Lincoln. He grew up in the Compton area of LA. If you didn't join a street gang, you didn't survive...but Lincoln hadn't and was somehow still breathing. As a matter of fact, he'd successfully coexisted, and when he earned his badge, he took down those he thought were the worst—leaving the others to live by their own rules. But let's be real, the man had to have gotten dirty somewhere along the way. No one was *that* good.

Lincoln blinked hard and gazed out the window, as though he thought about a particular incident he'd rather forget. "This trip came at the right time, Darcy. Turkey's put out the word he's gunning for my partner and me, and the best thing to do is place some distance between all of us. Turkey would never look for me here."

Lincoln's face coated in head-to-toe frustration while I secretly said in my head, *Please come, and let me shoot a gun*. "At least, you've got two weeks to relax," I said smiling.

"I don't understand the term, dear," he said and chuckled. He fished his hand down in his pocket, pulling out a pack of Wrigley's Spearmint chewing gum, offering me the first piece. "Do you want some gum? I chew four packs a day when I'm anxious."

I'd had four cups of coffee in two hours. There was a good chance my mouth smelled like a cigarette butt.

———

A trip to the restroom later, I wheeled my bag outside and telephoned Murphy to communicate we'd landed safely. Then I punched in 411 and got the number for Lola Medina. Did I have a plan? No. Did I pray one would materialize if she answered? Heck, yeah.

The airport felt hotter than Hades. My underarms took on a strange funk while sweat rolled down my back like a leaky faucet. Twitchy with apprehension, I dialed and after five rings was greeted with a cough that resembled an asthma attack, and then an aggravated sigh. "Hullo?" she muttered.

Somebody pinch me. "Lola Medina?" I asked.

She didn't have to voice anything. The vibe through the receiver smelled of suspicion. After a New York minute, she stiffly said, "Yes?"

I picked at my nails—hoping to sound professional—and then spit out a reply. "I'm going to find your son." What I recognized as Spanish curse words filled the dead space, followed by an avalanche of tears and a disconnection. Talk about tearing at your heartstrings. For some reason, I remembered the chapter in *Alice in Wonderland* called *Pool of Tears*. Alice had fallen down the rabbit hole and is trapped, depressed, with no way out, and swimming in her own sadness.

I choked down the hysteria but told myself three times, *You're doing the right thing*. Maybe that explained away my own brand of conviction, but people like me didn't boast a lot of success stories. We were the ones who got patted on the head with a look of sympathy that said, *Nice try*. I surprised even myself with the strategies I'd use, but for some reason I had the consuming need to help the woman. Trouble was, I needed to formulate a plan of action before my good intentions went haywire and bit me in the rear.

Lincoln and I met eyes while he checked out the bestseller section at Hudson Bookstore. He returned a hardback book to its shelf and waved me toward him, but as I bent down to retrieve my bag, I inadvertently knocked it onto the rolling sidewalk. I quickly jumped onboard to retrieve it, but three businessmen suddenly clustered together like sardines in a can. Squeezing around them, I hurdled over a toddler, veered left, and ran into what felt like the entire offensive line of a professional football team. The air left my body in a hiss—my heart pounding so loud I think they heard it in Africa.

"Watch out!" Offensive Line screamed. Offensive Line stood two heads taller than me, attractive enough in a pinstriped black suit, but was pit-bull mean. And here I was, trying to be a hero. I fought the urge to slap the jerk because he went on and on about how stupid I was. Maybe so, but no one liked a face-rubber. When his voice reached a more threatening octave, my fear grew like a fungus. My word, he planned to hit me...his intentions written all over his blood-red face. When he backed me up against my luggage, I choked out an apology, but he snorted and launched spittle in my eyes followed by another, "You're an idiot."

Right when I told him to kiss my you-know-what (seriously, I just let that crap fly), Lincoln exploded onto the scene with the snarling face of a butcher. With one angry hand, he leapt over the railing, corralling my runaway bag and inserting himself between us.

"Why don't you pick on someone your own size?" he sneered. The man took one gaze at Lincoln's flexed fists and looked like he'd just wet his pants. On paper, it shouldn't be a fair fight—he stood massively larger than Lincoln—but anger was a funny thing. If you had enough of it—with the attitude to back it up—you could suddenly appear one hundred pounds heavier and shrink the size of your opponent to a bedbug. "Apologize to her," Lincoln demanded. He paused for effect and then bellowed, "*Now.*"

Holy crap...my neck broke out in hives.

The man babbled incoherently—like some Appalachian native handling snakes—while Lincoln continued to carve him up with his eyes. After a few seconds of Holy-God-help-us, I thought it was over, but then Offensive Line dumbly crowded Lincoln's personal space. Lincoln threw his head back and laughed like the talking doll Chucky, plotting a plan for world domination. He curled his fingers into a fist, and I dove between them.

Chapter Six

WIPEOUT

Serendipity Country Club is the filet mignon crowd. Trouble was, I grew up in the beans and franks crowd. Where my street was littered with plastic toys and dead trees, beautiful landscaping crisscrossed through the grounds that'd make God Himself envious. Here, your home was maintained for you. There was twenty-four-hour security with a manned gatehouse, and visitors didn't get in unless their name was on the invite-list.

Holy cow, can you just say exclusive...

Stationed along several lakes that make up the Lake Butler chain, residents could boat, swim, or water-ski on the body of water of their choice. A private dock in the middle of the neighborhood allowed people to skip from one lake to another via a group of navigable canals. All we had to do was chart where we were going and *ba-da-bing, ba-da-boom* an inlet would take us there.

Colton, Dylan, Zander, and I were in their sleek, red, and black twenty-one-foot ski boat, cruising on Lake Butler. Dylan had just finished skiing and attached a double-seater tube for Zander and me. Once he clicked it in place, we cannonballed into the H2O as Dylan hoisted himself back inside the boat.

"Have a good trip," Dylan said, winking as we settled inside.

I threw him the peace sign as Colton revved up to our mutually agreed upon speed of twenty miles per hour. Twenty miles per hour seemed like child's play to me, but to Colton, it was flirting with danger and a trip to the morgue.

Water splashed around us like the French outrunning the guillotine, but it didn't faze me one bit. In truth, I loved the onslaught of the spray. It could jar me awake from an otherwise spiritually numb existence. I'd practiced shutting myself off for years. Sometimes it worked. Others, I was left raw with an open wound time refused to heal.

The lake was crowded with boaters. Teenagers joyrode up front, an elderly couple puttered near the shoreline, and dozens of others skied in the main path. Zander and I tangled our hands together as we skipped across the waves, but right when I closed my eyes to YOLO the moment, I heard Colton bellow and felt him zigzag the boat.

Literature claims there was a foreshadowing of bad before it happened. I watched "bad" unfold in slow motion before my eyes. Colton maneuvered his boat sharply to the left but not before he hit the wake of those on the opposite side. The tube bounced once, twice, and the third time we went airborne and zoomed like a hovercraft. Zander's head bonked with mine, our arms and legs twisted like a pretzel, and we both dove face-first into a watery grave.

And that was all she wrote...

I stiffened and went limp, my head banging with an instant case of the dizzies when I crashed into the water. Clawing for the surface, my eyes burned with unshed tears as I tried to make sense of what'd happened. It felt as though someone had hit me with a semitruck, backed up, and then ran over me again. Water entered and exited every orifice of my body, but all I could manage to do was think, *Whoa*.

Whoa...and my God I need a clean suit.

Alternating between bloody and woozy, I viewed someone shuck their orange life vest and dive off the side of the boat. Something warm, thick, and rancid ran into my mouth, and I briefly thought about Lincoln's text and the hanging victim—wondering if my head had popped off my shoulders and splashed like a fish in the lake.

Spitting out blood, my mind started singing the "Kumbaya" song.

Someone's cryin', Lord, Kumbaya, it sang. *Hum, hum, hum, hum-hum, Kumbaya.*

Holy. Moly. Even my involuntary thoughts were stupid.

"Talk to me," a voice murmured. I finished the song and concluded the Lord probably didn't want to hear me sing.

Someone said again, "It's me, sweetheart. Talk to me."

Shaking my head brusquely, my eyes blinked open as Dylan wiped my face with both his thumbs. "Lord?" I choked out.

"No," he murmured and chuckled. "I *do* have some supernatural characteristics, but I'm not that high up the chain of command."

"What happened?"

"You wiped out and took a little trip to la-la land. You nearly scared me to death."

I spit again, running my tongue across my upper teeth, ensuring they still clung snugly to the gums. My nasal cavity had swelled, but when I tried to sneeze it open, all that came out was a dribble of snot.

"Do I need stitches?" I snuffed.

Dylan caressed the bridge of my nose once more, tilting it back to peer inside, finally shaking his head in the negative. "I don't think so."

At fifteen, I had the joints of a professional football player with a mass of arthritic injuries: ulna, cheekbone, finger, wrist, and ankle —all breaks, no stitches...well, darn.

As I tread water, I cursed, "Holy crap it hurts."

"Aw, Darc," Dylan moaned sympathetically. "Come here, and let me love on you." Dylan was the take-charge type. When I continued with the dead fish routine, he clutched me to his wet, muscled chest, and I briefly went bye-bye. I longed to hug him. Kiss him. Roll all over him. Not necessarily in that order. It had to be a concussion speaking because these just weren't my thoughts— although no woman with functioning estrogen could deny the pull.

"Darc?"

What sounded like a moan hung in the air...my word, I think it was mine.

To my silent protest, he gingerly lifted me back in the tube as he and Zander climbed in afterward.

"Sorry," Zander said, laughing and retying his hot pink trunks, lounging back against the black seat. "I tried to dodge but was in the middle of an unscheduled enema. It was awesome."

Yeah, enemas were the bomb.

I lay flat-backed on the tube, like roadkill that had recently been splattered. After a few bleary moments and more Kumbaya, Colton docked at the wharf, pulling us by the rope to the side of the boat. His eyes focused on Zander and me only briefly but spent most of the time shooting daggers straight through the heart of Dylan. Wearing red swimming trunks, they appeared vastly washed out compared to the hue of his angry face.

"Dylan!" he screamed, pointing at his jaw. "Don't *ever* dive off the side of the boat again when it's moving! You could've gotten ripped apart by the propeller. For all I care, you could've been sliced in two, but if you make your mother cry, you're a dead man."

Dylan hoisted himself onto the wharf, extending his hand for me, too self-assured in his own abilities. He calmly said, "I cleared it, Dad."

His father gently grabbed my opposite elbow, pulling my punch-drunk behind to a standing position. He muttered to himself, his voice a little more in control. "Quit being so cocky, son. One day, it's going to come back and bite you."

Dylan definitely shot off some cocky, but it was just that he never really failed at anything.

———

Homes in Florida could be pink, peach, coral, or some other random rainbow color, and it remained acceptable. Outside of a few historic areas in downtown Cincinnati, if you painted a house pastel in the Midwest, people would swear you were having an LSD flashback.

The Taylors' fifteen thousand square foot home away from home was located off Serendipity Club Drive. Dylan's family called it home several weeks out of the year, including spontaneous week-ends and major holidays. Plus any other time they wanted to enjoy the Benjis they probably used as toilet paper.

A French architect designed the mansion, and when Colton discovered it was named *Maison de Saule*, or *Home of Willow*, he yanked it off the market quicker than a shark devouring chum. I gather he considered it a good omen that would keep his globetrotting sister home. Trouble was, half the time no one even knew where she parked her stilettos.

I called Willow the goddess of love because she played matchmaker to anyone she met. Oddly, she seemed to be the one who couldn't find true love herself. She'd been dating polo playing, Viscount Henry Ainsworth of the British Highlands. Sounded important and royal, but for all we knew, he could've bought the title off the Internet.

The outside of *Maison de Saule* looked like your typical Florida home with palm trees, magnolias, and white stucco. The inside was white and airy with a contemporary Grecian flare. Large columns, reminiscent of the Parthenon, supported the structure that included a den, media room, living room, nine baths, library, and office. The kitchen came equipped with stainless steel Sub-Zero refrigeration, black marble countertops, top-of-the-line Wolf gadgets, and a bar area that seated eight.

Outside, a four-car garage and unattached guesthouse sat to the left of the property. An infinity pool adorned the backyard with a lanai overhead, hot tub, and beautiful view of the golf course winding around the lake. Perhaps what I liked best though were the seven bedrooms. The majority had french doors that opened to a marble lakefront terrace, perfect to watch the sunset framed by willow trees.

Since boating stopped before it truly got going, the four of us finished out the afternoon poolside. Lying on a black padded chaise, Sydney sashayed out fifteen minutes earlier wearing a white string bikini that qualified as little more than dental floss. Colton asked her to change. She hadn't moved a muscle, and odds were she wasn't going to. My black halter top bikini clung more to the concept of "covering your flaws."

Colton still acted somewhat skittish, and it wasn't just the plane or boat ride. He'd also pulled his father's fist out of Offensive Line's mouth. "Are you sure you're okay, dear?" he asked.

My brain stutter-stepped for the last hour, and I didn't know if it was: (A) I'd finished off a jar of olives; (B) I'd tampered with the Cisco Medina case; or (C) I couldn't stop wondering who lived on borrowed time in LA. Not to mention (D), whose freaking head fell off? That was too many variables to juggle to nail down only one.

A light rap rattled the outside entrance, and Kyd Knoblecker moseyed in before I could answer. Kyd and his family were the next-door neighbors. Kyd thought he was long lost family. If it were up to Dylan, however, he'd be lost in a meat grinder.

Kyd paraded over to the bottom of my chair, sitting at my feet—looking at me as if he'd eat me alive. "I heard my girlfriend was here," he murmured. "I've missed you, Darcy."

Stutter.

Stutter more.

Annnnnnnnd prove to the world I was an absolute moron.

Since my tongue took a time-out, I gave him a mindless wave.

Kyd graduated in May, and in what appeared to be a fit of insanity, he'd developed a crush on me. Throughout the year, he'd phone, email, send naughty texts at holidays, and pledge his eternal devotion and desire to impregnate me with a dozen kids. I'd rather be impregnated by a five-headed gargoyle, but he didn't seem to tire of the begging.

Dylan stretched over, mumbling in his father's direction, "Can this day get any worse?"

"I heard that, Taylor," Kyd said, adding a laugh.

Dylan jerked his head around, firing off a lethal stare. "Good. Consider me a bullet in a loaded gun."

I understood Dylan's concern. Kyd had a playboy look about him. A little taller than me, he sported designer everything with a pick-up line tattooed to his tongue. He also wore a smile that said, *It's a matter of time before you succumb to the wile.* Reputation claimed a lot of girls had buckled under the pressure. With blue-green eyes and sandy-blond hair, Kyd definitely was model-handsome. Even in an untucked T-shirt, his chest rippled and bulged in all the appropriate places. And the lower half of his body wasn't bad to look at either. His legs were lined with long, lanky muscle. Not too big. Not too small. As Goldilocks would say, *Just right.*

Kyd's eyes dipped to my stomach, lingered for a while, and then went up to my eyes with a lusty growl. "Did you miss me?" he drawled.

"Yeah," I said, grinning and finally locating my voice. "I thought about you right around the time the nausea hit mid-flight."

(giggle-snort) My God, I loved myself...

"I've been known to produce butterflies," Kyd said, smiling broadly. "Nice pedicure."

Kyd was a moron. Marjorie painted my toenails, alternating between red, white, and neon blue. It was dreadfully unskilled, but I didn't want to discourage her Picasso aspirations. "Patriotic," I said, followed by a shrug.

"I love patriots," he flirted.

When Kyd wound his hand around my foot, Dylan shot up growling, straddling his chair. "It's going to be the color of your face in about five minutes. Drop her foot before I shove *mine* up your—"

Oh boy, Dylan said the donkey word.

"Does anyone else think this situation is as transparent as I do?" Sydney said huskily.

"Stop, Syd," Dylan demanded. "*Please.*"

"Whatever, little brother," she purred. "Just keep paddling along that river called DE-NIAL, and see if you get anywhere."

Colton sucked in a breath and sighed in interruption, trying as always to be Mr. Manners-And-Dignified. "How are you, Kyd?" he murmured, rising up to swipe his hand.

Kyd stood up, returning the gesture. "I'm well, Mister Taylor. Thank you for asking."

"Don't you have some place to be?" Dylan bit out. And there you have it, folks. Dylan's mouth started running on steroids. He wanted what he wanted, and everyone else needed to step out of his way.

Kyd slowly shook his head, almost in a purposeful taunt. "Actually, I don't."

Dylan warned, "Trust me, you do."

"No," Kyd refuted doggedly, "I've found what I was looking for... blonde, leggy, tanned, great teeth. That spells at least one date. Frankly, it might spell a trip to Cincinnati." That was the biggest load of bull-to-the-crap I'd ever heard. "How about it, Legs?" he said grinning.

"I considered trying a speedball once but then thought, *nah*, not worth the risk," I joked.

Sydney burst out laughing. Colton muttered, "Good Lord, I need an aspirin."

"Your mouth," Kyd fake pouted, "another reason why I want to date you."

Kyd continued the rakish grin, vacillating back and forth between Dylan's rising anger and my apparent reaction to it. Frankly, I was uncomfortable for two reasons. I didn't like to be the object of discussion, and I didn't want Dylan to go *Texas Chainsaw Massacre* on him. Kyd either liked inflicting his Casanovaish tendencies on girls or was an out-and-out idiot who didn't care if he lost his teeth. Maybe both.

"You're jealous," he said, smirking to Dylan. Dylan didn't confirm nor deny, but the statement definitely left him irritated. "Regardless," Kyd said shrugging, "it's my understanding that Darcy is single."

I am, I mumbled in my head.

Dylan gave him one of those stares that said you might technically be right, but there's a whole file of information you're not operating under. Kyd threw his head back—his laugh a little heavy on the theatrics. "Oh, my," he said. "I do believe you're green with envy."

I gasped, "Crap."

Sydney purred, "Suicide."

Dylan's father surprisingly remained quiet. It dawned on me, in that moment, he was more concerned with how his son handled poaching in his territory. What didn't I understand about the rules of Manland? Granted, most of my friends were males, but I'd never understand why some guys barely said, "Hello," and then immediately attacked what they thought was yours.

"You know who you remind me of, Kyd?" Dylan spat.

Kyd lifted a shoulder, indifferent. "Not in the slightest."

"You remind me of Darcy's grandfather's goats."

I choked on the Coke I'd been sipping, suddenly wanting to nosedive into the nearest volcano. Those goats were the stupidest creatures ever created, and in my opinion just sucked up green space best reserved for the cows.

Kyd folded his arms across his chest, looking confused. "I'm sorry," Dylan said to him. "Let me clarify the comparison...

Winston's asinine goats. They eat garbage and whatever else is in their path. And you know what? Their young are called *kids*. What I'm *doing*," he stressed, "is called a little bit of housekeeping, baby goat. Every once in a while, you need to take out the trash."

Dylan's father laughed loudly but quickly cleared his throat. Then he chuckled again and tried to swallow it down with iced tea. Vintage Dylan. No one did smart-mouth better than him.

"Dylan, that's *rude!*" I screeched. Surprise, surprise, he ignored me. "You're being a hypocrite," I huffed. "Girls flirt with you all the time."

"That's different," he said with a loud snort.

"How's that different?"

"It just is," Sydney whispered for him.

"I'm going," I told him.

Dylan rolled his eyes, giving me a dream-on look. "Are you sure about that?" he murmured.

My heart went atwitter, and I blinked back the haze of confusion. Why did I want to crawl inside my best friend's eyes? Problem was, whenever he got bossy I found myself acting like the head of the class in canine school. All barky and sitting on command. A few blinks later, I decided to embrace the inevitable. Dylan didn't want me to go...ergo, my spine became Jell-O.

"I'm sorry, Kyd," I muttered. "The answer is no."

Kyd turned smooth operator, echoing Dylan's question. "Are you sure about that?"

My mind dropped anchor, all operations on standby. I didn't possess the skills to even have that conversation because when I looked back at Dylan, every inch of my body started thrumming.

Huh...weird.

"I, um..." I scratched my head. "It's just," I said, gazing over toward Dylan. "Well, we *always*," I started again. "It's just one of those thingys, Kyd," I blurted out.

"One of those thingys," he repeated and chuckled.

"Yeah, one of those thingys."

Kyd's face ripened with determination, his jaw setting high, while his blue-green eyes tempted a girl with everything immoral. "Let's take this thing slowly," he said grinning. "Come over for Daddy's annual crawfish boil tonight. Sevenish."

A sound of pure bliss rolled out of Colton. "Crawfish boil?" he murmured with a smile. One thing about Colton, he'd eat anything you'd place in front of him. I'd seen him devour the gonads of a sea urchin.

"N'awlins style," Kyd drawled out. "One hundred pounds of fresh crawfish arrived this morning. We'll have all things deep-fried, Cajun, Creole, and jazz. My parents would love to entertain all of you, and once a year is not enough for Miss Legs, and it *is*," he emphasized, nodding toward Dylan, "*Miss*."

Dylan grunted, "I'm surprised you understand the term, Kyd. Don't you have a girlfriend?"

And that, in itself, lit the fire to the conversation in the first place.

Your move, Kyd.

Thing was, Kyd didn't have a leg to stand on. He *did* have a girl-friend—an unbelievably pretty girlfriend. Best friend of his sister, Yankee, and notoriously jealous. But they were an on-again, off-again kind of thing, with loads of replacements in between. For her sake, I hoped it stayed in the off-again phase. In short, that made Kyd a fastard—substitute a B if you're the cursing type. See, fastards weren't just bad boys. They were bad boys who had a Mrs. Fastard on the sly. Dylan had been waiting for the perfect moment to point that out. I was surprised it took him so long.

Kyd looked like he tried to understand quantum physics when he barely understood basic math. "I'd never cheat on Darcy," he finally said.

SURE, YOU WOULDN'T.

Dylan stood up, forcing Kyd to do the same. "Well, she's not on the market. Thanks for the invite, but we're busy."

Colton leaned over, placing a firm hand on the back of Dylan's thigh. Obviously, he'd hoped to rein him in, but the resigned and defeated look in his eyes said he didn't think that was possible.

"No, we're *not* busy," his father interrupted. "Thank your parents for the invitation, Kyd. We're looking forward to it."

"No, we're not," Dylan hissed.

"Oh, Good Lord, boys," his father said, frowning at them both. "Play nice."

"My brother doesn't want to play nice," Sydney said, laughing sultrily.

"Well, he can't kill Kyd," Colton grumbled. "Your mother doesn't like dead teenagers by her pool. It's the hospitable thing to do."

You could've heard a pin drop. When the air thickened with an overabundance of testosterone, Colton pushed himself out of the seat, downing the last of his iced tea. He slapped Dylan on the back. "Come on, son. Run the neighborhood with me. That flight left me a little jittery."

Dylan fumed, "I don't need to run. I'm actually relaxed." He wasn't relaxed. He was wound tighter than a steel drum bouncing on a trampoline. You know, just this side of the insane asylum.

Colton cleared his throat, and after Dylan pitched one last murderous stare in Kyd's direction, something unknown passed over his face that immediately snapped him out of the turmoil. He bent down into my space, tenderly cupping my face in his left hand. "Listen, sweetheart, block everyone out for a second. You're your own person, and I'd never stand in the way of your happiness. It's just that he makes my radar beep, and I want to protect you. I've got your back, yeah? And I just..."

Dylan's voice was so low and mesmerizing, it vibrated. He said something else, but by God I was stuck in the vibration. After a slow blink, he leaned in even closer and brushed our cheeks together—our version of a kiss.

The hormonal floodgates opened.

I needed to find a backbone or I needed to...

Aww, crap. I didn't know what I needed.

Colton snagged his sneakers from under his chair, quickly laced them up, and took off at a full-sprint through the side entrance. Dylan casually strutted inside, presumably to scout around for his shoes.

Sydney's voice graveled out, "Exactly what *is* your relationship, Darcy?"

I shrugged and curled to my side. I had nothing but baby kittens and moonbeams filling up my heart where Dylan was concerned. But I wasn't a fool. I had a feeling dating someone like him would bring me to my knees. It was absurd. It wasn't safe. It was illogical, and I'd have to seriously reevaluate my entire belief structure. Biggest opposition? We were too diametrically opposed. He was kind, dependable, and probably a knockout in the lovemaking department. That put him light-years ahead of me on the road to happily-ever-after. I was so ADHD, what if I never caught on to doing the wifey thing? You know, at least the part men really cared about?

"He's my best friend," I told them. And I just...loved him.

Kyd frowned and added, "Maybe you need to define those terms to Dylan. He doesn't seem to understand them. In fact, he acts like you're dating."

I suppose Dylan and I *did* act like we were dating. We had routines. He brought me coffee...I brought him the sports page. He gave me his dessert...I gave him my leftovers.

Come to think of it, we didn't act like we were dating...we acted like we were married.

Chapter Seven

THE LOUISIANA PURCHASE

Serendipity had secrets.

Probably why the coroner was parked across the street and detectives strung yellow crime scene tape through the yard. I didn't see what had happened, but the setting was definitely the aftermath of something deadly and momentous. The fact that it occurred at Gertrude Burr's home didn't shock me either. New to Serendipity, her reputation preceded her. She was a homewrecker and left her last neighborhood in Jupiter, Florida, because she not only wrecked a marriage but the six-figure car of her adulterous lover. Legend had it the bumper was left hanging from a street sign. Evidently, women could perform miraculous feats and don superhuman strength when they were so motivated.

Two men with "Coroner" on the backs of their black jackets wheeled a stuffed body bag out on a stretcher to place in the back of a black Suburban SUV. It bounced vertically twice when it hit the sidewalk, and an arm shot up out of the zipper at ninety degrees. I nearly wet myself and quickly grabbed the binoculars I'd snatched from the study earlier. Focusing on the body, one man rested a hip on the gurney, putting the full force of his weight on the arm, coaxing it to bend. The arm contrarily wouldn't move, so the man opposite him leaned across the stretcher, attempting to angle the arm at the elbow. The victim—hand size insinuated male—had been dead for some time because it shouldn't have been that difficult to get it to budge. When they finally got the victim zipped in the bag, Gertrude and a tall, stately man exited the house speaking with an officer who expeditiously took dictation on a notepad.

Gertrude's face looked hollowed out, like a skeleton that'd been scared out of its own skin. The profile of her companion appeared unusually perturbed and not what the situation called for. He was both ruthless and apathetic or had almost expected things to happen. He held himself with an exorbitant amount of self-confidence—it lay in the strong curve of his spine, the elevation of his chin, the broad expanse of his shoulders. Even though he wasn't law enforcement, it was apparent he steered and controlled the conversation.

My curiosity grew like a malignant cancer. Did I have time for something else amidst Cisco Medina and whatever the heck it was Lincoln was into?

In a word, no...but I'd make time.

Situations like that were what made me expand the roster of whom I hypothetically employed on my staff. I couldn't be everywhere at once, and since Murphy hadn't been willing to part with any XY chromosomes—giving me brothers I could bully around—I developed a brotherhood of my own.

Call me Darcy Walker, AKA a Cincinnati mob boss.

My life, Grand Central Station for Freaks.

Inductees into my brotherhood had a certain swagger, with an undying loyalty to all future members—my discretion, of course. We had, for lack of a better phrase, a handshake. Not a high-five or secret whisper in the air, it was the modified chicken dance. It consisted of two beaky hands, two flapping of your wings, two hip shakes, and then a chest bump. We looked weird (okay, we looked like certifiable boneheads), but as long as I found people willing to be crazy, it was a no-brainer.

I had four proverbial brothers, and Zander stood in the bathroom next to me begging to join the mob.

"Let me join the coalition, Darcy," he said, staring into the mirror and attempting to style his tawny-colored hair. "It's the least I can do since I bloodied your nose."

Removing the binoculars from my neck, I pitched them in his direction and finished flat ironing my hair. Other than a few cowlicks, my hair hung poker straight. Stylists, however, claimed girls had to flatiron their tresses to show the extra effort. By the smell, all I did was singe the ends.

"You're doing this *for* me?"

A deviant grin curled the edges of his lips. "I'm doing it *for* you."

Wearing only a pair of black nylon shorts, his chest was concave and totally devoid of testosterone. I hoped things jelled together, but it didn't look like he'd headline the girls' locker room talk anytime soon. "What do you have to offer?" I asked.

"A lifetime of eyes and ears, spying on anything Dylan does, and who he does it with. If it's NC-17, you'll get all the tawdry, raunchy details in 3D and high-def. And yeah," he said, chuckling and jerking his head toward the window, "I noticed the excitement, and I'm all over that."

Adrenaline spiked through me. Praise the Lord. It was a gift from Heaven.

Lifting my shirt, I drenched my underarms with Lady Speed Stick and applied a touch of blush, saturated my lashes, and rolled on two coats of pale pink lip gloss. "Do you love me?"

"One hundred percent."

"Will you keep my secrets?"

He leaned up against the doorjamb, taking two fingers, symbolically locking his lips. "Until death," he promised.

"My other brothers?"

"Family."

"Deal," I said. We did the modified chicken dance...twice for good measure.

Zander jumped up and down, acting as though he'd just seen his first naked girl. Puckering his lips, he sauntered three steps closer, aiming right for my mouth. Suddenly, the room felt hotter than a bonfire. The boy might only be twelve, but he threw off enough hormonal heat to warm Poland. "Do we ever get to kiss?" he moaned flirtatiously.

I had to think about that. There was a four-year age gap, and I was two months shy of sixteen. *Nah*, I quickly decided. Dylan would de-ball him. And it was officially incest. "Maybe if we travel to the mountains."

"Run that by me again?" Kyd asked confused.

What-evvvs. I explained the benefits of joining the brotherhood for the third time. Frankly, there were no benefits other than bragging rights, and bragging rights existed in my own warped, little mind. Well, that wasn't totally true. If he needed me to have his back, I'd have it and then some.

Thing was, Kyd wanted me to have something else...

"Repeat after me," I said and laughed. "Darcy's the boss."

"Darcy's the boss," he echoed. I *sooooo* wanted to say Jester, but that identity needed to remain on the down-low. When we landed, Colton reminded me his laptop belonged to me all week. Feeling industrious, I typed and re-typed a let-me-explain letter to *troyoncrime*. When I realized there was nothing to explain, I deleted it, paced the floor, and banged my head against the wall until it bruised.

Time. Give me time, people, and I'd rock Orlando's world.

"You're in," I told him.

"Is this a secret?"

"Not really," I said, lifting my shoulders in a shrug, but if it were true to the mob, it should be.

"I like secrets," Kyd moaned. "Can we seal the secret with a kiss?"

"No!" I said with a giggle. "That's sort of creepy." Both of my new brothers were incestuous. If I had bylaws, that'd be the first clause included: no making out with the family.

The whole concept totally flew over Kyd's massively touchable, blond head. "What time are you coming over?"

Kyd was killing me. He'd called three times in three hours, and our new blood tie insinuated he could step it up even more frequently. *Maybe I should go over early*, I rationalized. If anyone knew the dirty laundry in town, it would be Herbie and Minda Sue Knoblecker. Good thing because I felt slightly dirty.

Waiting until Dylan jumped in the shower, I quickly slid into black shorts, a painted on tuxedo T-shirt, and black flip-flops with sequins adorning the top. Knowing I needed to give accountability for my whereabouts, I sought out Lincoln while he shaved. He motioned me inside the bathroom as he finished up a phone call with his partner and Dylan's godfather, Patrick O'Leary.

The earbuds of my iPod were threaded in one ear, listening to Godsmack's "Voodoo." Lincoln held the title of the world's most suspicious man. True to nature, he pulled the white cord from one ear and listened for about five seconds, and then yanked it out with a snort. "What's this *shiii*—stuff?" he corrected himself instead of saying the s-h-i-t- word.

"Godsmack's Voodoo," I said, smiling and taking it from his hand.

"Godsmack?" he echoed.

"Voodoo," I said, grinning bigger.

"Of course, it is," he grumbled. "Darcy, this is Paddy. Paddy," he paused, "Darcy."

"Hey, Paddy," I said.

Paddy answered in an Irish brogue. "Hawareya, doll?"

Paddy slurred his three-worded "How are you" into a three-syllabled sound. Nice to talk, but seriously, I didn't have time for chitchat even if it appeared rude.

"Good," I said, "and you?"

"Grand. I heard you've grown up quite a bit." Well, he might think differently if he knew the bullcrap I'd been bathing in.

"Finish up," Lincoln told him. Scooting around Lincoln, I fell onto the toilet, trying my best to remain calm. Wasn't working. My legs bounced up and down, my heart beat irregularly, and before long, I'd developed an eye twitch that felt terminal. Lincoln pressed his razor to his cheek and carefully swung the blade downward, mimicking the movement until one side of his face smoothed. Rinsing the blade, he duplicated the process on the other cheek.

"Our girl told me Turkey's proposin' a large land deal," Paddy said. "In other words, this third family wants to buy their books of business or a portion of it, at least. And if the deal isn't legitimate, we're lookin' at a turf war beyond turf wars."

"Hmmm," Lincoln responded.

"Yeah," Paddy said and snorted. "Hmmm is about right."

I didn't have time for *hmmms* because time tick-tocked away. Except something was scheduled to go down, and my imagination polluted my thoughts of what that could be. Were they referring to that midnight meeting? With the man making unreasonable demands? And *hellooooo*, what about the body in the video whose head just happened to pop off?

"You saw the video, right?" Paddy asked.

Talk about timing. I couldn't breathe. Move. Do anything other than swallow my own dang tongue. "Yes," Lincoln muttered, surprisingly unaffected. "Just because he stole the video doesn't mean he now has the right to make demands."

Let me summarize...so the guy making demands snitched on the goings-on of a psychopath? A psychopath who liked to film his own psychotic exploits? Stupid and dangerous, but idiots like him kept people like me entertained.

Lincoln suddenly jumped subjects, bracing one hand on the sink with a faraway look in his eyes. "What in the world is a viscount, Paddy?"

Oh, boy. Talking about his daughter's boyfriend was one subject I needed to get out of like yesterday. "Ah, I don't know, Linc," Paddy said sighing. "Whaddya think, Darcy?"

Heck, if I knew. I wouldn't recognize a viscount any more than I'd recognize a balanced meal. I offered him a shrug—my face saying Henry Ainsworth embodied the dumbest viscount of all viscounts.

After a few more sentences where they contemplated whether Henry was a closet serial killer, I finally spit out that I'd ditched Dylan like a bad date. Both wanted to know if guns were in the Knobleckers' home. Did they do drugs? Were they ex-convicts, pedophiles, or sociopaths? When I joked that they were in the witness protection program for assassinating Viscount Henry Ainsworth of the British Highlands, both belted out a laugh and kissed me on my way.

Not before Lincoln gave me a wicked grin, acknowledging it wouldn't go over well with his grandson. *What the heck*, I'd told him, *I'm a verb*. Plus, in the back of my mind screamed the fact that I'd called a grieving mother, promising the impossible.

My conscience dealt with a lot...not delivering, I couldn't stomach.

Five minutes later, Zander and I stood stoically in front of the Knobleckers' front door.

Seven cars lined the drive: two Cadillac Escalades, a Dodge Viper, some sort of souped-up European contraption, a red Corvette, a black Maserati, and last but not least, a silver Maybach. Several professional athletes lived in Serendipity, and Kyd made friends fast. He was personable, fun loving, and always ready for a nighttime pick-up game. Thing of it was, that's when Kyd did his best work. Turn the lights down low, and Kyd, the womanizer, came to the forefront.

I rang the doorbell, wondering if God himself would answer the door in his robe. You know how life's made up of the haves and have-nots? Serendipity's made up of the haves and have-mores. Herbert Knoblecker won the Powerball when it hit $250M in Louisiana five years earlier, and his home indisputably ranked as one of the largest have-mores in the neighborhood.

Giving my underarms a quick sniff, the socially awkward part of me halfway turned to bolt when the door opened with a sharp-dressed Kyd. All I could think was, *Down, libido, down.*

"Wow," he said. Kyd looked me up and down and whistled. "You look scrumptious."

"Yeah, my brother thinks so too," Zander grumbled.

I elbowed Zander in the ribs. It wasn't the time for him to protect what he assumed was Dylan's domain. We were on the job—anything was acceptable when we were on the job. I could beat myself up over it later.

Kyd's hair lay slightly damp and clung to the sides of his face, framing cheekbones that could cut you. With a brisk headshake, he finger-combed it in place over a face that would never be ordinary. For some unknown reason, I gulped down a burning desire. Kyd, no doubt, was a good-looking guy. Let me amend that: a very, *very* good-looking guy (he deserved two adverbs). Maybe I needed to rethink that no-kissing-of-the-family clause because my lips suddenly begged for something to do.

"What are you thinking?" he murmured. "Your face blanked out for a moment."

"Just thinking about my bylaws," I mumbled.

Kyd chuckled. "I love the way you think. It's just so—"

"Warped," I finished in an embarrassed giggle.

"No, Legs," he said softly. "You're one of a kind."

No, that's him, I thought. Kyd had adorned himself in blue and khaki plaid shorts to the knees and a navy T-shirt. On his feet, however, were one hundred dollar flip-flops. Lord have mercy. Mine were the Walmart special.

Placing his hand on the small of my back, he steered the three of us toward the party. We followed him through a maze of antiques, traditional leather furniture, and expensive light fixtures. Everything shone brilliant and glittery and would probably take my father's weekly salary simply to replace a light bulb. When we made it to the kitchen, we stepped around several ladies dressed in black who were lighting up chafing dishes filled with dirty rice, red beans, bourbon chicken, gumbo, and jambalaya while throwing fresh seafood in ice buckets.

Kyd opened the sliding glass doors.

First thought? Gasp.

Second? Run for the freaking hills.

About forty people fraternized and sipped beverages, smiling one thousand-watt, beautiful people smiles. In the left corner, a jazz ensemble picked out a ragtime funk that included a trumpet, clarinet, and trombone. A bow-tied pianist hunkered over the keyboard while a drummer and guitarist rounded out the rhythm section. A soloist growled through his song, making eye contact with anyone who would gaze his way. It looked like the French Quarter 2.0, and by the smell of the cuisine, everyone was destined to leave five pounds heavier. Red, crab-shaped lights outlined the porch while fire-breathing Tiki torches lit up the black-bottomed pool. The ambiance was fun, festive, and stimulating to all five senses...perfect for a party.

Even more perfect for a bloated stomach.

Zander made a beeline for three girls his age.

"Look who's here, Daddy," Kyd bragged as he led me to his father.

Wearing three pounds of gold necklaces and a pinky ring that weighed five, Herbie's loafers squeaked like a rusty door hinge as he waddled toward us. The night air was hotter than Africa, and his off-white linen shirt was peppered with perspiration while his matching shorts stuck between hairy thighs.

I took a long, hard look at Herbie. Maybe I liked him so much because he reminded me of *me*. He came from humble beginnings, and God knew I understood the term of being humbled. People like us always searched for the opportunity to prove we belonged and not an oxygen poacher from the real movers and shakers. Kyd and his sister had assimilated well as the nouveau riche. Herbie, however, still made mistakes. He would definitely benefit from that speech "less is more." Right then, he looked like a cross between a nervous pimp and sweaty rapper.

He set down a can of Red Cream Soda and greeted me with a warm handshake. "Herbert Knoblecker. "Soft K," he said. I'd known Herbie for years, but he always insisted on informing the world he understood phonetic spelling and that the first "K" was silent. I had a friend—acquaintance really, because she personified evil—who introduced herself in the same fashion. With Herbie, it was endearing. With her, she was downright witchified.

"Hey, Herbie," I said, offering him with a smile.

"Ya taller than me now." A munchkin stood taller than Herbie. He'd tapped out at five foot two and close to two hundred pounds. He yanked me over in an aggressive hug.

"Daddy's affectionate with people he likes," Kyd apologized.

"I like him too," I said laughing.

Herbie released me with a frown, boring a question into my eyes. "Where are the Taylors?"

"On their way." *Probably digging my grave*, I omitted.

"Ye sure? I called Colton this afternoon, and he promised they was comin'. He said he couldn't wait for the jass."

My guess was he wanted to *kick* my *jass*, but that was just me.

Leading us to the poolside bar, Herbie offered me a Coke. Our server was South American, tiny, and markedly dark. "Gracias," I said, saluting my drink toward her, bringing the glass to my lips.

"Habla español?" she said and grinned.

"Si," I answered. "My nanny taught me. She's loco and likes magia bajo la luna."

She poured Kyd a soft drink while he moaned, "I'm in love."

"Magic under the moon?" she verified.

"Voodoo," I clarified. "She's trying to give me boobs."

Kyd spit his Coke out in a horizontal geyser, soaking the front of his father's shirt.

Herbie wasn't even fazed. "I fashion myself a witch too," he grumbled. "I've got a nasty fungus I've been trying to get rid of on my—"

Kyd nearly yanked my arm out of my socket, hauling us away before I discovered the location of Herbie's fungus. My eyes darted to the sliding glass doors. The Taylors' ETA was thirty minutes past let's-kill-Darcy ago, and my heart grew tight and constricted with each passing second. I could feel it in my bones that somebody wasn't happy.

It didn't take three guesses to figure out whom.

Who I recognized as Leroy "Big J" Jefferson, bellowed for Kyd to join him. Big J played professional basketball for the Orlando Magic and stood around seven feet tall of Black testosterone. Bald as a cue ball, he came clad in a shirt so geometrically colorful he looked like a Colombian drug lord.

A crawfish boil station sat about fifteen feet over from the bar. Big J had parked himself next to it with a smile on his face that looked as indecent as something found on the Vegas Strip...guess he liked seafood. A dark-skinned female chef dropped squirmy crawfish into a boiling pot, delivering death-by-ladle to the crawfish not smart enough to stay out of the net. After they died, she dumped a load on Big J's plate next to corn-on-the-cob and boiled potatoes. Big J bit off the crawdad's head and sucked it dry until its pink casing crumbled in his hand.

The fact that I didn't barf was nothing short of miraculous.

Kyd raised one brow. "Come with?" he asked, momentarily wondering if I was too finicky. Honest to God, I didn't shy away from new experiences, but I'd rather puncture a lung than for a crawfish feeler to latch onto my tonsils. Plus, I needed to talk to Herbie...preferably alone.

"I'll keep Herbie company," I said.

Kyd pivoted toward Big J, resting his hand alongside my cheek. "Don't go away, Legs. Give me one minute."

I gave him a lot of teeth.

The wind kicked up a notch, drying the perspiration that had pooled at the base of my neck. I looked "amaze" when I left the house—okay, scientifically and socially acceptable—but outdoor parties in Florida were inviting catastrophe. The humidity had grabbed ahold of my hair, and it stood about an inch off my scalp, hookerfied.

Zander said he was quote-unquote all over the action next door. The boy hadn't asked anyone anything—and frankly had gone phantom—so I made that first on my list of questions for Herbie. "What happened across the street at Gertrude Burr's house?" I asked.

Herbie practically frothed at the mouth, his double chin jiggling like a gelatin mold. "Gertrude came home and found a man floating facedown in her pool. He was blue. Dead. Wrinkled like a darn raisin. End of story."

Huh. "Did she know him?"

"Never seen him before."

"A man was with her as she talked to the coroner and detectives. What's his name?"

"New boyfriend, I've never met 'im. I invited both of 'em over, but Gertrude was so shook up that she took a pass."

That would suffice for the moment, but prudence said I needed to get the scoop on Cisco Medina's disappearance before the hometown fuzz arrived. "Herbie, what's the deal with Cisco Medina?"

As expected, Herbie knew exactly whom I referred to and gave me the dark, sordid details. His own version included child trafficking, Devil worshipping grandparents, holes in the ozone layer, and what he feared included alien abduction.

"Did ye know there's a trust in his name that funds private investigators?" he said proudly. "I give 'em $10 Gs a month."

Ten thousand? I gulped. "That's pretty steep."

"If we can git that little boy back from the aliens, it'll all be worth it."

I guess he had a point. "Did you know him personally?"

He downed the last of his Red Cream Soda. "Not real well. Ye should talk to Kyd. He's a friend with his daddy, Hank. Hank works in the kitchen at the Club."

Well, well, well, clue number one said the mother had something to hide. Clue number two washed dishes in the clubhouse. It's times like these I took my cue from the universe that my bad behavior was called for. Maybe that was the way I justified my actions, but hey, to be successful at times you had to kill your conscience.

Herbie took a long whiff of air. "Why looky here," he said, grinning bigger. "Minda Sue's arrived. She took a little extra time to get dolled up. I kin smell her."

I drew in the aroma, almost barfing up my intestines. "What's she wearing?" I asked and coughed.

"Chanel Number Five, Beautiful, Clive Christian Number One, and good old-fashioned Timeless from Avon. She never can decide, so she wears 'em all. Don't she smell like sweet tea and pralines?"

I had visions of a funeral home crossed with fabric softener and mossy wheat field. I coughed again. "It's definitely unique."

"Well, *she's* unique. Minda Sue won Miss Congeniality in the Yambilee Festival. She smiled and all I saw was movie star."

All *I* saw was silicone: big boobs, big butt, big hair, and whatever junk they sucked out of her trunk I think they shoved into Herbie's. She basically had the body of a well-endowed eighteen-year-old with the face of a woman stuck in a wind tunnel. Minda Sue was clothed in head-to-toe Chanel, wearing a white sheath dress with two little "Cs" on the front pockets. She'd paired it with black flats that appeared two sizes, too small and a diamond necklace that had *Herbie's* written out in cursive.

Classy...all the way around.

"Well, I do declare," Minda Sue greeted. "It's none other than Miss Darcy Walker herself. Kyd's in *love*, and he said ye was single. Would ye like to go out on a date?"

Yikes. Talk about your forward momma. Right then felt like the Louisiana Purchase.

Chapter Eight
BACKUP PLAN

"**K**yd's my blood brother," I attempted to explain. "I don't date brothers."

Minda Sue's face filled with confusion. My guess was her brain got zapped along with her true hair color. Either that or my lexicon of norm needed a serious overhaul.

"Come on," she said smiling. "Let's talk while ye eat."

Linking her arm in mine, we ambled to yet another food station. Seafood and hot sausage po' boy sandwiches were made to order, meatballs and green beans simmered high, and mac-and-cheese bubbled next to a fruit salad and fries. I wanted to take my tongue and lap it across the table like a dog.

Shocking that I located some self-control.

Picking up a sausage po' boy from a silver tray, I globbed some macaroni on my plate and grabbed four meatballs, plopping one in my mouth with a toothpick. It happened to be one of those times it proved best to leave me at home. If I didn't cause the catastrophe, I somehow attracted one.

Minda Sue bent over for a napkin, tipped my plate with her boobs, causing a meatball to tumble down my neck and somehow work its way inside my bra. As everyone let out a collective gasp, Minda Sue dabbed my chest...Herbie fondled my chest. I danced a little jig until it rolled down my stomach and onto the floor. That was what happened when a girl didn't have cleavage, folks. The floor was a straight shot.

"I'm sorry, Darcy!" she shrieked.

"That's okay," I said. I gazed at her chest and added, "Nice boobs." I mentally smacked my own mouth. Please tell me I didn't say that out loud. When Herbie's chest puffed out with pride, that pretty much affirmed that I had—and he was thrilled with the upgrade.

Lifting my shirt to clean my stomach, Herbie knocked my hand out of the way and spit on his napkin, rubbing in a wide-eyed oblivion across my abs. One would think I'd feel violated—and perhaps that was a testament to misshapen morals—instead, I had an overwhelming need to laugh.

Minda Sue twirled toward her husband. "Where's Oinky?" she gasped, looking at the meatball between my feet.

Herbie whistled and out from a white pet door cut into the side of the house toddled a gray and black pot-bellied pig. Grunting his way over, he gobbled up the meatball.

Oinky was domesticated, but his DNA suggested warthog. You know how they say a person chooses a pet that resembled them? Herbie either adhered to that rule or exercised it subconsciously... they looked like twin pygmies. Both were dark-skinned, short with squatty, little legs, and hairs they could braid, hanging from their schnoz.

After Oinky's tongue took a few swipes at my toes, he snorted and fell over to his side with a tooting thonk. Herbie quickly set him aright as he grunted back through the door.

"You've got to excuse, Oinky," Herbie said. He laughed, embarrassed. "He's got the vapors."

What did I care, I had a case of Darcy's-dead-meat-coming my way.

Minda Sue suddenly got that pistol-wielding momma face again. "Where were we?"

Herbie slapped me on the back. "Darcy was tellin' us why she cain't date Kyd."

Minda Sue tried to frown, but the Botox made it impossible. "Why not? Kyd told me ye went through some ritual that involved a chicken, but it didn't involve real blood. That means you're good to date. Right?"

I nibbled on my sausage po' boy, attempting a response. "I suppose, but it still kinda feels like incest."

Herbie snorted, gazing at me like I was an idiot. "You mean like kissin' cousins? *All* cousins kiss. Ya just got to make sure it ain't on the lips."

I scratched my head, wondering if that was true.

"He also said ya do whatever Dylan tells ye," Minda Sue interjected. "Is Dylan ye brother?"

I couldn't help but sigh. "Dylan *won't* be my brother, but I want him to be," I said.

"Well, would ye date Dylan?" she pushed.

"No." *Possibly*, I thought. "He's too *much* like a brother." Although, he'd been acting sort of strange, which I found kind of odd.

Minda Sue took one intimidating step closer, and my fear escalated to the highest level of somebody-kill-me-now. "Well, if he's too much like a brother to date, then why don't ye date a blood brother that ya barely know? That seems like destiny."

I was confused because it sort of made sense.

Herbie shook his head adamantly while he fingered a meatball off my plate. "But if they're related, then they cain't date," he said in a gruff. "I know some of that stuff still flies but not with me. I suppose if they're fourth, fifth, or sixth cousins that don't really count. The royals roll that way in England."

All I'd wanted was to gossip about Orlando, and I suddenly wondered if Murphy had made me a dowry.

Minda Sue stomped her black leather flat onto the patio. "But they're not cousins, Herbie. They're brothers even though Darcy's a girl."

"No," I said giggling. "I'm the godfather."

Herbie grunted as a nearby server placed fries and gravy onto his plate. "Well, that changes evrathin'. That's a vertical family tree. We ain't doin' no one-branch family tree, Minda Sue." Suddenly, I had an eeeuw moment but let it pass. "Tell me where your kin's from, Darcy. I've got to make sure we're only cousins because this brother and father stuff could be a deal breaker."

I scooped up some macaroni and tried not to laugh. Good God, I loved these people. "I'm a Cincinnati native. Word on the street says we're from the Walker line that came from Great Britain. Somewhere along the trail, we mixed blood with German and Scottish ancestors. My grandfather claims one of our relatives was on the Mayflower."

Herbie's eyes dilated tenfold. "*The* Mayflower?"

"Plymouth Rock," I confirmed.

He elbowed his wife in the ribs. "Well, that's top shelf, Minda Sue. Kyd deserves top shelf."

Both of them beamed like they'd hit the jackpot all over again. Grandpa Winston somehow scored the manifest. Who knew how, but at least it boasted a good story on family history day. Evidently, my great, great—*however many greats*—grandmother fell in love with a Cherokee Indian scout and married him. One of their offspring hooked up with a Walker along the marital trail. So my identity confusion was something I was born into in spite of my "dark walker" name.

True to the melting pot, my family was the Chergerbritishscotch —the mutts that sounded like a mixed drink with whiskey.

"So you're a mongrel?" Herbie asked.

"A mutt," I said.

"The best coonhound I ever had mixed blood with a toy poodle. It made for a weird bark and hairy bottom, but that mutt was good in the hunt."

I reached up and smacked him a high-five.

"I believe the correct word is multicultural," Minda Sue said snootily. "Turn around, Darcy."

I had no idea why she requested but provided a slow revolutionary turn anyway.

Minda Sue gave Herbie another expressionless face. "She don't have birthin' hips, Herbie."

I swallowed hard. Dear God, I didn't want to birth *anything*.

"You had *great* birthing hips, Minda Sue," Herbie bragged. Minda Sue's hips were three feet wide with a four-figure lipo job. No doubt, she could've birthed a cow.

"It don't feel right, Herbie. Kyd weighed thirteen pounds. You've got to be able to push somethin' that big out, and that ain't right to do to a young girl."

I choked on my last meatball as Herbie pounded on my back. It popped out and bounced three times before landing in front of the rhythm section. "Then I'm not a good purchase," I coughed out. "Kyd deserves the best, so just keep me as your backup plan."

The Knobleckers pondered my lack of birthing equipment as Herbie ran a thick hand down my hip. "I don't know Minda Sue. With legs like that, a baby could walk outta the womb. Let's not count her out yit. Can we think about it?"

I tried to find a smile, but it lodged somewhere between thirteen pounds and an incestuous relationship with my blood brother. "Sure," I said, smiling sweetly. "We don't want to rush into anything."

The Knobleckers took one last gander at my legs and wandered over to their other guests. When I turned, I caught my reflection in the sliding glass doors. Casting a reflection back were Dylan and his father. Both were garbed in what I called look-at-my-six-pack-black —black shorts, matching polos, and leather slides. The first had a disgruntled scowl—the second, a satisfied snicker.

Insert the fidgets. Lots of fidgets.

I slurped up a spoon of mac-and-cheese and traipsed over to join them, speculating whether Dylan had a gun.

Colton grinned. "We've stood behind you and listened to the majority of your conversation, dear. Work for me when you gradu- ate. If you can maneuver dialogue around like that, then I'll make you a millionaire by the time you're twenty-five."

"Tough negotiations, huh?" I asked.

"Extremely," his father said laughing.

"Hey, D," I said, giving him the teeth. *Pray, Walker. For God's sake, pray...pray...pray*. Dylan crossed his arms over his chest, stubborn as a freaking mule. "No hi?" I pouted.

Dylan's voice went tight. "What are you up to? I can feel it in my bones the Darcy Boat is about to hit an iceberg."

I scooped up more mac-and-cheese, offering it to him, which he not so politely ignored. "Whoa, back it up, Prince Charming," I said. "This little Cinderella can fend for herself. And although that iceberg comment is degrading, I'm willing to overlook it if you'll be my brother. Be my brother," I said, winking flirtatiously, "and we'll have no secrets."

He rolled his eyes so high he saw his own brain.

Colton jabbed him in the side. "So my son won't be your brother, eh?"

"Nope," I said, munching my food, "and it hurts my feelings."

"Exactly what's the reasoning for hurting her feelings, son?" Colton acted like he was smiling inside. Dylan looked like he wanted to punch his smiler.

"I'd like to know that too, D. What gives?"

Dylan eyed the crowd, searching for something to annihilate. He came off as primal, emotional, looking for a cave to crawl inside and growl. Something emanated from him that was carnal and all male. Someone who protected what was his and got ticked off as heck when someone messed with it. I cocked my head in wonderment, realizing I was staring at my father. I wanted to laugh. I wanted to run away. Heck, I wanted to fall into his arms because I always knew what I'd be getting. A love that would forever be true—but a love that could steal my last breath.

Colton sighed deeply, shook his head with a frown, located his wife, and strode away.

"The last thing I'll ever be is your *brother*, Darcy," Dylan bit out. "We need to have a little talk."

I inwardly shivered. "A walkie-talkie?"

Dylan's eyes narrowed into beady, snake-like slits. "A walkie-talkie," he repeated. A walkie-talkie was basically when Dylan forced me to listen to whatever he thought I needed to change in my life. The practice evolved from battery-powered walkie-talkies we had as children to the teenage shut-up and listen.

As I stumbled to keep up with his stride, Dylan pulled me onto his lap in an empty chair in the corner. He told me not to leave without telling him, not to jump without asking how high, and not to kiss anyone I wasn't related to. Then he stared. He stared for a good thirty seconds and started up again, whispering the biggie of all biggies, "You hurt my feelings, sweetheart. You really, really did."

Darn him, darn him to heck.

As I offered the mother of all mea culpas, something even worse happened. Have you ever been punched in the face? Like really punched? No? Me neither, but I swear the universe made a fist and launched one right in my jaw. Kyd's sister, Yankee, literally plopped down on Dylan's other knee and inched me out in an attempt for both.

I felt like bursting into song...(NOT).

Dylan bristled but was nonetheless mannerly. I snorted at his convenient display of propriety though. In my opinion, he should've spit on her, but I got the feeling most boys couldn't control themselves when two girls moved in their lap. When I attempted an escape, his hand grabbed onto the bottom of my shorts and tugged me back in place.

Dylan's fingers were warm, demanding, and almost sensuous. Crud. That might be the first time ever the word sensuous entered my brain waves.

"Hi, Yankee," Dylan murmured. "How are you?"

She gave him an overly sweet smile. "Wonderful, now that you're here."

Cue the barf.

Cupid's arrow'd struck Yankee when she turned fourteen, and apparently, the chubby little cherub still released his bow. But where Dylan was concerned, Cupid seemed to have an unlimited supply of weaponry. Yankee had a turned-up nose, her lips were full, the bottom one slightly fuller. From what I gathered, she was the cheer captain too. I wasn't even the band geek. You had to be talented to be a band geek. I could barely play the air guitar.

Yankee also looked like she hung with the wheatgrass and carrot juice crowd. About five foot four and maybe—*maybe*—ninety pounds, her weight was distributed in all the appropriate places. Enter Darcy Walker: Neanderthal-tall, loudmouthed laugh, so-so features with a dirty-blonde head and boobless torso. Plus, my body would die of shock if it consumed wheatgrass and carrot juice.

She'd dressed in a black tube top, heels, and a white micro-miniskirt. In short, it looked garish, but from what I'd observed, teenage guys lived for garish.

"Hello, Darcy," she said, smirking snidely and finally acknowledging my presence.

"Yippee-ki-yay to you too," I mumbled sarcastically. "Would you like the other knee?"

She looked at me like I was a circus freak. "How thoughtful of you to offer," she said. I had a feeling she'd take it anyway.

I wriggled around again, but Dylan slid his hand up my shorts, locked onto my thigh, and roughly sat me back on his right leg.

"That wasn't necessary," I grumbled angrily.

Dylan placed his lips underneath the curve of my chin. His breath blew hot and angry with an immediate demand that I pay attention to it. "I beg to differ," he murmured.

That tickled, but I was determined to not let him know it. A broken longneck bottle lay at our feet. Yankee picked it up, the prism of light caught in the reflection of the Tiki torches. She and I locked eyes, lost in a world of territorial dispute and cold innuendo. *What do you plan on doing with that glass?* I silently asked her.

I'm not to be messed with, she mutely responded.

My heart palpitated twice. I wasn't afraid of the girl. H-to-the-e-l-l no. I just wished it was socially acceptable for me to drown her in the pool.

I frowned at Dylan and whispered, "Are you aware another girl is in your lap, Romeo?"

"Hmm," he murmured, leaning into my ear. "And what, pray tell, would you like me to do about said other girl sitting in my lap?"

"Hold her down while I drown her."

Dylan lightly laughed. "Now, sweetheart, that would make me an accessory to a major crime."

"So?"

"So I think you can't stand it when I'm not one hundred percent yours."

I snorted, hitching my chin up a notch. "In the spirit of us telling each other what we think," I muttered, "you can't stand it when *everyone* is not one hundred percent yours."

Another light chuckle. "Ahhh, sweetheart, you wound me."

Dylan murmured in a sexy-as-heck voice that only he could produce. I slid my eyes over angrily, telling him to kiss my big, white arse. He threw his head back, laughing.

"You're only doing this because you're mad at me," I pouted.

"I've been mad before, and it's never held any historic or intrinsic value."

I opened my mouth and closed it, even more irritated than

before. We listened to Yankee brag about her clothes, brag about boyfriends, and brag about bragging. Then thankfully, Kyd zoned in on my predicament and rescued me from his sister who was obviously a narcissist.

He whistled in my direction, and before Dylan could protest, I pushed off in a harried frenzy. I meandered through some Fortune 500 types, witnessed Zander kissing a brunette behind a plant, goosed Grandma Alexandra, and smacked Dylan's mother on her tight, little behind. Big mistake...she pulled me by the elbow over to the corner for a speech on proper decorum. I almost laughed. Murphy quit giving that speech when I was eight.

All I knew was sometimes my impulses were larger than my desire to dodge any punishment meted out. When she viewed Zander rolling around next to us (seriously, he went horizontal on some chick), she let out an "Eeek," and I counted it as my chance for escape. Tripping over my own feet, I stumbled headfirst into Big J's knee and a plate of crawdads. Even though they were dead, their pink creepy-crawly feelers still latched onto my hair. I wanted to faint, scream like a girl, or yell for the male with the most testosterone to save me, but even I had standards. When I danced around to dislodge them, I knocked Big J's iced tea out of his hand, which rolled down my back, soaking me to the bone.

What the mother of God...

Big J gasped, pulling me up, gaping at his empty cup, horrified. "I'm so sorry!" he apologized. Bending down, he fingered a crawdad out of my hair and pitched it onto his empty plate.

"That's okay," I said grimacing. "I have klutzy tendencies. Accidents are normal for me."

He tipped my chin between his thumb and forefinger. "Babe, you're about as normal as a two-dollar bill. And *you* are?"

Kyd plucked a napkin off a server's tray, trying unsuccessfully to dry me off. "It's Darcy," Kyd answered.

Big J's mouth dropped wide. "Dylan's girl?" he verified. *Not anymore*, I thought.

Kyd laughed. "She's about to become *my* girl."

I gnawed on my lower lip.

"Is that right?" Big J asked oddly, addressing me. "I always thought something was going on between you and Dylan. I texted him earlier. Why don't the both of you play golf with Kyd and me tomorrow afternoon?"

Kyd acted as if he'd been given the keys to the candy store. I didn't particularly want to play any sort of game with Kyd, but I wasn't above using his amour to introduce me to Hank Henry. Besides, Kyd had a girlfriend. His cheating, fastard butt ought to know better.

Kyd commenced with the begging, bending down on one knee. "Say yes, Legs. Let me go to bed with a smile on my face."

If I said yes, perhaps I'd run into Hank Henry in the clubhouse. If I said no, then let's face it, I'd be stupid.

We were standing next to a dessert tray. Leaning over, I picked out the fluffiest beignet, deciding to savor the moment. "Wouldn't miss it for the world," I said, giving him a lot of teeth.

After your basic I'll-meet-you-here, nobody-be-late conversation, I decided to clean up and answer nature's call. Cramming the beignet in my mouth, I strolled inside the house and hoofed it down the tiled hallway toward the bathroom. Moments from peeing down my legs, I abruptly stopped, hearing a voice I recognized murmur nearby. I peeked inside Herbie's private office—one foot in the hallway, one foot pushing the door slightly ajar.

Lincoln.

His body was hunched over the corner of a wooden desk the size of a compact car. One hand spread wide over its ornate surface. The other braced his weight on a corner. The time rolled at eleven something at night. Not even close to the midnight meeting I'd assumed meant West Coast time, but evidently, some pre-planning was in the works. He grumbled "Paddy" over and over. Unfortunately, Paddy did more talking than listening, which made it virtually impossible to piece together the specifics of what I knew contained a juicy backstory.

Dressed in dark clothing, Lincoln appeared unrecognizable in a darkened room. But Lincoln was one of those people who threw off about ten feet of personal space when you were around him anyway. If you were good at reading vibes, you could've been blind and still detected his presence. Powerful people threw off energy without saying a word. It spilled over everything else.

Lincoln muttered, "Surely, he's kidding." The only thing I could figure was the man making demands, still conducted some outrageous bargaining. The conversation was emotionally charged, to say the least, but even though I had my ear to the door, I knew I needed to get closer.

Inching the door ajar, right then Lincoln shot straight up, moving to peer out the window for a view of *Maison de Saule*. Maybe he wanted the comfort of home, or maybe he knew he'd never really be on vacation one way or another. He put two fingers in the blinds and abruptly released them, muttering a threat. "Tell him this, Paddy. Tell him if he doesn't do as we've suggested, he can never count on us to bail his sorry ass out of any problem again. He has to pick a side, and he'd better choose wisely."

Wonders never cease, I thought. Why was it bad guys always hooked up with other bad guys even if the good guys were offering a way out? From my perspective—and that included little information —the man just committed a major boneheaded move and possibly suicide.

"Is that right?" Lincoln said, laughing sarcastically. "Tell him I couldn't care less about his life span, or if his neck is sliced from ear-to-ear. The only reason I'm negotiating in some back channel diplomacy is because of what it will provide *me*. Either way, what he has is *mine*, no matter what right Cardoza thinks he has to it." There was a huge awkward silence, and I took that as my cue to leave. Pivoting on my flip-flop, I was jolted back to the conversation by the biggest cursing-like-a-sailor incident the world had ever known. No, seriously. It was like *South Park* on steroids. Eff this, effity that, the F-word taking on all parts of speech. "Is that so?" Lincoln sneered. "He should be more scared of me than Cardoza, and tell him if he mentions my family again, I'll disembowel him personally."

Chapter Nine

LIVIN' ON A PRAYER

*B*obby Gerber called, confessing to the accidental deaths of Frick and Frack. He claimed he wanted to see if they could fly...the moron. He climbed on the top of my dresser and threw them in the air. They unexpectedly collided with the ceiling and cracked open when they crashed to the ground. I mean, really... shouldn't that have been obvious? And what kind of freaking centrifugal force did he throw them with? The recount sounded so bizarre I didn't believe it to be a fabrication or something else more iniquitous. MacArthur? He happened to be a nosy little gerbil that liked to bathe in blood, apparently.

At least, that was cleared up, but it made me recycle the hermit crab tears. Ugh, I hated crying, and I hated crying at bedtime even more.

I stumbled out of Sydney's room and crept quietly down the hall. It was close to three a.m. I still assumed the, *Midnight tonight. He either talks or he's dead* text referred to Pacific Standard Time.

Whose days were numbered, and who was the hit man?

After I listened to Sydney's rundown of her tumultuous day with bound-to-get-his-heart-broken, I knew the only way to make the three a.m. EST date was to consume caffeine...and binge eat. So I'd alternated between stale doughnuts and shots of espresso.

The espresso went through me like motor oil.

After half a dozen trips to the restroom, I finally saw a dim light click on down the hall in the den. I eased over the cool marble flooring, past Colton's office and the laundry room, and hid behind a white pillar until my vision adjusted. The house was full of structural pillars. It added to the Greek and Romanesque mystique. The one I stood behind happened to be the largest—about eight feet in circumference—so my guess was if it went down, the place would crumble like a house of cards.

In the middle of the room, Lincoln perched on the edge of the white leather couch, his elbows resting on his knees. Gum wrappers were igloo'd at his feet and a cup of coffee balanced on the edge of the ottoman in front of him. He must've been sitting in the dark for hours because it was the first time I'd noticed signs of life...and believe me, I'd been looking.

His cell phone was cradled between his neck and left ear, a baseball cap pulled down over his eyes. It was quiet—like horror movie quiet. The quiet a girl hears right before someone jumps out from the dark and knifes her life away. After a few moments of holding my breath, Lincoln shifted his weight into a fighting stance, leaning forward as though he was ready to throw his entire weight into something or someone...enough weight to silence them permanently.

"So he gave you very little in the face to face?" he asked frustrated. He went silent for a bit. "Well, we already suspicioned as much, Paddy. That information doesn't really place me one step ahead of Cardoza."

More talking on the other end.

Lincoln snorted and finally said, "That doesn't frighten me either, and I've been itching to get my hands bloody too. In fact, I want to frigging take a bath in it."

My brain scrambled for a second, and then I looked at my fingers, counting every digit twice, moving on to the wrinkles along the knuckles. As Lincoln raised his voice and growled, "I don't care who or what stands in my way," I counted the prints on the wall and panes in the glass windows. When I finished, I started with my breaths: in-out, in-out, slow and easy, times that by four.

God help me, that wasn't a good sign. It was an OCD frenzy.

Lincoln then mumbled low. I found that odd since he was in a room alone—at least, he thought so—until it occurred to me he must have been delivering one last threat he didn't even want the walls to hear. With a breath heavy enough to knock over an elephant, he looked to the ceiling—like he prayed for guidance—and slowly shook his head.

"Then on with the original plan," were his final words. He ended the call, carefully laying his cell phone next to his coffee cup while he buried his face in his hands. Things didn't look good for him—or perhaps they didn't look good for the other person, and Lincoln knew it was a do-or-die situation.

——————

Serendipity Golf Course was built on a rolling terrain and was known for its fast greens. In other words, someone hit the ball, and it rolled like a mother. That was okay by me because I felt as hyper as a Mexican jumping bean. We toured in a cart, but half the time I hoofed it to my ball just to get rid of the excess energy. That's what happened when the hyper had a case of the nerves, people. The energy latched ahold, and the brain functioned on a constant misfire.

A pack of gum and eighteen holes later, I still couldn't erase Cisco Medina from my mind. How in the world was I going to make good on my pledge (to *troyoncrime*) to provide new information? I longed for some sort of omniscient clarity but found comfort in the fact that I was a verb.

On even holes, I decided I could make a difference in the world. On odd holes, I concluded I was an idiot. Since we ended at an even eighteen, I took that as a sign from the universe to motor on. I'd beaten all of them. I finished even par on a course I hadn't played since spring. A narrow defeat, but you know what, I knew my limitations. Dylan led the pack until all three guys decided they would play from the professional tee box. Let's just say they weren't ready for the circuit. Clubs took flight, profanity scorched my ears, but that was what happened when your ambition was bigger than your club size.

Or jockstrap.

I was thinking that was the *real* problem.

Feeling somewhat like a champion, I then became obsessed. Unfortunately, it never ended well when I became obsessed because the preoccupation never went away until it was laid to rest...or someone beat the crap out of me.

Metaphorically speaking, of course.

Dylan pitched our bags in the trunk of his mother's pearl-white Mercedes SUV. Both of us wore khaki shorts and white golf shirts— my hair in a ponytail, his underneath a tan ballcap. He glistened with pure masculinity with dang little perspiration, while I was in full-on sweat mode, smelling like a salt mound.

A shower had to wait...

Kyd had a connection to Cisco's father. If I didn't act soon, opportunity would dissolve like my makeup had on hole two. As we prepared to say our goodbyes, Kyd acted like a sugarholic with a brownie. He couldn't and wouldn't let go. Call me a manipulator, but I decided to strike while the iron burned hot.

I lovingly touched Dylan's arm, throwing in some bedroom eyes with a come-hither wink that crumpled my contacts. "Let's eat here, D. I'm starving." That happened to be the truth. Lunch consisted of half an apple, processed cheese, and a cold cappuccino. As I faked crippling hunger pangs, I topped it off with an extremely suggestive bear hug and an innocent smile—well, at least my attempt at one.

He tenderly ran his index finger down my nose, sliding a muscled arm around my waist. "Sure thing, sweetheart," he murmured. "I love you and want you to be happy."

Dylan brought out the heavy artillery...I love you.

When his gaze burned over me, I knew that statement was also for Kyd's benefit. Still, I didn't know how big of a deal I should make of the declaration. I mouthed, "Always," realizing it was one of those cross your fingers and hope for the best situations. As uncomfortable as it might be, I needed Kyd to answer some questions. Sure enough, Mr. Do-The-Right-Thing switched on the charm. "Would the both of you like to join us?" he asked.

That was like waving a T-bone in front of a hungry Rottweiler.

Kyd took a tiny step in my direction, flirting. "I wasn't ready for the day to end," he said with a sigh.

I rolled my eyes in my brain.

"I'm in," Big J added.

We made our way over to the clubhouse, containing a gazillion square feet of throw-your-money-away opportunities. Dylan threw his arm around my shoulder as we hustled into Bogeys, one of the more casual dining rooms. Even at "casual," I couldn't help but feel like an outsider. Dylan was my link to that side of living, and even if I woke up with dollar bills coming out of my boobs, it would never be me.

While we waited to be seated, Dylan chatted with Big J, and I took the opportunity to dive-bomb Kyd with questions. More specifically, I needed him to introduce me to Hank Henry. First, I had to get past Dylan though. As awful as it sounded, one surefire way to drop his defenses—short of jumping rope nude—was to hold his hand. If his fingers were wound in mine, he stupidly assumed I was in a heeling position.

I slipped my fingers in his, and yes...*I batted my eyes*.

Made me want to puke.

Dylan sighed a blissful sound, as though I defined the perfect female. As he pulled my fingers to his lips, I shut down the guilt and swung my head to Kyd. "Do you know anyone who works here?" I asked.

Kyd lifted a shoulder in a shrug and watched Dylan's lips on my palm, not making secret his desire to de-tongue him. "Just about everyone," he clipped, "but you're the only one I really want to know."

(cough, bullcrap, cough)

"Herbie and I talked about Hank Henry," I told him, ignoring his words. "It's horrible what happened with his son, and it's wonderful what your father's doing."

Kyd lost the flirtatious attitude. He checked his watch, almost as if he tried to cut the line of questions short or was supposed to be somewhere else. He explained, "Daddy likes to do nice things, but unfortunately, he tends to trust people too easily. In this case, he got it right."

I agreed. "Herbie said Hank works in the kitchen. Is this the particular one?"

Kyd motioned toward the silver double-doors, swinging in the rear. "He does. He's simple, Legs, and I feel sorry for him. I try to run interference whenever I can."

Bingo for Darcy. I smiled.

Kyd and I pored over the details of the case, and I unfortunately didn't gain any information that I didn't already have. But hearing the heartbreak firsthand left me a little empty inside. At least more empty than normal.

When we were seated, Kyd ordered fajitas. Dylan ordered a cheeseburger and fajitas, and he'd probably have the remains of my five-layer nachos. Big J practically ordered the entire menu.

Twenty minutes later, I'd devoured my food like a caveman and picked at the scraps like a chicken in the farmyard. I longed to be in the kitchen, and short of masquerading as a cook I hadn't found a path there yet. "Is your meal, okay?" Dylan asked. He wiped his mouth with a white napkin, angling my chin toward him.

Wow, I had a hard time looking him in the face even when I was sort of up to no good. My answer came slowly as I gave him a genuine—although guilty—smile. "It's awesome, and it's Mexican," I said smiling. "What more could a girl ask for?"

Then I threw in a quick hug.

As I scooped black beans onto a chip, Kyd expelled an audible gasp, closing his eyes with an old-ball-and-chain expression. I zoomed in on Mary Cartwright, the absentee girlfriend, slithering over to our table.

Just when you thought your day was boring.

"Here comes Mary," Kyd warned almost as an afterthought. He stopped constructing a fajita, dropping everything at once, like his appetite had been flushed down the toilet.

"More like Typhoid Mary if you ask me," Big J whispered to Dylan. Yeah, I agreed with the pun. Mary looked like she had death on her mind...mine.

Mary had been suspiciously absent at the party last night. I found it weird, but by the expression on her face, she found it even weirder. Obviously, there were nuances to anyone's relationships, but not inviting your significant other to an annual shindig couldn't be a nuance in a healthy one. Dressed in a thigh-high, pink mini, and a tight T-shirt that said, "Make Love, Not War," Mary was nothing but a contradiction. Her long curly blonde hair and sky-blue eyes represented the classic princess...a shapely princess...she, however, was the evil witch queen.

Big J fingered in his pocket and pulled out his cell phone, scrolling through texts, acting as though the situation with Mary was status quo. All I knew was I needed a boob job and some Rolaids.

Mary stopped in front of Kyd, hands on her hips, sneering, "Hey, Kyd. I've been trying to contact you all day. I know you must have an excellent excuse for ignoring me."

No lie. His hands shook like cellulite legs on a treadmill. After hesitating, he mumbled, "Sorry."

Mary narrowed her gaze with an air of judgment, flipping her hair for good measure. I must say, I'd only seen that in the movies. Way more dramatic in person. "Very monosyllabic," she said in a huff. "You're going to have to do better than that."

"Sorry actually has two syllables," I dumbly mumbled. Thankfully, she didn't hear.

"We were playing, Mary," Kyd muttered.

She let out a snarling *humpf*. "Is Darcy your *plaything*?"

I snarfed Coke through my nose. "I plead the fifth," I said, coughing and rubbing my nose. Besides, I wasn't even positive I knew what that meant but was certain it included naked bodies. My word, was no one virginal anymore? Kyd handed me his napkin in apology as I sopped up my chin. Trouble was, that napkin had a jalapeño nestled inside. I sneezed three times and coughed twice. Then my eyes went wild like a crazy person begging for sanity.

Mary's tone grew even more condescending, nearly peeling the skin from my body. "Are you here as my boyfriend's date?" she repeated, leering at me. "God knows he's always had a thing for you, but I'd assumed he was going through a dumb phase."

Maybe I should choke the life out of her. Unfortunately, my vocal chords paralyzed, so I couldn't defend myself with words either. I was in over my head. I looked to Kyd (no help), and then at Dylan who calmly wiped his mouth and slowly laced his fingers through mine. Like a lion, he was fiercely loyal. In one instant, he poured all of that hot-blooded animal magnetism onto Mary. My temperature shot up. The room swayed. I swear, if there'd been a nun around, she would've dropped her robe and begged, *Make me a bad girl, Dylan...please*.

"Hi, Mary," he murmured.

Another hair flip. "You approve of this?"

Dylan didn't care what anyone thought of him, but that didn't mean he couldn't pick up on your emotions quicker than you could feel them. He lifted my fingers to his lips.

"No worries, Mary. Darcy will always be my date, and if you're to be angry with anyone, be angry with *me*. I invited Kyd and Big J, and by the way," he said with a wink, "you look lovely tonight."

She did look lovely, and thankfully, Dylan had the skills that could defuse a stick of burning dynamite.

"Is this true, Kyd?" she snapped, scanning his face.

Kyd didn't say anything. Instead, he swayed like a bulldozer had run over him. Dylan rose up, casually pulled a wooden chair from an empty table, scooting it between Kyd and me. "Have a seat," he said to her. "It would be nice to catch up."

Mary twirled the gold chain around her neck, gushing to Dylan as she sat down. "It's great to run into you. Yankee told me she visited with you last night."

I just bet she did.

He smiled graciously and listened to Mary's latest egocentric escapades as I excused myself to find the restroom. The clock said seven o'clock. Darcy still had nada. Not knowing what to do, I decided to march into the kitchen. I mean, how bad could it be? Granted it was a lofty goal, but I guess if you were in the shooting mood, you might as well shoot for the moon.

I squeezed between two tables, making my way to the rear of the restaurant. Once I pushed open the doors, my nose was blasted with the smell of food and too much heat contained in one place.

So much for being a cook...

My conspicuous lack of expertise in a kitchen was evident. I knocked over a tray of ice water, bent over to help the server, and then rose up—cracking my head on his elbow. Scrambling to pick up the broken glass, I subsequently tripped yet another server, fool enough to stand by me. Before I could mutter, "Sorry," minestrone soup dripped down my white shirt from yet a third party.

Someone held out a towel and dabbed at my arms. "Girl, you're a walking disaster," he said chuckling.

Yeah, I was a keeper. When I smeared a carrot into the fabric, I gave up figuring I made things worse. "I guess you're not going to hire me now, are you?" I said.

"I'll just tell the boss it was me. I'm not the most coordinated of individuals either. I'm Hank Henry," he said and smiled. I blinked. Opened my mouth. Then did the whole ritual again three times. Lo and behold, I stared speechless into the face of the man I'd been searching for...call me lucky. Or destined for a bullet of some kind.

Hank looked nice enough...but what did I really know? There was a lumberjack look about him: big, burly, and getting by on his own brawn. His face was round like Cisco's, with light blond hair, clothed in head-to-toe Serendipity black. On further review, I didn't think he was the "bullet kind" because even though he had a ready smile, his eyes were undeniably sad—like they'd seen more pain than any one person deserved.

We cleaned up the broken glass, shoved it in a tan plastic container and onto a cart bound for the industrial-sized dishwasher.

Focus, Walker, I told myself. "I'm Darcy," I said.

"Nice name."

"Different, I suppose. Do you have a minute?"

He inspected his watch. "Walk with me, I'm on a break. What is it you'd like to know?"

Everything.

He pointed to the back entrance of the kitchen. Hank said a few goodbyes as a cook threw a bag of what I assumed were food scraps into his hand. "She's with me," he said to a frowning coworker.

No doubt we were breaking Department of Health Codes, but what the heck, I reveled in dodging all things healthy anyway. As we strolled outside, the heat beat down like we were revolving in a microwave. "Are you feeding a pet?" I asked, wiping the sweat from my brow.

He nodded. "My dog bunks over at a friend's home while I work. I like to take him a treat on my break."

After talk about essentially nothing, God help me, I couldn't find an appropriate opener. "So have you had your dog long?"

"My son picked him out at Christmas." He paused, looking down at his feet. "I lost my son six months ago."

Insert a kidney punch to the back. "What happened?" I asked even though I knew the answer.

"Cisco just vanished," he explained, his eyes brimming with pain. "It was big news for a while, but I'm afraid people have forgotten him...but I won't."

My word, he'd just pulled a page out of the *Darcy Walker Playbook*. I thought back to my own childhood. Wherever I happened to be, I looked for someone who was never going to come back. Heck, I *still* did. But it hurt worse when those around you forgot what your pain was about. That stunk, on like a billion different levels—a billion levels too painful to name.

It seemed like a millennium had gone by before I found my voice. "No one has any information?" I whispered.

A yellow finch desperately hung onto a magnolia bush as it whipped around in the wind. It reminded me of Hank: trying to hang onto something amidst an element he had no control over.

He stared blankly at his black sneakers. "A group of private investigators check in with his mother, and a detective calls to give me updates. But that's all I'm going on right now. I just let Lola take care of it."

I decided to play along. "Lola is Cisco's mother?"

He nodded. "It never worked out between us, but we talk." He gazed at the sky, clearing his throat. "I just hope whoever has him..."

He stopped mid-sentence, unable to continue. I then remembered what Lincoln said. Retrace Cisco's steps. What did he like? Who were his friends? Did he have any enemies?

"Tell me about him." I waded carefully through the conversation, careful to put everything in the present tense.

Hank's eyes lit up like the sky during the Fourth of July. "He always smiles, and he's smart. But he's not like other boys. He does like to play ball, but he likes bugs and stuff. I got him this ant farm, and he'd sit by it for hours and watch them work."

"What else?"

"He likes frogs and geckos, so I bought him a book to help him identify the ones he caught. He went to the park to look for them."

"What park was that?"

"It's right by his house off Conroy Road. Some older kids there weren't so nice to him because they thought he was weird." No, "weird" was when your six-year-old sister was a freaking nudist. Liking frogs and geckos was refreshingly normal.

I stumbled around, finally asking what I'd been dying to. "Would any of them...*hurt him?*"

He adamantly shook his head. "No, they just laughed at him."

Glancing down at my watch, I knew Dylan must think it was the longest bathroom break in history. Either that or he'd buy it was bad Mexican.

Hank sensed I needed to go. "Hey, we didn't talk about you working here. I'm sorry, let me introduce you around."

I squeezed his forearm, adding a warm smile. "You know, I've already got something else in mind. Thanks for speaking with me."

We both were livin' on a prayer. Final assessment? Hank was hiding nothing and honestly struck me as a little milquetoast. He took people at their word, and as Kyd claimed, seemed simple. But what did I learn? He trusted Lola. Lola spoke with the private investigators regularly, but Lola, however, sent funky vibes to Troy. If I had any hope of procuring more information, I needed to get closer to her.

Hustling back inside, I pulled my iPhone out of my pocket and stood in the nearest corner, dialing in her digits I'd memorized. My stomach dropped all the way to my feet when I got a "Beep, this number is no longer in service."

My word, I'd caused the woman to disconnect her phone.

Shoving that guilt far down into my conscience, I dodged a cook sliding a plate of fries under the heat lamps and spun around a server balancing three plates on her arms. Heavy-footing it to our table, I noticed that Kyd, Mary, and Big J had departed.

Dylan, however, moved like a hamster on a wheel. He checked his wristwatch, running a hand through his hair, giving a description of me to a more than accommodating teenage girl. His hand went up to his neck mimicking a five foot nine posture, motioning that I had blonde hair just like hers. When our eyes met, an exhale of relief washed over him, quickly followed by his trademark what-in-the-heck-were-you-doing look because I don't trust you.

"Hey, are you okay?" he murmured when I made it to the table. "You practically fell off the grid."

"I kind of ran into some soup," I mumbled and shrugged.

His eyes darkened as they scanned over the goopy brown stain, and for some reason, I got all warm inside. Fever warm. You're-in-trouble warm. Dylan pulled me forward by the lapels of my shirt, and the rest of the room melted away.

"Lucky soup," he said grinning.

"Two things are infinite: the universe and human stupidity; and I'm not sure about the universe."

—*Albert Einstein*

Chapter Ten

FREAK SHOW

*W*ell into the wee hours of Monday morning, I was crashed on the white leather couch I'd made a makeshift bed at midnight. Across from me, Lincoln haplessly recited the skills of criminals—career criminals—specifically Turkey Cardoza. He'd finished polishing his gun, Jackal, and I didn't think he was totally awake. He talked too freely, and if he harbored the secrets to national security, it was probably best they took him off the night shift. No word yet on what went down in his midnight meeting, but he'd been uncharacteristically loose-lipped. I remained hopeful I could piece something together in between the incessant rambling, and the quote, "I need more bullets."

He'd called Willow twice with no answer, and it was my guess he didn't want to sleep because he knew he'd wake up and relive the same pain all over again. I knew from firsthand experience sometimes the term "a good night's sleep" didn't erase what was wrong in your world. All it did was bring the problem into the next day.

He mumbled, "Turkey's not dumb, Darcy. He's set up some legitimate businesses, which a lot of the time makes it hard to pin the bad onto you. The weird thing is that no one has taken him out because of his conflicting loyalties. I'd take him out on his mouth alone. That tells me he has something substantial on all three families."

No objection from me there. It always amazed me how the

ponkeys in the people-you-love-to-hate camp could slide by without a scratch. Especially someone as triple-dipping as Turkey in his business dealings.

"You'll get him," I encouraged.

Lincoln gazed down the barrel of his gun. "Willow's boyfriend?" he grumbled. Oh boy. I laughed to myself. On one hand, he talked about a career criminal. On the other, he referred to his daughter's significant other.

Funny thing was, he seemed a little trigger-happy on both accounts.

"No," I clarified. "Turkey."

He took one last swipe at the barrel and shoved it back inside its leather holster, snapping it up nice and tight. "Yeah," he muttered. "The man has some sort of plan, but I can't wrap my head around it, yet."

You know, I decided to spit it out. I curled under my blanket and sipped on coffee, trying to act disinterested and merely conversational. "So the midnight meeting didn't go well? He didn't talk?" I remembered Lincoln saying, *Then on with the original plan.* Well, what did that plan entail? To live to a ripe, old age or get acquainted with a casket?

He gave me one of those looks that meant he was on to me, overly tired, or rehashing details he'd rather keep buried. He exhaled, rubbed his eyes with his palms, and shook his head. "We shouldn't have trusted that guy," he muttered. "I can't protect him if he doesn't give me information." *Aaah*, I said to myself. The man was an informant who chickened out at the last minute. "Sometimes," he continued, "people don't take an out when you offer it to them. You can't help someone if they won't let you."

I needed help, but my mind couldn't formulate the perfect phrasing. The good girl part needed to confess I'd investigated the Cisco Medina case on my own. The bad girl part said, *Who gives a donkey's butt?* My conscience was playing hooky, so the bad girl got a free pass.

I blinked three times, wondering if I'd walked in the middle of a dream or real life nightmare. Herbie Knoblecker lay on his front yard flat on his back, like a corpse. Fear crawled up my body like a tiny spider making a web. My God, he'd had a heart attack, someone shot him, or it was conceivable he'd choked on his breakfast.

I cupped my shaking hands around my mouth. "Herbie!" I yelled.

No response from his end.

Instinct took over, and I ran down the ribbon driveway, my bare feet wincing as soon as they struck the hot pavement of Serendipity Drive. Fueled by pure adrenaline, in no time flat, I knelt over him checking for wounds. Wearing a white, nylon jogging suit, no blood trail lay evident anywhere. The only thing evident was the perspiration beaded underneath his nose. That left his heart...I think. I'd performed CPR on Resusci Annie before. Could I remember how to do it? What if I did it wrong? Did a bad technique even matter?

"Herbie," I said loudly, jostling his shoulders. My throat dried up when that got me nowhere. "Herbie!" I shook again.

Nothing. I reluctantly unloaded a hard slap, and when I didn't even get a groan, I traced two fingers down his ribcage—readying for chest compressions—when Herbie suddenly snorted awake. He slowly propped himself up, one elbow at a time. "Mornin', Darcy," he muttered, meeting my gaze. "I fell asleep in my yoga."

I shook my head, questioning if I'd heard him right. "You wh-what?" I asked. Sure enough, he repeated it again.

"I'm communing with Mother Nature," he muttered. "I need her help with my fungus."

His fungus. I exhaled, patting my pounding heart. I collapsed by his side in complete and utter amazement. The man merely fell asleep on his lawn. Sleeping on the lawn was normal, right? Let me answer my own question...that would be: No. Problem was, my thinking had been skewed toward the bizarre for so long that I always jumped to the worst conclusion. I had no clue how to live another type of life. I saw things...I reacted. I didn't see them...I manufactured a story. I wished them to be there...they were. All I knew was bizarre crap had happened to me since birth. Finding Herbie asleep on his lawn epitomized a prime example of the "weird but true." Trouble was, the sane would never believe it.

Herbie rolled to his side—a marvel, in itself—and farted. "Ya have a witch nanny, right?" he asked.

Sweet God in Heaven. I pulled my red tank up over my nose, wishing I'd stayed in bed. Things had gone beyond ridiculous, and suddenly I needed a sedative. "Yeah," I muttered.

"Do you think she can help me with this?"

Before I could blink, Herbie hefted his rotund body up on his knees wherein he simultaneously dropped his drawers. I closed my eyes on impact. I'd never seen male body parts, and Herbert Knoblecker's were not the male body parts I'd have chosen as the introduction. I'd always imagined some stud muffin who'd rival a thoroughbred would do the honors, not an overweight munchkin with gas problems.

Cracking one eye open, relief washed over me when his doublewide butt stared in my face and not his front package. "See this?" he muttered, craning for his backside.

"Unfortunately," I croaked.

"What *is* that?"

The "that" in question was a scaly, red patch of skin about three inches wide that started at his waist and went south. Thank God, my view stopped at "The Great Divide."

I took a step back. "Maybe it's athlete's foot."

"On my hiney?"

"That stuff can migrate," I lied.

"Like birds?"

"Like birds."

"How in the world did I get a bird fungus on my hiney?"

"Anything's possible with all the preservatives in food."

Herbie took a few moments to process the lie I'd just fed him. He scrunched up his nose, rolled the words around in repeat, and finally said, "Ain't that the truth."

After a few more grumbled sounds, he pulled up his pants and immediately locked his eyes on my chest. He narrowed his eyes and widened them, blatantly sizing up my lack of female endowment. "So your witch nanny can't give you boobs?" he grumbled. "My granny used to do a lot with frog eyes. If this cream of yours don't work, then mix in some bull frog eyes, and those things will puff up real nice."

I closed my eyes for a second.

Opened them.

Made a mental note.

I was desperate, people. If it took the death of a million frogs to give me boobs I was all for it. While I stood up and offered Herbie my hand, he instead stayed on the grass and actually buried his face into it and spoke. After a few muffled words, he staggered up, and as God as my witness, commenced with yoga moves—what I thought would've been anatomically impossible. He launched into what resembled the warrior pose but looked like a fat snowman. Next was the half frog except it reeked of the Kama Sutra. After a few more seconds of failure, he attempted the scorpion. With a few grunts of, "Help me, Mother Nature," he fell into the downward facing dog. His white nylon pants split down the seam, and his hairy rear end exposed itself for God and everybody. I coughed behind my hand, swallowed, and then coughed again because the laugh was begging to live.

My word, I was destined to see the man's rear end.

"Did the breeze kick up?" he asked.

"No, but the smell did," I mumbled.

When Herbie resurrected the fungus conversation, I was struck with an instant migraine. The last I'd glanced at the clock it was after five a.m. Law-abiding citizens and good moral teenagers were tucked away, snug in their beds. But teenagers like me were doing what we always did...the forbidden.

I'd tripped Colton's security system ten minutes earlier, wanting to walk-off an intense sense of failure. The process of escape wasn't especially hard. For Colton, it was the year of the zodiac. The Taylors spent a long weekend here last February, and I happened to be on the phone with Dylan when he and his father were beeping themselves back into their home. In the background, I heard Colton mumble, "Aquarius." It was August, so I boldly typed in "Leo" and prayed like a monk. After a green light beeped the all clear, I merely opened the door. Before I could symbolically pat myself on the back, Herbie's not-so-dead corpse caught my eyes.

Someone was bound to wake soon and find that I'd gone

AWOL. A search party would ensue. I'd get airmailed back home, spanked, grounded, flogged...etcetera. The way I saw it, I might as well make the best of my time with Herbie. When I walked back through those doors, all hell would break loose.

"Kyd told me you're financing some private investigators to look for Cisco Medina, Herbie. What do you know about them?"

"Not a lot," he admitted. "The money's taken outta my account the first of the month on automatic withdrawal."

"Are we talking about one firm?"

Herbie stopped whatever double-jointed yoga pose he'd been attempting, wrinkling his face, deep in thought. "One, maybe two."

"Can you remember their names?"

"One was somethin' like Find it, Incorporated, and the other I can't remember. Gertrude Burr will know. She's good fer a grand a month."

Talking to Gertrude just shot to the top of my to-do list. Our dealings were slim and closer to none, but it would provide a good excuse to ask about the man floating in her pool. Murphy didn't raise a fool though. Gertrude might give me the other name, but the real information would come from the bank.

"Who's your contact, Herbie?"

"Eleanor Talley at the Bank of America. She takes care of evrathin'."

Eleanor Talley. Maybe Eleanor could cough up information, but a bank manager wouldn't speak to a teenager unless *I accidentally*, I emphasized in my mind, called on her personal line. When I asked for her direct number, Herbie jabbered it out, closed his eyes to recheck, and recited it again more confidently. I repeated the numbers twice in my head, commanding them to stick.

My plan consisted of getting my big girl voice on, explain that Herbie was a personal friend, and tell her my inner-do-gooder was dying to donate a hefty sum. I'd impressed myself. I actually had a plan that didn't include rushing into a place and hoping it didn't burn down.

"It's really nice what you're doing for that little boy, Herbie."

Herbie breathed in deep with a look of satisfaction. "I like to think of myself as that silent *k* in my last name. I can be involved in something great as long as I'm surrounded by the right letters."

I felt more cerebrally challenged than normal. Yoga with Herbie and half a dozen texts from Kyd—apologizing for (surprise, surprise) Mary—was way too much brain activity. I putzed around until lunch, and after a meal of chips and BLTs, Dylan twisted my arm into playing sand volleyball.

My hair was the bedhead special, sort of parted and looking like the star of a freak show. Sweeping it back into a high ponytail, I switched into a yellow bikini, hoping to even out my tan and darken up my stretch marks.

As we stepped onto the sand, I took a gander at my partner. Dylan was usually polite, maintaining civilities, with the moral code of a martyr, but when his competitive juices started flowing, all of that "yes, ma'am" and "no, ma'am" behavior flew away in the wind. He'd perform a few stretches and neck rolls, look you up and down —smiling like a death row inmate suddenly let out on furlough. As though annihilating you, he'd relish as a chance to "walk the crazy" in him. In that respect, we were alike.

I. Absolutely. Hated. To. Lose.

The sun blazed high overhead and beat us like a punching bag. After thirty minutes of play, I was soaked to the bone, and Dylan's black board shorts stuck to his hamstrings like a second skin. Right as we readied to leave, Kyd and his best friend, Tricky Neptune, sauntered onto the sand, challenging us to a game.

Trouble...

Trouble, trouble, trouble.

Tricky had that nickname for a reason. Rumor claimed he was a safecracker. A little under six feet, Tricky had the physique that would keep his extracurricular activities cloaked in the dark. He was built long and lean and extremely agile with chestnut brown hair, black eyes, and a tan so deep it reminded me of a Fudgsicle. Tricky exuded confidence. Where most teenage guys tripped over their hormones, Tricky frolicked in them. Case in point, he wore a candy apple red Speedo cut down to a perfectly muscled...well, use your imagination. God knew I did.

"Nice tattoo," Kyd said, whistling in my direction.

I nervously giggled...Dylan growled.

Kyd referred to the fact I had a faded, henna tattoo right above my booty—a tramp stamp. The image initially consisted of angel wings surrounded by lightning bolts. I mean, what good were angel wings without a lightning bolt, right? Well, one lightning bolt and wing later, I concluded that idea had been royally stupid. Go all the way, or don't go at all. I looked like a hoochie convention reject.

After a few rounds, Kyd suddenly slammed a ball in Dylan's direction. Dylan launched himself high, throwing all his weight into the hit, spiking the ball to the sand directly under Tricky's feet.

Tricky stood there stunned, puzzled why his reflexes had failed him. "Are you workin' your mojo, D?" I said with laughter.

"Is it working?" he asked grinning.

When Dylan set loose his smile, I never knew what to zero in on first: lips, dimples, or teeth. I usually swapped fascination on all three characteristics in between deep breaths and wheezy coughs. I swallowed the frog in my throat, shrugging as I served the ball over. We volleyed back and forth a few times—Kyd stuffed a ball, Dylan stuffed two—when all of a sudden the air supply thinned out. I wasn't sure what it was...a message from God, or maybe even survival of the species. All I knew was Kyd locked on my bikini like a divining rod seeking water.

He soared through the air, his face hard and determined with me as the intended target. Before I could defend myself, he took us airborne, and I flapped like an idiot, landing spread-eagle in the sand. I couldn't breathe. I couldn't think. And Kyd lay on top of me enjoying my feathers. Running both hands seductively down my sides, he firmly planted them on both hips. Heck, I'd never felt anyone's hands on my jeans let alone my bikinied bottom.

"How's *that* feel, Legs?" he whispered into my ear.

I just got shellacked. It actually felt painful.

Dylan growled overtop Kyd like a bloodthirsty lion. "You must not value your life, Kyd." Kyd had no opportunity to respond. In one breath, Dylan picked him up by the back of his flowered board shorts, throwing him fifteen feet in the air like a rag doll. Kyd came down with a thud, and momentarily, I think, went night-night.

"You're toast," I heard Tricky half chuckle, half sigh.

Dylan expelled a humorless laugh. "Toast is only a minor burn," he threatened. "I'm going to start the process by breaking his back and then each of his fingers, leaving him to blister in the sun." He glanced down at me, and I lay motionless. "Take my hand," he ordered.

Trouble was, my hand quit working. I looked at his hand and then to mine, and God help me, I didn't know what to do with either. Dylan gently pulled me up, my toes gripping the sand for support. While he dusted me off, I spit out a mouthful of beach.

"I'm sorry," I coughed out.

Dylan frantically searched my face, trying to understand where I was going with the dialogue. Who the H knew. The important thing was to rein in Dylan's dark side before it chomped down on Kyd and ripped off a bite. I wiped my mouth on the back of my wrist. "Don't h-hurt him, D," I coughed out again. "I know he's a fastard, but he's still my brother."

The imaginary dart he threw in Kyd's direction said he wasn't in the bargaining mood. "He's not going to hurt, sweetheart. When I'm done with him, he's not going to feel *anything*." Dylan's eyes span the length of my face. "Are you sure you're okay?"

"I'll be okay," I assured him. Once my lungs figured out how to suck in air.

Dylan took my face in his hands, his eyes tender, his voice super-barbaric. "Go to the car," he fumed.

"Go to the car?" I echoed in surprise.

Dylan acted like he contemplated something complex and was frustrated because he couldn't make it simple. Out of the blue, he smacked me on the rear, as though congratulating me for a game-well-played and was sending me to the locker room. We met eyes—mine wide with surprise, his naughty as all get-out.

For a moment, the world stopped moving. Fire fell from the sky, the earth split in a quake, and the wallflower got to dance with the hottest guy around. Things were perfect. Destined. Deliberate. Then like an insecure teenage girl, I feared the flimsy elastic on my swimsuit made my cellulite butt a sideshow. Dylan had smacked it. His hand might be grossed out.

"Put on some shorts," he demanded, narrowing his eyes. Well, I guess he answered that.

"That bad, huh?" I whispered.

He suddenly appeared distracted. "...*What?*"

I dropped my head, embarrassed. "Nothing."

Ever compliant, I shuffled over to guide my feet inside my white short-shorts. *Darcy, Darcy, Darcy*, I said to myself. *You really need to invest in a 360-degree mirror*. When I picked up my shorts, staring back at me was the rotting head of a man buried in the sand.

Chapter Eleven

SKILL OR JUST DUMB LUCK

There was weird, really weird, and so freaking weird there was no word for it. I didn't think it to be a figment of my imagination, and like a fool, I lightly touched the gruesome spectacle with my toe. It felt hard, yet squishy-soft at the same time, and definitely not attached to a spine. After a few nail-biting seconds of doubt, my mind accepted the obvious...Oh, Lordy... *Eeeeuw!* It was real.

And on whose body did it actually belong? I racked my brain trying to determine what'd happened when the answer remained obvious—someone or something had cut it off. I wanted to run, jump, and scream—cry for mommy, suck my thumb—my body just couldn't decide which to do first.

"I f-found a h-hhead," I whispered. My voice sounded like an old, leaky tire. Hissing and squeaking with each stuttered syllable. I didn't think Dylan and Kyd would've heard anyway. Their mouths were moving at full throttle.

"Go out with me," I heard Kyd say. "Please, Legs. Just jump right in with both feet."

"What about Mary?" I heard Dylan bark.

Kyd genuinely sounded flabbergasted. "Who?"

"Your girlfriend?" Dylan stated as a question.

Flies had begun to buzz, landing on the dead man's brown hair and face. I swallowed down some bile—convincing my lunch to stay put—but as soon as I swatted one fly, two replaced it.

Tricky and I were two peas in a pod, thinking and doing the same things. While Dylan and Kyd remained oblivious to anyone except the other, Tricky unexpectedly dropped down into a crouch next to me.

"Is it dead or what?" he whispered.

"Or what," I answered.

I went on autopilot, knowing full well I should've lost bladder control or at the very least been screaming bloody murder. Luckily, I found my happy place and was able to cope when normal people would've been paralyzed with fright. I wasn't sure what that said about me—that I was sometimes more comfortable with the dead than the living—but I decided to embrace it and consider it a gift.

Damp and covered in sand, the head looked like a science experiment, already presenting itself in varying stages of decay. The stench rang potent, and the remaining flesh was either falling off or bluish-gray. The man had died in fright because the expression on his lifeless face indicated one of surprise and extreme pain. His hair was brown, eyelashes were thick, and one blue eye sunk deep in its socket. The other was glazed over into nothingness. Sandy pus lined the pocket of the collapsed eyeball and bloodied capillaries spiderwebbed the whites of his eyes. His contorted lips were ajar, showing perfectly porcelain teeth, and in the corner of his mouth was a scrap of paper rolled up like a cigarette.

My God, that was sick. I mean, what was the purpose? Tricky and I met eyes—simultaneously glanced at the paper—and back at one another once more. Our wheels turned, and our wanting to read that paper was like asking an aardvark if he liked ants. As if to ask silent permission, when I gave him a nod, Tricky fingered a twig next to him and lightly shoved it between the man's teeth, tipping the letter to the sand. Before we could do anything else, I was instantly jarred from the trance by Kyd's motoring big mouth.

"Listen, Taylor," Kyd sneered, loudly and obnoxiously. "One day soon you're going to have to let her go."

"Let her go?!" Dylan said with a loud snort. "What I do is absolutely none of your business, and the last person I'd 'let her go' to is you."

Kyd snorted back. "I know she's your best friend, but I've got her back."

Dylan's voice lowered an octave. "First of all, no one will ever have Darcy's back like I do, and it's what you're doing behind it that worries me. I don't trust you, Kyd. You use people. You change girl-friends like you change clothes. And you're not going to work that shtick on Darcy."

Kyd laughed. "What if she wants me to work it on her?"

Okay, he was cute, but I didn't think I wanted his shtick.

"She doesn't!" Dylan barked. "And screw you for the connotation."

Dylan grunted and cursed in the primal sounds of cavemen. Dylan had a mouth on him and belted out a line of expletives that would peel the polish right off my toes. My mind thankfully bleeped out most profanity. Weird because God knew I sinned everywhere else.

Thing was, Kyd was a brother, and I had rules with brothers... sort of. Reaching behind me, I sunk my fingers in the sand, searched around, and found another stick, handing it to Tricky like you'd assist a brain surgeon. He put the two together like chopsticks and unfolded the paper, hoping we could get it read before Dylan and Kyd tired of their pissing match.

"I don't date brothers," I answered in Kyd's direction. "Of course, I'd like to deepen our relationship, but for now," I paused, "that's it."

"So it's not a no?" Kyd clarified.

Dang it. Kyd had a one-track mind. I finally glanced up, gazing in Kyd's blue-green eyes, firmly replying, "No!" Then it dawned on me, I didn't know what the no was actually for...a refusal or a maybe in the future.

Dylan went ballistic—perhaps he interpreted it as a *maybe*—roughly shoving Kyd backward up against the net. To him, our rela-tionship was a no-fly zone, and Kyd stood in violation of federal laws. I opened my mouth, not having a clue what would come out next. Did I eventually want to date someone? Sure. Would it be Kyd? Um, he was taken.

After some careful maneuvering, Tricky pried open the note while I continued to keep Dylan occupied.

"It's like this, Kyd," I joked. "I'll probably do whatever Dylan asks me to, and before I push up daisies, that might mean I'll be chained to a radiator in his basement...where no one will ever see me, and I'll die of boredom."

My word, Dylan didn't even issue a denial. He might technically be one of the good guys, but a part of him was nothing but the Devil himself. I heard rumblings about the shama lama, ding-dong (all that boy-girl stuff I didn't understand), and Kyd briefly adopted that oh-crap look. Unfortunately, it immediately transformed into differing degrees of cockiness where he thought he could down Dylan's wild bull.

The fastard was on his own.

I nervously scrubbed the sand from my arms and legs and prayed. I prayed, people. I prayed for the head and for peace on Earth and the merriest of all Christmases. Finally, Tricky unfolded the note, without getting our fingerprints on it at all. Blowing some sand from the wording, imagine my surprise when it listed Gertrude Burr's name, address, and underneath...the surname Medina.

A breath stuck in my throat.

Talk about luck.

It was luck...and then some.

I'd told Troy I had something Saturday morning—that qualified as a "no show" in my book. Add Gertrude's name? That was a gold mine of epic proportions. I just didn't understand the specifics yet.

Tricky and I had one of those unspoken moments where we debated "what was right" versus "what would quench our curiosity."

Neither of us cared what was right. In the flutter of an eye, I made the quick decision to phone Gertrude Burr first. CPR wouldn't be the answer—it was obviously too late for anything—so I figured we weren't in danger of committing manslaughter by our lack of attention to a medical emergency.

Before guilt could take root, I pulled my iPhone out of the pocket of my shorts and dialed.

———————

Gertrude Burr wore a white skirt and a pink, sleeveless sweater. A Prada designer bag on one shoulder, she was using the side of her silver Porsche Carrera as a crutch. Taller than average, her black hair swept back from her face in a sophisticated ponytail with platinum jewelry cascading from both arms and ears. Other than her penchant for married men, she represented your typical high society philanthropist. Right then, however, she looked sweaty and bug-eyed—a woman on the verge of a nervous breakdown or swallowing a bottle of pills. She'd already eaten off four nails and had moved on to number five.

"Do you know who it is?" I asked her.

The color completely drained from her face. Thankfully, when I'd phoned earlier, her first instinct was to dart over and take care of business herself. I feared Serendipity Security would accompany her, but so far, so good.

"It's Howie," she whispered behind her shaking hand.

"An old boyfriend?" I asked softly. Gertrude burst out crying, snot flying from her nose like a gushing fountain of pain.

That answered that.

Words could either heal or be catastrophic. Thank heavens Tricky was born to talk to females because suddenly, I was an emotional idiot. Tricky patted himself down, my guess, looking for a handkerchief, but where he planned on finding one in a red Speedo remained a question for the gods. He settled for putting his arm around her quaking shoulders. "I'm so, so sorry," he apologized smoothly. "Your pain must be unbearable."

Gertrude sounded like she'd been sawed in half.

My conscience took a shot of bourbon. I'd made her cry, and by God, I wasn't done with her yet. I kicked my bare feet around in the sand, shoving down the guilt, debating what I needed to do next. I had two things on my mind: the author of the note and the names of the PI firms searching for Cisco Medina. Gertrude, as traumatized as she was, held the answers to both. Before I could say anything, Dylan appeared behind me like a rabbit out of a hat. I didn't have to see him. I felt the hairs on the back of my neck singe.

"What in God's name..." *bleep...mother bleeping...bleep.* "Mother Mary," he prayed, crossing his chest, breathing deep to calm himself. "Is that a head?"

Well, it sure as heck wasn't the Easter Bunny.

He latched ahold of my elbow. "What are you doing, Darcy?

Please tell me you aren't doing anything," he murmured, trying not to raise his voice, with very little success.

I pivoted around, giving him a tsk-tsk frown, right as Kyd (and his dropped mouth) thundered up behind him in a catatonic stupor. If they hadn't been arguing, they would've known exactly what had gone down. "I'm not doing anything with the head," I said self-righteously. "I saw it and tried to spare you the gory details...you're welcome."

I made a kissy *mwah* sound in his direction. Dylan narrowed his eyes, giving me a look like he'd smack some sense into me later. "Is that the truth or the version you want me to know?" he growled.

Good question. "What do you want it to be?" I asked grimacing.

Another smack-some-sense-in-me-later look.

Flies danced around Howie. Dylan gulped hard. When spectators began to get curious, Mr. Do-The-Right-Thing immediately popped the trunk on his father's nearby Bentley, retrieved a towel, and gently laid it over the remains. It made a modicum of improvement, but not a lot, and thankfully, whoever had been moderately interested went on their merry way.

Dylan took a few moments to ponder what had happened, swallowing again. "This doesn't upset you?" he asked incredulously. Stranger things had happened, I was sure. Although, I couldn't think of any at the moment. When I just shrugged, he snorted disapprovingly. "For once, it would be nice if you cried, had normal reactions, and wanted me to comfort you, sweetheart. My God, is that too much to ask?"

So I wasn't the general populace, big deal...I thought he knew that. "What do you want me to do, D? Fall at your feet and beg you to make it all better?"

"I swear, you have balls," Dylan said, snorting under his breath. "I honest to God think you have balls."

I laughed...my word, that was funny, but even I knew it wasn't the time to laugh.

"Darcy!" he yelled, embarrassed for me.

Gertrude looked like a tree about to snap in the wind. She wailed a big sob, making it evident she was moments from a strait-jacket. Tricky tightened his grip as Dylan sighed deeply, realizing our one-on-one conversation piled on the pain for someone who'd already been wounded deeply.

When I gave him a sheepish shrug—like Welcome to Darcyville —he studied me with intermittent fascination, as though I was a yet unnamed species. Ending with a frown, he immediately located his cell phone to call the authorities.

Looking like he'd been to Hell and back, Dylan took two deep breaths and reached for my hand. I wasn't sure if he felt I needed it, or if he did, and my job was to play along. His large hand engulfed mine, and once I squeezed back, he pulled me under his arm and located his concerned-citizen voice. I didn't waste time trying to talk him out of it. That would've been futile. What I needed to do was gather information from Gertrude before the cops came and ruined everything.

I decided to go for broke, knowing my logic made zero sense but hoping it garnered something substantial anyway.

I quickly asked Gertrude, "Is that note in Howie's handwriting?"

"I can't tell," she whispered, "but maybe." For the sake of argument, let's just assume she was right. That meant he'd been attempting to see her and needed the address. Even if it wasn't his handwriting, he obviously didn't put it in his mouth after decapitation. I mean, duh. Who would want to do that and then send him to Gertrude like a birthday present?

"Do you know why he would want to see you?" I asked. "Or why someone would want you, specifically, to find his head?" She shook her head no. "What about the man in your pool, Gertrude? Could this be related?"

Another, "Maybe."

It hit me like a boulder I had been speaking about a head to an ex-girlfriend—who probably had residual feelings—and I acted like it was the weather report. I had the irrational urge to launch into nervous giggles. I didn't know if the situation was funny, or if I'd finally coming to terms with the fact that my mind wasn't normal.

Dylan murmured, "Yes, ma'am," into the phone three times and ended with our exact location.

Time had run out.

I blurted, "Do you think Howie has anything to do with the Cisco Medina case?"

Gertrude lost some of the tears, a bitter hostility punctuating her words. "Cisco Medina?" she repeated exasperated. "Livingston & Associates have helped the case, and I recommended them to that Herschel man. As a matter of fact, Howie worked for them. This has nothing to do with anything other than Howie and his lifestyle."

"His lifestyle?" I asked confused.

"Pooky will find out the answers," she said and sniffed, suddenly in her own world. "He always does."

"Pooky?" I said. That irrational urge to laugh came back with a vengeance.

"My pooky bear boyfriend," she said, crying harder. "He hates Howie."

Well, did Pooky have a reason to want Howie dead? I thought. I pushed her to clarify, but Gertrude had gone off the deep end, weeping and groaning to herself.

I couldn't help it, but a sigh tumbled out. I didn't want to see a head, but a feeling grew in the pit of my stomach that things wouldn't end well. Cisco, Gertrude, the man in her pool, and a bodi-less-Howie were related in some way...a relation I planned to expose. Situations like that broke down to one of two things: skill or just dumb luck. I wasn't sure I had either, but I did have the dumb part down.

Chapter Twelve

WOULDA, COULDA, SHOULDA

A priest wouldn't touch my latest dream with a ten-foot crucifix.

It was early Tuesday morning, and my nightmare had been so horrifying, I needed a dose of Dylan to calm my nerves. His bedroom sat at the west end of the house. As the rest of the house, it was timeless sophistication, but like its occupant, it held an air of modern masculinity. Every designer element from the pewter fixtures to the snowflake, gray paint reflected young, virulent male.

Once inside, my eyes shifted to the floor-to-ceiling windows reflecting a moonlit view of the lake. When the night sky was clear, we could lie on his bed and gaze at the stars. Sirius, located in the constellation of Canis Major, is the brightest star in the Milky Way. From Dylan's room, we could almost reach out and touch it. Perhaps on some metaphorical level, I needed its brightness to shine on me.

Something that would provide answers...

Flush against the wall stood a gigantic platform bed adorned in a black satin comforter and sheets. A large flatscreen TV had been mounted in front of it, and a desk fit for a king sat in the right corner. On the opposite wall existed a bathroom that had black granite countertops and a walk-in-shower with a faint smell of chlorine and shower gel. Over in the far corner, a black leather recliner occupied the space that appeared to be Zander's bed for the evening. He snored rhythmically, curled on his side, one arm grazing the floor. The nook also included a mini-library, housing the books of a deep thinker.

Dylan journaled. Leather bound notebooks lined the shelves from as far back as grade school. No doubt, the subject matter grew deeper, but it wasn't unlike him to pull one out and pore over it for hours. They weren't under lock and key—which was carte blanche to a snoop—but I had no desire to invade his thoughts. I'd always figured there'd come a day when the time was right. I'd just never felt it knocking at my door.

I couldn't make these things out clearly at two in the morning—the only thing for certain was a snoring Zander. The reason? I'd lost my glasses. My nose had been on the trail for fifteen minutes, and I hadn't unearthed anything but a letdown.

Stealthily puttering inside, I knelt down by his pillow. Dylan lay flat on his back with his hands propped behind his head, the black satin sheet spilling around his waist. That qualified as Shangri-La, and I sat within groping range and should probably cop a feel for female-kind. Unfortunately, the angel on my shoulder eeked it was morally wrong. Plus, Grandpa Winston said, *If you look on a naked boy, you'll be struck blind*. Well, that momentary blindness could be worth it because Dylan had a washboard stomach, and Darcy wanted to wash some clothes.

"D," I said, giggling and lightly touching his abs, "just lie there, and enjoy yourself, baby. I'm going to do a little laundry."

Dylan took one deep breath, rolled to his side, and tunneled the fingers of his left hand through my hair. "Sweetheart, are you okay?" he murmured softly.

Dylan had just busted up my moment of immoral domesticity... the bugger. Truth was, I *wasn't* okay. Insomnia was a pain when Howie screamed for someone to sew his head back on. "I can't sleep," I told him, "and was hoping I could sleep with you."

Dylan lightly laughed, stretching over to check the time on his alarm clock, leaving his palm curled along the side of my face. "Darc, we can't do that. My father will crucify me."

"I can't settle down," I whined. "Can I just lie here on the floor?"

Dylan sat up and swung his legs around when I realized my hand rested on his muscular thigh. *Down hand*, I told it. *Be a good hand and get on down*.

Wearing what I assumed were dark shorts or boxer briefs, my goody two-shoes angel went red-faced and jumped up and down for me to find my manners. Frankly, I wasn't sure why it even mattered. I was one step from legally blind and barely had on much more than underwear myself. I sported a white cotton camisole with matching boy shorts. Feminine enough, but then again, I didn't understand feminine anyway.

Before bedtime, Dylan had been pensive, deep in thought, like he tried to deflate something that had been expanding and brewing for a while. It wasn't just Howie either. My guess was Kyd lay at the root. Dylan had somewhat dialed down his anger...the key word being "somewhat." All I knew was when Kyd knocked on the door to check on me—seriously, did he not know who I was?—Dylan was silhouetted in the hallway like a wild animal, lying in wait.

"I can't let you sleep on the floor," he murmured adamantly. "Take my bed, and I'll sleep elsewhere."

"Why can't I sleep in here if Zander's on the recliner?" I said, squinting toward the corner chair. "That *is* Zander, right?"

Heck, it could've been a life-sized figure of King Kong for all I knew.

Dylan glanced over to the nook, nodding with a slight laugh. "Sounds like him."

"Please?" I begged. "I'll even sleep by the door. It'll be like a slumber party."

Dylan scratched the back of his neck, debating the chances of discovery. "You're breaking my heart. I hate it when you beg, Darc, but we can't. I know it's *odd*, but it just *is*."

I hated odd, and I wanted to kick is's can.

"*Pretty please*," I pleaded again.

Dylan outstretched both arms, dragging me into an embrace. Cupping one hand around my head, he let the other hang leisurely at my hip. I tiptoed up, clasping both arms around his neck, and briefly shut my eyes into the curve under his chin. "I'm just so tired," I mumbled, "and I need to feel close to you."

That'll do the trick. I smiled to myself. *Just stroke, stroke, stroke that whopping ego*.

"I love you too," he whispered into my hair. I wasn't positive how long we stood there. I could've stayed like that for a million years and never complained. It felt peaceful, perfect, and unusually pleasurable...especially when Dylan hummed a lullaby. Dylan could sing like an angel, but when he hummed, it unveiled a supernatural elixir. I yo-yo'd in and out of consciousness realizing the last thing either of us wanted was to break contact. "What's wrong with your room, sweetheart?" he finally voiced.

It was too far away from him, that's what. I bunked on the opposite end of the hall with Sydney. She talked/fought/made-up all night on the telephone. I didn't mind, but proximity-wise, it felt like a country away from the Big Man.

"Nothing. I prefer the couch, but Lincoln's in the kitchen with paperwork sprawled out all over the floor."

One would think my curiosity would be killing me, but actually, it wasn't. Whatever was going on in Lincoln's world remained his business. Turkey Cardoza could kiss my Chergerbritishscotch keister, and unless he came to Orlando, I was done with him.

"Grandpa's up?" Dylan shrieked. "If Dad won't go for it, I can promise Lincoln will spit nails."

I didn't know how it happened. Maybe it was paternal instinct on overdrive, or maybe it was because he worked as LA vice. But the moment my arms clasped tighter around Dylan's neck, he stiffened and gasped toward the door like a clairvoyant episode goosed him in the butt.

"Good morning, Grandpa," he murmured.

I circled my hand in the air in a smiley-faced wave. I couldn't see crap, but I didn't need to. As Lincoln thundered forward, no doubt he appraised our lack of clothing and calculated exactly what had gone down between these four walls.

Nothing. I sighed to myself. *Abso-freakin-lutely nothing.*

"What's going on, son?" he questioned at a rolling boil. He paced another few steps until his jaw hung parallel to Dylan's.

Dylan exhaled a breath. "I was having a nice dream about a nice girl saying nice things, Grandpa. Obviously, it wasn't Darcy."

I laughed, not even close to being offended. "It wasn't?" I said.

"Not even close."

"Darcy, you're not supposed to be in here," Lincoln bit out.

"I'm not?" I said. He gave me a heck-no look. "I thought you were an equal opportunity grandpa," I said frowning. "Zander's in the recliner, and now you're saying Darcy Walker doesn't have rights. Well, I'm the Susan B. Anthony of slumber parties, and I'm taking what *I've been denied*."

I stomped the floor for emphasis.

"Darc," Dylan whispered nervously. "Not the time."

Glancing over to a still snoring Zander, Lincoln's voice barked angrier, "You don't have rights!"

I opted for the truth, giving him a flippant answer. "If you must know, I asked Dylan if I could sleep with him." I laughed like a naughty truck driver, smacking Dylan's rear end so hard he fell forward and off to the side. Both his hands mauled my chest, breaking his fall—OMG moment—neither of us knew what to do. "See?" I said, giggling like a truck driver. "He can't keep his hands off of me."

"Oh God," Dylan muttered, gasping for breath. "You've just sealed my fate." Running a hand through his hair, he scrubbed it down his jaw, stupefied.

Lincoln sounded homicidal. "Good grief, child, you can't sleep with a boy!" Even exhausted, my mind worked it from every conceivable angle.

"We do in Cincinnati," I said, lifting my shoulders in a shrug.

Dylan snapped to attention, something frightening filling his voice. "Darcy Walker! We *do not* have that type of relationship!"

True, but I really didn't know *what* we had, and the joke was too good to pass up. Dylan occasionally kissed my forehead. We hugged longer and deeper than most. I sat on his lap like a girlfriend, and the exact words that commitment-phobes choked on—*I love you*—we'd been saying since we were six. Sneaking into his bedroom and talking to him in the wee hours seemed as normal as anything else in our relationship.

Trouble was, our normal was abnormal to the rest of the world.

"My father warned me about boys like him, Lincoln," I motor-mouthed on. "The love 'em and leave 'em kind. I just pray our unborn baby doesn't make the same mistakes I have."

All at once, everyone (but me) started cursing.

Bad words.

Filthy words.

File that under *Uh-oh*.

Lincoln clutched Dylan ferociously by the wrist. "Is this true, son? Answer me, boy!" Dylan pointed at my face—his eyes demanding a retraction—but a flicker in his smile insinuated he might actually be enjoying the drama.

When my grin grew wider, he finally released a tired sigh. "No, Grandpa," he murmured. "This is just Darcy *being Darcy*." He turned to me in his party's-over voice. "I'm tired, sweetheart. You know I love you, but I don't want to do this at two a.m."

"But we're best friends," I complained, sticking my lower lip out in a pout. "If I can't sleep, then the Best Friend Rule says you're not supposed to sleep either."

Dylan rubbed both eyes with his palms. "No one's ever told me that." Poor Dylan. I laughed to myself. He truly was the walking dead, and a few more minutes of my guilt trip would have him apologizing and tucking me into bed.

I sniffed. "Well, now you know, and it wasn't like I saw your happies anyway."

Happies was Darcyspeak for testicles. One deep grunt from Lincoln, and I opted against a definition. Dylan giggled, tweaked my nose, and rubbed his knuckles over my scalp like one of the boys. Yeah, true love...soak it all in.

Lincoln stretched both hands high and rapidly plunged them through his hair. Maybe he worried or maybe he debated yanking it all out. He notoriously pulled all-nighters when consumed with a case and never looked tired during the daytime hours. Turkey Cardoza—*coupled with me*—had left him emotionally drained. "I need some coffee. Follow me, dear," he paused, motioning over his shoulder. "You're not sleeping in my grandson's bed."

Not what I wanted to hear. "Can I at least sleep on the floor?"

Lincoln stopped to mull over my request. These were the situations grandparents struggled over. Number one, they'd raised their kids. They were tired, and it was easier to give in and let the grandchildren have their way. Number two, they'd also screwed up their kids. So they were operating under a lot of guilt and woulda, coulda, shouldas.

"No," he muttered, deciding to take the conservative route. "If you can't sleep, then come to the kitchen, and I'll make us both a sandwich and a pot of coffee."

Good. Coffee usually relaxed me. For most, that was a contradiction. Coffee could be like mainlining steroids.

Lincoln's fuzzy silhouette left the room, mumbling he didn't understand teenagers, let alone our relationship. When I went in for one last hug, he bellowed, "Hands off, you two! I don't get it. I swear to God, I don't get it."

I obeyed, metaphorically kicking and screaming the entire way.

———

Since Saturday evening, it had been a nightly routine for Lincoln and his partner, Paddy O'Leary, to pore over the case of Ronald "Turkey" Cardoza. Why they thought I was trustworthy was unfathomable, but they didn't seem to mind that I'd crashed their nightly business meeting. Minutes earlier, I'd sworn off Turkey altogether, but Lincoln seemed so ensconced in his life, it piqued my interest again…ugh, I was a messed-up person.

I played it cool, acting only partly interested—or even asleep—but secretly I tried to piece it together myself. Turkey had been in and out of juvenile detention starting at age nine. His petty thievery and vandalism grew into money laundering and cooking books for the mob. Somewhere along the way, Turkey established legitimate businesses: a chain of laundromats, used car lots, two restaurants, but rumblings placed his person at the scene of three murders. One would think that someone who brokered deals between two competing mob families would be above being the triggerman though.

There's always the option that Turkey had a facet of his personality that simply liked to kill. Lincoln felt Turkey crawled up from the lowest level of Hell but unfortunately couldn't place him definitively at the crime scenes other than by word of mouth. Therefore, there wasn't enough proof to stick. My feelings with the Cisco Medina case were exactly the same. Something was twisted in Cisco's world that included Gertrude and a headless Howie—but I didn't have a name yet of the person hiding behind the curtain.

Lincoln had been on the telephone for fifteen minutes listening to Paddy's fast-talking Irish ways. Half the time, Lincoln left him on speaker while he shined his shoes or made a sandwich. Instead of sandwiches, we ordered Chinese takeout and were eating on our respective couches. I didn't know we could get Chinese takeout at that late of an hour, but maybe that was merely when they cleared their freezers of all the dead cats.

Sliding my glasses on my nose—I found them in the kitchen trashcan—I shoveled Kung Pao chicken in my mouth, concentrating on Paddy's words.

"But how in the world," he said frustrated, "is the guy always on camera where the crime *isn't* when we have witnesses who swear he blew somebody's brains out across town?"

Lincoln took a generous bite of Mongolian Beef. "Just another braid in an unwanted emotional entanglement. Our only prayer is that he gets lazy."

As he ambled to the kitchen to grab a drink, that left me alone with Paddy. Paddy expelled a few Irish epithets I didn't understand. "And the biggest jaw-dropper of all," he grumbled, "is that Turkey's six kids are all good. Private schools, church on Sunday, not even a detention slip from best we can tell. Shouldn't some of that crime have passed down, Linc? I mean, really. It's almost like they're squeaky clean."

That got me to thinking. Does where you come from really matter in life? My ultimate opinion was "no." My father put the bookie life behind him, so it could be done, but it depended on how deep your influences were and whom you considered your lifeline. Not to mention, which part of your personality you wanted to win in the end.

I snuggled deeper under my white fleece blanket, chewing some rice. I asked Paddy, "Did you ever think that there might be two wild Turkeys?"

Paddy didn't respond, and you could almost hear the *dun dun du-dunnn*.

———

I didn't know what time it was...only that it was late—or early—however, you wanted to term insomnia. Lincoln slept soundly across from me, but my brain wouldn't blackout. Pulling Colton's laptop out of its leather satchel, I tapped it "on," hoping Troy was still all hey-let's-work-together or at least wanting to flirt. My fingers rapped on top of the keyboard as I waited for Jester's account to load. My hands were still empty of information—at least damning information—but I'd typed a message earlier to see what he knew about the PI firms. A quick scan of the yellow pages gave me nothing, which caused me to doubt Herbie's recall even more.

What would I do if Troy hadn't returned my email? Better yet, what would I do if he *had*? I waited for a heavenly epiphany to show the next course of action, but Heaven wasn't speaking. My guess was it kicked me off the walk-thru tour.

As my email program loaded, my eyes wrapped around the inbox like a commode-hugging drunk.

Then I saw it...and dropped a jaw.

DATE: August 13, 03:00 a.m.
TO: Jester from Jesterville
FROM: Troyoncrime, Orlando Sentinel
RE: Private Investigators
Hi Jester,
Fix It, Inc. is the name. Anything on Lola???
Troy Brown
Better known as the man of your dreams

The man of my dreams. I snorted. Flirting aside, the information threw me. Herbie had said, Find It, not Fix It, but I should've figured as much. That came from a man who thought Cisco was having dinner with the aliens. The time stamp marked the message at three a.m. Troy was obviously a fellow insomniac, so I decided to type up a response. I wasn't risking anything—perhaps the familiar feeling of failure—but unfortunately, my feet walked that tightrope and fell into the abyss regularly.

DATE: August 13, 03:05 a.m.
TO: Troyoncrime, Orlando Sentinel
FROM: Jester from Jesterville

RE: Private Investigators
Dear man of my dreams,
I promise to deliver on Lola. Where is Fix It located?
Jester
The woman who's been waiting a long time

I struck the enter key and prayed he was in the buying mood.

DATE: August 13, 03:08 a.m.
TO: Jester from Jesterville
FROM: Troyoncrime, Orlando Sentinel
RE: Private Investigators
Dear woman who's been waiting a long time,
Fix It, Inc. is the company name of a group of private investigators. Elmer Herschel set up the trust, so he would know more. According to my source at the police station, this group is ex-military and rumored to be mercenaries-for-hire. All I know is the police department hasn't worked with them since the beginning.
Troy Brown
Better known as the man worth the wait

Peculiar. Wouldn't the police routinely share information? Mercenaries or not? My guess was Troy had already heard about the tragedy of Howie, but if I played my hand too soon, then he might send it on to press. Going to press early—without irrefutable evidence—could make the guilty jump the country.

DATE: August 13, 03:13 a.m.
TO: Troyoncrime, Orlando Sentinel
FROM: Jester from Jesterville
RE: Private Investigators
Dear man worth the wait,
What about Livingston & Associates? They're supposed to be working the case too.
Jester
The woman worth waiting for

. . .

I nearly hurled when I keyboarded that byline, but if the boy wanted to flirt, then far be it from me to rebuff his advances. My inbox beeped.

> **DATE:** August 13, 03:18 a.m.
> **TO:** Jester from Jesterville
> **FROM:** Troyoncrime, Orlando Sentinel
> **RE:** Private Investigators
> Dear woman worth waiting for,
> Never heard of them. I'll check them out.
> Troy Brown
> Better known as the man dying for a face-to-face
> (Who am I kidding...I need a big break.)

Finally, a language I understood.

> **DATE:** August 13, 03:23 a.m.
> **TO:** Troyoncrime, Orlando Sentinel
> **FROM:** Jester from Jesterville
> **RE:** Private Investigators
> Dear better known as the man dying for a face-to-face,
> Find out where that company is headquartered.
> Jester
> Your big break

I wasn't sure why I typed that. Call it a supernatural gimme, or call it the ebb and flow of my early morning grasp of reality. Either way, it was a sad state of affairs when Darcy Walker was someone's life-line. I slurped the last of my coffee and considered my options. Door number one: do nothing, and then always wonder. Door number two: do something with the small amount of information I'd acquired. Door number three: flip a coin. Leave it to the universe.

Chapter Thirteen

WAKE-UP CALL

aking me required yelling through a bullhorn, but for some reason, I could always hear a text. Dylan had provided that rise-and-shine service for years. Here in Florida, however, I didn't need additional assistance. The bloody sun rose to attention before seven a.m.

Freaking sun. I despised it. Made me think it hated the people near the equator.

I heard grease splattering, a mixer growling, and the smell of eggs and bacon in the kitchen. The saliva in my mouth multiplied like guppies, but why hadn't my normal alarm yanked me out of bed for his favorite meal of the day? Why??

He was gone...

After I drowned my sorrows in three thousand calories of farm animals, I got dressed for what Susan Taylor informed me was "Shopping Surgery," the unspoken truth being, "Darcy Reassignment Surgery." Evidently, she'd promised my father she'd help me purchase school clothing. I gave her one of those girly smiles that said, *I just can't wait*, and zombie-walked into the bathroom, feeling it grow harder and harder to breathe.

Once showered, I dressed in my I-don't-care look, which consisted of a wet ponytail and my glasses. To give the semblance that I cared a little, I rolled on bubblegum lip gloss. As I stuffed a red jawbreaker in my cheek, I dialed Murphy to say "hey" and pulled on some jean shorts, coaxing a white tank over my head with the phrase "Blonde Happens" in the center. Reaching inside Sydney's closet, I stepped inside a pair of black leather flip-flops and shoved Dylan's Ranger ballcap on my head.

Hours earlier, he, Colton, and Lincoln loaded into the Bentley to travel to the University of Florida to watch an open football practice. Dylan was the best athlete I'd ever seen. He lettered in all three sports and was named a First Team All-American in football our sophomore year. Football had always been his dream job, and traveling to U of F told me his dream might ultimately sever the "'til death do we part" thing between us.

"You didn't want to go?" Sydney purred as we settled inside her mother's Benz SUV.

"I didn't know," I surprisingly admitted, and why exactly *was* that? Granted, he saw red when Kyd dropped by, but when I woke him in the middle of the night, he seemed extra touchy-feely. I should've made sure we were kosher then, but I tended to be of the if-it-ain't-broke, don't-fix-it camp.

Evidently, it broke into a million little freaking pieces.

Sydney legitimately seemed as confused as me, cocking her head to one side, thinking so hard it made my head hurt. I quickly added, "I'd be in the way."

She rasped huskily, "Those are probably the last words that would ever come out of my little brother's mouth."

I leaned my head against the window as we backed out of the driveway. For some reason, I had a feeling of dark foreboding that I couldn't shake. Like the day wouldn't end well. "It's probably for the best," I added quickly. "He needs to do things without me."

"What if he doesn't *want* to do things without you?" she countered, smoothing her red sundress. One could only wish, but it didn't appear he'd had problems weaning himself away.

Shoving that fear to the back of my mind, I tried to embrace the shopping mood. Problem was, I'd rather be chased by a chainsaw. After a fifteen-minute drive, we pulled into the Mall at Millennia. Well, more specifically, a bunch of clearance racks. Susan could shop-the-heck out of clearance racks. At Bloomingdale's, I picked up two cotton polo shirts, sand-colored UGGs, fur flip-flops, a pair of resurrected Nike Classic Cortez sneakers, brown suede Pumas, and a few perfume samples that threw me into a sneezing fit. Three hundred-plus dollars later, we bought cinnamon pretzels at Auntie Anne's and piled back into the Benz to hit one of my favorite outlet stores: The Gap.

I stood in the dressing room, shorts at my ankles, shirt halfway over my head when my phone burst into Milli Vanilli's lip-syncing train wreck, "Girl, You Know It's True." Add some ooh-ooh-oohs.

A look at the caller ID: Kyd...ugh. Oh, boy, wasn't that awkward.

"Whassup?" I answered.

"Hey, Legs, whassup with you?" he said laughing.

I thought about saying, "I'm tromping nude through The Gap," but that felt kind of icky. "Just dillydallying around."

"Well, I'm being proactive."

"Proactive," I repeated.

"Yeah, I wanted you to know that we have a deep connection, and I plan on deepening it even further over the next two weeks."

I choked down a gulp. Kyd had his bad boy on, and unfortunately the thought wasn't totally repugnant. Looking in the mirror, I came to the conclusion I might be a lost cause. My fashion sense left little to be desired, but I knew things were supposed to match, even down to your underwear. But when everything fits too short, even the idiots got the picture.

"And FYI," he continued, "I dropped over the last of the beignets earlier since I noticed you had a sweet tooth after your third. Dylan's grandfather grunted a 'thank you,' but he wasn't exactly talkative."

More than likely, he had been protecting his grandson's turf. "He has a lot on his mind," I offered as explanation. First off, Turkey Cardoza, followed by a close second of, *Why did Darcy find a head?* No one seemed to buy the fact that it was Darcyville, but it was.

The crackle of papers rustling filled my ear as I pulled on the fifth pair of skinny jeans Sydney threw over the changing room door. I punched both legs through, pulling them to my waist. "What are you working on?" I asked.

Kyd choked out a sigh, like the last breath exited his body. "I'm going over course catalogs for a dozen schools. I have no idea where to go, but I definitely want to be a psychiatrist."

A groan slid out. "A shrink?"

"You have issues with psychiatrists?" he asked and chuckled.

I had tons of issues with psychiatrists, but I guess that was because I had tons of issues myself. I did the talk-and-go gig for two years, but I didn't think it accomplished anything other than reducing my father's bank account.

I tugged on a navy T-shirt that had a red and white bull's eye in the middle of it...oh, the irony. I gave him a politically correct, vanilla response. "I think it's an admirable career choice."

"Why do I feel like there's something you need to talk about?"

Our conversation would fall under the category of *There Are No Words*.

When I zipped up the pants, once again they were too short, so I ripped them off and slinked on another pair. "Psychiatrists aren't supposed to push, Kyd. Rule Number One."

"Ah, the smart patient."

I'd never thought of Kyd as a psychiatrist, probably because I always dodged what I felt were insincere proposals. Perhaps I needed to take a step back. He definitely was careful with his words, tenacious, and unusually observant. I guess if you were going to be a shrink, the please-come-again factor would be to your benefit.

"Why a shrink?"

He stopped for a few breaths, and I knew he searched his soul. "Good question," he said passionately. "I suppose I want people to reach their goals. Life is full of unfulfilled potential, Legs, and if I can help clear away some of the..."

I crawled onto the bench and didn't even hear the finish to his reasoning. There definitely was another side to Kyd those two weeks out of the year and the occasional card and phone call never unearthed. Frankly, if I were smart, I'd hook up with him just to unearth all the things that went down on a daily basis in my head. But Kyd had a girlfriend despite his good heart. Something was awry between them, but at the end of the day, he'd contemplated cheating and had emotionally cheated already.

Two words? Heartbreak Hotel.

"Wow," I said and whistled. "You're a fastard, but a part of you is like...umm...a good person."

He went breathless. "And you..."

Sometimes feel alone in a room full of people. I sighed to myself.

A light rap tapped on the door as the conversation headed to a raw place. "Gotta go," I muttered, exhaling in relief. "Call you later."

I killed the call the moment Dylan's mother peeked inside. "Let me see, Darcy," she murmured. A glance down at my ankles showed the usual. Too short and floodwater ready.

Susan Taylor laughed. "Oh, dear," she said, squatting down, attempting to pull them further south. "I love the shirt, but that's the longest inseam they have."

What~evvvs...I usually wore my aunt's castaways anyway. Problem was, she was a redhead with the sex appeal of a pin-up. I had the sex appeal of an onion.

Susan picked up the T-shirts, shorts, and a few sweaters, and made her way to the checkout counter. I tried on one last pair of jeans, rolling them up as capris when Sydney stepped back inside.

"That could work," she purred. "And let me add, thank God."

"Maybe I should ask Dylan," I muttered.

Sydney burst into laughter, her voice resonating in a growl. "My little brother thinks your derrière is divine. Trust me, his imagination is going to work overtime."

She fixed her hair in the mirror, looking more confident than I'd ever be. My aunt and uncle were attorneys and Sydney had interned with them since she was sixteen. Sydney had a plan: four years undergraduate and then three years of law school. Find a husband and then her first and only child at age thirty. I didn't have *any* sort of plan. I would be sixteen in October, had never kissed a boy, gone on a date, and was probably a bona fide fool because I didn't have the gumption to venture out and do it.

Perhaps that was why I obsessed over a child who time seemed to have forgotten. Right then, he didn't have anything, and any ambition he'd had hopefully hadn't been snuffed out permanently.

Slipping back in my clothes, I followed Sydney outside, spotting her mother who held up four hoodie sweatshirts in various colors. I gave her an emphatic thumbs up. As she filed into the line half a store long, I grabbed a dozen ultra-low girl shorts underwear and moved on to accessories. Somewhere between throwing three scarves around my neck and a houndstooth bucket hat on my head...I saw (big gulp)...Cisco Medina.

No lie. Cisco Medina.

I'm numb. Shocked. Afraid I'm going to die on the spot.

Thank the Dear, Sweet Lord, I thought...but right then, I didn't know what to do.

I glance east, west, north, and finally south—all directions deluging me at once—because it was almost like someone had sling-shot him, and he landed next to me. A rational person would say it was your imagination. A crackpot would claim you were high. But for an idiot like me? I had to hand it to myself...every once in a while I hit paydirt.

Cisco slumped over painfully at the shoulders, picking at his nails and pulling at his shorts—racked with nervous habits. His face shape was round like his father's, housing inquisitive, bright brown eyes that appeared older than his biological age. To add to the shock, his hair had been dyed corn silk-blond. So whoever abducted him did their homework because if the gist of the game was to assume a different persona, they'd attained success. He was dressed like a skateboarder, and Cisco was a nature buff. He wouldn't be wearing Vans shoes, looking for a skate park.

I took a tentative step closer and discovered his nose had freckles down the bridge with a black mole the size of a baby pea under his right eye. Those were characteristics too descript to be a coincidence.

"Cisco?" I whispered. His eyes grew as large as saucers, with a little nod.

Right when he opened his mouth, a woman rushed to his side and jerked him toward the front of the store by the elbow. I was positive she hadn't heard me, but my idiot side emerged, and I froze in the revelation. I couldn't move, scream, or do jack squat. Had she wanted a child so badly she stole someone else's? She didn't appear psychotic. She had brown hair ponytailed under a ballcap with a medium height and build, in your traditional mom clothing of jeans and a T-shirt. The only things appearing strange were her expensive Italian high heels. Almost like she'd been in such a hurry, she grabbed whatever she found closest to the door.

Last night, I flipped a coin and left my course of action to the universe. Heads was a go. Tails was a no-go. I didn't have a coin at the time, and frankly, the universe and I weren't always on good terms. But as I thought about it, it didn't matter what a fifty-fifty chance dictated. Certain things in life you shouldn't contemplate.

Be a verb, Darcy, I said to myself. *Be a verb even if it means you pee your pants.*

Like mosquitoes on water, the undergarment rack suddenly was a customer breeding ground. I stood elbow-to-elbow with tourists wanting the panty deal of the day. Taking a few vertical jumps to keep him in sight, the twist in my gut said time ran short. Knowing the best route was to cover ground fast, I shifted my body into fifth gear throwing my hat, scarves, and underwear at a horrified Susan Taylor.

"Darcy!" she shrieked, catching part, watching the others flutter in the air. Big mistake! And I knew it as soon as my hand decided to throw them.

My pink and white polka-dotted underwear launched like a rocket and touched down on an angry Muslim's head. His left eye peeked through a leg hole, but anger's one of those emotions identifiable on any continent. I didn't know Sunni cleric but was pretty sure what he mouthed sounded like, "Capitalist call-girl slut."

And that was the rated G-version.

To dodge a baby in a backpack, I bumped into a teenage boy slurping a cherry Icee, causing it to fly like a bird. Slipping on the slush, I face-planted into the baby's spit up. Covered in a slimy yellow film, I wiped away the snot and told myself it didn't matter to verbs. Verbs kept moving. Verbs didn't care. Verbs had a job to do. Trouble was, I didn't have a plan once I caught up to them.

Since I was already hugging the floor, I army-crawled past two teenage girls and brushed against a southern gentleman who offered me a helping hand. After declining with a smile, I flipped the bill backward on Dylan's cap, focusing all my energy on Cisco's puttering feet.

"Darcy!" Mrs. Taylor shouted again. "Stop!"

My mind was stuck on shuffle. I needed to think...and think fast. The good news was Cisco remained in town. Why keep him in town though? If you merely wanted to nab a kid and fulfill your warped maternal desires, wouldn't you move to another venue where it was safer? That fact alone made me think the woman operated under another agenda. The bad news? If she was smart, she'd left her car somewhere close.

Half my body hung out the door when a security guard parked his two hundred pound, nightstick-packing frame in front of mine. A hurried glance up revealed a nametag that read "Jim Bob." Jim Bob *looked* like a Jim Bob. Or better yet, an angry weeble. He had no neck, his hair was balding, and his expression froze solid like an ice cube.

"Hi, Jim Bob," I mumbled. If I didn't get an E! True Hollywood Story out of the mess, I was going to be one angry female.

Jim Bob narrowed his eyes, crossing his arms across his navy mall cop uniform. "Quick getaway?" he muttered.

"Not quick enough," I said, sighing deeply. I peered between his legs, and a cursory look down the hall produced no Cisco. What the freakity freak should I do now?

"I believe you have something that belongs to me," Jim Bob grumbled.

My self-respect? "Excuse me?"

He pointed to the neon-coral scarf dangling from my neck. Ah, shoot. It looked like I'd been practicing the five-finger discount.

"You left the store with my merchandise around your neck," he told me. Totally defeated, I begrudgingly pulled myself to my feet as Susan rushed to my side, looking like a momma bear when someone threatened her cub.

"Is there a problem, Officer?" she asked with a warm smile, laying a hand on my lower back.

Jim Bob tightened his hand on his nightstick. "Your daughter has sticky fingers," he grumbled. She didn't cower one bit, but her expression said she wondered how she drew the short straw and had custody of me for the day. I frankly wondered that myself, but I didn't plan the excursions. It was just that when you were a verb, the call to action took you places.

Sydney pushed through the crowd. "Why would she *steal* a *scarf* that has a *hole* in it?!"

I should've known her inner-fashionista would be the first line of defense. Sydney unwound the scarf from my neck, motioning to the cavern that had frayed at the bottom. A good chance existed it happened mid-crawl, but if it could get me out on parole, I knew enough to keep my mouth shut.

"Thieves don't always take the time to discriminate," Jim Bob muttered.

Sydney held her chin high, her black eyes like daggers in his jiggly gut. "Well, *we're* the discriminating type. She deserves a refund."

"A refund?" Jim Bob echoed in surprise.

"A refund," Sydney seethed, flipping her hair in a circular swish of PO'd.

It was one of those situations where I was supposed to wax poetic—say things that would make people think I had a good heart and intentions—Jim Bob, however, appeared to be inoculated against poetry.

He said, "You didn't pay for it."

Um, no kidding. Jim Bob pitched his head toward the manager ringing up a patron. No more than mid-twenties, he wore relaxed fit jeans and a navy short-sleeved polo, collar upturned, and untucked at the bottom. Preppy. VIP. Unfortunately, the keeper of my fate.

The manager ambled over to join us as Susan fished out her black American Express Centurion credit card. It wasn't only unlimited, it put a whole new spin on the term "no boundaries." I could buy a freaking third-world country on that card's clout alone.

"Hello, I'm Susan Taylor," she introduced herself, placing the card in his hand. "We were shopping when my *daughter*," she said tightly, smiling in my direction, "got distracted. We actually weren't finished yet."

I heard the cash register cha-ching in his head.

Susan Taylor had the gift of persuasion and could talk her way out of a jail sentence when she had fifty carats of stolen diamonds in her purse and the nuclear football under her arm. At the end of her two-minute montage, the manager was eating out of her hand.

"I didn't try to steal it," I mumbled as we took a place at the head of the line.

She found a smile but nonetheless said, "I believe you, but I'll need an explanation."

I unloaded it right then. "I was running after Cisco Medina."

The manager smiled pleasantly as Susan pitched a stack of long-sleeved, layering T-shirts and turtlenecks on the counter, along with some socks. "Who's Cisco Medina?" the manager asked me. And that was the *real* problem.

———

I repeated the story to Lincoln, throwing in the part about Jim Bob and the panty-hating Sunni as comedic buffers. I wasn't certain it provided entertainment. There was a brief lull in conversation, but that could've been the interlude where he rued the day he'd answered my call. He breathed deep, rehashing a blow-by-blow account to an extremely impatient Dylan. "Yes, son," he repeated exasperated, "Darcy's okay." A long pause. "No, she didn't find another head."

If only I were that lucky. I laughed to myself.

"What can we do, Lincoln?" I interrupted. "I need you to believe me. I know what I saw."

Lincoln blew out an aggravated sigh. "Just because I'm quiet doesn't mean I doubt what you're saying. I'm merely thinking. Let me log into NCIC when I get back home."

"NCIC?" I repeated.

"National Crime Information Center. It's a nationwide computerized index that gives law enforcement access to tags, pawned items, drivers licenses, warrants—"

"Etcetera, etcetera, etcetera," I interrupted.

"Etcetera, etcetera, etcetera," he repeated chuckling.

Lincoln explained that each state had their own database and fed information into a nationwide system in case suspects crossed state lines. It was available to people like him in the field, but it required FBI clearance to access it.

"When are you coming home?" I pushed. I wanted things done like yesterday, and the last thing we needed was for Cisco, at the spur of a moment, to jump the border.

"Don't expect us until around midnight, but let me make a few phone calls."

Huh, wonder what they had planned? *Well, Darcy Walker.* I smiled to myself. *You have a full day planned too.*

Number one was to crack the code into that database. Number two? Eat a beignet.

Chapter Fourteen

DIRE STRAITS

My legs were crossed, sitting in the Lotus position in the middle of Dylan's room. I prayed for patience but was denied. I was tired of passing emails back and forth, and regardless of the consequences, it was time to chat voice-to-voice with Mr. *troyoncrime* himself.

Anonymity be damned.

Or darned...I hoped that wasn't cursing.

I punched in his number and waited...nothing but voicemail.

Ten minutes earlier, Herbie phoned to say a bank representative informed him that Fix It, Incorporated was, in fact, one of the PI firms on his monthly statement. God love him, he didn't ask if anyone else was listed, but I decided to cut my losses and leave that part of the equation to Troy. A quick scan of the phonebook did actually legitimize Livingston & Associates (who Gertrude said Howie worked for), but a telephone call only produced an automated message.

Who knew, maybe they were at "Howie the head's" funeral.

Did you send flowers to stuff like that?

"Troy, it's Jester," I said. "Did you have any luck on the private investigative firms? I'm working an angle here," sort of, "and that information will be invaluable. And guess what," I paused, "I believe Cisco Medina is still in town."

I think that covered all the bases. Disconnecting, I quickly changed the voicemail on my iPhone to, *Jester's not in the house. Please, leave a message after the beep.* Then I recorded my own idiotic beep merely because I couldn't help myself.

"Dire straits" and I were thicker than thieves, and patience had never been one of my virtues. Heck, I didn't have any virtues, period! But sitting idly by didn't jell well with my hyperactive tendencies. Where I'd planned to crack the NCIC database, finding a free moment was tantamount to getting lost in New York City during rush hour. Everyone was up everybody's muffler all day, and short of taking my laptop to the bathroom with me, that idea remained wishful thinking.

I leaned forward thinking fifty push-ups might exorcise the fidgets from my body. After completing twenty-five in the army position, I started twenty-six cricket-style with my elbows pressed tightly to my side.

"Knock, knock," someone said, rapping the door with their knuckles. Glancing up, I saw none other than Kyd Knoblecker. "Zander told me you were here," he said and grinned.

Aww, and Zander's days would be numbered like the dodo bird if Dylan discovered the mutiny.

I squeezed out a smile, resuming a count.

Kyd kicked off his flip-flops sidling closer, obviously thinking he'd get some real face time. Maybe that was what I needed. Kyd *was* a psychiatrist...in a junior bridesmaid sort of way.

He swooped down, tickling his nose in the crook of my neck. I breathed deep. No one had *ever* been that close to my carotid artery other than Dylan, and Kyd acted like he considered taking a bite. "What perfume are you wearing?" he growled.

"Dryer sheets," I mumbled.

"Tasty," he murmured.

Why did I attract fastards? I'd jumped from Liam Woods to Kyd Knoblecker. Both were taken. And honestly? That was offensive. I should tell Kyd to hit the road—or bite my big, white booty—but I needed him. And by God, I guess I was a user.

Change the subject, Darcy. "You're friends with Hank, right?" I asked.

He propped his back against the bed, crossing his legs at the ankles, picking up the controller for Dylan's Xbox 360. "Good friends."

"What happened between him and his ex-wife?"

Kyd shot bad guys on *Call of Duty Black Ops 2* as I slowly neared the forty mark. "Lola gambled a lot and basically blew through everything they both had. Hank's job situation has always been shaky, so even though they had joint custody, guardianship to the grandparents was the route they took when Lola lost her rights. Hank can see him whenever he wants. So although it made him sad, he could deal. It's a shame. I actually like both of them."

Huh, I had no idea Kyd knew both parents.

I took a deep breath to finish out the last ten. "Where does she work?"

"I don't know," he murmured. "She's great with numbers, and that's what got her into trouble in the first place. Lola gambled with powerful people in town, and sometimes she gambled *for* them. That's all I know." No doubt that led to her losing custody of Cisco, I surmised. The newspaper article claimed she placed him up as ante during a high stakes poker game. She was either grossly negligent or overly confident she could win him back.

Kyd laid down the controller as I finally tapped out at fifty, huffing and puffing, lying supine for a few seconds. After a few beats, I resumed the Lotus position and ripped open a bag of chocolate chip cookies beside me. There was only one left, and in a bag of roughly thirty, that meant I'd polished off twenty-nine and somehow avoided a carbohydrate coma.

After the last bite, Kyd took my hand, his eyes growing heavy-lidded, flickering with what I thought was...*want*? Nah...couldn't be. The boy had Mary-I'm a freaking goddess-Cartwright. That wasn't even close to Darcy Winston Walker—yeah, my middle name was a cigarette. But flirting aside, he legitimately looked like he desired me. That little voice in my head that screamed he was a lying rat fastard couldn't peel itself away from his face. Kyd's sandy-blond hair played a nice contrast to his golden tan. Dressed in an old white T and black athletic shorts, he was a card-carrying member of the jocks of the world. Sure, I was a mutual jock, but my brain spoke nothing but nerd.

He held my fingers to his lips, speaking into them. "Come here when you graduate. We can do University of Florida, Florida State, University of Miami," he rattled off. When I tried to tear my fingers away, he narrowed his eyes, slightly tightening his grip. "Don't pull away from me," he begged in a whisper.

Verrrrrrrrrrrrry interesting.

For some reason, that felt like a veiled comment about Mary.

I withdrew my hand, wanting a love triangle like I wanted a punctured lung. "I'm a hometown girl, Kyd. Plus, college is probably out."

He snorted. "You're joking, right?"

"Ha-ha," I lied.

"Then I'll join you," he said convincingly. "My parents are going nuts because I haven't made a decision yet, and I should already be enrolled."

My turn to snort. "You'd leave paradise and move to Cincinnati?"

Kyd took a deep breath, acting like a boy desperately in love. Focusing all of his energy on me, he scooted closer—so close that the heat radiated from his body like a Bunsen burner. "I expect I would go to Podunk, Alaska if you were going to be there."

Podunk was out because I couldn't leave Marjorie. I remember the shock when out-of-the-blue circumstances left me flying solo. It felt like I had an anchor around my neck while someone pushed me overboard.

Kyd dropped his eyes to my chest, his gaze tearing into me. Yup, he was a fastard. Fastard, fastard, fastard. "What's wrong?" he asked. "Is it the, um, head?"

Not even close, perv. I almost laughed.

Kyd was obviously still reeling from Howie. I'd successfully tucked him away in my *Things Not Meant to be Understood File*. Word on the street though—according to Lincoln and his inside connections—claimed that Howie had gotten into trouble with gambling debts. I found it interesting that he and Lola had the same pastime.

My stomach started to pitch when Kyd kept pushing the issue. He said I appeared to be experiencing some serious post-traumatic stress and was in danger of snapping at some weird, inopportune time. I *so* didn't want to go there...not even in my subconscious. I wasn't even pseudo-ready for that conversation and doubted I'd ever be.

"Trust me, I've experienced worse than Howie," I muttered, and I wasn't referring to the dead man I found in the spring.

I was referring to my mother.

Kyd immediately got his shrink back on, drool dripping like a leaky valve.

Dylan had a putting green outside his room on the lawn. I grabbed a pair of golf balls and two putters from his closet and tossed one of each in Kyd's direction. The testosterone in me needed to kick some serious gluteus maximus. Plus, I needed to break the hormonal mood and walk down Horror Movie Lane I had no desire in resurrecting. Putting was generic enough, right?

We stepped outside the french doors, seeing who could get closest to the hole in one shot, eight feet out.

Kyd broke into a smile. "Ladies first," he charmed.

I dropped the ball, lined it up, and sank it in one easy stroke. I stood back up with a cocky laugh. "Taking candy from a baby," I bragged.

Kyd crossed one ankle over the other, balancing his weight on the club. "If I make this shot, you have to answer a personal question, same for me."

"Okay," I said with a shrug, but evidently he hadn't learned the first time.

Kyd squatted down, taking a dominant eye's view. He then stood aright, gripped the club, and followed through on a putt that did a quick 360 of the hole before it bounced inside with a thunk. "Do you love Taylor?" he asked, standing aright.

Dylan made me feel unconditionally and irreversibly loved—unfathomable and unsurpassed. There was no hesitation in my answer. "More than anything."

His confidence deflated like a hot air balloon when someone released its air. "Ten feet out this time," he said and frowned.

I expelled a ferocious snort. "You're stacking this in your favor, Kyd. I didn't even get to ask a question when I scored the first time. If I sink this one, I get to ask two."

Kyd said, "Sure." The cocky gleam in his eyes wasn't convinced I could make it, and frankly, I wasn't so sure either. Suddenly, my palms dripped with sweat because I didn't know what he deemed personal. I bent over gripping the club, swung through, and watched the ball slowly travel to where it teetered at the edge and finally plopped in.

"Nice shot," he groaned.

I did a face-rubbing victory dance. "First question," I said. "Do you love Mary?"

He answered easily with a nod. "Yes." *Huh, funny way to show love*, I thought. "Question number two," I added. "What do you want from *me*?"

Kyd drew in a sharp breath, dropping his eyes to his feet. "That's the burning question," he said with a sigh.

I narrowed my eyes, wondering why the boy acted more confused than me. "Line it up," I said.

Kyd sank the ten-foot putt like his life depended on it—except he didn't immediately come up with a question. His eyes narrowed and then softened, tightened again, and I got the feeling he'd insert more psychobabble. "Love can be a confusing emotion, Legs. Sometimes it's hard to distinguish between friendship versus attraction versus out-of-this-world." He paused to sigh, his eyes drowning with emotion. "Do you understand?"

Sounded simple enough. "Yeah," I answered.

"Are you *in love* with Taylor?"

Boy, he went for the mother of all mothers, didn't he? I laughed and held up two fingers. "That's two questions, Kyd."

I wasn't sure I even knew the differences between the two anyway. The gist of it, I suppose, settled around whether you'd like to make out with someone. I thought about that for a while and figured if I made out with anyone, Dylan would definitely be my first choice. Trouble was, I didn't understand "making out" either.

Kyd balled his fists, and I almost heard him count to ten. "How is that two questions?" he barked.

Whoa, strung out to die, he was. "You asked if I understood, and I answered yes," I explained.

Kyd gurgled some strange sounds, acting as if I'd just kicked him between the legs. "I'm guessing you can haggle well because you're constantly working things to your advantage. Your turn," he said in a clinical voice. "Twelve feet. If you miss, just remember you have to answer."

I walked off twelve feet, lined the ball up, flexed my knees, and carefully tapped it toward the empty cup. The ball took the lip and rolled down the hill into the lake.

———

It was a little past the witching hour.

Earlier, Grandma Alexandra and I took a stroll outside attempting to right the things that were wrong in our lives. She wanted Willow home. I wanted Cisco Medina home. Neither of us possessed the immediate power to make those things happen.

Like always, when the physical exercise didn't tame the beast in my brain, another option was to read. Right then, I lay on my stomach with my chin propped in my hands, reading *Atlas of the Stars* on the couch. For the last few hours, I'd missed Dylan terribly. My mind worked double time questioning: one, why he'd left without so much as a note; and two, how many hearts he'd broken in the span of a few hours.

Sure we'd spoken briefly, but let me emphasize *briefly*. It was more a recap of what I'd seen regarding Cisco and him responding, "I see."

And let me ask...what in the mother-trucker did "I see" mean??

I longed to regurgitate the day, first starting with Kyd. Kyd was all over me like white on rice. He'd tried to kiss me three times and —gasp—I kinda-sorta almost let him. No, I didn't answer his question about being in love with Dylan. I hoodwinked him into thinking I'd tell him later when I better understood myself. Just thinking that statement made me laugh because a huge possibility existed that might mean never.

"Hey," Dylan murmured, swaggering through the door on cue. My eyeballs stuck on pause, as muscled leg after muscled leg elegantly strut its way toward me. Who was I kidding? Kyd could have his rice. One of Dylan's killer grins shot me right back into desperation. His dimples were deep, and when they were accompanied with sleepy, bedroom eyes? Let me tell you I understood why good girls sometimes had bad thoughts.

"Hey, yourself," I greeted, grinning back. I swung my feet happily back and forth like I was looking at Santa Claus.

Dylan touched his heart with a wink. "Hey, hey to you too. I didn't expect you to be up, but I'm happy that you are."

Susan and Alexandra fell asleep two hours earlier. Sydney was connecting with her newest victim, and Zander snored underneath the pool table, holding the eight ball in his right hand. Honestly, I couldn't explain how my eyes remained open. I operated on three hour's worth of sleep, but couple that with my Cisco-high, and I might not sleep anyway.

Dylan wore royal blue athletic shorts and a new Florida Gators T-shirt carrying what I knew—without asking—was a duplicate one for me. The color was gray with a big, green, smiling gator in the center.

I moved my plate of cookies and chocolate milk out of the way, making room for him to settle down.

"I missed you and wanted to talk to you," I explained. Dylan collapsed next to me with a sigh, and I automatically slid over to hug his neck.

"Aw, honey, I missed you too," he said and squeezed. "You've been behaving?" Not really. There still had been no word from Troy, and it wasn't for a lack of trying. It didn't bother me in the least to wear him down until he listened. I couldn't do that with Cisco however. I had no idea which rock to turn over first.

Dylan dragged his cell phone and wallet out of his pocket, laying them on the glass end table beside us. Although he planted a quick peck on my cheek, darkness settled over me, and I was reminded of the sense of foreboding I had earlier—the sense that the day wouldn't end well.

Sheesh, it felt like a breakup was coming.

Chapter Fifteen

FASTARD MAGNET

*D*ylan sighed, briefly closing his eyes. "Darcy, we need to..."

Right then, his cell phone vibrated, and as I leaned over to retrieve it, the picture of an unbelievably cute blonde flashed with each ring. She had big blue eyes, a smile even bigger, and my guess was the rest of her attributes were bigger still. At the end of the day, Dylan was a guy. Guys liked boobs. Guys liked butts. It was a law of the universe.

"She's pretty," I whispered, reluctantly placing it in his palm. He declined the call, but not even ten seconds later his cell jingled again. Another girl. Redheaded. And by the flirty look in her eyes, she had an attitude (and the skills) that knew how to make a guy smile.

A nervous twitch settled in my left eye.

"She's even prettier," I muttered, sighing lower, massaging my brow. "Jeezle, Dylan. How many girls did you meet today?"

"A few," he said with a shrug. I had to give props to the redhead because when he didn't answer, she persistently dialed again.

My mind was thinking it, and my mouth couldn't help but say it. "I guess the end of our love affair is nearing."

Dylan jerked his head back like I'd just sucker punched him. "... *What*?" he barked surprised.

"They're calling already?" I tried to explain. He tilted his head in my direction with one arched eyebrow, curiosity his dominant expression.

"Does that bother you?" he asked. *Heck yeah*, I said to myself. I didn't want to lose him.

"I just didn't expect it."

Dylan struck a key and sent the call straight to voicemail. "You had one thousand people on your Facebook page in a little less than a month, sweetheart. The people on my account and in the contact list on my cell phone I actually *know*." *True*, I thought. The wonders of the Internet let me keep tabs on people I wouldn't normally rub shoulders with. Hopefully, my good feelings about some of my "friends" weren't unfounded, and they weren't the ax murderers Dylan feared.

"I know mine." Sort of.

Dylan bristled like a porcupine. "Not enough. There are about five hundred people I'm going to delete personally. Men my father's age have no good reason to be friends with a teenage girl. That's sick." My body angled to touch his arm. He scooted away to keep it from happening.

"Well, you just made friends with people *you* don't know, and they're already calling you, D. Take it from a girl, that's far more chummy than my Facebook page."

Dylan rolled his eyes sarcastically. "You're being a hypocrite."

"Why are you being so *mean*?" I asked exasperated.

Anger flashed in his eyes, consuming him. That wasn't good, people. Dylan didn't get angry often, but when he did, I either laughed uncontrollably or ultimately wanted to cry. "I'm not being *mean*," he snapped. "It's just that you're frustrating me, Darcy."

"D, I love you." I swallowed down some instant dread. "Why are you doing this?"

His eyes went wider than mine, almost like he fought through an intense pain. "Don't you get it, Darcy?" he said in a gentler tone. Heck, I didn't get anything other than an ulcer.

As I sat paralyzed like a moron, he went vertical and swiped a hand through his hair, angrily throwing the T-shirt into the corner by the TV. Almost like the purchase was a waste of time or an embarrassment. I pushed off the couch, my arms outstretched. He pulled back, denying physical contact.

Shoot...Crap...

I dropped my arms, confused. "I'm frustrating *you*? I don't even know what I did *wrong*! All I did was comment about two beautiful girls, Dylan. Don't I have a right to know?"

Once again, he rolled his eyes so high they might as well have been stitched to his hairline. "Do you have Kyd's number on your phone?" he barked.

Headed south.

Just pack your bags, the conversation was headed south.

Like the idiot that I was, I froze. A fact I blamed on being stoned on cookies.

"No comeback?" Dylan said with an amused snort.

"He's my brother," I whispered.

Dylan paced over to the television, turned it on...turned it off... and pivoted and jutted his finger angrily in my face. "I'm sorry," he sneered sarcastic. "I totally forgot that he had his hands all over his new sister's behind yesterday. Her string-bikinied behind, I might add."

Wow. Wow. Wow.

I thought I'd successfully dodged that conversation with the discovery of Howie's head. Evidently, Dylan held a grudge. "He wasn't successful," I muttered.

"Oh, he felt success," Dylan grated out. His eyes darted out the window in the direction of Kyd's home. *Dear God*, I prayed. He was ready for round two.

I whispered, "It didn't mean anything to me."

"And that's supposed to make me feel better?" he spat. "Honestly, Darcy, why can't you see what he's up to? It's disrespectful to you and frankly disrespectful to me."

"So you're more worried about you?!"

"No!" he screamed, adamantly shaking his head. "I'm just completing the thought!"

My lips went numb. Dylan and I never fought—not like this— and it was our second blowout in the past four months. The first had been over Brynn Hathaway—a girl who'd had him on her radar since junior high—who'd practically landed on top of his mouth and sucked out his soul. In all fairness, I could add fastard Liam Woods to the mix. Liam, however, was out of the picture, and unfortunately, my fastard magnet self had somehow attracted Kyd.

"Well, here's a thought for you," I stated, feeling the beginnings of anger. "If it's any consolation, he didn't have his hands on my behind today. In fact, he was nice, encouraging, and extremely understanding." Okay, so he tried to kiss me three times but backed off when I ultimately sprouted feathers and clucked like a bird.

Dylan scrubbed a hand down his jaw, pointing to the floor angrily. "He was *here*? In *my* house? Why didn't you *tell* me?" The climate in the room transformed from a sweet homecoming, to one of torqued-off teenage angst. He wanted to body-slam me. I wanted to ram his head through a glass table.

I pointed a shaking finger in his face. "I didn't have a chance to! Both girls called past midnight, Dylan, so talk of my day was usurped by the party you obviously had!"

Dylan's eyes flashed with an emotion I'd never seen. It wasn't pain, it wasn't anger, but it definitely contained a remnant of both. He ran a thumb under the strap of my tank top, tugging it, and then releasing it in angered frustration. "Were you dressed like *this*?"

I was dressed for bed, wearing ocean-blue boxer shorts and a matching spaghetti-strapped tank. My hair was in a halfway down ponytail. My glasses were smudgy, and to top it all off, I had choco-late milk and cookie breath. Add a pair of blue wool socks, and you weren't talking silver-screened siren. You were talking two-year-old kid.

"No!" I answered confused. "I'm dressed for *counting sheep!*"

I stepped backward. Dylan immediately stepped forward, giving me a proprietary glance.

"Exactly what *did* you do and how close did you *get*?" Dylan's eyes raked across the floor looking for evidence of something. There was no drug paraphernalia, no movie ticket stubs from first-time dates, no *nothing* except a girl who'd been debating whether she had the energy to brush her teeth or boycott it altogether.

"For God's sake!" I then screamed. "We played video games and putted a golf ball!"

He lowered his gaze with a no-more-Mr.-Nice-Guy look. "He wants to do more than putt a golf ball, Darcy. He wants to be *me*."

"No, he doesn't."

"Yes, he does," he said louder.

"Hold on, Attila the Hun. I offered a long time ago to make you my brother. It's not my fault that you repeatedly refuse."

Dylan expelled a string of expletives, his voice coming out in a brutal growl. "The last thing I'll ever be is your *brother*, Darcy. This whole situation is absurd. I warned you about his type, and if memory serves me correctly, you swore that you understood. That's a lie, and I absolutely *hate it* when you *lie* to me."

I grabbed a handful of his shirt, squeezing it between my fist. "Listen, bud, you don't own me, and I never swore to you that I wouldn't talk to him again. Plus, it's not like we don't know what those girls are after. You just *met* them. Obviously, they thought it was okay to call, and why wouldn't they? You told them to smile and say freaking *cheese*!!"

I shouldn't care *what* he did, *who* he did, whether it was Rated-G or hardcore porn. But dang it, why did I?

All we did was demolish the other with our eyes. Dylan eyed a football Zander had left on the floor. He gave it a swift boot, ricocheting it off the wall. It knocked over a lamp, which by guestimate cost close to a thousand dollars. When realization hit what he'd done, he thundered over, picked it up, and verified that it had shattered. One of two things would happen. Dylan would feel remorse and perch the lamp back on the end table, or Dylan would feel remorse and launch it again. After one long pause of deliberation, he torpedoed it up against the wall where it left a divot the size of a softball. Drywall and plaster crinkled to the ground like a bucket of spilled marbles.

"Well, my phone calls aren't dates!" he spat back. I flinched and jumped backward like I'd stepped into a bear trap. "Do you want me to delete their information?"

My face said yes, but my mouth said, "No."

"How magnanimous of you to concede like that," he deadpanned sarcastically. "You usually only concede when you're guilty of something, Darcy. Exactly what *are* you guilty of? Did he *kiss* you? Did you wait until I left to jump right in with both feet?" he marked in air quotations. "I know you're remarkably clever, but honestly, this is a little low even by your standards."

Any residual hurt was officially extinguished. I'd missed him. So much so that I napped in his room to merely smell his sheets. My thoughts surprised me.

"It wasn't even a *date*!" I screamed. "I feel like you're punishing me for something, Dylan. Tell me what I did, and I'll apologize!"

"Can you tell me why Kyd came over here last night?" he asked. "And I don't buy the fact that he was checking on you after you found the head. You were the least affected."

Oh, the cluster conundrum I found myself in. Tell the truth, I'd be busted that I used Kyd for information. Don't tell the truth, I'd be deeper into an argument I didn't even understand. I was amazed that what I thought was a tender moment last night meant nothing when he opened his eyes at the start of a new day. The answer was he thought Kyd and I had some lurid, secret affair going on. Granted, it felt like that, but a relationship with Kyd was the least of my concerns.

"It's not what you think," I said, gulping down the panic.

"Then give me a reason to think something else," he said, his voice losing some of its edge. "If it was so innocent, couldn't you have talked to me about it? We're friends, sweetheart. Best friends. We talk...at least, we used to."

In the blink of an eye, Dylan's anger suddenly abated. Just went away...poof, kaput, gone. His chin quivered, and he looked like he'd break in two with the vulnerability. I shook my head. Scratched the back of my neck. Dylan was nothing but raw passion, but his unusual display of emotion had surprised even me. He was up...he was down...his heart beating on the outside of his chest. My God, he had PMS.

"You're torturing me," he whispered. "Don't you understand?"

Duuuuuude. Still don't really get it.

I opened my mouth, closed it, and realized whatever I said would probably make things worse. If I thought I understood the spectrum of emotions that could encompass an argument, I was sorely mistaken. I'd gone from shock, to anger, to desperately wanting to wipe the tears that fell freely down his face.

My words were gravel in my throat. "D, why are you crying?"

"I'm not crying," he refuted, frustration returning. Guys didn't cry like that...especially not in front of girls. His chest heaved as if an elephant sat on it and smothered his last breath. Had I seen

Dylan cry before? Sure, but it wasn't to that extent nor something I'd ever advertise. Dylan's expression said his world was ending, and he'd fight to the bitter end to keep it from happening.

His chin trembled more. "Tears are flowing down your cheeks, D," I whispered.

He opened his mouth to speak, but immediately a thought pummeled me that whatever he intended to say would be a half-truth. "Listen—" he said softly.

"Don't lie to me," I dumbly interrupted.

Dylan looked like I'd smacked him. "Wow," he said with disbelief, "when did you get so cold?"

Someone other than me started working my mouth. "Me, cold?" I retorted. "Well, you weren't much into goodbyes this morning, now were you?"

Dylan slowly lifted his chin, stubbornly. I'd lost the argument—or conversation—or whatever the heck it was we were doing. I'd bated him back into debate, and nothing short of a zombie attack would stop him from making his point.

He took another step toward me. "Evidently, I need to spell it out to you. Kyd's after you, Darcy, and why wouldn't he be? You fascinate people. You're beautiful, unpredictable, and smart," he said, pointing to *Atlas of the Stars*. "That's not exactly what I'd call a beach read, but on this one, you're being *so dumb*," he emphasized, "I don't even know what to say. He has a damn girlfriend. You did this with Liam Woods. You're going for guys who are already taken. Don't you think you deserve someone who considers you the ultimate catch?"

"I don't really want to be caught," I mumbled.

"So you just like the attention?" he asked wide-eyed.

Whaaa...? Huh? No!!

I was just using them, I wanted to scream, but Dylan would never understand it. That was the difference between us. I had no problem keeping secrets. Dylan, however, liked to live so honestly it was oftentimes unpractical...at least in my world.

I longed to touch him but balled my fingers into a fist to talk myself out of it. I could've shut him up a hundred different ways—tickle him, tackle him, shake him...kiss him. Strange, that the latter seemed the most enticing.

Instead, I opened my big, fat mouth and took the argument to the highest level of stupid. "Is it time to move on?" I choked out. "Just say it, Dylan. We both knew this day would come."

Whatever I said, it wasn't the explanation or dialogue Dylan had hoped for. Where he'd cried in frustration earlier, his eyes were then a teary mask of pure anger—anger he intended on stoking until it blew the whole dang place up. He closed the gap between us, the air crackling with passion about to pop. One moment I thought he'd throw me to the floor and devour me. The other, I was convinced he'd bend me over his knee. Three words came to mind: Behavior. Never. Lies. Something was definitely boiling between us—outside of the argument—and it would never go away until we explored it or beat it out of one another. And I didn't think that would include a hug or sweet, tender kissing either. It would be a raging forest fire. One fire ignites, and you think you've got it under control, only for another to spring to life somewhere else. Trouble with passion like that, it either illuminated your world or burned itself out. When the last ember cracked, you opened your eyes and wonder what happened to all of those pretty, little trees.

"Darcy," he started.

The way he said my name, like a desperate prayer, turned my stomach...I'd hurt him as much as he'd hurt me.

"Don't," I begged, pushing both my hands against his chest. For once, I wasn't the motormouth that wouldn't shut up. Where before I'd been struck with the feeling that whatever he said would be a lie, right then I knew it would be the cold, hard truth. A truth my churning gut said I wasn't ready to hear.

Dylan ignored my wishes, his tears resurrecting themselves in torrential waves. "Interpret this as you will, Darcy," he finally seethed, staring down in my face. "The contacts I made today were players, one coach, cheerleaders, and a few girls rushing a sorority. But if you continue to make our relationship a threesome with people like Liam Woods or Kyd Knoblecker, then consider me moved on. Consider me so frigging moved on you can't remember what I look like."

I tried not to let it sting, but it felt like a honeybee just zapped me with its tail. A cry strangled in my throat, and I quickly spun to view his grandfather leaning up against the wall who'd overheard part—if not all—of the entire exchange. Lincoln pressed his gaze over my shoulder, and if Dylan could've turned into stone, one blink from his grandfather would've left him fossilized. What the freak was that? Can someone tell me what the freak *that* was??

"Take a walk, son!" he growled, his brows creased and fists flexed.

I didn't have to turn around to see if Dylan walked away. My heart felt him leave the room.

I needed an excuse to explain why I was a simpering, dimwitted idiot. Heck, maybe I needed an excuse for myself. The quickest thing that came to mind as a cover was to focus on Cisco—who was probably crying more than me.

"I *s-s-s-saw* him, Lincoln," I whispered, voice cracking with emotion. "I *r-re-ally* did."

He pulled me to his chest, curling a finger under my chin, tilting it upward. "I believe you, kiddo. But is there anything else that we need to discuss?" I just shook my head, surrendering to the tears I'd been holding at bay.

The crux of the matter? I was losing my best friend.

After I did my thing in the bathroom, I curled up on the couch and eavesdropped on Lincoln talking to Paddy. The only thing good to come out of the day was I knew Cisco was alive and the name of the national crime database was NCIC. Come Hell or high water, I was going to get my hands on it. So while plans of mischief occupied one side of my brain, the other was plagued with the uncertainty with Dylan. What in the heckity heck had just happened? We'd never had a conversation with so many negative interjections.

Lincoln terminated the call, looking at me. "Sit," he murmured, motioning to the space on the couch beside him. Trudging over, I brought my blanket with me, leaving it to hang loosely around my shoulders. My eyes slid to the clock on the wall: two a.m. Shoot, I was fried.

"I made some calls for you today," he murmured.

My mood perked up. "You did?"

Lincoln narrowed his eyes, almost offended. "You're the sharpest kid I know, dear. If you said you saw him, you saw him." Sharpest? Not really. Nosiest? No doubt about it.

Pulling my legs up to my chest, I folded my arms around them and hunkered down, all ears. "Spill it."

Lincoln located his glasses and shoved them onto his nose. He then switched on his email account and nonchalantly typed in the password "Willow." Wasn't profound, but I guess it was predictable. He missed his daughter, and without saying it, my feelings were he slept on the couch opposite mine to be one step closer than everyone else when she came through the door.

He scrolled through several unread emails, clicking on one with a subject of Cisco Medina. He skimmed over it, and then read it aloud.

TO: Lincoln Taylor
FROM: LAPD
RE: Cisco Medina
DATE: August 13, 02:22 p.m.
Hey Linc,
Orange County and the FBI launched a nationwide whodunit, but in the past few months, they've come up with nothing. My source at the Bureau tells me the guys on the case are a little leery of the mother's account of the days leading up to the abduction. Yes, she was spotted on video at Walmart, which ruled her out as a suspect, but she's throwing off a guilty vibe. They think she knows something she's not divulging but didn't want to feed that to the press.

"In other words," I summarized. "No one can come up with a *who* that *done* it."

Lincoln pinched the space between his eyes, shifting his gaze to the clock on the wall. Willow should've been here at dinnertime—she wasn't. "That pretty much sums it up," he murmured, "but I had your information passed onto the Bureau and the cop working the case. Evidently, the number of mistakes and miscommunications involved in this one are mind-boggling."

"How so?"

"For one, the grandparents' English is so bad, by the time an interpreter was called in, the daughter showed up, and they clammed up altogether." I must've looked confused. "That's not necessarily odd in cases like this, Darcy. When a child isn't located right away, sometimes people get paranoid—even good people. And dependent upon how a lawyer advises them, sometimes law enforcement is left alone investigating people who don't truly have a connection to the case."

"But they've both been cleared, right?"

"Yes, of physically nabbing him themselves," he clarified. "In most abduction cases, it's the other parent, but these two check out. Lola and Hank both saw him regularly, and on the day in question, he simply went to the park as he did every day. Nothing was physically out of the ordinary, which unfortunately appears to be the situation most of the time."

That synced up with what Kyd told me earlier, and the email about Lola sending off funky vibes also corroborated what Troy suggested days earlier.

Note to self: find out the funk, and you just might find that little boy.

"What other miscommunications?"

Lincoln powered-down his laptop and shoved it underneath the ottoman. "Apparently, the first detective working the case retired last month, and his replacements aren't quite up to snuff. People are playing catch-up with grandparents who are no longer in town."

Lincoln leaned forward fishing his cell phone out of his left pocket, thumbing in a number for whom I knew was Willow. Watching the desperation in his eyes was a flashback to the pain of seeing it in my father's when my mother wasn't around anymore. That stuff never went away, and time rarely salved away the feeling. He shook off a wince when I assumed he received her voicemail.

"Will, it's Dad. Give me a call." He paused and choked out, "I miss you."

A precipice of pain morphed over him as he terminated the call, pitching his phone into the seat beside him. Right then was where the normal reached for your hand and cried with you, but dang it, I felt like that little Dutch boy with my finger in the dam. Somebody needed to get a grip on the chaos before it got even worse. I couldn't help Lincoln with Willow, and although I'd sworn off Turkey Cardoza (sorta), if that could relieve some of his stress, then I was all-in.

I linked my arm in his, resting my head on his shoulder. "Thanks," I told him. "I know you've got a lot on your mind. Is everything okay with you?"

He turned his cheek toward me, his face calling me out on the argument I'd so far refused to discuss. "Is everything okay with *you?*" he echoed back.

We blew out a mutual sigh. Not by a long shot.

———————

There was a reason your parents said to not read or watch scary things before you went to bed. You couldn't sleep, or if you could, you played those images on a loop in your dreams and wound up crashing in their room.

Lincoln was sound asleep with his briefcase wide open on his lap. Made of high-impact silver aluminum, it was the type you hand-cuffed to your wrist with a preset password. CIA league...or at best, James Bond. If you had a lapse in memory, the only way to click it open would be using a force just slight of a mini-Uzi.

Squatting down on the rug, I quietly laid it on the ottoman and rifled though several colored photographs inside a Cardoza file. The pics resembled a natural disaster. Debris lay in every direction, piled on top of one another at weird angles—splattered on the walls, the floor, the ceiling—but I couldn't make out the exact nature of the original structure until my mind registered the debris was human.

I prayed ten thousand prayers in the span of a few seconds.

That wasn't a campfire horror story. It was graphic and disturbing.

You know, awesome.

The file contained two sets of photographs according to a date-stamp on the edges, and the man or woman—I couldn't tell—had literally been blown to bits. It didn't look to be your typical mob kill, in-the-head/in-the-heart, because whoever perpetrated unloaded a submachine gun or stuck a bomb in the vic's mouth and detonated it, offsite. Chunks of flesh and bone hung from the white walls, and blood streaked from floor to ceiling in what appeared to be a warehouse or building under construction. A nail gun lay in the middle of the mess next to an empty paint can that had flesh alongside its handle. A wedding ring, with part of a finger still inside, sat beside a Nike sneaker.

The photographs from a few weeks earlier suggested a male. The bone structure seemed larger and the jeans and shirt were undeniably styled for men. In those photographs, the method of killing was different. He'd been bludgeoned, having died long before the killer decided to stop with the blows. What remained of his face looked black and blue with a cheekbone protruding through the left side. I stared at it for several minutes but eventually looked away, my stomach cramping into knots. For some reason, it was worse than the body parts. The person had felt each delivered blow and probably begged for his life.

These types of criminals don't rob convenience stores. We're talking sick, sadistic, loony bin bound—or better yet—destined-for-Hell type of killers. On the back of each photo was a serial number of some sort and a sticky note in Lincoln's handwriting that said "Bonnano, Giuseppe, or Carlotto." I lifted the ink pen from the end table and inked the information onto my left palm. When finished, I placed the photographs back inside the silver briefcase, snapping the lid shut.

I tried to breathe. Find normal. Shove away the insanity. Falling onto the couch, I tugged the cover up to my chin, realizing the thick fleece blanket was white like the blood-soaked walls. Kicking it onto the floor, the chill was fierce, but getting another blanket meant I'd have to navigate the dark. The dark normally didn't scare me. Right then, it clawed at my sanity. I settled for curling into a fetal position and closed my eyes.

Chapter Sixteen
THE GUESSING GAME

*A*ffection is defined as a strong fondness, a feeling of respect and deep devotion. Humans need it, animals crave it, and civilizations flourished when they held it as a core value. You didn't know how much you needed affection, though, until the warm part of your life suddenly ran Russian-cold.

Closing up the newspaper, I downed the last drop of black coffee, needing a little bit of affection myself. Morning rituals in my home were simple. You poured a cup of coffee, grunted a goodbye, and hit the ground stumbling and definitely not running. All of the Taylors...excluding Sydney...woke up happy to meet the world. Like me, Sydney was a vampire. Her best work was done under the dark of night.

It was midmorning, and the morning ritual here looked like an assembly line of love. Before the Taylor men went anywhere, they "loved up" the people they were in love with as if they were the most precious resource on the planet. They weren't afraid of public displays of affection, and the object of their PDA acted like the luckiest person in the cosmos.

Some days I found it sweet. Right then, I wished I could pepper spray all of them.

Lincoln hopped into the kitchen, pulled on his sneakers, and cupped Alexandra's face in one hand, kissing her lips. Colton followed thirty seconds later, repeating the same mannerism with his wife. Dylan strolled in, and suddenly I felt feverish. My vision doubled. Got dizzy. Wanted to hurl. My God, I wanted to be on the receiving end. But then again, I wanted to shove my foot up his boom boom, hoo-hah masterpiece and break it off. He had on a red golf shirt and khaki shorts with his hair parted on the left, causing his cheekbones and eyes to pop out in a *wow*. He gave half a grin, but I just sat there, speechless.

Leaning up against the countertop—watching us like the peanut gallery—were his mother and grandmother. Both were dressed for tennis. Obviously, word in the camp traveled fast of our verbal free-for-all. Grandma's eyes were wide and peeled for round two. Susan, however, took a slow sip of her coffee, eyes studying her son closely. My guess was she instigated an apology or subliminally willed one into his mouth.

He pulled me out of the seat by my forearm, his face with that indentured-servant thing going on. "I love you," he murmured.

My breath caught in my throat—the L-word was one heck of an opener.

I think I whispered, "Always," but maybe I told him to "KISS MY A-S-S" in all capital letters.

We stared at one another for a moment, my chest squeezing with the bad memories. Dylan captured my face in his hands, tilting my head back so I couldn't look away. I was struck with the intimacy of the moment and the feeling that he wanted to kiss me. My heart thumped against my ribcage. *Do it. Don't do it. Do it,* I thought. Surely, to God he wouldn't, would he?

But it was Dylan...he'd do whatever he pleased.

Finally, he murmured, "What's on your agenda for the day?"

The day's mantra: mystery, suspense, fun, scared out of my mind, throw some imaginary kissing in there, OMG-I'm-afraid stuff... repeat, repeat, repeat.

"I'm going to relax by the pool," I answered quickly. But to qualify the mantra, I planned to snoop and tap into Lincoln's computer. I needed more information on Cisco. Plus, I needed the full names of the dead in Lincoln's photographs. Bonnano, Giuseppe, and Carlotto were still inked onto my palm, but I wasn't sure what that meant. They could've been the victims, but then again, they might've been the perpetrator.

"Play with me, sweetheart," he murmured and grinned. Dylan had dressed for golf. Normally, I'd hit the links with him, but the day's schedule was jam-packed with sin.

I'm busy, I said in my head.

Out loud, I said nothing.

My lack of words floored him. Abso-frigging-lutely floored him. His shoulders dropped a fraction, but then he drew me to his side, crooking his arm around my waist. "Listen," he murmured, "if you'd prefer to relax around here, then have a wonderful day, but I'd like to apologize, sweetheart." I slid a glance over to the females in the family and neither looked like they had the urge to scramble away. As a matter of fact, they simultaneously nodded I needed to hear him out. "You fell asleep before we said goodnight, and you never crawled into my room for a late night chat. And frankly," he said, wincing and briefly shutting his eyes, "I didn't sleep that well. Actually, I didn't sleep at all. I need to make things right with my favorite girl."

No kidding. We had a fight, and it was a doozy. Nonetheless, a part of me wasn't truly sure what it was because, at one point, I wanted to roll around with him on the floor...you know, panting... like dogs.

My voice was a thready whisper. "You were angry, and if I would've known you were going to go all Rocky Balboa on me, I would've laced up my gloves."

The hurt in my chest ballooned all over again.

Dylan spun me around to face him, tenderly murmuring, "I know. My behavior was barbaric, and I allowed my emotions to turn me into someone who I didn't even recognize. Please," he begged, "hug me. Let me remind you that's not who I am...not with you... not ever."

To say I was perplexed sounded trite. All I could manage was a stare because I didn't know what to say, and I wasn't sure my arms understood what had gone down either.

When I still did the Statue of Liberty routine, he painted on another heart-stopping grin, his amber eyes sparkling. "Do you want me to grovel?" In no uncertain terms, would I pass up the chance to watch Dylan Taylor grovel.

"Groveling might be nice," I said, sort of smiling.

Dylan dropped to one knee, tenderly stroking my fingertips until my hands were completely swallowed by his. The hurt in his voice rang palpable. "I'm sorry, Darc. I love you, and I'm never going to get tired of telling you that. Nor will I ever leave you for anyone else. Please, forgive me." A light slam of the door let me know we were officially alone. Dylan gave me his patented I'd-take-a-bullet-for-you face, but the quiver in his chin suggested his vulnerability might be greater than mine.

My voice trembled as I whispered, "I missed you last night."

Dylan slowly nodded, apparently reliving a painful memory. "I know. My heart is bruised too. Three times, I tiptoed in to check on you, but you'd already fallen asleep. As much as I missed you, I didn't want to disrupt your peace. You're even more beautiful when you sleep, sweetheart. It nearly took my breath away."

If I thought about it, I looked like crap. My clothes were rumpled. My hair was hookerfied. One sock was MIA, and my breath smelled like a stale cup of whatever had been living in that espresso machine. My energy level tapped out at a two on a scale of one-to-ten.

That didn't imply beautiful. It said I needed a do-over.

"Three times?" I asked.

"Three times," he said, adding a wink, which was his way of telling me things would be okay.

"I figured that was Lincoln," I said, pulling him back up.

"Lincoln snored next to you. He's waiting on Willow, Darc. She was scheduled to be here days ago, and I now understand how it hurts to wait for someone who never comes."

Ah, jeezle. I was seconds from dissolving into a driveling idiot. Besides how Dylan conducted himself as a person, I was addicted to his words. Problem was, his brutal honesty at times was hard to stomach. I'd been content with sweeping situations (like Kyd) under the rug, including Dylan not saying goodbye the day before. Dylan never swept *anything* under the rug. If he didn't cover it immediately, I could bank on the fact he'd eventually dig it up and beat the crap out of it.

"It's okay," I softly told him.

He drew both my hands to his lips, his voice resolute. "No, sweetheart. It will never be okay for me to make you cry. You had questions. I should've made sure you had answers. Let's make a deal to never go to bed angry or confused, with anything on our minds that we need to talk over. Deal?"

My guilty conscience poked me in the ribs—he'd had questions too. Still, I grabbed his pinky finger and wound it through mine—that served as answer enough.

After we made plans to ride the mechanical bull at Cowboys that night, we had a marathon hugging session, resting our foreheads together. I couldn't help but pick up on the fact that sentences begged to be released from his vocal chords. His arms and body were relaxed, but I sensed his soul was anything but. My chest thundered in anticipation, but I watched him swallow down an emotion I wished he'd share. He released me with a tight squeeze and jogged to the door.

Here I was, at ten-something in the morning, totally alone. A golf game was minutes from happening and tennis scheduled out the day for the women of the family. Sydney wouldn't be up for hours, and a look out the door had Zander shuttling to the course with the other guys.

Once the coast was clear, I shoved my lucky hat on my head, snatched Lincoln's laptop, and perched it on the kitchen counter, plugging it in an outlet. While it fired up, I opened the refrigerator and grabbed ham, pulled pork, cheese, mustard, and pickles, finishing with crusty bread to make a Cuban sandwich. Stacking everything inside the bread, I drizzled on butter and placed it in the sandwich press, counted to one hundred and twenty, and burned my left hand. After I said part of the s h i t word, I apologized to the universe because God knew I had more sin on the horizon.

Tossing it on a paper plate, I took a seat on a barstool and cracked open a Coke, trying to think like a kidnapper. The lady at The Gap didn't strike me as psychopathic, so conceivably Cisco hadn't been physically abused. And since I was proof-positive he remained alive, that left it to the personal: (A) the woman wanted a child; or (B) the grandparents truly were messed up in things as the newspaper suggested. If it were (B), the confusing part, once again, was why would grandparents steal a child they were already legal guardians over? They sure as heck wouldn't get any kind of ransom from the parents—so if they weren't the kidnappers, that only left fear.

But what could they fear?

Biting off a big chunk of sandwich, I stared at the screen, knowing my posing as Lincoln Taylor carried some major jail time. As I thread the earbuds of my iPod in my ears, I piped out "Crazy Train" by Ozzy Osbourne and decided the payoff would be worth it. Singing in a tone-deaf splendor, I hit the icon labeled NCIC and struck in "Willow" when prompted for a password. Nothing. Erasing the word, I next typed in "Colton." Once again, nada. That left the nickname of his son and gun, "Jackal." Pecking out those six letters also rendered a big fat zilch in the success department.

"Think, Darcy, think," I said out loud.

Lincoln dressed in dependable colors. When he wore brown, it was brown from head to toe. If he wore black, he decked out like the creature from the Black Lagoon. He viewed the world simply. Simple people were usually loyal to the bone, and being in the undercover game, I'd guess, made him cling to the realities he knew to be true. It wasn't abnormal for him to go underground for weeks with no one knowing if he was dead or alive. My feelings were he wouldn't bombard his brain with an inordinate amount of details.

So who better to know you than your best friend?

I'd memorized Paddy's digits several nights earlier, and although the rooster had barely crowed on the West Coast, I dialed anyway.

"Paddy," he mumbled on the second ring.

"Hey, Paddy, it's Darcy."

"Hawareya, doll?" he slurred out.

"I want to get Lincoln a birthday gift." Dumb opener, but it's all I had.

"It's his birthday?" he slurred, a little more awake.

"No, I just wanted to get a jump on the sales. Do you know his favorite color?"

"Uh, no."

"Favorite book?"

"No."

"Favorite sport, TV show, clothing brand?"

"No, no, and good God no."

"Well, how about his favorite food?"

He gave me a whole lot of nothing until he finally muttered, "Something dead, but there was this one time we both got tired of it floppin' around, so he snatched it up, and bit its head off. So I guess it could be *semi*-dead."

What...the...?

On any other day, I'd delve into that subject matter, but right then wasn't conducive to my time constraints.

After Paddy proved he might be the worst best friend in the world, we ended the call. A quick look at the rest of Lincoln's icons didn't immediately strike me as out of the ordinary. He had a copy of Microsoft Office, icons for two antivirus programs, access to the Internet, and a white birthday cake image in the lower right hand corner.

My forefinger struck the rain slicker yellow birthday candles and up popped an alphabetized list of about one hundred names. Lincoln had five sisters. If Willow was his email password, perhaps his sisters were the others? It was worth a try, and as far as I knew, I had four hours or so to peck to my finger's delight.

Jumping off the counter, I ran through the living room, jumped over my missing blue sock in the hallway, and bounded into Sydney's room. Sydney's room was fit for a demigod. Like Dylan's, it was modern, but hers had a flair for the dramatic. The walls were painted in pink blush with fuchsia fabric headboards on both white twin beds. Clothes strung the top of a red couch, a black lace bra hung from the white fur lampshade, and magazines were scattered on the bed, which hadn't been slept in but one night.

Sydney lay on top of the white satin sheets, flat on her back in a red babydoll nightgown that looked sultry and sexy with a racy edge. Evaluating my own ensemble, I couldn't help but laugh. I'd never be sultry and sexy with a racy edge. There was a good chance I had happies shoved up under my ribs just waiting to fall out.

"Pssst," I whispered. Just a slight rustle.

"*Sydney*," I whispered louder. Nothing but a moan. I placed my hands on her shoulders and shook. No movement whatsoever. I jostled her harder.

Sydney rose up on her elbows, sliding her red satin mask up to her forehead. "What time is it?" she muttered. Time to break into Lincoln's computer, that's what.

"What are Lincoln's sisters' names?" I asked sweetly. That could go one of two ways. Sydney would tell me to kiss her keister, or she would mumble the answer and still tell me to kiss her keister.

"Margaret, Anna, Celia, Calliope, and Evie," she mumbled.

"In that order?"

"That's the birth order," she said. Sydney sighed and pulled her mask down, fluffed her pillow, and then rolled to her stomach... muttering a few curse words.

Running back to the computer, I typed in all five sisters and once again came up empty-handed. I closed the lid, immediately massaging my temples. *Holy cow*, I thought. Lincoln loved his grand-children, and guess who just had a birthday in the month of August? A smile lit up my face as I boldly typed in D-y-l-a-n.

Access granted...

Baby Jesus, let me fall down and worship at your baby crib. I laughed.

I'd just been granted access...and was rubbing shoulders with the F—*freaking*—BI.

Once I keyed in Cisco Medina, I captured the pertinent details on a scrap sheet of paper. He was abducted from a city park near Conroy Road in the city of Orlando. Letting that page idle, I activated another session of Windows Explorer, and typed in *googleearth.com* for an aerial view of the vicinity. Zooming in, I observed playground equipment, parked cars, trees and shrubbery, but nothing really substantial. Zooming out, I spied a laundromat, bank, gas station, apartment complex, and Albertson's Grocery Store—nothing out of the ordinary that you wouldn't find in suburbia anywhere.

Flipping back to the case details, Cisco's grandfather reported him missing at five p.m. Sunset around that time of year was roughly an hour later. So Cisco—in theory—still would've been visible to someone. He wouldn't have been swallowed up by the dark. Trouble was, that someone very well could've been the person who nabbed him.

All at once, I felt the immediate need to blow some cash. Padding back to the couch, I grabbed my purse and fingered inside my wallet, pulling out my father's MasterCard.

———

A hypothesis is an educated guess. You theorize if "A" happens, then "B" will result. If you test the theory and get a positive result—or it comes true—you have a scientific fact backed up by experimentation.

Trouble was, I didn't possess the know-how to make an educated guess on anything. But I knew someone who would...Kyd. Grabbing my iPhone, I punched in Kyd's digits with my thumb.

He picked up on the first ring. "I do, Legs," he breathed out.

"What?" I asked, giggling and collapsing back on the bed.

"I'm thinking sunshine and skimpy bathing suits for the honeymoon."

Why did I feel like I'd be dodging that proposal for the rest of my life? He'd only said two sentences, and already I wished I could shove him in front of a moving car. But I needed him. It made me feel horrible—like a bloodsucking user—but not horrible enough to murder my plans.

Leaning back on the pillow, I threw an arm behind my head and contemplated how to get the names of Lola's contacts. Kyd stated the day before that she gambled with powerful people and even played cards in their stead. The only way Kyd would gain additional information, however, was to question Hank who clearly was still in pain. I didn't want to inflict any undue stress on the man, but I had a gut feeling it might mean something.

"Would that be so bad?" he murmured.

"I'm fifteen!" I shrieked.

"Almost sixteen," he deadpanned. True, my birthday was October 15th, but that still wasn't considered legal in the good ole U.S. of A. Maybe that was the way they did romance in Louisiana. Heck, Murphy was raised in Kentucky, and a few in his hometown were born with an engagement ring on their finger. But I was a Midwestern girl from Ohio. We tried to hold onto that single status at least until mid-twenties, and then we grew paranoid our best days were behind us.

Helloooooo, eHarmony...

"You're frustrating me," he muttered. Funny. Dylan turned the same phrase last night.

"Maybe you need to try another pick-up line."

"Name what you want, and it's yours." Aaah. I smiled. Sweet satisfaction.

I went for the direct hit. "I need the names of the people Lola Medina used to, or better yet, *still* plays cards with. Make it happen, Kyd."

"Strange request," he said, suddenly quiet.

"To some, perhaps."

"Obviously, the human mind fascinates me, or I wouldn't want to be a psychiatrist, Legs. But I have to admit you are hands-down the most fascinating individual I've ever run across. I could spend a lifetime rummaging around in your grey matter."

I blushed, feeling like something indecent had just occurred between us. I didn't want Kyd in my grey matter, but fighting the attraction had proven difficult. It was like being a vegetarian and never wanting a flaming piece of steak. Only a moron wouldn't recognize the juicy smell.

Kyd promised me he'd have their names by the end of the day.

My thumb lay on the "end" button when Kyd got in touch with his pushy side. "Have you given any thought to coming down here for college?"

I rolled my eyes, pulling a pillow over my head. "I'm kinda stuck in the present right now."

"Just hear me out," he encouraged.

"Kyd, I probably won't go to college," I spit out.

"Ever?"

"Ever."

I heard the clock ticking away in Kyd's brain and fleetingly wondered if he took notes to place in his *Darcy Walker File*. You know, childhood trauma, low self-esteem, let's feel sorry for the girl with no mommy. "Legs, we need to work on your self-image," he said softly.

"My self-image is fine," I lied.

"Well, if it's fine, then we can talk about college..."

I chewed my left pinky nail, almost to the cuticle. I didn't have many options. If I didn't give Kyd what he wanted—or at least a version of it—he'd call non-stop and interrupt my thinking time... diabolical as it was. Problem was, a good chance existed that talking to him negated Dylan's and my request to not hurt the other. Fortunately, or rather unfortunately, I ascribed to the concept it was better to ask for forgiveness than permission.

At least for the time being.

"...so I'll see you in a few?" he asked.

What Dylan didn't know wouldn't hurt him, right?

———

As far as Kyd knew, I was researching a summer project on murderers versus contract killers, versus serial killers. I thought he'd dehydrate from salivating. When the boy said he loved the brain's complexities, I mean, he LOVED its complexities. For some reason, he acted like the sun rose and set in my brain—or lack thereof—these days. But spending time with him became a mistake of cosmic proportions. Amidst the talk of born killers, killers driven by circumstance, loyalty, or employment, I dodged my growing feelings infested with an all-consuming guilt. I'd butchered the détente with Dylan—at least, in the fact that I hadn't explained Kyd's and my relationship. Heck, I hadn't explained anything. So while my chest heaved with regret, I had a great, big hormone screaming, *Somebody kiss me, somebody kiss me, somebody kiss me.* Thing was, I didn't know if it was Kyd per se or the fact my estrogen met up with his testosterone. I didn't feel entirely ready for a boyfriend (at least my brain wasn't), but maybe I was *readyish.*

When Kyd left after a couple of hours, I pushed aside the guilt and immersed myself in what we'd discovered. Since the two murder victims in Lincoln's briefcase were associated with Turkey Cardoza, then that meant they were mob fallout. Both murders more than likely were for-hire, but the person contracted obviously garnered some sort of pleasure in causing the pain.

As a starting place, we'd searched the names on the backs of the photographs. I typed in Bonnano, Giuseppe, and Carlotto and uncovered an article that said the two largest Italian families in Los Angeles were the Bonnanos and Carlottos. As far as I could tell, Giuseppe was not the name of an organized syndicate, and the third family Paddy referred to—the family Turkey allegedly represented— could have been sending the Bonnanos and Carlottos a message. A message that they were bigger and badder than the both of them. In fact, it wouldn't surprise me, if they'd ordered the hits vis-à-vis Turkey.

Mobsters were a counter culture all unto themselves. Their values and behavior norms weren't like our own. What they did appreciate, however, was a larger show of strength. Blowing someone to smithereens who meant something to their enemy was a ballsy show of power. Without having names, I knew, beyond a shadow of a doubt, we weren't dealing with your average member. The two that were dead, more than likely, were high up the food chain or even a Bonnano or Carlotto themselves.

To prove myself right, I conducted an advanced Google search on the words: murder, Carlotto, and Bonnano. As suspected, one man from each family had died in the past year. The newspaper article stated the usual—no leads, no witnesses, just unsolved crimes that were obviously handled within the system of the mob. If my logic proved right and Turkey Cardoza committed the murders, Lincoln said there were witnesses who saw him on the scene. The newspaper hadn't interviewed those witnesses, or there was a chance the newspaper truly didn't want the story.

It got murkier and murkier.

With the FBI database at my disposal, I ended by searching on Gertrude Burr and Howie whatever-his-name-was. To my surprise, Gertrude had a file. It wasn't extensive—containing only a few speeding tickets and a former request to file bankruptcy—but no cross-reference whatsoever about previous severed heads in her past. When I searched on Howie and the dead body in her pool, conversely, the strangest thing happened. Another screen popped up where I had to have special clearance within the special clearance.

Talk about a buzzkill.

Chapter Seventeen

KARMA

*A*nd the crazy continues...

Grandma Alexandra grabbed two handfuls of my hair, looking at it in horror. "Oh, Jesus," she whispered.

Oh, Jesus, was about right.

Orlando was a real butthead temperature-wise, and I swear, the birds panted out profanity. Feeling our skin peel away in the heat, Sydney and I'd decided to swim. Like total morons, we swam right after the pool had been shocked—in other words, when it had been doused with a bucket of chemicals that weren't supposed to kill us. We didn't think it would matter, but apparently, it was a no-no for blonde hair. My hair was seaweed-green, which might be karma kicking my two-faced arse. Kyd was one thing, flirting with the F— *freaking*—BI and lovin' every minute of it was another. Problem was, my beauty happened to be a work in progress, and I'd nuked any headway Mother Nature had thrown me out of sheer generosity.

"For starters," Grandma said cheerily, "let's condition it. I condition mine weekly."

I couldn't find a logical reason to object. She went to the pantry, pulled out a bottle of extra, extra virgin olive oil (hellOOO, oxymoron), cracked it open, and massaged it into my hair. Before I knew it, half the Mediterranean was draining down my face.

Alexandra threw off such a dominant aura you found yourself

doing whatever she said even if it felt stupid. By no means was she dictatorial. She had just learned to survive as a first generation American. She did everything for her parents—even keeping their books before she was a teenager—and I'd always suspected that's where Colton and Willow inherited their business savvy. Her early childhood experiences left her self-assured, but oftentimes people like that thought they had the answer to the whole enchilada. I mean, look at me. I felt so cocky about successfully tapping into her husband's computer that I ignored the pool gods, and my hair resembled mustard gas.

When finished, she gently turned me toward her and confidently said, "Go outside and sit in the sun. The heat will help."

When I resumed my post poolside, I punched in Dylan's speed dial. "How far out are you, D?"

He seemed quiet. No flirting, no "Hi, sweetheart" on pick-up, just a breathing so shallow he might as well have bought the farm. Finally, he breathed a two-worded, "Almost home."

I'd showered, washed my hair three times, and dressed in my Gators T-shirt along with my favorite pair of cut-off jean shorts. They were too short, the white bottoms of the pockets falling lower than the inseam. In Murphy's words, "heavy on the hoochie."

I twirled a strand of hair around a finger, holding it up to my eyes. "The pool turned my hair green."

Another equally unnerving pause. "You're blonde, Darc," he finally said, sighing.

"Not anymore. It's some kooky shade of yellow. Kinda like mustard gas."

At last, a chuckle. "I'm sure it will be fine. So how did you entertain yourself in the four hours or so I was gone?"

I made deals with the Devil, and if he asked if that bothered me, he probably wouldn't like the answer. Thing was, I found success, and when a person found success, it was easy to overlook one's transgressions—a practice that continued to serve my conscience well.

When he murmured a deep, "Darcy," my iron resolve cracked like Humpty Dumpty. Something lined his voice that felt unwavering and nonnegotiable. He was trying to will me into submission. Did he know? My word, my heart started thumping like the feet on a rabbit. Dylan was silent. I was silent right back. I mentally made out a grocery list, picked at my nails, and then imagined my hands blistered to the bone doing ten years in a Siberian Labor Camp.

"We're in the driveway now, Darc," he said quietly. "We can talk in a bit."

Five minutes later, the garage door activated. Wrapping a white towel around my head, I trudged into the kitchen, giving a whole new meaning to the phrase walk-of-shame. No Dylan. Instead, I found Lincoln, standing with arms crossed over his chest, leaning up against the doorjamb.

Jesus, Mary, and Joseph...*he knew*.

"Hey, Lincoln," I whispered. "Where's D?"

"Cooling down," he said, low and deep.

Cooling down, I thought. What did that mean?

Lincoln ignored my request for specifics, sitting down at the kitchen table, unlacing his white sneakers. *Busted*, I thought. Just like that, the air sucked out of the room. "You're acting odd," I choked out.

"I'm a cop, Darcy. I can smell trouble a mile away. When Paddy called and said someone was messing with my *FBI clearance*," he emphasized, "I thought, who do I know who's sharp enough to crack my password and stupid enough to break into government property?" I grimaced but didn't admit to anything. "Exactly," he grumbled. "This has your fingerprint all over it."

True, left to my own devices I did have a tendency to get into trouble. But I still intended to smack Paddy around upon introduction. I raised my chin a fraction. "What proof do you have?" I asked defensively. The one thing I *did* know was you'd better have proof of culpability before you accused anyone of anything.

"He has your transcript," he said, holding up his index finger, "check stubs, IQ scores, your father's credit rating, and photographs of you with my grandson," he finished, holding up all five. "Believe me, he *knows* it's you."

I grimaced even deeper. "He knows I've got bad grades?"

Lincoln removed his shoes, peeling off both socks. He balled them together and pitched them over the couch. "He thinks you're bored out of your mind on a daily basis."

"I kinda have attention deficit."

He narrowed his eyes. "We all do, but my feeling is you only apply yourself on things you get obsessed with. You're obviously extremely industrious, and his assessment is that you may have deviant tendencies. Plus, we know your father has a lengthy juvenile record in his past."

He gave me the apple-doesn't-fall-far-from-the-tree look. I tried my best to not seem like an apple, but I'm pretty sure I looked all red and shiny.

"Murphy's a good man," I mumbled.

Lincoln breathed deep, his eyes closing with a heavy sigh. "I didn't say Murphy wasn't a good man. In fact, I *know* he's a good man. I simply said he needed to entertain himself too."

Ahhhh, Murphy's past...he used to gamble his brains out. Impulses like that never truly went away. A person merely replaced it with something else. For Murphy, it was food, fantasy baseball, and fantasy football...you get the picture.

Colton thundered through the kitchen door, ready to ram bamboo shoots up my fingernails. Tromping past me, he opened the refrigerator and poured a glass of iced tea, shoved the pitcher back inside, slamming the door even louder. "I don't know what to do with you," he complained, his black eyes narrowing. "You woke up in this mood, Darcy, and don't think that I don't know it was you who bamboozled me out of my shoes."

Sheesh, I almost forgot. Before I went to bed, I literally threw Colton's new leather golf shoes on the roof of the house. Why? The Devil told me to. When he discovered them missing before breakfast, I even scoured the premises like a concerned citizen but admitted to nothing.

I'm going to Hell.

I'm going to rot down there with the fastard that shot Bambi's mother.

When it was clear I stood on the losing side, I finally fessed up. "What is this, the righteous mob?" No one laughed. "Okay," I said, sighing deeply, "clearly you don't find the humor in this. At least, promise you're not going to tell Dylan."

"Dylan already knows," Lincoln muttered.

Son of a beast...all I needed was TAPS and the twenty-one-gun salute.

One day soon, he'd issue a pink slip on our best friend status—mark my words. No one could take the continual drama that I brought along with me.

Lincoln rattled off how they'd busted me: I'd erroneously called Paddy. I'd repeatedly messed up his password, which flagged the bigwigs, and I'd left a paper trail the length of Hawaii by ordering clothing from his laptop via Murphy's credit card. His partners performed a trace. Ugh, elementary mistakes.

"How'd Dylan take it?" I whispered.

"Dylan hyperventilated on hole eleven," Colton tag-teamed. "My son sat in the middle of the fairway, head between his legs, in utter disbelief what his favorite *girl*," he said, snorting sarcastically, "was doing."

Oh, God, I prayed. How much time would I be looking at? Ten years? Twenty? Home for the holidays? "Can you grant me clemency or something?" I begged wide-eyed. "Community service? Work release? Promise of good behavior?"

"A trip to the clink is what you need," Lincoln muttered. I didn't want to debate my moral depravity, especially when it was so obvious.

"Are you going to tell Murphy?" I mumbled. Oh, boy, that wouldn't produce anything but pain and suffering for all parties involved. My father had a way of making inanimate objects rue the day they were birthed into the imagination.

Colton narrowed his eyes. "That indicates I can't control you, and calling your father will not only have you on the next flight home, but it will destroy my son, plus everyone else in the household." He lowered his eyes, speaking even lower. "You're going to behave."

I wanted to vomit. I needed to upchuck all over the floor and be done with it. *They* knew, and *I* knew I'd be victim of my impulses until the day I died.

Lincoln chuckled when he eyed my panic. "Lighten up, dear. No charges are going to be filed, but you owe Paddy an apology. On the bright side, we'll give you a job when you graduate. You might have a talent for profiling, and under my tutelage, the sky's the limit."

A fist slammed on the table...Colton's.

"Darcy is *not*," he interrupted, with emphasis, "going to pursue a career in law enforcement, Dad. You'd better count yourself lucky your grandson didn't hear that. God only knows what he's truly capable of."

Both abruptly stopped to ponder, flinched like they'd been hit in the head by a two-by-four, ending with a mutual shudder.

"What if I'd be good?" I interrupted.

Both were still stuck in the moment a good twenty seconds later —Lincoln looking at the ceiling, Colton into dead air.

"I have to do *something*," I mumbled.

Colton gave his head a hard shake, scrutinizing my reaction. "Find something else," he said. "I swear, dear. You and Sydney are going to kill me. I can't ground you, and I try to ground Sydney, but she merely tolerates the conversation. The boys *never* give us any trouble." I disagreed. Dylan never gave them any trouble. Zander, however, had been kissing girls since age seven, and I was pretty sure he'd mastered the European portion of the art.

"You're mad," I mumbled.

"I wouldn't be a good father if I wasn't."

Colton had never figured out that I hadn't been born from his DNA. Believe me, it had its perks. Times like these...*notsomuch*.

"They're on the roof," I blurted out, trying to smooth things over. "Your shoes are on the roof. You should've seen them when you backed out of the driveway. It's honestly not my fault that your peripheral vision sucks."

My word, was that what I called a concession speech? I'd basically called the man an idiot.

Lincoln chuckled but squelched it down by swallowing water. Colton tabled his drink, talking überly slow. "What else...do you need...to confess?"

"Your password is Leo," I said. Knew it was a mistake as soon as it fell out of my mouth. I actually waved my fingers in the air, trying to symbolically shove the faux pas back in.

"You've not been staying in your bed, I presume," Colton exhaled. Well, duh. There was no rhyme or reason to why I said the things I did. I had foot-in-mouth disease. I opened my mouth and inserted my foot.

I'd rather kiss a blood-sucking leech than deal with Dylan when he was upset.

I whispered, "Are you miffed with me?" Dylan's feet were outstretched, crossed at the ankles as he lounged on the couch in his bedroom. His body claimed he was relaxed. The clenched muscles in his neck screamed he was far from nirvana.

"I've been waiting for you," he said quietly. Dylan lightly patted the seat next to him, and like man's best friend, I trotted over and melted into his side. After Lincoln and Colton read me the riot act, I waited for Dylan to materialize...he didn't. I pouted. Cried. Apologized profusely. When that didn't accomplish anything, I slogged to his room, and here I was—salivating. Shirtless, he only sported gray athletic shorts, and suddenly, I wanted to snack on his boom-chicka-wow-wow abs.

Weird, I thought. All of those mixed emotions were confusing and plain, ole weird.

"Why didn't you stick around?" *For the flogging*, I said in my head. Dylan took my hand in his, holding it to his cheek. "I can't stomach to see someone discipline you, so I took a shower. Then I felt like I didn't have your back, so I jumped out and toweled off only to talk myself out of it." A panicked look crossed his face like he didn't understand his own actions—as if foreign to his genetic code. "I'm a laidback, confident person, Darcy, but with you I break out into a cold sweat and get so insecure it scares me. I don't like being scared," he said on an exhale. "In fact, I... "

He paused, not finishing the thought.

Now he seemed embarrassed...or mad. I wasn't sure if he was mad at himself, the situation, me, or all three. Problem was, the rules in Darcyville didn't always mesh with societies'. For someone like Dylan—who prided himself on religiously doing the right thing —just hanging with me required thinking outside the box. By the looks of things, maybe one too many times. "Where you're concerned," he continued, "my first instinct is to come up swinging. It always has been. Do I care? No. Will that change? Never. I admire your moral courage, sweetheart, but it's extremely difficult for the people who love you. Ultimately, I suppose I wanted to see if you'd tell me," he finished.

"I tell you everything," I said. Eventually. *And, by the way, I'm going to need a second to pull that arrow out of my heart.*

Dylan was a master at the guilt trip.

Dylan took a deep breath, emotions playing all over his face that I didn't have the names for. "You do," he admitted, "but most usually it's after the fact."

"It's *just*..." I said. "*It's just*..." I tried again. "Well, what should—"

Dylan was a good listener, compassionate. He not only answered your questions. He answered those you were too afraid to ask. He tenderly sighed. "It's just that you're sure of yourself, and now you're afraid of the information."

The tears took me by storm, and when I tried to speak, all that came out was garbled embarrassment. Before my feministic side disapproved, I went old school and crawled onto his lap, burying my face in the side of his neck. Yep. Old school. Girlfriend behavior. When females let the males in their lives solve whatever had gone wrong.

"Ah, Darc. Don't cry," he soothed, rubbing my back.

"I know what I saw, D. I really, really s-saw him."

Dylan made slow circles around the middle of my back. "Sshh, I believe you. It'll be okay."

Dylan needed to join the rest of us back on planet Earth. Things weren't okay...and they wouldn't be okay until Cisco had black hair again.

"I'm just so frustrated." I sniffled. "I wouldn't have gotten caught if I'd figured out the password sooner."

"No, but your actions were tantamount to breaking a half dozen laws."

"Does it matter if it was for a good cause?" I justified.

Dylan pulled a tissue from his nightstand, gently placing it in my hand. "Unfortunately, yes," he murmured. "My grandfather is sworn to uphold the law."

I adamantly shook my head, honking my nose like a foghorn into the tissue. "He won't do anything."

I hoped.

Dylan sighed so hard it had to have hurt. "No, he loves you, and his partners found it entertaining. But just because you have friends in high places, that doesn't mean you can keep sticking your neck out like you do. I swear, sweetheart, one of these days it's going to get chopped off."

Chapter Eighteen

A SATIRICAL AFFAIR

*S*omeone once said, *Beauty is in the eye of the beholder.*

The originator of that slogan had people like me in mind. I'd gone to bed hoping I woke up a pussycat doll. Instead, I was HAZMAT suit material. My hair looked like nuclear waste. My hoping hadn't garnered much success in life...but I was due.

I was soooo freaking due.

It didn't sit well with my self-image when we ate at a restaurant called Ember last night either. I'd never seen so many beautiful people in one location in my life. It was like Venus opened up and dropped them by the handful. I made plans to return when I wasn't so visually offensive.

And even though Dylan was dying to ride that mechanical bull, we didn't make it to the country bar like we'd planned, opting to swim at the clubhouse. I got the impression the family wanted us close to home. In other words, "Don't let Darcy off the leash."

I opted not to buck the system and just save my breath.

Kyd texted before bedtime and reported that Lola traveled in well-connected circles. She played with a congressman, mayor, and a few local businessmen and women. He claimed someone named Ivanhoe was her confidant and knew her every move—if he didn't orchestrate them himself. I got the feeling Lola willingly made herself a puppet, which could be good, I guess, if the puppeteer pulled her in a direction she didn't mind going. If he didn't? Well, perhaps that, in itself, was Lola's problem.

Troy phoned and said he'd had little luck finding information on Fix It, Incorporated but had a friend at the Better Business Bureau digging around...were the guys legit, etcetera. He also landed another interesting find: Livingston & Associates declared bankruptcy three months earlier, and no one answered his endless knocking. Could that be why Howie started gambling? He needed the money? Howie was definitely involved in the Cisco Medina case because the note in his mouth had Medina scrawled on it. Unfortunately, I might never know the extent of his involvement since his former employer had gone belly-up. Whatever the case, my fascination with Howie came to a premature end. As industrious as I was, no way in the world could I get past the extra security screen within the NCIC database, and after my latest hack-in, Lincoln probably had it booby-trapped anyway.

I liked Troy, believe it or not—in spite of the flirting. He'd just graduated from college and was trying to make a name for himself, waiting on that big break. He sounded desperate, and desperation was one word I'd recognize in Braille. But who were *we*? All we knew was the stench around the case was like smelly cheese, and if we had any talent in life, it was that our noses never steered us wrong. Problem was, my big girl voice—i.e., my adult voice—didn't always come into play. I slipped in and out of teenage vernacular when excited. Troy had to have noticed the *omigoshes* and *no ways*, or maybe his lack of comment was a true testament to his distress.

After breakfast, Sydney and I borrowed Willow's red convertible Audi R8—what I liked to refer to as "Six Figures of Oh. My. God." She peeled out of the driveway, hit I-Drive, and drove off to the nearest beauty salon. We found a Cosmetology School close by. Stepping through the door, I swallowed the golfball-sized lump in my throat.

Beauty and me...a satirical affair.

————

While my stylist prayed to the hair gods, Sydney strolled next door to a tattoo parlor and phoned when she spontaneously decided to ink herself. I didn't do anything drastic with my hair, but regarding the overall assessment, it probably wasn't a good sign when the stylist threw in a brow waxing for free. She either felt my hair was beyond help or was too nice to say I had a freaking unibrow. Mid-makeover, I decided a tattoo might be fun. My last go-around with a henna tramp stamp proved catastrophic. Real ink might be the answer. Trouble was, when the decision stood before me, I had to determine quickly what I'd like to have on my body for the rest of my life.

Pat Benatar's "Hit Me With Your Best Shot" blasted me in the chest as soon as I cut through the door. I'd never frequented a body shop, but the place wasn't the sleazy, needle-infected joints of the motion picture industry. These were high-class artists, probably pulling down a hefty paycheck. Sydney sat in a black swivel chair in the rear, talking to a woman who looked like she ate eyeballs for breakfast, skulls-and-crossbones for supper. Around Sydney's height, she had the build of a swimsuit model with short, spiky pink hair, and cat-shaped orbs for eyes. At quick count, eight piercings stabbed one ear with multiple tattoos down her back, peaking outside her blue, lacy tank top.

Three other artists inked away on other clients, which left one lone station directly across from Sydney. I skipped back and jumped into it.

"Hi, I'm Spike," Sydney's artist said, smiling at me. "Hector will be with you in a sec." Sydney excitedly perused picture books, while admiring the navel stud of Spike who'd exposed her rock-hard abs for appraisal.

"Spike?" I asked grinning.

"Kimberly," she said, grinning even bigger. "Spike sounds—"

"Like I should avoid you in a dark alley," I interrupted.

Spike threw her head back and laughed, unleashing an infectious personality that, no doubt, was the life of the party. She was naughty, brazen, and had a to heck-with-the-world attitude. My word, I'd found my long, lost sister.

Almost on cue, Hector entered the room, swinging through rainbow-colored wooden beads, dangling from a back office. "Hey, chicky," he said with a big smile. "You here for me?"

Hector was very Latino looking with long, curly black hair and tattoos down both arms in red and orange flames. The Virgin Mary capped out one deltoid. El Diablo topped the other.

I gave him a lot of teeth. "Yes, I'm here for *you*."

Hector immediately cleaned his station, spritzing antibacterial fluid on the counter and wiping it clean. "What's up?" he asked. "If you're here for me, you must need something kept on the down-low. People who sit in my chair usually have secrets."

Oh, goody. As luck would have it, destiny picked the right chair.

Destiny or stupidity.

I said the first thing that popped into my mind, realizing it was a long shot he'd know Lola Medina personally. But then again, her son's disappearance had been big news here for a while, so he'd at least have a valid opinion. "Well, how are you on the low-down?" I whispered for effect. "Because I'd like the scoop on Lola Medina."

Hector shivered and stole a glance at the door as though he expected highway patrol to crash through with submachine guns. His breathing intensified to 5K level, and he stood straighter, defensive. "That's a pretty big, dangerous scoop you're after," he muttered, "and you're dressed very Midwest...tank top, tiny shorts, and a nice, sexy legitimate tan." Actually, I'd dressed in jock-girl chic —green Adidas from head-to-toe—but I'd never turn down a compliment that included the word sexy. "Why are you concerned with someone who can count cards who has a little boy missing?" he said frowning.

Better yet, I thought, *why do you act like you know her personally?*

I twirled my hair as if bored, trying to keep it factual. "Just curious, and by your reaction, I'd say you know her well."

"Maybe I *do* know her," he said evasively.

"Well, then you'd be happy to know that I'm positive I saw her son."

Hector's eyes bugged wide, his mouth dropping open like a Venus Fly Trap's. "Are you a cop?"

"I'm fifteen!" I said, laughing incredulously.

Hector loosened up but still cocked an inquiring eyebrow. "Your eyes say you're innocent, but your smile suggests juvenile detention."

I had visions of working on the chain gang earlier. Evidently, I needed to work on my appearance. I gave him a flirtatious wink. "Takes one to know one."

Hector tweaked my nose. "Okay, chicky, so we're both bad news. What's your name?"

I looked over at Sydney who thankfully appeared to have forgotten I'd accompanied her. I saw no harm in giving him my alias. "Call me Jester...on the down-low, of course."

"Okay, Jester...on the down-low," he said and chuckled. "You're cute, but I'll only give you information if you help on my commission. So what'll it be? Tattoo or piercing?"

With no forethought whatsoever, "Can I make a call?" tumbled out of my mouth.

Hector said, "Be my guest," and rearranged his piercing tools while I whipped out my iPhone and speed dialed Dylan.

"Let's get a tattoo," I said when he answered.

"Interesting opener," he said and chuckled. "That's the last thing I would've guessed was going to come out of your mouth. My first guesses would've been, *I love you, let's get married, I think you're the hottest guy around, and I'm dying to procreate*."

Yep, vintage Dylan. I chewed on my lower lip, stopping when my mouth filled with the metallic taste of blood.

"Tattoos tell everyone who you are," I diverted.

Dylan groaned, "You're not putting a tattoo on your cute, little body."

"What if we get matching Ds?"

He stopped to think, sighed, and then jumped back on the moral high horse. "Maybe someday, just not today."

"*When?*"

Dylan's voice went harsh. "Exactly *where* are you, and why is the *when* suddenly important, Darcy?" I looked at Sydney who laughingly took a finger and made a switchblade movement across her throat. Not sure whose throat she referred to. Hers or mine. She resumed her perusal of Spike's piercings when it dawned on me she might be leaving the place looking like a pincushion.

"So you're in?" I laughed in his ear.

"I'm going to perform a little litmus test," he murmured. "Do what you want to do, sweetheart. Have fun."

The world had ended. If it hadn't, then I was pretty darn close to a sinkhole that had my name on it. "Is this reverse psychology?" I asked.

"Is it working?"

"No."

"Then I'm merely supporting your impulsivity," he said chuckling. "That's love, sweetheart. Love at its finest."

"Is it painful for you to be so supportive?"

"Shredding me in two."

Dylan's voice grabbed mine. Latched ahold. Traveled to my insides and settled some place in the pit of my stomach. He was toxic to me and destroyed my resolve to grab the bull of life by its bucking horns and hang on. "You're toxic to me," I groaned.

Dylan chuckled naughtily, and I instantly had an X-rated picture of the two of us alone—sweaty, heavy-breathing, furniture overturned, maybe some bruises...oh, gosh, I literally slapped myself in the face. "Think about that, sweetheart," he murmured as if he'd read my mind. "Wouldn't that be a great way to go?"

I slammed the phone off.

Rather than chance him calling, I switched off my phone altogether. Sydney's immediately rang. She fumbled around in her purse, looked at the number, and shut it down with a sigh.

"We're in trouble," her voice graveled out.

"I know," I said, giggling nervously...on more than one symbolic level. "So what's the verdict?"

She lifted her shirt, pointing to her navel. "I'm getting my navel pierced." *Ouch,* I shivered.

Hector and Spike pulled out their selection of jewelry: gold dangly squids, gold Mother Marys, and gold almost Olympic-sized barbells. Description? Not expensive enough for Sydney.

Predictably, Sydney wrinkled up her nose. "Do you have any real diamonds?" her voice cooed. "I don't want any cheap, tasteless knockoffs."

The merchandise didn't appear cheap to me...although, Jesus's mommy didn't need to lounge in my belly, and my navel didn't anticipate doing the clean-and-jerk anytime soon.

Hector narrowed his eyes on Sydney, frowning. "Can you pay for real?" he asked. Seriously? Her trust fund could buy the strip mall on the interest of one month alone.

She glowered, thinking him an idiot. "Does it look like I can pay?"

Hector took the time to eyeball her up-and-down, adding up everything from the clothing, to the haircut, to the pedicure. Not to mention the unseen underwear that weren't the Hanes-packaged-deal like mine. After he made a decision, he turned and opened a drawer of what I assumed contained his secret stash. Lifting out a black velvet box, he stole a glance toward the door, popped it open, and pulled out two diamonds with long studs, the optimum size for belly button rings.

I just threw up in my mouth.

"Five hundred dollars apiece," he said firmly.

Sydney drew them up to her discriminating eye. After the visual pat down, she closed her black orbs and sucked in a mouthful of air. As if communing with her inner-diamond.

"They're legit," she purred. "Four hundred dollars, and it's a deal."

Hector shrieked, "Five hundred dollars *is* a deal! They're a carat apiece!"

"They're also fenced," I said and laughed, meaning it as a joke.

By the giggle that erupted from Spike, I hit the nail on the head. Hector pointed a thick finger in her face. "Don't judge, Spike. My extracurricular activities provided you with a nice Christmas." Spike closed up her red tattoo book with a wink. My guess was she enjoyed whatever his sticky fingers gave her.

I tried not to act overly eager, but dang it, I liked getting things on my terms. "You're a businessman, Hector, and I can appreciate that." I said. "But you have no overhead, and they're stolen. Let us help you out."

Hector wasn't amused. He snapped the box shut with a loud whack. I shuffled in my seat, trying to act as unhappy and irritated as he was.

Registering my balk, he reluctantly flipped the box back open, laying it on his workstation. "Five hundred," he said stern. "And I'm not going lower. My little girl needs clothes."

"Four hundred," I countered again.

Sydney tried to keep her inner-diva in check, but the vixen reared her head anyway. Throwing her four-figure bag over her shoulder, she pushed out of her chair and hitched up her chin, heading for the door.

Hector tugged on the space between his eyes. "This is highway robbery. Where are you from anyway? Did you just get out of the pen?"

"We're from Cincinnati," I answered. Hector still had that I-need-to-think thing going on. Well, he needed to get a move on because it wouldn't surprise me if Dylan was burning rubber as we spoke. "Okay," I said softly. "We'll do things your way. Three hundred and fifty total, and it's a deal."

Spike snorted, doubling over in laughter. "My God, I love you," she snickered.

Hector went berserk. "You lowered the offer again!" he bellowed in exasperation.

Heck, I didn't know why I lowered it, but occasionally, Murphy's genes staked a claim in my body no matter how hard I tried to avoid them.

"Look at it this way," I explained. "You're due a raid, and we'll help lower your inventory and losses." Growing up with a father in the insurance industry at least provided me with appropriate buzz-words. And like a good citizen (facetiously spoken, of course), I wasn't above using them to my advantage.

"What's in this for me?" he growled, narrowing his eyes.

Good question. Not a lot, really. "If you answer my questions, then you can be my brother."

I explained the benefits of being in my brotherhood. Hector gave me a devious smile. He knew the definition for benefits more than anyone. I kept secrets for you. You kept secrets for me. When I whispered I'd give him a bonus for his little girl, he was sold.

"I do need another sister, I suppose, but *she*," he grumbled, nodding to Sydney, "is a man-eater. I want nothing to do with her." No kidding. Plus, she looked hungry.

After I inducted him into my brotherhood, he and Spike pulled out their piercing tools as Sydney sat back down. "Are you certi-fied?" she asked rather snottily.

"APP," Spike said, pointing to a five-by-seven framed certificate on the wall.

"And you're sure you're sterile?" Sydney pushed. "Let's light them up to make sure, and that way I can check the diamonds. Cubic zirconium will crumble." Heck, I didn't know if it would crumble—she probably didn't either—still, Hector left through the swinging beads, bringing back a piece of equipment resembling a flame thrower.

I burst out laughing. "And you have that *why?*"

He gave a wicked shrug. "Sometimes a person needs to change his looks fast." Cue the nausea. You always hear these kinds of stories, but it's a totally different situation when you meet the people who participate in them. "I don't get to use this often," he said, "but here we go." He hit a switch on the silver contraption, and a foot of blue flame lit up both diamonds that Spike had placed about six feet away from us on the black tile floor. Nope, they didn't disintegrate. So, if anything, they were good fakes. Plus, all things viral and bacterial went bye-bye.

Sydney stretched over for my hand as we raised our shirts for numbing cream. "Ready?" she purred raspily.

My nervous giggle was a yes.

After Hector and Spike loaded their guns, they gave each other the eye and simultaneously pulled the triggers. For once in my life, I understood what the birthing process must feel like for pregnant mothers. There was a pop, deep burn, and warm ooze, and then the doctor told you it was over while you proudly looked down at the object you were bringing home. But reality set in, and you immediately questioned if it was a good idea or perhaps the dumbest thing you'd ever done.

"That's it?" I asked with a wince.

"That's it," Hector said. "How's it feel?"

"Stupendous," I lied.

"Grounded," Sydney said, laughing loudly.

Hector chuckled as the cold dread of stupidity washed over me. I should've consulted Murphy. "Pay me," he said, "and I'll answer your questions."

Sydney and I pulled one hundred and seventy-five dollars apiece out of our wallets, and behind her back, I threw in an extra fifty bucks. Murphy sent me with eight hundred dollars. I usually only spent half, but that way Murphy'd feel like he provided for his child, while unbeknownst to him, he provided for someone else's.

Rationalize it, Darcy, I thought to myself. *That's how bad people make it through the day.*

"About Lola," I started.

Hector peeled off his rubber gloves, throwing them in the waste can. "I've tatted Lola before. She has a picture of her son on her left wrist."

"Annnnnnd," I pushed.

"Annnnnnd," he mocked, "it's the type of tattoo that took multiple attempts to get it right. It's in full-color."

"So you got to know her well."

"Yes, and my impression is she's the type of person who knows too much for her own good. She's crafty and brags how great she is at swindling people. Whatever she does, there's a reason, so it wouldn't surprise me if she knows exactly what's going on."

That comment, I wasn't prepared for. "You think she took her own son?"

"I didn't say that, but she probably has information no one else has. The grandparents are gone. Maybe they're trying to get away from *her*."

Interesting thought—one I hadn't considered. "Where does she live?"

He sprayed disinfectant on the surface of his table, wiping it with a paper towel. "Last I heard, Lola lived near her parents off Conroy Road. Even though her parents have custody, I don't think they booted her out of his life entirely."

Howie's face—er, head—floated into my mind, and once again I remembered the note in his mouth not only listed Gertrude's name and address, but the word Medina. It was a long shot, but if Hector knew about Lola, a good chance existed he knew of Howie. How in the world, pray tell, was I supposed to phrase a question about someone's severed head??

In typical Darcy fashion, I dove in forgoing a preamble. "So I found this head, Hector." Hector's jaw dropped. "Howie's head. Have you heard about Howie?"

He grew silent for a moment while he slowly finished cleaning his station. He carefully put everything away, one instrument at a time, deliberately delaying an answer. "Everyone's heard about Howie Cantrell and the missing body," he said stiffly. "Question is, how do you know about Howie?"

Good grief, he wondered if I was the executioner. I somehow kept my laugh to myself. "Like I said," I reiterated, "I found him."

"Mother Mary," he prayed. No kidding, I hoped Mother Mary found it as upsetting as I did.

I relayed the story of the note and how Gertrude divulged Howie worked for one of the PI firms she funded. Hector didn't have an opinion one way or another—he'd never heard of Gertrude nor had he heard of Howie before his head hit the gossip waves.

He said, "If there was a note that said Medina, I can guarantee you it definitely referred to Lola."

"Want to guess on the specifics?"

Hector crossed his arms over his chest, back to eyeing me suspiciously. "All I can say is that Lola's name is synonymous with trouble. A severed head in her path is probably not abnormal for her every day."

I reserved judgment since severed body parts seemed to show up in my life too. Other than that, I got nowhere. All he did was corroborate the never-ending merry-go-round of Lola's bad news antics and illegal affairs. I needed to find the one thing—or person —who tied Lola to Howie and Gertrude.

An idea percolated. "Do you know the people she gambles with? Like an Ivanhoe?"

Hector's relaxed candor morphed into one of paralyzing terror. He whipped out a cancer stick so fast I would've sworn he'd been born with it attached to his lips. Grabbing the blue BIC lighter near his station, I flicked the roller for him, the red flame dancing at the end of his cigarette. With one long draw, he shivered nervously, acting like someone had run a machete across his heart and threatened to leave it there. "Ivanhoe," he muttered, "is bad news, chicky. Don't go looking for him. All I know is wherever Lola is, there's always a lot of money."

I scratched my head in my mind. If it had been money-related, how could Cisco's captors gain dollars if no ransom had been placed? When I asked for Hector's spin, his face went blank. He'd honestly given me all he had...except on the Ivanhoe part. He made clear—with a clenched and set jaw—that he'd rather wear a toe tag than dive into the world of Ivanhoe. There were no other options, except to find Lola.

Chapter Nineteen

A BROTHERHOOD OF LIES

A lie is a deviation from the truth. Some believed that a little, white lie was innocent, but purists believed that anything— even the slightest omission of cold, hard fact—remained the same as the blackest of offenses. Right then, my brain lied to me. It was one thirty-three a.m., Friday morning. The time suggested I should be sawing logs, but my mind couldn't find the "off" switch.

"He's asleep, Paddy," I whispered.

"Aww, doll," he apologized, "I keep forgettin' you're on East Coast time. I'm sorry to wake you. Just have Linc call me first thing."

I pulled my ink pen from behind my ear, penciling a note on a nearby napkin. *Call the Irish, or your shamrock's going to lose its happies*, it said. When I finished, I folded it into a tent and placed it on top of Lincoln's glasses. Both of us had crashed on our respective couches, the sandman loving him and hating me like a bad case of eczema.

Guilt blasted my conscience when I remembered I owed Paddy an apology. "Hey...umm," I stammered. "I'm—uh...well, you see ... *uuuugh*."

After several aborted attempts at an apology, I finally blurted out, "I'm sorry for tapping into Lincoln's stuff."

I felt like a total donkey.

A pause hovered in the air. "Listen, doll," he eventually said and chuckled, "you're a smart girl. A *very* smart girl. Just stay on this side of the law, and we won't have any problems."

There were all kinds of smart and all levels of dumb. Unfortunately, I happened to be familiar with each of them. "Technically I'm smart, Paddy," I stated, "but so many other variables live in my brain that I can never settle down long enough for good things to jell. I've tried to conform, but from what I'm told, psychologists insist that might prove difficult. The best I can probably offer society is the promise to not reproduce."

It felt like a knife stabbed me in the heart. I waited for it to happen...the judgment. It was a universal law in Darcyville. I told someone who I was—what really went down between my ears—and then the unrelenting whispering followed.

There was another pause with Paddy finding his voice first. "Aww, doll, that would be the worst thing you ever did. The world needs more people like us. One day, I'll tell you what I did pre-Lincoln. It wasn't always on the up-and-up, but he'll be the first to tell ya that some days my past comes in handy."

I wasn't sure what the prerequisite was for working in vice crimes. Killing easily? Selective consciences? Disguises out the yin-yang?

"You're fifteen, right?" he asked.

"Almost sixteen."

"College in a few years?" Most of my efforts in life were self-imploding. College sounded like rubbing my nose in everyone else's success.

"I already have a PhD in bullcrap detection, Paddy. I don't see a need for another degree."

Paddy chuckled and mumbled a surprised, "Hunh. Then you really need to think about your future."

He had no idea that was *all* I ever thought about. I was in high school. At least once a week some teacher told students that what we did mattered. What grades we made...what choices we made... what friends we hung around with. They drilled into our heads that *everything* counted—even the things we didn't want to count. Talk about pressure, it was crippling.

"Lincoln and I could use you," he continued, "and you've given our colleagues something to rib Lincoln over. He's one man who's hard to fool."

No, his heart beat like pure snow, and mine beat so black it was scary.

After Paddy and I cut the call, I cleaned and organized the house. I finally conked out only to be wakened when Howie's head —escorted by my two dead crabs—crawled up my chest, hissing the name of his murderer. Scared senseless, I brewed a cup of coffee, and instead of it relaxing me, I became so jacked-up it left me in a state of suspended animation. Like always, my first instinct was to find Dylan. I slipped a white terry cloth robe over my Angel-sleep T and stole off to his room, rubbing what I knew were bloodshot eyes.

Dylan gave me a drowsy smile as I knelt by his bed and caressed the hand lying outside the sheets. I painstakingly swallowed. He was brutally handsome and vexingly perfect. The kind of beauty that could make a girl commit hara-kiri because she'd lost her mind. "Hey," he whispered.

"Hey," I whispered back, dropping a kiss onto his hand, "I can't sleep."

"Neither can I," he said, lightly laughing.

"Can we talk for a minute? *Please?*" Although physically tired, when I looked in Dylan's face, there existed a natural and satisfied serenity about our relationship. I highly doubted either of us would ever find that comfortable feeling with anyone else.

Easing quietly under the blankets, I disrupted him as little as possible before he had a chance to kick me out on my psychotic tail. Dylan rolled over to his side, tucking my back into his chest, crooking his arm under my head as a pillow.

A small ray of moonlight, peeking free from the clouds and bouncing off the lake, illuminated his room. There had been a thunderstorm earlier, no stars were in sight, and the land of sunshine had become a gloomy shade of gray.

Like my mood.

"What's bothering you?" he murmured. Dylan's voice rumbled in a sleepy sort of way...*cute*...it sounded too stinking cute.

Oh, where to begin? "Everything, I guess. I'm worried about things I can't control. I organized the refrigerator, alphabetized the spice collection, and color-coded Sydney's nail polish according to the spectrum of the rainbow." He laughed. "I polished Lincoln's gun, Jackal—"

"Oh, God...don't tell him that," he groaned. I didn't plan on it. Another few moments elapsed with us both simply listening to our breathing. He finally asked, "What can't you control?"

"School," I answered. Cisco Medina, I omitted. Everything Hector told me. Did Fix It, Incorporated really exist? Where was Howie's body, and were there really aliens, blah, blah, and imbecilic blah. Not to mention, what the heck had Lincoln been working on?

"*And?*" he tenderly pushed.

I blew out a sigh. "You're going away someday while I stay home. I don't ever want to be without you, D. I worry sometimes."

And I need you to love on me.

"Shhh," he soothed. "That's crazy talk. I'll never leave you, sweetheart, and I'll never move somewhere that makes you uncomfortable. We're a team." Whoever wound up with Dylan would be one lucky girl. I had plans to kill her. But I knew the best friend creed demanded I love her as much as I loved him.

My chin quivered, and I hit the skids immediately. I didn't want to cry, but Dylan could pull my emotions to the surface quicker than anyone. "Promise me," I begged.

"Pinky promise," he murmured into my shoulder. "Rest, Darc."

"It's just..."

Dylan chuckled in my ear. "You're not ready to rest yet."

"I always miss you," I explained. Dylan and I didn't say anything for a while, and it didn't feel weird. We had a wonderful relationship. There was never any awkward silence or excruciating subtext... we could just *be*. I was the first to speak. "Why is talking in the dark just so..."

"Intimate?" he murmured.

I would've chosen the word raw, but intimate worked. "Yeah," I agreed.

"I don't know, sweetheart. Maybe because all you have are your thoughts. It's just you and the other person's—"

"Heart," I interrupted.

Dylan released a soft sigh, pulling me even tighter to his body. "My thoughts exactly," he whispered. "The face draws you in. The heart makes you stay. And you have a warm and beautiful heart that I love very much."

All I could think was ditto, ditto, ditto.

Dylan ripped me in two. Every. Single. Time.

"Do you think you'll ever feel as close to anyone else as you do to me?" I asked quietly. A dozen heartbeats went by, and Dylan grew so quiet I feared he'd fallen asleep. "D?" I said. Nothing but nothing. "Are you awake?" I rolled over, tenderly touching his face with my fingertips. My hair tumbled and splayed across his chest, and for whatever part of his body had been asleep, Dylan all of a sudden appeared wide awake.

A hush drew out between us, and a sense of urgency filled the air. Something else entered the room—something neither of us understood or was comfortable acknowledging. Finally, he murmured, "I'm not asleep, sweetheart, and no. I don't think I'll ever feel as close to anyone as I am to you. You're amazing. The most beautiful thing in my world and the most intense, honest, and fulfilling relationship in my life."

Honesty might be lacking, but I could wholeheartedly agree on the other adjectives. Trouble was, we said things you usually only claimed about your significant other. These weren't the things you said to your best friend.

"I feel the same way," I agreed anyway. "That's why I don't ever want it to go away."

I got another beat of silence from Dylan as I stroked the hair at the base of his neck. Dylan claimed it relaxed him, but he suddenly seemed tense. He gently pushed his head into my hand, as though he couldn't get enough of the feeling. With a deep breath, he murmured, "We don't have anything to worry about. Close your eyes, sweetheart, and rest for a while. I'll make sure we'll always be together."

All at once, sleep won its battle. Maybe those were the words my subconscious waited to hear. I crawled even closer to where there was barely any space between us, like I longed to connect with the one entity that would always complete me.

———

Sydney and I were laying poolside while I ran my finger around my diamond belly ring. It sparkled like a prism in the sunlight, and frankly, I felt so dang proud of the purchase I could barely contain myself. No, it didn't go over well with the Taylors, and it went over even worse with Murphy...until he'd discovered I'd swindled a crook. Then he became so impressed, he hung up and bragged to his friends.

Murphy Walker...Father of the Year.

While I watched Dylan flip burgers on the grill, an unexpected waft of entitlement filled the air, and without even turning my head, I sensed Yankee Knoblecker had slithered onto the premises. She wore a teensy-weensy pair of shorts with a poison-green belly shirt that showed off a six-pack stomach. Her smile was totally saccharine, and in my opinion, offensive to all powdered sugars of the world.

She marched by us like we were the hired help, eyes locked on Dylan's—um, hamburgers—the entire way. Sydney and I stole a look at one another, and I had a sick feeling we were going to witness firsthand the tactics Yankee would employ. As Dylan obliviously jammed away to Van Halen's "Beautiful Girls," Yankee turned him around, tiptoed up, grabbed his T-shirt in both her hands, and (gasp!) kissed him.

She kissed him, I whispered to myself.

And it was swoon-worthy...slow and torturous and deep with intentions.

Dylan's one arm hung limp, while the other still held the spatula. Bright side? At least, he didn't spank her with it. Yankee sidled even closer to where nothing lay between them but Dylan's shirt and her lack of one. After what felt like forever (it was twenty-four-point-something seconds, people), Dylan briskly shook his head, shocked and tongue-tied.

But it wasn't like he spit out her lipstick.

"You like?" she said, smiling up to him. "It's what the shirt said to do."

Seriously, some people had no shame.

I felt responsible. He wore a T-shirt that said "Kiss me, I'm Greek." Colton strolled into breakfast wearing it, and Dylan whispered he wanted it. Times like that, I wish I had no skills because within minutes that shirt was mine. It had been as simple as telling Colton he looked like a drooling Jabba the Hutt.

Dylan gave her a half a grin and a quick, awkward one-handed hug—mumbling something that was best I didn't hear anyway. Yankee blushed but kept her bony arm around his waist as he flipped over the burger I didn't want at all.

"Stupid shirt," I mumbled.

"She bothers you?" Sydney stated as a question.

"*PUH-LLLLLEASE!*" I joked.

Sydney purred out a laugh. "Dead give away, Darcy. You always joke when things get uncomfortable." No kidding, and seeing the clock strike midnight on the day couldn't hurry up quick enough. I worried about Cisco...was more convinced than ever that Lola was the key...and had to watch my best friend lock lips with a hard-bodied munchkin. I needed to think of something to make the day profitable because it was only noon and already smelled like failure.

I chewed my pinky nail. "She doesn't bother me," I lied. "He just deserves better."

"*You're* better than her," she rasped. *Maybe in a perfect world*, I thought. Sydney reached down beside her chair for a sip of the sweet tea she'd left there. "Do you want to talk about it?"

I'd avoid that conversation like the plague. Yankee's hair was perfectly-perfect while mine still had a green sheen. Appearances suggested she didn't sweat, and I'd only been outside ten minutes and perspiration had mustached underneath my nose. Plus, my legs were stuck together at the thighs. When someone's legs stuck together at the thighs, that usually meant they contained some extra meat. But who was I kidding. Dating? I didn't understand anything about dating. I was knee-deep in emotions I couldn't begin to fathom.

When Sydney told me Dylan was anxiously looking my way, after half a minute, I finally geared up the nerve to glance his way. By then, he was likewise distracted. While he politely—and almost too easily—spoke with Yankee, I snuck inside and snatched two dough-nuts and slipped out the front door to visit the Knobleckers. Besides, I didn't want his stupid hamburger when I could talk Herbie into grilling a hot dog. A girl had to have standards, and right then I hated cows.

My conscience told me it was tit-for-tat, still I found myself looking for Kyd. When I discovered he wasn't home, Oinky and I hooked up and right then shared hot dog number two. Oinky was a peculiar little pig, but the fact that he grunted his approval at whatever I confessed caused me to initiate him into my brotherhood. He couldn't communicate that my actions were bat-poop crazy.

And that maybe...loose emphasis on the *maybe*...I had feelings for my best friend.

"Is this kosher?" I asked Herbie.

"Ya Jewish?" he asked surprised. "Ya never struck me as a Jewess."

With hot dogs, I was. But right then, I merely asked out of Oinky's well being. I might've made him a cannibal of his own species. "Just curious," I answered.

"Ballpark frank," Herbie grunted proudly. "Do you want all meat?"

Not really. It tasted just as good, granted in a different way. I guess I was a hot dog snob. "No, it's great," I said.

"I've got some cow tongue in the freezer if you'd like somethin' else."

I had an eeeuw moment but shivered it off.

"Maybe later," I said and smiled. The three of us sat at a fancy picnic table in the back of his house. Herbie's banana-yellow board shorts fell a good six inches below what nature intended as his waist. I still wore a brown bikini but had thrown on a white mesh cover-up. Modesty dictated I dress more appropriately, but once again, it was Herbie. I'd seen the man's fungus-ridden rump. We were close enough to wear our birthday suits if we so chose.

I gave Oinky a bite and returned it to my mouth. "On second thought, I'm going to throw that tongue on the grill," Herbie grunted, turning toward the house. "I'll be back in a minute."

Okay, I needed to leave. I'd never seen a cow tongue, and I was pretty sure I didn't want to smell one. Still trying to make the day successful, common sense told me I needed to get inside the apartment where Cisco Medina lived.

"I need to get inside that apartment, Oinky. Like really, really bad."

Oinky grunted in approval as I whipped out my iPhone and commenced to dial.

Phileo in Greek meant brotherly love. It could be biological, or it could be symbolic of a strong affection one had toward someone who wasn't a relative. To me, phileo meant an I've-got-your-back type of love, and right then I needed that lying-for-your-sibling type of thing.

Kyd answered on the first ring. "Miss Legs," he growled suggestively. "What can your brother do for you?"

"I need to speak with Tricky."

Kyd went wordless. "And the reason for that?" he asked flatly.

He's your brother, Darcy, I said to myself. *Tell him the truth.* "I need some help breaking and entering."

Kyd broke into laughter. "Neptune's your man, but what exactly are you up to?"

"It's for a good cause. I'm sorta fixing something."

"So it's philanthropic," he said and chuckled.

"Think of me as Florence Nightingale."

"Right." Then he paused, and a very weird vibe stretched between us. "Exactly where is Taylor?"

Oinky looked at me, I looked at him, and we both knew that could pose a problem. "Not with me," I replied. "So if you run into him, you need to...you *need* to..." I paused with a grimace, "you need to...*lie*."

Kyd moaned like he'd just downed an aphrodisiac. "Legs, that will be my pleasure."

After giving me Tricky's number, Kyd promised he'd call back that night. Possibly a mistake, but my experience with Kyd said he'd crash the evening anyway.

I pecked in Tricky's digits while I patted Oinky on the head. "Tricky, it's Darcy," I greeted when he answered. "I need to break into an apartment."

He didn't miss a beat. "What part of town?"

"An apartment complex off Conroy Road."

"Do you need any help?" That certainly was one good idea.

"Would you?" I could hear Tricky mumble something to someone as he paced.

"Absolutely," he finally answered. "But now isn't the best time. I'm playing basketball up by the club, and by the way, your best friend is here looking for you."

H-e-double hockey sticks. Mother-trucking son of a ball buster. "Dylan?" I shrieked.

"Uh-huh."

Pray, Darcy. For God's sake, drop to your knees and promise your first-born son.

"Does he know you're talking to me?" I asked with a grimace.

Tricky let out whispering laugh. "I'm not an idiot, babe. Of course, he doesn't know. Do you want to speak with him?"

Heck no! I stole a look toward *Maison de Saule*. No one had to tell me it was on the list of "thou shalt nots." Heck, it was probably on the list of "thou shalt nots" for people that didn't even read the Bible. But that was the funny thing about lying—you told one and the second didn't seem like that big of a deal. I swiped the bun crumbs off the table into the grass, bouncing my legs nervously up and down. "I need you to occupy him," I begged, "and *lie*."

I felt my soul grow blacker by the second.

"I'll try. He's not exactly what I'd call pleasant."

Er, no kidding. I didn't expect him to be. "Can I call you when I arrive so you can walk me through the process?"

"My phone is on. Be careful though. I recently did a job over there and ran into a guard dog."

Figures...and an idiot like me wouldn't consider that a deterrent.

"I was not the lion, but it fell to me to give the lion's roar."

—Winston Churchill

Chapter Twenty

NINE LIVES

When I looked at an aerial view of the park, only one apartment complex was in sight. So if Cisco's grandparents lived near the park, chances were good it had to be that one. If I got into their apartment, I hoped to determine their pattern of behavior. Bills they needed to pay, people they needed to see, blah, blah, and senior citizen blah. I'd look for anything out of place or out of the ordinary. Hopefully, that would lead to Lola, and if Hector was right, Lola might know exactly where her son was.

As I showered, Dylan knocked on the bathroom door, saying he'd like to speak with me. Said something about Yankee meaning nothing...to let him explain because he felt like a hypocrite...that he'd screwed up but didn't see it coming...etcetera, etcetera. I told him I had a headache. I didn't have a headache, but women seemed to work that line successfully throughout history when they needed some me-time. Apparently, Tricky wasn't successful, but asking him to stall Dylan was like asking a T. rex to chew on a twig when he wanted to chomp on a side of beef.

He was lucky he made it out with all his limbs.

When I finally stepped outside, Dylan was singing in his shower as though he hadn't a care in the world. I didn't take the time to decipher the tune—knowing him, it was some sappy love song that would make my teeth hurt. Wrapping a towel around myself, I sprinted to Sydney's room, changing into what I felt was appropriate apparel: black shorts, black spaghetti-strap T, Dylan's Ranger cap, Ray-Ban Aviators, and my beloved Chuck Taylor sneakers. When my last zebra lace was tied, I stood up and gazed into Sydney's mirror with a cheesy smile. If the apartment were equipped with some sort of doomsday device, then at least I'd go down looking like an American hero.

Roaming into the kitchen, I opened up the fridge and removed a hot dog from its packet, grabbed a plastic baggie from the cupboard, and slipped back into the bathroom. The only drugs in the medicine cabinet were Tylenol PM capsules. The back of the box stated that adults should take two, and I prayed those directions applied to canines.

After I shoved a pill in each end of the hot dog, I placed the wiener in the baggie and crawled out the window, landing in a bed of mulch. I river-danced my way across the flowerbed and hurdled the hedge while I thumbed in the number for the Yellow Cab service. I took off at a leisurely jog toward the gated entrance, not wanting to be too conspicuous, while wanting to make my date with destiny.

———

The place was dump city. Paint peeled from the metal railing, and rust bled through the blue enamel still hanging on. I paid the cabbie and requested he wait, hightailing it up to the manager's office. Placing my hand on the doorknob, I twisted it both ways only to deduce it was locked. The windows framing the door were smudged, and a swipe of my hand didn't make it any easier to peer inside.

Glancing overtop the door, I spied a small window that had been busted out. There didn't appear to be any residual glass, but if the goal was to get inside, it looked to be my only option. I raised myself up on the railing, balanced both feet, and took a hulking jump until my body was suspended half-in, half-out. Wriggling my hips through, I felt like a newborn—I birthed myself through that narrow hole and fell out with no body control whatsoever, screaming.

I crashed into a dive forward roll, lost my sunglasses, and busted my nose while Dylan's hat flew several feet in the air. I bear clawed my way to it, getting one heck of a rug burn in the process. It didn't take a rocket scientist to conclude things weren't going well, but what I lacked in skill I prayed the universe rewarded me for enthusiasm.

Once I retrieved Dylan's hat, I shoved it back on my head and unlocked the door for good measure. Appraising the space, I journeyed to the reservation desk and tapped the silver bell on the orange countertop. When I yelled "Hellooo" and got an echo's worth of nothing, I decided to do what came naturally.

I snooped.

To the rear sat a desk. I wandered behind the counter and thumbed through bills, a bank statement, and an unopened letter in a light green stationery. A coffee blot covered the return address, but from what I could tell, "O-S-E" were the last three letters. When nothing struck me as out of the ordinary, I snapped a few pictures with my iPhone and cut through the door on the back wall.

Assuming it was the manager's apartment, my stomach lurched at the squalor. It smelled like a rotting compost bin full of beer bottles, moldy dishes, dirty socks, and what looked like a dead rodent. Dodging a dive-bombing fly, I swatted at a cobweb and hopped over a stuffed animal pelt that appeared at one time to be a cow. Its head had been lobbed off, and all that remained was brownish-green fur and collapsed udders. Before I had a chance to vomit, two voices boomed from behind, and a deep bark told me I was seconds from coming face-to-face with a guard dog.

I panicked.

Prayed.

Hoped it was all in my head.

It wasn't—barreling through the door, like I'd just stolen its last bite of kibble, was a Rottweiler mix someone had sicced on me. The black hairs on its neck were up like a hyena's, and its brown jowls dripped a long string of slobber. Nervously ripping the plastic baggie in two, I threw the hot dog toward the door. After a sniff and a growl, the fleabag gobbled it in one bite, ran his tongue over his lips, and maintained his protective stance at the door.

Holy shizzers. I was toast.

Animated talking filled the space outside, and common sense

told me the moment was do or die. *Say you're lost, Walker*, I said to myself. *Smile and act like the dumbest blonde on Earth.*

A man and woman ventured inside. At least, I think I'd term him male because he was the most idiosyncratic creature I'd ever encountered. His head was watermelon-round, and a black permed ponytail lay at his neck like the tail on a horse. Wearing shorts too tight and a dingy wife-beater, his ensemble showcased the hair on his shoulders, knuckles, and elbows. Top that off with buckteeth, and he just might've owned the corner on weirdness.

"I'm lost," I said, smiling and breaking the stare down.

"Did we leave the door open?" he grunted, glancing back at the door.

"No, I kind of fell into the place. I was looking for the manager."

"That's me," he muttered. "I'm Elmer Herschel." Elmer gave me a bone-crushing handshake. Here I was palm-to-palm with the landlord who set up Cisco's trust, and I couldn't contain the smile. "This here's Polly Teasdale. She's got a job at the bank." He pointed to whom I assumed was his girlfriend...couldn't tell. She gave me a "Hi." Nothing more.

Polly had an overall gothic look about her: black hair, black lips, black eyes, and black nails. She even wore a black polyester dress with three-inch black wedge sandals. Problem was, she was a plus-size girl living in petite-size clothing. I saw a little bit more of Polly than I cared to.

I tore my eyes from her spilling boobs when fleabag growled. "Has he had all of his shots?" I winced at the thought.

"I vaccinated Doo-rod for rabies about ten years ago."

Sheesh. "I hear that was a good batch."

"Yeah, me too," he agreed. Doo-rod stepped up the growling.

"Is he hungry?" I asked.

"Maybe."

"What's he eat?"

"Scraps, neighborhood children," he muttered. Oh, jeez. Next thing I knew, Doo-rod fell in love with my leg and mounted my knee. Not. Gonna. Happen. I staggered backward, violently shaking him off. One more time, and I'd kick him in the puppy-maker.

"He likes you," Elmer said chuckling.

"I'm flattered," I lied.

"So if you're lost," he said, "where were you headed? Elmer wants to know." First off, I needed to lie. Secondly, the fact he referred to himself in the third person made me fear some sort of dissociative behavior. And thirdly? What the heck was a Doo-rod?

"I'm here to feed the Medinas' ferret," I lied again.

He arched a brow. "They were in 23B, but they don't live here no more. Those people weren't no good. They did something with that little boy, and their place is a junkyard."

"Did you have it cleaned?"

Elmer glanced at his black digital wristwatch. "No. They've only been gone for a month, and they've got two month's deposit on record. I can't legally do nothin' until that runs out. So unless you're here to ask Elmer out on a date, I don't have time for this right now."

When silence filled the conversation, Elmer gave me a shrug. "You are sort of cute. You'd have to do something about your hair before I'd take you dancing though." Ponkey.

"My hair's fine," I said, snorting loudly. "Besides, I'm in a relationship."

"Whatever," he said shrugging. "There's a shirt sale at Walmart, and I need to get going. My new woman wants a man to dress good." If he wanted to impress the gothic girl, Walmart might be too conservative. But if Elmer wanted to get a jump on the crowd, then more power to him.

Especially if it got me out of here alive.

———

The only thing Elmer provided of substance was 23B and his personal phone number. What he didn't know was that I snagged his set of keys on the way out the door. Perhaps I should reserve opinion on my own personal luck because if the key fits?

Well, I'm just sayin'.

Good things were around the bend.

While I threw a twenty-dollar bill at the cabbie to stay put, I watched Elmer and Polly climb into a beat-up brown Ford Pinto. Once I made sure they hadn't seen me, I moved across the parking lot over to the opposite building. My iPhone sang as I jogged up the second flight of stairs.

"Start talking," I said, not recognizing the number.

"Jester, it's Troy."

Troy, I thought. I guess I'd multitask. "Whassup?"

"I should probably take this time to flirt with your sexy voice, Jester, but I'm too befuddled by what I've discovered. Fix It does not exist, at all." I stopped dead in my tracks, speechless. "Jester?" he said.

I shook my head, trying to regain focus. "What do you mean it doesn't exist at all? As in there's no shingle over the door or a man behind a big wooden desk?"

"Exactly. The only thing I can come up with is a typo existed on the original story printed, or there's a possibility it's an acronym that stands for something else."

"The bank's obviously still taking the money, right?" Because Herbie still sent ten grand a month to catch the aliens.

"Believe me. I'm going to find out."

We disconnected. I'd think about that later.

You could always count on a Florida shower. It was a given. Unfortunately, one burst from a cloud as I made my way up the stairway. I took the slippery steps three at a time, until I stood right smack in the center of 23B. Hooking my sunglasses onto my shirt, I squeaked the rusty door open with the key that said "Master" on it. Stepping inside, the view wasn't exactly as I'd expected. Elmer insinuated the place would be a junkyard. Their apartment, however, legitimately smelled nice. No dirty dishes, no piles of laundry, and no signs of any criminal behavior were anywhere. Sure, it looked Lilliputian, but to those who didn't make much money, it looked like a squatter's paradise.

Altogether there were four rooms—a living room with a foldout couch, a kitchen dinette, and one small bedroom and bath. A little small for three people, but the place was uncluttered and clean. Even the stack of used children's books had been nestled neatly inside a worn wicker basket, up against the wall. Point blank, Elmer had lied. It was possible he could've mistaken their place with another tenant's, but if not, why discredit them?

I opened the closet and rows of little boy's clothing lined the wall next to a few articles of adult dresses and men's trousers. The kitchen sat to the right, so I navigated next to the butterscotch refrigerator and cracked it wide. Inside were four cans of soda, milk that had curdled, two sticks of butter, but that was it. When I closed the door, a white piece of paper fluttered to the yellowed linoleum. Snatching it up, I read a handwritten note that said: *Lola, 8 p.m. Saturday*.

Why did I think that meant something?

Stuffing it in my front pocket, I moved to a brown door that had to be the pantry. I popped open the space and realized it was likewise sparse. It contained name brand Apple Jacks, canned black beans, corn, a boxed taco mix, bag of rice, and white kitchen garbage bags. Not much, but that didn't surprise me either. Most senior citizens didn't have money to stockpile. Their purchases usually carried them through 'til the next month.

A white plastic trashcan sat in the corner. Peering inside, I nearly jumped out of my skin when I spied a pair of rubber gloves, one empty plastic bottle, and a box of Clairol Nice 'n Easy Born Blonde. Well, lo and behold, seek and ye shall find. I'd just hit the jackpot with evidence of someone's quick color change. And guess who had blond hair...Cisco!

Holy Mother of All Things Holy.

What was a girl supposed to do *now*??

Closing the pantry door, I crouched low in the middle of the room, trying to get a feel for the place. Scanning the area, I imagined Cisco eating breakfast with his grandparents and talking to his parents on the sunshine yellow phone mounted on the wall. I watched him read, color, laugh, and wondered why anyone would kidnap a child—and why someone as talentless as me thought they could make a difference. Before I got all mushy, paranoia gripped ahold of my chest like a vise. Something didn't feel right. I listened for the sounds of footsteps, anything at all, while my pulse beat loudly in my throat. I heard a door slam and a frighteningly familiar gait. Ah, bugger me. I could use a magic carpet because by the feel in the air, Mr. Do-The-Right-Thing had made the scene.

"What in God's name are you doing?" he bit out.

Snooping, a little bit of B&E, minus the B-part.

And I absolutely hated it when he brought God into the conversation. No, Dylan wasn't perfect, but he did actually talk to God on a regular basis. He bowed his head before meals, looked to the sky for acknowledgment of great plays, and asked for guidance before making big decisions. My guess was he and God weren't having a rip-roaring time at the moment.

Funny, I was.

I stood up, turning around with a giggle. "Fancy meeting you here."

Dylan leaned against the doorjamb, both arms crossed over his chest, wearing his stubborn-as-a-mule look. Cocky. So exasperatingly cocky and cute. "Answer me, Darcy," he demanded.

Always with the formalities.

"I don't like it when you're bossy, Dylan," I said frowning. When he rolled his eyes, I tried another tactic. "You look cute today. New shirt?"

He still wore the Greek T-shirt I literally talked off his father's back. You know, the one Yankee swapped spit over and practically swallowed him whole. "You're changing the subject," he murmured.

"I was hoping you were grateful." God knew Yankee was.

"Start talking."

"I *am* talking."

"Then let me spur the dialogue. From everything you've been up to, I take it this place belongs to the Medinas. Be glad Sydney saw you sneak off. My father would be mid-conniption, and Lincoln would've shot you in the thigh. I told Murphy I'd take care of you, Darcy, but you're making it rather difficult."

"I kinda got lost."

"You kinda got lost."

"In another person's house," I pseudo-lied and giggled.

"In another person's house," he echoed. Dylan had this annoying habit of repeating my phrases during an argument.

"Kill your mockingbird, D. It's annoying."

He narrowed his eyes. I fidgeted like ants were in my pants and cracked the fingers on one hand. When he didn't bat an eye, I moved on to the other.

"You're lying to me," he murmured. Yup.

"No," I clarified, "I'm telling you a fib. You know, creatively stretching the truth."

Dylan's smile moved up a fraction of an inch. "They're the same thing."

"No, they're not. Fibs are for people who don't have any options."

"No options, huh?"

"It's a tough place to find yourself."

Dylan's voice lost some of its edge. "Your first option would've been to tell *me*."

I snorted. "That's never a fun option, Big Man. You tend to be a killjoy."

Dylan blew out a jagged sigh. "I tend to be more rational, but I've never set out to kill your joy."

"You're making this sound awful," I mumbled.

"Darcy, this is illegal, and let me remind you, they have rights. You shouldn't be here."

"Well, *I* have rights, Dylan," I pointed. "I have the right to life, liberty, and the pursuit of happiness, and this made me happy."

Why did stuff like this only make sense to me?

Dylan crooked his finger, motioning for me to join him. Honestly, it was more like demanded. I shuffled over, proverbial tail flopping between my legs.

Dylan expelled a tentative breath, as though he negotiated with emotions best kept in check. "I don't want to argue with you. I'm still recovering from our argument a few days ago, and that was enough for a lifetime." He drew me into his chest, engulfing my entire frame. "Now show me some love."

Sometimes Dylan's demands sounded hot, but I didn't think I could handle all of his love if he ever got the urge to unleash it. His hugs alone were maddening. Nuzzling my nose in the curve under his chin, I fell into every rippled inch of his torso. Somebody smack me, but I had the strange desire to lick his neck, bite it, and suck him dry. "How did Sydney know?" I muttered, slicing my own daydream in two.

His answer was, "*Mmmm*." After a few beats of us just breathing, he located a reply. "First of all, she's got eyes in the back of her head, Darc. Secondly, you jogged to the entrance and jumped into a cab when I was in the shower. Thirdly—"

"There *is* no thirdly," I interrupted laughing.

He released me to look in my eyes. "Thirdly, is that you're just being *you*."

"You're making me sound like Sydney," I mumbled.

"Sydney's high maintenance and should only date someone with a strong constitution. You, however, need to be chained to a tree in the backyard."

I debated another lie, but when your hand was caught in the cookie jar, you might as well admit you like cookies. "Does this place look shady to you?" I asked.

Dylan glanced around while he ran a large hand down his jaw. "No. It looks like a home where they treasured what they had."

"They didn't do anything wrong. This place proves it."

Dylan grew serious, wanting to hear my reasoning. "Talk it out with me."

"Think about it," I explained. "If they took the child, they're not going to hire a mom with expensive shoes to shop at The Gap. That woman holds the key. Plus," I added, motioning to the closet, "about two weeks worth of little boy's clothes are in the closet. They wouldn't leave them, and if they did, they're not going to shop at one of the most popular outlet malls where they can be seen. Nobody's that dumb." (I hoped.)

"What else?"

I motioned to the wastebasket. "An empty bottle of Born Blonde is in an otherwise empty trash bag." Dylan furrowed his brows, peering inside the trashcan to check it out for himself. "If you were covering up your tracks, you sure as heck wouldn't throw that bottle in there."

"What if they had to get out of the place quickly?" he refuted.

"Perhaps, but it doesn't feel right. The place would have some residual mess. According to the paper, the Medinas left over a month ago. Why would they come back here for one day just to dye someone's hair? And the biggest clincher of all, why dye it blond anyway? That's some seriously messed up stuff, D, and frankly, it's like they're being set up."

Dylan herded me out of the apartment like it was on fire.

We were in rush hour, and traffic had slowed to a crawl. Debating how to get his grandfather involved, unfortunately there was no choice except to admit I did a little bit of B&E minus the B-part. Hopefully, I got points for that somewhere in eternity. As usual, Dylan wanted to fall on the grenade for me and claim he willingly participated, but I didn't feel comfortable with him manufacturing a lie. No one would've believed it anyway. No doubt, my solo effort was aging me, but as much as I loved Dylan, I missed my normal partner-in-crime, Vinnie Vecchione. Vinnie wouldn't care to do what I had planned next...nor would he care that it might eat up eight of his nine lives.

Chapter Twenty-One

FREUDIAN SLIPS

There were sins...and then there were *sins*.

In Dante's Divine Comedy, the mortal sins—or bad ones—were comprised of seven different types: lust, gluttony, greed, sloth, wrath, envy, and pride. I was sure at one time or another I'd committed all of them, but I banked on the fact that slothfulness wouldn't trip me up at the moment.

Once Dylan and I unloaded the groceries we purchased on the ride home, I snuck into the library to call Herbie. Colton's library was immense, complete with a red onyx, Italian stone desk, custom-made to order. I shook my head at the wealth. Murphy purchased his desk at one of those naked furniture places and stained it himself among a Hillbilly cursing fit. No way in the world could he afford a rare rock that he put a leather chair behind.

As I smoothed down the white draperies, I reminded myself Lincoln said to plug away at what didn't feel right. The two PI firms made me want to cry foul. One was insolvent. The other conveniently contained a typo in the news copy and remained nameless. Sounded fishy to me.

"It's Darcy," I said when he picked up.

"Herbert Knoblecker. Soft K," he greeted gruffly. Huh, I had no idea he did that on the phone too.

"Herbie, tell me about Fix It."

"Did you go see Eleanor?" Not yet. Kinda hard when I didn't have your own set of wheels.

"No," I answered. "I hoped you could give me a contact name at the two firms the trust is financing."

Herbie belched. "I know the contacts for one of the PI firms. I happened to be in the bank on the day the account got set up, and they were there. One guy was Felix. Felix Xavier, I think. The other man called himself Will. The woman," he paused, "was Scarlet. That one I know fer sure. She had black as coal hair with candy-apple red lips. Men have plans fer lips like that. Ye don't forget a Scarlet, ya know what I mean?"

"That's what they tell me." Herbie gave me more information than the first time, and the newspaper claimed that Elmer set up the trust. Elmer seemed denser than your average dunce cap, but logic said if he set up the trust, then he also hired the investigators and was their contact. "Gertrude told me she recommended Livingston & Associates to Elmer Hershel who set up the trust. Do you know much about him?"

"Who's Elmer Herschel?"

Good God. An answer I suspected. When I heard Dylan yelling my name, I hung up and stepped outside, returning the gesture. At the most, it bought me a few minutes. At the least, he'd bust down the door. I tapped in Troy's number, leaving the three names, which possibly comprised the Fix It organization.

I scrolled through my contact list and thumbed in Kyd's digits. He remained my only connection to Lola, and perhaps, like Herbie, possessed something more of value. The note I lifted from the Medinas' residence burned a hole in my pocket. Sliding the note out, I reread how Lola had a Saturday meeting of some sort at eight p.m. The plan germinating in my head said I needed to bust up that engagement, and the only way to find out the specifics was to push Kyd until he broke.

"Call the godfather," I said, laughing when he didn't answer.

My cell phone belted out Milli Vanilli as I reached for a random leather-bound book on the bookshelf. When Kyd answered with nothing more than heavy breathing, I ignored it and immediately explained I needed information—information required under the brotherhood rules he had to provide.

It went through one ear and right out the other. "Tell me what you're wearing, Legs."

You know what, I didn't have time for small talk. Plus, I heard Mary whining in the background—so flirting with me was a major dirtbag move. "Lola does something at eight p.m. on Saturday, Kyd. What is it?"

The flirting came to a screeching halt. "Why in the world do you care what Lola Medina's doing?"

"Please, Kyd," I begged. "I have my reasons."

Kyd gave a few more beats of the silent treatment followed by a massive groan. "Ah, Legs, I can't turn you down when you say please. Hank always complained about a regular poker game at that time, and it continued into the early morning hours. He said it was the beginning of the end."

"Take me," I said.

"You're kidding." I wish I were.

I heard his blood pressure rise through the receiver. "It's the weekend, Darcy. Do you know how hard it's going to be to ditch Mary?" Not as hard as it would be to ditch Dylan. He sighed. "You're sure you can make this happen from your end?"

Good question. I was going to die trying. "Just meet me at the club at midnight," I told him.

"Why meet at midnight when the note said eight p.m.?"

"As you said, their little party goes well into overtime."

"Why do I feel like this trip has sin at its core?" he groaned.

Probably because it originated with me.

———

One steak, baked potato, and a few obligatory bites of salad later, I decided to relax by the pool for some sun therapy. Lincoln lay on his back next to me, his right hand holding his heart, the other massaging his forehead. At my urging, Dylan had just informed Lincoln of my latest caper, he'd termed it. Lincoln was uncharacteristically reserved and kept answering with an, "Uh-huh."

Uh-huhs, in my meek interpretation, were bad.

"Darcy, promise me you won't go back to that apartment again," he said emotionless.

He cocked an eyebrow up in question on an otherwise stoic face. "Why?" was in his eyes, but Lincoln knew he'd be wasting his breath. Right then was me being me...dragging the rest of the world down with me.

"I promise," I said.

He rubbed a hand down his jaw, but I realized with his next statement things were far from over. In fact, I received a glare that said, *Conversation imminent*. "I'll have someone check it out," he murmured, "and then you can give an official statement about what you witnessed at The Gap and a timeline with this story. I'm serious, though, dear. My patience is wearing thin. It's not good when my patience wears thin because that only leaves me with a couple of options."

I contemplated confessing the date I'd made with Kyd, but my tongue wouldn't cooperate.

When I offered a guilty-as-sin nod, his cell phone chimed, interrupting with a text. Lincoln fished it out of his pocket with a sigh, took a double take at the number, gasped "Oh God," and thundered back toward the house. Like he was going to put out a fire even larger than the one I'd created.

From out of nowhere, tears came like the summer rain.

My shoulders shook. Bent forward. Twisted and contorted oddly. Right then was me to the extreme. I snorted back the embarrassment but unfortunately was stuck on shuffle, repeating it once more. I was in over my head and didn't know what to do except flail around in the water. Kyd would take me somewhere. Apparently, he knew the "somewhere" or would figure out the "somewhere" along the way.

But what would I do when I was *at* the somewhere?

Just a tiiiiiiiiiinnnny detail that I needed to nail down.

Most people couldn't see their sins, or they refused to see them. Life had taught me early on that the spirit and the flesh were two totally separate entities. Sometimes the spirit was willing, but the flesh was weak. So in other words, just because you could *see* your wrongs, it didn't mean you were capable of *changing* your wrongs. We were on a constant collision course with both facets of our personalities. Oftentimes, I found myself standing back as a third party watching the struggle, not having a clue who would win in the end.

That was the day's method of business...I functioned as an observer in my own life.

Blowing my nose on the black and white striped beach towel, I tried my best not to dissolve into a blithering fool. Dylan perched his toes on the side of the pool, his white trunks blowing with the wind, his muscles powerful as he readied to dive in.

"It's going to be okay," he said.

One of the things I loved about Dylan was his inability to hold a grudge—not with me, at least. Here's to hoping he stayed stupid a little while longer. Things would only be okay if we found Cisco, and I quit tempting fate with a plane ride back home.

After he hugged the tears away, Dylan swam a dozen laps and toweled off right as Yankeezilla opened the outside pool entrance. The last thing I needed was her blowhard mouth. As usual, she was swank and über-hip, wearing a floral strapless sundress I recognized as one Willow had in her closet. On Willow, it looked sophisticated and sexy. On Yankee, it left nothing to the imagination. Her mammary glands were spilling out like the udders on a freaking cow.

Dylan met her lascivious gaze, giving her a wave as he shook out his thick, black hair and sauntered inside. His smile looked innocent enough—in fact, it was rather benign considering their earlier lip lock—but I would've preferred a go-to-heck-and-die face. "Wow," she whistled out, when he closed the french doors, "nice abs." Yankee plopped down in the chair next to me as Sydney slid into the one Lincoln had left vacant. Sydney showcased a hot, little black bikini that looked painted on. Curves galore. I wore a silver swimsuit, which unfortunately fit a little baggy upstairs.

"No doubt about it," I mumbled, sticking out my chest.

"Is that some sort of Freudian slip?" Yankee spat. Heck, *was* it a Freudian slip? I didn't know how to answer, so I didn't. "Not answering is Freudian slip number two," she added sarcastically.

As far as I was concerned, Yankee could cram her Freudian slips up her crammer. "Go away," I muttered.

Yankee held her chin high, ignoring the request. "Are you my competition? I'd think if you were my competition, your relationship would be a little more *clearly defined.*"

The girl had a point, but let's look at things rationally. Dylan had better hair than me. Even if I *was* interested—which I wasn't (I think)—no girl wanted to be with a guy who had better hair than she did. That left my dating options to baldheaded men and halfway hairless dogs. Still, I found it disconcerting that all I'd been thinking of lately were dirty adjectives when he came to mind.

"So if Darcy knows nothing," Yankee said and smirked, "what do *you* know, Sydney?"

Sydney slowly sprayed her arms and legs with an aerosol suntanning lotion—procrastinating a reply—like Yankee was an annoying little gnat she waited to swat away. Wow, how rude, but Sydney was a master at maintaining the upper hand.

"My brother's private life is private," Sydney purred, "but I'll let him know of your interest."

Yankee unveiled a chilly smile, unaffected. "I'll hang out nonetheless. That kiss," she said giggling, "tasted out of this world."

Tasted. I groaned. Couldn't she have picked another verb?

Sydney shoved the can underneath her chair not taking the time to even meet Yankee's gaze. "*You*," she clarified, "kissed *him*. My brother was simply caught off-guard."

Yankee giggled louder. "Oh, he reciprocated."

Had he reciprocated...?

By the looks of things, he had. At least, he had for twenty-four point-something seconds, and if that defined being caught off-guard? Well, let's just say I didn't want to be around for anything that was scripted.

Sydney shrugged off the comment. "Suit yourself. Girls constantly woo Dylan, and no one has successfully landed him. Watching him shut you down just might perk up my day."

"Maybe he hasn't been wooed enough by *me*," Yankee said with a smirk.

Sydney narrowed her eyes, snorting. "No one knows my little brother as well as I do, and he's definitely not interested in your woo."

I threw a hand over my mouth to keep from laughing. Yankee angrily jerked her head to me for corroboration of the story. I gave her a blank stare. That got me to thinking. If Dylan *did* want to date her, I'd have major problems with it. If she treated Dylan's sister like that, how would she treat the best friend? I didn't claim to be the teacher's pet in charm school—so I sat in no position to judge—but Yankee's behavior made Sydney look like a saint. Sydney defined brazen, but she was rarely confrontational for confrontation's sake.

Okay...maybe she was *sometimes*.

Yankee hung out until the silence became deafening. After ten minutes of pure awkward, she dramatically flipped her hair and went home, her mile-high pink stilettos clickety-clacking on the charcoal-colored pavers.

A few minutes later, Dylan and his mother came outside headed for the car, freshly showered, decked out in shorts and polo shirts. They were going for "a drive." Emphasis on the quotations. Over the years, I'd learned that signaled code for something else in their family. Could be good, could be bad.

"How's the most beautiful girl in the world?" he asked and grinned.

"Missing you," I said, fake smiling. *Um, hating you*, I should've said.

"Come over here, and let me love on you."

Standing up, I gathered all my strength and bumped my right foot into his thigh, knocking him flat-backed into the pool with a thunderous splash. There was little premeditation, but if I were brutally honest, I held him responsible for Yankee. Evidently, she brought a hibernating jealous streak out of its cave.

He broke the water, yelling. "Darcy Walker! You little brat!"

"Don't use my name in vain, D," I said laughing. "That's a sin."

Dylan whipped his head around, ridding the hair from his eyes. "In no way are you deity. Why did you just *do that*?"

The Devil made me. "It was an accident," I claimed. On purpose. "An accident," I said again.

Dylan splashed a huge tide of water in my direction, but I jumped out of the way.

"Pack it up, sweetheart," he growled. "You're on a plane tonight."

"I'm already packed," I said with a shrug, "and I don't care," I finished, adding a lie.

Dylan treaded water, acting like he wanted to hold me under. "Try that again, Pinocchio," he hissed. "I just picked up a pile of your dirty clothes and threw them in the washing machine. Out of the grace and goodness of my own heart, I might add." Dylan paddled over to the side, looking like a drowned rat.

"You're the best friend in the world," I said, grinning like an idiot.

"*Ex*-best friend," he emphasized angrily. "Watch your back, Darcy. When you least expect it, you'll get a calling card from *me*."

I laughed. "Blah, blah, blah, misogynistic blah. I'm not scared."

Dylan swam to the side and in a one-handed strength, skyrocketed himself to a standing position. Towering over me, he took my right arm and twisted it behind my back, forcefully shoving me facedown onto the chair. I felt his personality flip—the change rolling off of him in seismic waves. "Kiss me," he said, breathing hotly in my ear. "And you don't have to be gentle."

I looked back at his lips and was pretty sure I might've licked mine.

For a second, the world went on blackout. Dylan occasionally pushed the boundaries of whatever it was that we had together, but that went further than he'd ever gone. I mean, we had an audience, which had always been taboo. When I glanced to his mother, her face shot straight to blood-red, producing a frown that threatened physical pain. She reached to touch him and warily pulled away like it was too confusing to even try and dissect.

I smiled in complete satisfaction. "Towel off, Dylan," she told him exasperated.

Dylan left me laughing as he ripped his shirt off, stomping furiously inside.

His mother gazed at me and frankly didn't know what to say or do. "You two are *so*..." she said, pausing and looking for the right word, "*physical*," she decided on reluctantly, "I shudder to think what your relationship would entail should you ever date."

Okay, so Dylan roughed me up from time to time, but that was minor compared to the mental pain I inflicted on him.

———

All the good people were asleep. Lincoln had dropped off into his snoring period, so I banked on the fact it was safe to bunk with

Dylan for a while. I knew why I stood outside his door, so why was *she*?

"What were you two talking about?" I whispered as I passed Sydney in the hall.

Sydney pulled her bright pink robe together on what looked like another babydoll vixen number. "Ask my brother," she said in a gravel. "It's not my place."

As much as Sydney resembled her mother, she had her father's raven-black hair and dark, penetrating eyes. She could cut to the chase and was as blustery and protective as Dylan. And although she could grate on his nerves, he confided in her. But one look in her eyes, and I knew she'd die with whatever secret she was keeping.

Frankly, I wanted to ask, but I legitimately had a headache. My head always hurt when it thought about too many things, and right then some evil entity had sucked out my brain and replaced it with bad baby gremlins. They chomped and chewed and devoured what little bit of sanity was born in there.

After Sydney slinked back to her room, I made sure no one spotted me and crept inside like a cat burglar. The moon was full, casting a long shadow over the lake, and although my vision wasn't perfect, I caught the light bouncing like a prism of broken glass. I heard movement outside. I couldn't make out the exact source, but something scampered this way then that. Run, stop. Run, stop. As if tempted to stay, but something or someone made it feel unsure of itself.

Dylan lay on his stomach already asleep, hands up by his head hugging the pillow. He had that melt in your mouth thing going on, and the first thought that came to mind was: finder's keepers, losers weepers.

Dylan did offer payback—a calling card—like he'd promised. After his drive with his mother, he waltzed through the door, loved me up in his usual way, and then wrapped me in his arms and legs, launching us both into the pool. We rolled around for an hour. He meant it as punishment. To me, it felt like the foreplay of two porpoises.

Before I even uttered a word, Dylan jerked awake, instantly alarmed, rising up on his elbows. "Are you okay?" he murmured softly. Through the years, I'd always tried to sneak up on him. I'd tiptoe. Get my ninja on. Move with the wind to not disturb him. I'd never mastered the art of him not feeling me, as he said. On a night like tonight, I found that beyond comforting. Let's face it, the Darcy Boat was headed for an iceberg, and God only knew how many people would drown with me.

Dylan threw back the sheets, and I quietly climbed in next to him. He seemed extra affectionate tonight. His feelings were palpable—his heart beating so loudly I felt it touching my own skin. Sometimes Dylan's emotions streamed so strong he didn't even have to admit them. It could be a heartbeat. It could be anger he kept in check. Whatever it was, I'd simply peer in his eyes and what puzzled anyone else rang clear to me. Right then, he shot off nothing but one hundred percent, no holds barred, affection.

My night just got a little better.

While he slowly ran his left hand up and down my body, I instantly got struck with a feeling of insecurity. I was wearing old, gray sweatpants and a holey white T-shirt. I'd found them at the bottom of a laundry basket—nothing but B.O., sweat, and ketchup stains. Fluffing the pillow, I rolled onto my elbow to face him, once again wishing I'd worn my glasses.

"What were you and Sydney talking about?"

His hand stilled on my back. "Do you really want to know?" he said strangely.

Yes was on the tip of my tongue, but I couldn't bring myself to say it. "If it's between the both of you, then no." Wow, my nose must've grown two inches.

"Has Yankee's latest visit been bothering you?" he asked quietly. "Maybe it's time we have a conversation, sweetheart. I've needed to talk to you for some time, but I've not been able to find the appropriate moment or the words."

He tucked a tendril of hair behind my ear and lowered his forehead into mine. *Was* she still bothering me? Was that the reason I'd snuck into his bedroom? If so, what could we talk about? He'd kissed her. And if I were to make an educated guess, a little bit of France was involved. That wasn't you-grossed-me-out-and-I'm-just-being-polite behavior. It was wow-can-we-do-this-again kind of stuff. Could someone like Yankee actually be his "everlasting?" That was the word he used to describe the one destiny chose for you. If she was, a part of me wanted to find her and gut her insides. I'd heard the stories about Dylan and girls—seen them firsthand with Brynn Hathaway at school—but since I'd witnessed it again, any rumor would've been sufficient.

Curiosity, in this case, was a killer.

"Just hold me, D," I whispered, trying not to cry. "For once, I don't want to talk."

Here Dylan and I were—in a dimly lit room, no chances for discovery—and I was suddenly at a loss for words.

He opened and closed his mouth two times, ending with a long-suffering sigh. "I love you with an eternal intensity, Darcy, and if that's what you need, then okay...*for now*."

I'd always felt like an ellipsis followed Dylan's sentences...like there was something—or a dot, dot, dot—he knew that I didn't.

Chapter Twenty-Two

INIQUITY ENGINEER

Saturday night had arrived.

I stood in the kitchen chatting with Colton. The rest of the house surprisingly was sound asleep. How that managed to happen, I had no idea, but I wouldn't look a gift horse in the mouth. Colton's hair ran every which way but sophisticated, and his clothes were so rumpled together it looked like he'd dragged them out of a garbage can. My guess was he'd already snoozed a few hours and was searching for coffee to relax him.

Like me, it calmed him down.

Unfortunately, I had to account for my whereabouts as he found me inches from the door. I knew he hadn't changed the security code to something complex. I'd staked it out the last couple of nights, and it appeared to still be three letters. I hoped that maybe —*just maybe*—he'd left it the same or spelled Leo backward. A quick glance at the door showed the light still green and good-to-go. As luck would have it, he hadn't even activated it for the evening. I fought a smile because it appeared things were already in my favor.

Grabbing a white mug from the cabinet, he slid it under the Keurig and brewed a cup of Fog Chaser, still in his sleepwalking stupor.

"I'm going next door to take Oinky for a walk," I explained.

"Sounds like a fascinating evening, dear."

"We're going to paint each others' nails and tromp nude down the street while we rub our hooves together."

"Then let the Wookiee win."

"Huh?"

"May the force be with you," he slurred. *Star Wars*. I laughed...his favorite movie. I choked back a giggle as he took one, long sip. When Colton went on vacation, so did his brain. When Colton sleepwalked, his brain practically flatlined.

"Where's Dylan?" he mumbled.

"Around," I sort of lied.

"Just as long as he knows." Not yet and hopefully never.

After I reassured him that Dylan defined omnipresent, he shuffled over to the black cookie jar on the counter, removed the lid, and plunged his hand inside, placing a Benjamin Franklin in my palm. Why he felt Oinky and I needed a hundred bucks was beyond me, but Colton had one eye closed during our entire conversation.

When he stumbled back down the hallway, I shoved my bucket hat on my head to match my black miniskirt, halter-top sweater, and strappy sandals. Black represented formal affairs, and my getup was about as formal as my tomboy tendencies would allow. But I knew my ensemble wasn't complete. I needed a weapon, or weapons. I couldn't take Lincoln's gun for reasons of the obvious, and anyway that seemed more wrong than what I'd planned. Yes, I had Kyd, but at the end of the day, he might just be another pretty face.

In my opinion, I needed to prepare to live or die by my own two hands.

I rummaged around in the kitchen drawers and came out armed with a turkey baster and a butter knife. Neither would inflict mortal wounds, but they would buy some time and placate the angel on my shoulder who screamed I was stupid. Slipping the knife snuggly inside my waistband, I situated the blade running parallel to my right leg. When I took one step, it slid down my hip, pinging loudly on the tile. Quickly snatching it up, I grabbed a rubber band on the countertop, knotted it around the handle, and safety-pinned it to my skirt. When two aggressive jumps left it firmly in place, I figured I was good to go and ditched the turkey baster.

I tiptoed down the hall to retrieve my purse and iPhone from Dylan's room. We'd finally zip lined over alligators, and I had to say,

I didn't see enough reptilian debauchery for my liking. They were supposed to be mating, for God's sake, and we didn't see crap except for a few open jaws. We ended the day boating, and Dylan (thank God) fell into bed bone-tired. He lay in the same position he'd been in an hour earlier, facedown, hugging a pillow under his right arm. Dylan didn't technically snore, but he sure did breathe heavily when exhausted. I told him twice of my plans with no answer. Maybe that was why I consciously left my things in his bathroom. If he woke, it would be a sign to stay home. If he didn't, I'd interpret that as a green light to continue on. Well, fret not, my fellow deviants, he hadn't moved a muscle, and I was geeked up and ready to go.

Stepping up to his bathroom mirror, I pulled my cosmetics bag out of my purse and slid red lipstick on my lips. Taking a few swipes at my lashes with black mascara, I next patted on a minimal amount of pink blush. Lastly, I pumped body spray in the air, danced into it, and gagged two times ending with a snort. I tried to enhance my best assets, but a good chance existed that I looked like trailer-trash Barbie.

I could plan and think I had my bases covered for all scenarios, but occasionally I ran into a plot that blew my plans out of the water. What I did better than anyone was think on my feet. As I made my way back down the hallway, an unexpected someone proceeded to mess with my plan.

Zander groggily stepped into my path.

If only I had some chloroform...

"Whoa," he said and whistled, "you look delish. Are you taking me with?" Things could go one of two ways. I could tell him the invitation included me only—which it did—or I could tell him I'd planned for him to join me and to hurry and get dressed. Since rebels liked to drag someone down with them, I figured it wouldn't be a hard sell.

I simply agreed, "Yeah."

"Really?" he squealed. "Where to?"

"To a party with Kyd and Tricky." The boy acted slap happy, bouncing all over the walls—especially when I informed him that Dylan didn't make the invite list—and our blood clause demanded a silent oath he'd carry to the grave. My iniquity engineer side surfaced—just sin, sin, and more sin—but I really didn't see another recourse.

Zander ducked inside to change and seconds later stepped outside wearing a Cincinnati Reds shirt, baseball cap, matching athletic shorts, and black Adidas sneakers.

Everything that reeked of tourist.

...we were screwed.

Winding his fingers in mine, we took off toward the clubhouse armed with a butter knife, bonded by our pure idiocy. Ten minutes later, I concluded heels weren't appropriate for a walk on pavement. My feet somehow squeezed into a pair of Sydney's or Willow's Rock & Republic four-inch size sevens when I wore an eight. One heel wobbled, and the other might've given me an ingrown toenail.

Kyd and Tricky leaned up against his silver Toyota Land Cruiser, eyes agape that I had Zander in tow. Seriously, they *should* be agape, but bringing Zander happened to be one way to distance myself from Kyd's romantically challenged relationship with Mary. One look at him though, and the bad girl in me had to wonder. Kyd was meticulously groomed, and no doubt existed in my mind why Mary had fits of jealousy. Wearing dark shorts and a long-sleeved striped oxford, rolled and pushed to his elbows, his expensive tan loafers topped off a male you didn't see every day. He seemed almost too perfect, his blond hair waving gently in the breeze. Although attractive, Tricky appeared the exact opposite. Sporting all black athletic gear, his brown hair hid underneath a black ballcap, hiding his face. Tricky looked prepared for another day at the office.

"We're dead," he mumbled.

"Probably," Kyd said.

"Vamoose," I cheered.

Once buckled inside, we listened to Zander spout off the mascots for every college and university in the country. Like my Grandfather Winston, Zander held a plethora of meaningless trivia but barely made the C-list like me. Unfortunately, I couldn't rid that group of animals and inanimate objects from my mind. I never quite understood the complexities of my brain. Oftentimes my obsessions could be blessings—others, an overwhelming distraction.

Twenty-five minutes later, we rolled into the Orlando OBT area...one of the nation's notorious red light districts. Perhaps its reputation was why many crimes were easily overlooked. One kind of expected it. Orange Blossom Trail is a section of US 441 that ran north to south through the Orlando area and boasted the fact it was one of the twenty-five most violent places to live in the United States. It was a tourist trap and infamous as the city's ghetto. Figures. And here I was a minor, contributing to another minor's delinquency.

Ballsy.

Stupid.

Kyd must've heard my gulp from the back seat. He looked in the rearview mirror, kept his left hand on the steering wheel, and reached back and tenderly touched my knee. "Say the word, Legs, and we'll turn around."

My mouth couldn't do anything but produce another swallow.

Old hotels lined the streets while red, blinking neon signs alerted you to strip clubs. As we drove further south, we moved directly into the section called Whorelando. On one corner, a prostitute slinked. On the opposite, illegal drug trade transpired. A black Beemer idled as a gray-hooded drug runner handed him a baggie full of pills. People weaved in and out of the crowd like the process was as normal as walking down a nice area in Cincinnati. Apparently, assimilation was easy once conditioned to your surroundings.

Kyd pulled onto a side street and turned off the Land Cruiser. We'd parked in front of an old metal warehouse that had a newer, red side-unit attached to its side. Appearances suggested the building had been built for functionality and not for aesthetics, but here in OBT the idea of beauty wasn't thought of in terms of architecture. It mostly walked on two legs, was up your nose, or in your arm. The building stood three stories high and threw off the vibe that only idiots would venture inside. It appeared barren, other than a dimly lit section on the middle floor.

Suddenly, I felt grossly overdressed, completely out of place, and an overwhelming guilt for bringing a twelve-year-old boy along. I suppose I had no regard for my life. Perhaps I never thought anything presented a big deal because I'd already lived through every child's darkest fears...abandonment. Something like that aged you on the spot and killed the instinct that told you when you needed an adult's help. I somberly exited the car, and Zander crawled afterward like a nervous spider while I absently picked a few stray hairs from my sweater.

"You're scared," Kyd said, tracing a finger down my jaw.

"I'm not scared," I clarified. "I'm trying to figure out what to do."

He cocked an eyebrow. "You have no plan?"

I never had a plan. "It's a work in progress."

Lining the right side of the street were a navy Mercedes CLS-Class, a BMW 3 Series silver convertible, an army-green H2 Humvee, a green BMW Roadster convertible, and a red Porsche Turbo. On the opposite were a white Cadillac Escalade, a beige Ford Bronco, two black Chevy Suburbans, a black Aston Martin, a silver Bentley, a taupe Toyota Celica, and an old blue Honda Accord whose rims looked more expensive than the car. Next to the Accord sat a vehicle that resembled the Pinto rattletrap Elmer Herschel climbed into with the gothic girlfriend. But why would a lummox like Elmer Herschel rub shoulders with close to a million dollars of foreign and domestic automobiles? All the license plates were the normal seven-figured letters and numbers combo except one vanity plate labeled with a single X on the Red Porsche Turbo.

I said the numbers over and over along with the makes and models of the cars—trying to burn them into my memory. Tricky mouthed them out loud two times and acted as if he was bored. Tricky, by reputation, had a photographic memory. I suppose I did too, except I could never settle down long enough for any information to jell into something useful.

Kyd put his hand out like a stop sign as Zander and I attempted to make our way toward the back entrance of the building. "Hold on, Darcy," he demanded. "I feel like it's my duty as your brother to say something."

Zander immediately groaned, rolling his eyes. "You sound like Dylan."

Kyd shrugged with a frown. "Perhaps we're alike." Doubtful.

Reaching out to touch his hand for reassurance, I found it flexed and rigid...just like the rest of him. "I'm simply piecing some things together," I told him. "There's no need to worry."

Kyd grabbed me by the arm, dragging me to his side. "Give us some privacy," he said to Tricky and Zander. Both stepped about six feet over. "I don't want you hurt, Legs," he murmured when we were alone. "Lola Medina's nothing but trouble. She always *has* been, and here I am dropping you off in a seedy area as your brain runs amuck. I need more information, and for the life of me, I can't determine how you conned me into doing this. I'm having second thoughts, and as strange as it sounds, I honestly feel a bond with you."

Introducing Kyd, Romeo extraordinaire.

His eyes burned a light, drowning green. Almost tearful, like my pain filled him up so much that one step inside would pull us both under. Why was it that the guys who were players always knew how to talk to girls?

I gave him a lot of teeth, trying my best to look like a flirt. "It's the brotherhood," I said and grinned.

"*Stop it*," he warned. Heck, maybe he *was* like Dylan. "I care, and I have this drowning feeling you don't care enough about yourself to even think about your safety. What happened to you, Legs, that makes you not consider whether you'll live or die?"

How in the world should I respond to that? I exhaled six years' worth of disappointment and frustration but realized all that did was give me a headache. "To answer your question," I said tightly, "life happened. Sometimes, life doesn't give you a choice or ask permission. All you can attempt to control is how you respond to what it throws at you. What's going to happen is going to happen, Kyd. I appreciate the concern, but Zander and I will be fine."

Mother blankety-blank-blank, I cursed in my mind. I needed to take up cursing or find an outlet to release the guilt-slash-stress people inflicted upon me.

Zander jumped up three times in anticipation as I gave him a high-five. Dang it, I didn't know what we were doing but had a pretty good feeling I'd figure it out once we'd made it inside.

Zander hovered my every move. I moved an inch. He moved two toward me.

"First of all," Kyd grunted, "we're going to have a conversation about what life did to you. That statement is too morose and fatalistic for my liking, Legs. And secondly, Zander has to stay with me. It'll never fly with him going inside."

"*What?!*" Zander yelled.

I scrunched my forehead together, frustrated that he had a point. In retrospect, it possibly was for the best. If I conceded that point, then perhaps Kyd would lighten up on the demand to psycho-analyze me. I blew out a sigh, touching Zander on the shoulder. "It's okay, Hot Stuff," I said, offering a smile. "I'll tell you everything." Zander grumbled that he should've stayed in bed where he could've at least dreamt of naked girls.

Not shocking, the boy's first word was boob.

After a few moments of explicit instructions, checking to see if cell phones were charged, and what resembled a Come-to-Jesus Meeting from Kyd, he placed his hand at the base of my neck and drew me close. "I'm going with you," he murmured.

Kyd was a master at the serenade. When he parted his lips just a hair, my mind went blank and got stuck in a lightheaded swoon. "You feel it, don't you?" he said grinning.

Bracing my hands against his chest, I deliberately pushed off. I didn't know what I felt, to be honest, but it included sweat and a film I'd watched in human sexuality class. Kyd didn't need to go there...no, no, no. "Lola will *rr-recognize* you," I stammered.

"She's right," Tricky agreed. "*I'll* go."

Kyd's frame was suddenly riddled with anxiety. He acted as though he knew that part of the conversation was coming, and possibly that was what they'd planned anyway. "If anything happens to her," he threatened Tricky, "you'll answer to me, Neptune."

Tricky stifled a laugh. Without saying it, he implied he could take Kyd with one arm tied behind his back and blindfolded. "I've got it covered," Tricky said.

Kyd grumbled, "Thirty minutes and I'm following." Kyd tipped my chin upward, kissing the end of my nose. Before he could expand on his goodbye, I grabbed Tricky's hand and pivoted toward the back of the warehouse.

"Hey!" Kyd shouted. Tricky and I simultaneously turned on our heels. "Lola goes by the name Lynx. I love you..." Kyd might've finished the phrase with "both"—after all, Tricky held the title of his best friend—but whatever the case, I had a momentary pang of guilt. My body stopped doing everything. No breathing, no heart-beat, no brain waves, no nothing but a fifteen-year-old girl stuck in the middle of the biggest guilt trip imaginable. My behavior blatantly screwed my best friend code of ethics—don't take advantage of your friend's unwavering faith in you—but I ran on OCD adrenaline and very rarely did I make my way back from that.

The thought stung.

Tricky towed me across the gravel lot, ushering me into the darkened building. The metal door cracked open on the first push. *Odd*, I thought. They'd either expected someone or everyone knew it would be stupid to go inside, so why bother with a deadbolt. We hooked a left around a forklift and swung a right back toward the far end of the building.

The first floor consisted of cardboard boxes piled four-high. Rat poison surfaced in the aroma of the damp, musty smell. A set of stairs lay in the back left corner, with a double-door freight elevator in the right.

I took off toward the elevator when Tricky clutched my wrist. "No," he refuted, firmly shaking his head. "I prefer the stairs. That way I have a full view, and I'm never backed into a corner."

Made sense, I guess.

Tricky's arm encircled my neck, pulling me to him when I got that oh-crap look. "My job is to keep us safe," he said and winked. Tricky had some sort of potent virility thing going on. His silky, brown eyes looked even more furious with his black as night clothing. My heels placed me a good inch or so taller, but I had a feeling tall women weren't on his personal list of intimidations.

"M-maybe we should be brothers," I sputtered as we hit the second floor. Tricky dropped his arm, walking over to a window to canvass our surroundings. I followed as he palmed away grime, peering down into a flat-bottomed truck with a red cab that had two old mattresses piled on top.

"You're scared of me," he murmured. "I don't bite...unless you want me to," he added in a laugh. I *was* afraid...a little. What he happened to be capable of, I wasn't sure, but my gut said it included the fine art of the shama lama, ding-dong. Before he could decline, I performed the brotherhood ceremony when I discovered a pink Band-Aid on his index finger. Every once in a while I threw in real blood, and apparently Tricky had a four-year-old little sister who liked all things pink.

Once I ensured we were strictly platonic, I quietly followed him down the hall.

Of the several doors on the floor, only two were lit-up, muffled voices and the stench of heavy smoke flowing underneath both. I despised cigarette smoke, but Murphy smoked enough cigars that my lungs knew how to cope.

"Ready?" he murmured.

I really had no option but to hobo it back to the Taylors', so I gave him a big, albeit nervous smile. "Ready," I said and nodded.

Chapter Twenty-Three

X MARKS THE SPOT

*T*ricky's hand circled the first doorknob on the left, twisting it open.

Four men and one woman sat around a round professional-play poker table with a female dealer standing in the middle. Two Black men, about six feet tall and jointly five hundred pounds, stood with arms crossed over their chests, hawk-eyeing the chips on the green felt-lined surface. The muscle to ensure fair play, I presumed.

The first male my eyes landed on was balding with small brown eyes and a face so round he reminded me of the Pillsbury Dough-boy. All in all, he dressed nice enough. Khaki pants, khaki golf shirt, but something about him suggested he'd rather eat than work. The Bronco?

"Are you the entertainment?" he said gruffly to me. Oh boy, the pit of my stomach alerted me he didn't mean song and tap dancing.

Tricky possessively dangled his arm around my shoulder, kissing my forehead. "She's with me."

"Pity," Doughboy replied, sizing up my legs.

"Neptune, long time no see," another man interrupted. "I gather you got my message about another job."

Leave it to Tricky to provide legitimate justification when needed. Apparently, my newest brother was a contract-for-hire. Good to know.

Tricky answered with his best professional look and voice. "That's why we're here."

The man smiled and murmured, "We can talk once the game's over." Head-to-toe, he smelled of social climber. Dressed in a pinpoint cotton shirt, khaki dress slacks, and Italian shoes, one would think he had a lot of money to burn but looked too itchy, restless. If he did business with Tricky, he obviously needed someone to acquire an object he wouldn't—or better yet *couldn't*—pay for...like a convertible.

Tricky met my gaze, and I knew he debated how to introduce me.

"I'm Legs," I said, smiling and using Kyd's nickname.

Tricky nodded, not missing a beat. "Legs is expanding my own personal business. Show them what you've got, babe."

I recited their license plates numbers.

All of them.

Down to the county listed.

Top that, Doughboy.

Doughboy drew a long, deep snort on his stogy, white ash instantly snowing to the table. "I'm going to Vegas next weekend and could use someone with your particular," he paused, *"assets."*

Eeeuw.

"I don't play the slots," I said and grinned. That produced a chuckle from the rest of the room.

"I was talking about counting cards," Doughboy grumbled. "Maybe that's over your head."

I bobbed my shoulders up into a cocky shrug. "I just memorized the plates on a million dollars' worth of automobiles in less than five minutes. I think I can hang."

I had to say, I was proud of myself.

Social Climber plucked out the one empty seat. Tricky slid into it, tugging me onto his lap. The butter knife stabbed into my thigh, so I wriggled around replacing it in a more comfortable position.

Parked to my right was an older gentleman dressed in white linen pants and a short-sleeved linen shirt. He looked like he'd stepped off the pages of a historical novel. He scrolled through emails on his cell phone, letting out an occasional sigh while he checked his watch. He had that *Great Gatsby* thing going on—a Bentley would be fitting.

Seated beside him was a slim woman, slightly younger with short curly blonde hair. She wore a three-figure haircut and a four-figure dress, with a star-quality you were born with. In fact, the woman glowed. If Kyd was correct and Lola played with a congressman, I'd bet my life he meant "congress woman." She looked too polished, not missing a thing, and other than Doughboy was the only one who greeted us professionally. *Probably the Benz*, I thought.

"Good evening," she said and smiled.

"Evening," Tricky said, grinning back.

Opposite Tricky sat a mysterious, distinguished-looking man— even older, he was markedly gorgeous. Wavy black hair crowned his head, while all black custom-tailored clothing and loafers bottomed out the rest of the package. His features were chiseled to perfection, and his brown eyes looked like they belonged on some all-knowing creature.

"And you are?" he murmured deeply. *Smitten*, I thought. The man oozed unbottled charisma and class. Aston Martin, no doubt about it.

"You own the Aston," I said, adding on a grin.

Aston Martin did some sort of flirty thing with his eyebrows. "You are an unbelievably perceptive, beautiful, *young*," he emphasized slowly, "*woman*. Go away with me." Tricky's hand stiffened on my knee, but his easy breathing said he'd allow the conversation to play. In one breath, I flipped from impressed to one hundred percent grossed-out. Aston Martin appeared old enough to be my father, and apparently the group might share their earnings in every way conceivable.

"Tricky and I are exclusive," I explained.

"Every man has his price," he murmured, winking at Tricky.

"Not this one," Tricky warned.

"If you give me your card," I said, "I'll call if that changes."

He belted out laughter, pulling a black leather cardholder out of his back pocket, placing a thick, white card in my palm. My skirt had no pockets. Earlier, I'd hid Colton's one hundred-dollar bill inside my right sandal, underneath the heel. Stooping over, I slid the card on top of it.

"What goes on in the room down the hall?" I asked. Tricky squeezed my leg, giving me a bite-your-tongue look.

Aston Martin appeared totally disinterested. "Out of town business," he murmured.

"What kind of business?" I pushed.

"Any number of possibilities," Tricky answered, squeezing harder.

I decided to embrace my blondness. "You can never have enough business." I threw in a pause. "So why aren't you playing now?"

Aston Martin tilted his head to me. "We're waiting for Lynx."

"Lynx?" I repeated dumbly, knowing full well he referred to Lola.

He crossed one well-muscled leg over the other, straightening the seam. "The best card counter around, Legs. Lynx has a lot of problems right now, and she's promised many things she's having trouble delivering. She swears she's taking care of them, but if it bleeds onto me, I'll have to get involved." My body longed to nervously giggle, but surprisingly I kept my inner-idiot in check.

Blackmail? I gulped.

"So if she counts cards, don't the others she plays with object?" I asked out of curiosity.

He narrowed his eyes, not answering.

Not a heartbeat later, Lola strutted in. Dressed to kill.

What the mother of all mothers had I walked into?

Her black hair was meticulously styled, swinging in a modern cut that grazed her jaws and landed shoulder-length. She had an hourglass shape, poured into a tight, red dress that lengthened her petite frame. When she performed a triple-take on my face, I stopped breathing. Logic said the woman wouldn't recognize me, but I still reminded myself she'd heard my voice over the phone.

Tugging my hat down over my eyes, Tricky and I abandoned our seat, scooching up against the wall. When Lola eased into our empty chair, I zoomed in on her left wrist. Sure enough, a color headshot of Cisco decorated the skin. No sooner had she crossed her legs though than Elmer Herschel waddled nervously behind. I stagger. Fall into Tricky. Verbally say, *Beam me up, Scotty*. I was right. The Pinto definitely belonged to him, but I didn't know what to think. Frankly, I didn't think anything and just dropped my jaw, but the fact he accompanied Lola convoluted my perception of a grieving mother.

Elmer bow-legged it over to the corner and watched her every move.

After a few hands that Lola won, followed by a few taken by Doughboy, Aston Martin folded and retreated to the wall to stand by us. A quick glance at my watch showed the time as one-fifteen. I didn't have anything, and I'd already eaten up the half hour Kyd allotted and then some.

Lola undoubtedly was an interesting person. If she normally dressed like that, no way in the world had she arrived to the party in an average ride. *She's the Turbo*, I thought.

The car with the "X" license plate.

"Who's X?" I whispered to Aston Martin. Aston Martin sucked in a subtle breath, lightly frowning at my question. "I read the plates," I explained as benignly as possible.

"X watches the play through her gorilla's eyes over there," he murmured, nodding toward Elmer. Good comparison. Elmer had enough hair for a congress of baboons. Still, I had to think X might be the most stupid individual on the planet. Elmer wasn't intelligent. Plus, he dripped of sweat, and his brown T-shirt had a rim of perspiration underneath both arms. X must use him for something else, but at least, I knew X was a woman.

"Someone's playing *for* X?"

"Lynx *always* plays for her," he explained.

So Lola counted cards *and* played for people. That statement corroborated what Hank told Kyd. All I knew was it sounded like a surefire bet for the person doing the hiring.

"Who *is* X?" I pushed. Aston Martin narrowed his eyes, regarding Tricky and me like a mongoose befriending a cobra. When he wound a strand of my hair around his thumb, Tricky gave me one of those looks like he'd drop him if I wanted him to. But honestly, I wasn't sure how to proceed—tell Tricky to break his fingers or go with the flow because he seemed to be in the talking mood.

"X remains anonymous," he murmured, "but I have my suspicions."

Our host mindlessly rambled on how he admired my gumption

and slim frame, asking me to fly to Paris for some foie gras. *Foie gras*, I almost snorted out loud. The liver of ducks that had been force-fed to their capacity...not what I'd want to eat, not to mention so inhumane that those doing it should rot in Hell. One breath away from vomiting, I blatantly interrupted, saying I needed the little girl's room. Frankly, I wanted his hands off of me, and it was possible something more exciting existed down the hall.

Aston Martin opened the door, motioning that the ladies' room was at the end of the hall on the right. Tricky abruptly stiffened—wanting to accompany me—but Aston Martin pulled him back into a conversation. I tiptoed down the hall, stopping in front of the fourth metal door, cracking it open a few inches to the music of Nine Inch Nails—and the sounds of one man wailing, another demanding he cough up information.

Underneath a naked light bulb dangling from the ceiling, a middle-aged man sat bound and gagged at a square metal table with his hands outstretched before him. First thought: how would he give information when he'd been gagged? Then things slowly adjusted into view—those restraining him didn't want any noise. Two men in street clothes held him down by the forearms, a bloody dismembered finger off to the side. His black hair lay in a mass of sweaty curls, and tears streamed down his swollen face as he fought off the urge to slump across his arms and pass out. Above his head, a silver meat cleaver shone in the light, swung by yet a third man. The third man put the big in large. He was bald—his features so minuscule he didn't appear to look like anything human. Add stitches around his neck, and I'd swear he was Frankenstein's creation.

The victim's eyes snapped back and forth between the cleaver and the bloody stub spurting fluid in a constant stream. It took awhile for my brain to catch up to my eyes. I focused. Shook my head. Tried to blink it away. I wasn't sure what I thought I'd discover behind the door, but it certainly didn't include an amputation-in-progress.

Eh, that was a tad over-the-top...but in retrospect, what did I think I'd find when I snuck inside the building? A Bible study group?

Weight Watchers?

When the meat cleaver went up again, I screamed some animal-istic sound, threw the door wide, and yelled, "Wait!"

Dumb beyond dumb...

Nothing from my mouth was ever scripted. Obviously, I needed a publicist.

When everyone got that kill-the-blonde look, I knew I was in trouble. Something inside me immediately shut down. Surprisingly, I got calm. Here were my thoughts: Persevere. Gather information. Watch everything. My eyes quickly darted to the corner where a man and a woman were kissing—going at it like cockroaches in the bottom of a trashcan. Next to them, three expensively dressed females sat on a burgundy leather couch snorting cocaine. Their minds drowning in Cocaineland, they didn't care about my interrup-tion, but a rear door opened with a brawny man well over six feet tall who did. When our gazes met, his eyes glowed a piercing ice-blue—a blue I couldn't tear my sight from—and I had to remind myself he probably had plans to kill me. Everything about him was immaculate, from his navy suit, and short, gray hair all the way down to his spit-shined shoes.

He exchanged a few whispers with the man holding the cleaver and made five long strides toward me. I froze. Didn't move a muscle. Before I could back out of the room, he latched ahold of my wrist and angrily yanked me inside and slammed the door. That door slam would forever be emblazoned into my brain. It was a loud *whap*. Would it be the last sound of freedom? Once inside, he pulled me into a cloud of cigarette smoke, a switchblade immediately up to my neck. The smoke blinded my eyes...the burn causing them to blink automatically. I forced my lids to stay open because I didn't want to give him one second of me not being on my toes. Focusing on his face, even through the haze his inten-tions were clear. Shut her up. Make her forget. One way or another.

"Are you one of his?" he snarled. *One of whose?* I thought. "Answer me!" he barked.

"I'm not anybody's," I answered quietly.

"You've got that right," he seethed. "You're a distraction I don't need, and there's only one way to deal with you, girl. What body part do you not mind losing?"

The cold blade bit into my skin. One move in either direction and my carotid would be severed in two.

I was a dead woman. I wouldn't have a first date. I wouldn't go to the prom. I wouldn't be able to do anything more than sleep in the dirt and ponder what everyone was doing topside. I should be screaming or begging for my life, but something about the man looked familiar, and for the life of me, I couldn't place him. My pulse thumped in my mouth, and as I desperately tried to back out of the room, the cell phone attached to his belt buzzed at its highest setting. Still holding the blade to my neck, with one hand he unclipped it and checked the text message—and then swung a complete-180 into panic mode.

"Out!" he barked to the room. *Holy cow. Holy Jesus. Holy fat statue Buddha*, I prayed. Suddenly, I flew Mach 1 inside a litany of profanity. When he turned and shouted out orders, I threw the door wide and sprinted back down the hall into the gambling room, headlong into a desperately-seeking-Darcy Tricky. Bedlam had erupted. The table had been flipped over. Everyone snatched up their individual chips, and crammed them into six designated boxes.

I blew two air kisses to Aston Martin as Tricky jerked me back through the door by my wrist, taking a chair along with him. In four strides, we huddled at the only window in the hallway. Angry voices made their way up the stairs. The elevator hummed. People thundered toward us like a herd of buffalo. One answer was obvious. Down. Balancing the chair over his head, Tricky launched it through the window, glass crashing and raining to the alley below like a hailstorm. Next thing I knew, he booted out the excess shards, and before I could protest, he wrapped his arms around my waist and plunged us two stories into the back of the truck.

On occasion, I had good ideas. I clipped coupons and tried to stretch the dollar, but jumping out that window might've been the worst idea ever. Tricky flipped mid-flight taking the brunt of the fall. The butter knife ripped my skirt down the seam, and suddenly my booty fanned the air. I was pretty sure he felt up my behind, but after the mess I'd gotten us into, his imagination probably deserved the thrill. As soon as we caught our breath, he sprung to his feet, but when I tried to follow with equal fervor, I tumbled down into a bed of wet lettuce. My left heel broke off, and mayonnaise rolled down my elbow like a mudslide. Somehow, I had the sense of mind to ensure my hat was still intact...it was.

"God, thank The Gap," I said out loud. It was officially my lucky hat.

Tricky vertically jumped out of the truck, lugging me out with superhuman strength as we stared into the bright headlights of a squealing Toyota Land Cruiser.

Chapter Twenty-Four

TRAIN WRECK

*S*ometimes that light at the end of the tunnel's not the hereafter...it's a train.

We'd made it home in one piece, but as soon as Zander crossed the threshold, a whirly siren steamed like a locomotive while laser lights flashed like we were escaping Alcatraz. Good God Almighty, he'd set off the alarm.

"Darn," I mumbled.

"Sh-sh-sh-*shoot*!" Zander shouted, hitting the deck. I didn't need anyone to spell it out to me, the click of a handgun told me Lincoln was cocked, loaded, and aiming for a torso.

Zander stuttered as a child. When that happened, all he could manage was D instead of Dylan. I picked it up over the years because I didn't want the boy's infirmities to be more pronounced than they already were. In general, he grew out of it, but occasionally it cropped back up when he was scared. Problem was, the boy just yelled, "Shoot," when Lincoln had a gun. My guess was he opted against profanity, but in that situation, it might've been best if he let the four-lettered alternative fly.

"Don't even take another step, you *sonova*—" Lincoln cursed, adding the B-word. "Hands on your head or I'll shoot, you" *blankety blank...bleeping...blanker blanker*.

I laughed out loud...what an impressive line of expletives. Thank the Lord I had one of those laughs that belonged in a truck stop or brothel. Lincoln figured it came attached to me and ditched the anger.

"Dammit," he cursed, blowing out a sigh. "Get in here, Darcy."

I pivoted around, palms up, smile wide. Lincoln lowered his hand and did a click-click with his gun. Zander crawled into the house with his hands behind his head, fingers threaded at his nape. I limped in behind him, still wearing one heel, smelling like rotten mayonnaise...and a darn mattress.

I probably had bedbugs.

Lincoln fingered in a code and switched off the light show.

"I told him it wasn't safe yet," I said, shrugging in explanation when he turned around.

Zander got impatient and wouldn't wait for me to go through all of Colton's possible password changes. He boldly typed Leo into the alphanumeric keypad, and as expected, got busted by the hometown fuzz.

Amateurs, I grumbled to myself. *I'm working with stinking amateurs.*

Like a stampede of wild horses, the rest of the family finally made it to the party. Colton thundered to the door clutching a handgun in some sort of SWAT position. Susan and Alexandra crept slowly behind. Dylan exploded past all of them yelling, "Darcy, where are you?" with nothing more than a baseball bat and daunt-less determination. I burst into laughter...inappropriate laughter. I was probably riding coach on the next plane home—heck, probably in the belly of the plane—but I couldn't help it if my sense of adven-ture was different than everyone else's.

A quick eyeball of the crowd produced no Sydney. My guess was she didn't care.

Primarily speaking, Dylan's family remained impervious to what most recognized as dangerous. Even among the females. But what initial relief they'd felt when they discovered the source, was eclipsed by a maternal I'm-going-to-make-you-pay. Both women wore white silky nightgowns looking textbook angelic but with a visible demonic edge. The males stood in their underwear. Hard to take people seriously when they were standing in their underwear.

Grandma Alexandra immediately started speaking rapid Greek, collapsing at the kitchen table. They weren't words of affirmation.

The phrases were laced with Grecian obscenities. Before I could say anything, Susan angrily snatched Zander off the floor and shoved him into the chair next to his grandmother. Zander and I stole a glance at one another as we attempted to look grief-stricken and remorseful. It didn't work. We'd either killed our consciences or were one step from some serious mood medication.

Dylan's chest heaved erratically, and his left hand still gripped the bat—like it begged to take a swing at someone just to release the tension. Lincoln's body relaxed even further—peeling away its stress—when he saw the state his grandson was in.

"It's only Darcy, son," he explained to him, touching his forearm. "Relax."

Dylan had no inkling to relax. In fact, he took a gander at Lincoln's gun and acted like he wanted to grab it and blow a hole through his chest that he could walk through.

Dylan put the barrel to Lincoln's chin. "Let me tell you what *you're* going to do. You're going to get that..." *bleeping* "...gun out of Darcy's face!"

His mother shrieked, "Dylan, your language!"

"It's not cocked, son," his grandfather said calmly, "and it's lowered to my side if you haven't noticed." When that didn't morph Dylan into Mr. Nice-Guy, Lincoln slowly placed his gun on the kitchen table, palms up in surrender.

Dylan's father likewise lowered his gun, setting it on the table. "Watch your mouth, Dylan," he warned.

"*You* watch your *gun!*" Dylan bellowed louder, having to have the last word.

Colton's eyes lingered on his son's, and with a headshake, he shifted his gaze and bore a hole into mine. "Where in God's name have the two of you been?!" He realized the condition of my shoe, his mouth dropping. "And what in the," *bleep* "happened to your shoe?!"

Guess it was cursing night...no one sent me the memo.

I held out my right foot. "This shoe is Rock. This one," I explained, holding out the other, "*was* Republic. His heel fell off. I'm the Yoko Ono of the Rock & Republic dynasty."

No one found it funny...except Lincoln and Alexandra. His eyes briefly twinkled, she stifled a laugh, but the joke quickly fell flat when Susan's glare guillotined the mood. She didn't just guillotine it. She sliced me in two and fed the scraps to the neighborhood dogs.

Darcy, Darcy, Darcy, I said to myself. *You might've gone too far.*

"I told you I was going to see Oinky," I explained.

"You told me no such *thing*!" Colton roared.

I fished my hand inside my right shoe, pulling out the perfectly folded one hundred-dollar bill, which miraculously hadn't fallen out. "You gave me a Benji and said, 'May the Force be with you.'"

"I did *not*," he said, snorting self-righteously. "What self-respecting man says, 'May the Force be with you?'"

I held up both hands. "Hey, I'm not here to judge. If you need to go all Obi-Wan Kenobi once in a while, then more power to you."

I couldn't swear to it, but I think someone snickered. "You were sleepwalking again, Colt," Susan said, sighing and turning to me. "And, Darcy, I wouldn't call your explanation to a sleepwalking man exactly forthright."

Unfortunately, I had to agree.

Lincoln scrubbed a hand over the stubble on his beard, looking at his son sympathetically. "Aw, Jackal, I had no idea you still did that."

Colton mirrored his father's mannerism, likewise rubbing a hand down his jaw. "I do it when I'm troubled. Obviously, I'm troubled." Sleepwalking claimed the best of us. Last winter, I bunny-hopped down the driveway at five in the morning when I failed an English test. Murphy only pulled me back in the house with a promise of carrot tops and clover. No lie, people. I didn't even tell Dylan, the story was so freaked up.

"I won't tell if you won't," I whispered in a giggle.

"Darcy, you're exactly like Willow," Colton grated, ignoring the joke. "You both go off half-cocked and then one of the Taylor men are left playing cleanup."

I mumbled, "You're just angry at Willow."

His back straightened as he screamed, "I'm *furious* with Willow! You're merely the closest person right now with a semblance of rebellion."

Spoil sports. They'd ruined my perfectly profitable evening by inserting guilt.

God help me, I HATED guilt.

Dylan's voice dropped two octaves, "Don't push it, Dad," he threatened. Dylan went somewhere for a few seconds. While everyone exacted his or her piece of Darcy Walker, he'd checked out. I met his gaze, and the terror inside his eyes nearly toppled me. I'd scared him by leaving the house, and his amber eyes raced in all directions, questioning how he could roll back the clock and take back whatever was to come.

As much as I tried not to, I nervously giggled. "My hero."

Dylan's eyes cut to me angrily. Slowly and steadily, he placed his right hand on my chin, lifting it a fraction of an inch. "Don't hero me yet, Darcy. Don't think you're going to smile your way out of this or even laugh your way out of it. You're going to stand there, shut the frick up, and do exactly what I tell you to do."

As I turned to slump down the wall or crawl back to Cincinnati (I hadn't decided yet), the collective gasp of the crowd told me they'd seen my red-hot panties, peeking through the busted seam of my skirt. My word...my skirt was practically shrink wrapped even without a rip, and I'd just shown them my right butt cheek. I had no other choice but to burst into tears or own the embarrassment.

"Walkie-talkie?" I asked, wincing and turning around. The air blew at eighty degrees right then, but my arms and legs suddenly erupted into goose bumps.

Dylan's mouth dropped open to speak—one agonizing millimeter at a time—but his mother barked overtop him. "*I'm performing the walkie-talkie!*" she fumed, motioning to Zander and me. "In my *room! Now!*"

I was within minutes of getting the old heave-ho back to Cincinnati. The Taylors had been kind enough to take me on vacation, and for some bizarre reason, I remained hellbent on breaking all the rules. I didn't understand it, and God knew *they* didn't.

I whispered, "Can't Dylan come? I'll tell him anyway."

Dylan's mother pointed a furious finger at me, speaking very slowly. "This...is when...you shut your mouth, Darcy. I'm trying to keep you...and my son...alive."

Dylan's eyes grew wide and terrified—as though he contemplated exactly what atrocities his mother would be capable of. Laying the baseball bat down on the table, he shakily ran both hands through his hair and closed his eyes, physically in pain.

Running to Dylan would always be a conditioned response. Involuntarily, I hobbled over behind him and circled both arms around him, whispering, "I'm sorry," into his bare shoulders.

What a train wreck.

———

Five minutes into the walkie-talkie, community security interrupted, and an Orlando plainclothes detective sat in the living room. *Lucky me*, I thought, because I feared Susan Taylor more than OBT. According to Lincoln, he'd called the detective to run fingerprints in the Medinas' apartment, and he just happened to be in the area when Alcatraz lit up. Regarding the Medina case, as suspected, no prints were distinguishable, but the detective admitted the scenario suggested something unscrupulous. Well, Roger that. All the same, that didn't provide anything more than I already had.

I took a seat next to Dylan while Lincoln, Colton, and Detective Monroe Battle sat on the couch opposite us. Susan served coffee and cookies, but as I attempted a smile of appreciation (wrong move), I was rewarded with a look like I'd get the wooden spoon treatment later.

Figures. I deserved it.

Unfortunately, I didn't care.

"You went *where?!*" the detective shrieked.

"OBT," I answered again.

"Alone?" he verified.

"I can't drive," I said. "Not legally, at least."

Black, Detective Battle stood six feet with curly black hair, bedroom eyes, and ten extra pounds above his waist complements of fast food drive-thrus. His mustache was peppered with gray, and I guessed his age right around fifty. In jeans and a Miami Marlins gray T-shirt, he appeared tired but not overly tired. Like Lincoln, perhaps he required little sleep simply because his job wouldn't allow it.

"So you really jumped out the second floor of a three-story building?" he asked, adding a chuckle.

"Umm, yeah. We kicked out a window and went airborne," I

said, unfortunately giggling. "How about a woohoo for Darcy?" I inappropriately pumped both fists high in the air.

"For some reason, that makes total sense," Colton moaned in sarcasm. "I suppose I should congratulate you for not getting shanked by a mattress coil, but I have to remind myself you're quite the dumpster diving virtuoso."

I pulled down my hands, folding them neatly in my lap. "Actually, we dived into a flat-bottomed truck with trash in it," I corrected sarcastically.

"I stand corrected," he said, his voice dripping with even more sarcasm than mine.

Everyone rolled around in trash once in a while, right?? Frankly, diving into that dumpster last spring remained the top bullet on my résumé.

"Uh-huh," Lincoln said evenly. "Why don't you tell me who you jumped out *with?*"

I stole a glance over to Dylan whose eyes were invisible, buried deep inside his hands. Dang...he'd already figured it out. When I mumbled an embarrassed, "Um," Dylan unexpectedly cocked me with his knee, meeting my gaze, demanding I answer.

For a moment, I couldn't do anything.

Dylan was crazy good-looking, with a face that made angels weep and a body that burned nothing but nuclear. Lately, I'd tried not to notice his attributes, but when his mile-long legs were as lethally shaped and powerful as his, I couldn't deny the male in front of me. Yup, I wanted to hug every inch of his *godforsakenfreakingfine* body. Plus, he smelled divine when I smelled like...well, trash.

Nice legs, I mumbled in one of our silent conversations.

He rolled his eyes.

This is some weird crap going on between us, D. We probably should address it.

We need to address a lot of things, he countered coldly.

I coughed on my own tongue, instantly losing all desire for the dissecting of our souls.

I've changed my mind, I muttered.

Do I honestly look like someone who gives up when there's something I want? he said. "Answer the question," he demanded audibly, "and you and I will discuss what's between us later...in private."

I blushed (I think), or maybe I just had a voodoo hot flash. Everyone in the room had that look like they'd just lost a few seconds of their life, wondering what had gone down they couldn't put a visual to.

"Kyd drove. Tricky and I did the recon," I whispered. Kyd informed us on the ride home he'd dialed 911 reporting "terrifying screams" he'd heard coming from the building. When Tricky and I didn't present ourselves, he said he knew Tricky would go for the window. Evidently, they'd choreographed that kind of cut and run before.

"Tricky Neptune?" the detective asked. Stretching forward, he selected an oatmeal raisin cookie from the tray on the ottoman and took a big nibble off the edge. "Neptune always does it up in style."

"I'm going to kill them," Dylan seethed, reopening his eyes. He closed the barely one foot between us, hugging me to his shirtless side. It felt *goooood*, but I still smelled like mayonnaise.

"Sorry about the mayo," I whispered.

Dylan leaned over and carefully picked a piece of lettuce from my hair, wiping it on a napkin. "Shut up, Darcy," he warned.

Duly noted.

"I don't know this Kyd, but Neptune's a good boy," the detective added. "He works both ends of the law, and frankly, I let him."

Dylan roared, "He's seventeen!"

The detective shrugged, continuing to jot down notes. "Some kids show potential early on. You simply have to corral it."

Lincoln grinned, appraising his son. "Jackal did. He worked a lot of stings for his old man." For a brief moment, some sort of father/son thing went on. Both men were all business and dressed for the next day. Who in the heck did that at such an early hour? Frankly, I wasn't convinced they were entirely Homo sapiens, but my guess was they had a date with OBT.

"Well, Darcy's not going to use her *potential* while she's under my roof," Colton finally said. "That's not up for discussion." That would require some major effort on my part—probably futile—but I nonetheless gave him a lying smile that I'd try.

"Amen to that," Lincoln grumbled.

Suddenly, I had the urge to act like a lady, all smiles and so ingratiatingly polite it sickened the testosterone in me. I crossed my legs and realized I'd flashed my panties.

Squeezing my legs together, I leaned toward Colton. "Umm, I owe you a butter knife."

His black eyes flew wide. "A what?"

"My weapon of choice," I said, adding a shrug. "I lost it in the fall. Don't let anyone ever tell you that butter knives only cut butter, folks. My skirt is proof. I would've dug around in the truck, but we ran out of time, and I honestly couldn't tell you the last time I had a tetanus shot."

It took each of them a few breaths before they unscrambled what I'd just confessed. But I guess if the name of the game was to clear my conscience, it needed to be on the list of offenses.

Colton opened his mouth, closed it, but Detective Battle actually spoke first. He scratched his neck, saying, "What did you see?"

Man, I'd skin a puppy for a cookie, but I had a feeling they weren't there for me. "Can I have a cookie?" I whispered to Dylan.

Dylan automatically jumped to his gentlemanly ways, picking up the choicest double chocolate-chip, slamming it into my palm.

"Thanks," I said, trying not to laugh.

"Answer," he grumbled.

I took a big bite. "The people Lola gambles with. She calls herself Lynx, and they play in a warehouse off the main strip."

"How many people are we talking about?" Battle asked.

"Ten were in the room. Twelve with Tricky and me."

I spouted off the license plate numbers along with the makes and models of the automobiles. I described each of them as best my recollection would allow. Each person stopped to stare. I'd impressed them. Unfortunately, it didn't impress me.

"Extraordinary recall," the detective bragged, casting a strange look at Colton. "Do you normally have that?"

"Only on things I care about."

"Anything else?" he asked.

"I saw a light shining underneath a door as I headed toward the restroom."

"What were they doing in that room?" Lincoln added.

How did you say amputation-by-cleaver? When I couldn't find a discreet way to say it, I simply blurted out, "I witnessed a middle-aged man get his finger chopped off with a cleaver."

A string of profanity fell out of someone's mouth...not sure whose. Detective Battle put down his notebook, his cookie falling from his hand straight to the thousand-dollar rug. His brows knit together, and he glanced to Lincoln before focusing back on me. "You what?" he asked flatly.

I sighed and repeated, "I witnessed a middle-aged man get his finger chopped off with a cleaver." After a few minutes of what-the-heck, I provided specifics...from the two making-out like cockroaches, down to the women on the burgundy leather couch snorting a line of cocaine. "They were snorting blow," I explained.

Colton's eyes darkened like crude oil. "Did *you* snort blow?"

"No."

"What would you have done if they'd *suggested* you snort blow?" Lincoln interrupted.

Good question...ugh. "I guess I would've found a way to *not* do it, or at least act like I was enjoying it," I said quietly.

Dylan pushed off the couch and exited the room, the tension escalating to war zone.

"Did any of those people see you?" Lincoln asked stiffly.

"No," I lied. It felt right coming out of my mouth...wrong once I thought about it because there could be repercussions.

"Thank God for the little things," Colton said sarcastically.

Detective Battle steered the conversation back on track when Colton couldn't stop mumbling to himself about Willow, me, and how Dylan might shoot someone before he's eighteen. "Back to this amputation," Battle said. "Are there any other details you think I should have?"

"Tricky and I saw the light underneath that specific door... four rooms down...before we went into the card room. When those playing cards took a break, I got curious and asked a man what was going on inside. The quote I received was 'out of town business.' The business obviously required a meat cleaver."

"Who provided the quote?" Battle asked. I described the Aston Martin man, balanced the cookie in my teeth, and slipped two fingers inside my right sandal, pulling out his business card. What resembled egg yolk and ham shavings stuck to its front. "Salad," I said and giggled.

"Good Lord," Colton prayed.

Detective Battle glanced at the card and angled his body sideways, whispering to Lincoln and Colton. Colton slowly leaned forward and knocked the breath out of me with his eyes. "You're to stay in this house, do you *hear* me?" he bellowed.

No one said anything...we just let that threat sink in...and believe me, it *was* a threat of some kind. Dylan finally padded back into the room and sat down, breaking the mood, exhaling deeply. "Darcy hears you, Dad. Don't you, Darcy?"

Oh, boy, double formalities.

I slumped back into the cushion, pulling my hat down over my eyes. "Can't we come to a compromise? I could wear body armor or something."

His father seethed even lower. "Notice I'm not laughing, and let me make myself clear. You will *never* write the terms on negotiations with *me*."

Well, we'd see about that.

Dylan leaned forward, elbows on his knees, massaging his temples with his thumbs. "Maybe you should just kill me now, Darcy, because anything would be better than this. Talk to me," he begged hoarsely. "Tell me what you're lacking in your life that makes you flirt with death so easily. If you don't think anyone will miss you, you're wrong." For a brief moment, everyone melted away in the room, and Dylan grabbed ahold of my soul and wouldn't let go. "I'd be destroyed if you were suddenly gone from my life," he whispered. "Do you not want to *live*, honey? Do you not even care how we *feel*? How *I* feel? *Promise him*. Promise him you aren't motivated by a death wish that will claim your life before we're even twenty-five."

Dylan had some wicked guilt skills. Trouble was, his words weren't delivered merely to make me feel bad. He seemed desolate, his eyes completely bleak. He meant every, single word.

My eyes bounced to all three of theirs. Lincoln looked bewildered, Colton seemed madder than a hornet, and Dylan teetered on the verge of a psychopathic breakdown. Of course, I cared how they felt, and I *was* sorry. I just didn't know how to let it go. "Copy that," I whispered, twining my finger in his.

Reluctantly.

"You ran across the Grizzly, Darcy," Detective Battle explained. "You're lucky you made it out alive and a single woman. He *looooves* young girls." Dylan clicked his jaw, exchanging worried glances with his father. As far as I knew, he didn't act like a bear, but he did insinuate he had something on Lola.

Taking another bite of cookie, I added, "Grizzly has something on Lola."

"Grizzly has something on everybody," Detective Battle muttered.

"Could he know who has Lola's son?"

Detective Battle knocked back the last of his coffee and picked up a sugar cookie. "Perhaps, but blackmail isn't his style. If the child is even still alive."

That statement angered me. "He's alive, I saw him," I declared adamantly. "Grizzly told me Lola had gotten herself into trouble. He never mentioned her son, and that would be the first thing any normal person would mention."

"Grizzly isn't normal," he contested. "What else did he say?"

"He said Lola plays for someone named X."

"Does he *know* X?" Lincoln asked.

"He said he had suspicions."

Detective Battle munched the last morsel and looked at his notes. "The red Porsche Turbo, right?"

"Yes," I replied. "X is a woman, and he said if Lola didn't take care of her personal problems he would before it bled onto him."

"He said that?" the detective asked, eyes narrowing.

"Tricky and I both heard it," I clarified. Almost on command, the three expelled some sort of curse.

"Who owns the building?" Lincoln asked Battle, acting as though he already knew the answer.

Battle closed up his notebook, giving Lincoln one of those we'll-talk-alone stares. "The man on the card," he said. "Walter Ivanhoe. Grizzly owns half of the real estate in OBT."

I'd never been in the company of angels, but a heavenly chorus belted out a rock song and did a conga line over my head. I'd met the Ivanhoe—or should I say *the* Walter Ivanhoe—Hector had been struck speechless over. A smile tempted to show, but a glance at

Dylan—whose face was racked with grief and disbelief—made me opt for an appropriate, albeit fake, fear.

I wasn't afraid. Oddly, I felt aroused.

After the verbal smackdown, I showered in Bath & Body Works White Citrus, changed into turquoise blue leggings, my "Zombie Princess" T-shirt, and pulled my hair up into a wet braid. I sported my I-don't-care look. Trouble was, I cared a lot.

Even the contemporary space of a bathroom signaled perfection. A copper vessel sink sat atop a marble countertop, with fixtures that could probably buy a small country in Asia. Everything matched, from the spigots down to the doorknobs. The only thing out of place was...*me*. Glancing in the mirror, I thought, *My God, what have I just done?*

A man had lost his finger...and why? Did they finish the job? Let him go? And how had I compartmentalized things so well? I should be beside myself, or worse yet, moments from a tranquilizer.

Shell-shocked. That must be what shell-shocked looked like.

The Taylor house painted the perfect picture of Rockwellian peace. It was pitch black, nothing disturbed anywhere, except for the shadow of a floor lamp in the living room. Tiptoeing down the hall, I expected to find Lincoln working but instead found an android-like Dylan. No eye contact, no unnecessary movements, pretty much stone-faced and stone-cold.

I shouldn't have been surprised. What did I expect? Whistling Dixie?

Dylan pulled two quilts out of the hall closet, giving the fluffiest one to me, collapsing with the other onto Lincoln's spot on the neighboring couch. He was too quiet. Words were scarce if any at all. Our gazes met—his searching to understand, mine searching to explain. Dylan waited for something profound and insightful to spew from my mouth, something to piece together my behavior in terms he could understand...but it didn't.

With an exhausted sigh, he gazed at me as if he were seeing me for the first time. My behavior had been bizarre of late, but it wasn't as though I was a stranger to trouble. I'd dodged bullets in the spring and my school's detention several times by piping up the wattage of my smile. I'd even talked Murphy out of grounding me by faking some tears. I had a talent for talking my way out of jams, and Dylan had front row seats for many occasions. But I had to admit I'd never snuck out of a home and traveled to a venue that had been compared to the biblical hellhole of Sodom and Gomorrah.

The night had been a night of firsts.

As I watched him nod off, my heart ached for him to understand. Upon first glance, he appeared to be sleeping like a baby, but when I dared to investigate further, I observed a vertical worry-line between his eyes. No, Dylan didn't fall asleep thinking of me as his favorite girl in the world. I wasn't positive how he'd term me anymore—a vertical worry-line, perhaps. I whispered a heartfelt, "Sorry," in his direction, but he didn't hear. Once again, his words rang ominous. Was I victim of an unexplainable urge to shorten my days before the age of twenty-five? Kyd had suggested the same. Switching off the TV, I left my teeth to decay and snuggled the blanket up under my chin, while the truth reverberated in my chest.

I wished I was capable of letting it go...but I wasn't.

Chapter Twenty-Five

RESTLESS LEGS SYNDROME

wo days later, Dylan still hadn't let me leave his sight. I'd always believed we had the language of twins, but he took my Siamese twins separated at birth angle a little too seriously. The time ticked at half past midnight, Tuesday morning. We lay on his bed—my eyes watching a *Ghost Hunters* rerun, his at half-mast begging for sleep. He nodded off every thirty seconds, so I removed my head from his shoulder and rolled onto my elbow to stare at him.

"Do you still love me?" I asked and sighed.

"From sea to shining sea, sweetheart," he murmured with a moan. At least, he was back to calling me sweetheart. For how long? I didn't know, but prudence told me to take what I could get.

Lincoln had been on the telephone for over an hour talking to Paddy. Paddy phoned in a mood, and at last count, Lincoln had left him to pontificate three times into dead air, and Paddy hadn't even noticed. I'd padded into Dylan's room to watch TV, but he kept falling asleep. That's what happened when you got up with the chickens, people. Verification that early risers were stupid.

Trouble was, I happened to be in serious need of some action. Call me my own brand of opportunist, but before Detective Battle left the other night, I straight up asked him what he knew about Howie's head. His jaw dropped all the way to the ground, and he practically tripped over it. When I explained I'd found the head, he actually looked afraid of me. I laughed out loud. Not a good move because then I sounded evil. Long and short of it, he didn't give me jack about the head. He was lying too—the untruth written all over his dilated eyes.

Snuggling closer to Dylan, I ran my fingers through the thick hair at his nape. With my other hand, I fumbled around on his nightstand, retrieved my iPhone, and dialed Troy. One last cautionary look at Dylan, and he was dunzo. He'd fallen into his heavy breathing phase.

"Hey, Troy," I said, speaking lowly when he answered. "Do you have anything?"

Troy took a slurpy swig of a drink, sounding tired. "I wanted to call but feared it was too late. Bank of America's definitely still accepting donations, and Fix It, Incorporated is in actuality FX, Incorporated...written capital FX. A man in Miami known as Felix Xavier runs the joint. The FX previously printed as Fix It merely represents his initials. These guys have a stellar reputation, Jester, and when I called, they said the trail ran cold months ago."

To say I felt shocked was an understatement. "They aren't actively working the case?"

"Not like they used to. They bill if they're chasing a lead, but they haven't charged the trust for two months."

"So Herbie's money is just sitting there," I whispered to myself.

The borders in the puzzle were in place—Lola, Elmer, the Medinas, and FX, Incorporated, but who was the figure in the middle? Who was X?

How in the world did all of these things connect?

For one thing, Elmer said Polly Teasdale worked at a bank. I didn't know if Polly was the brains behind the operation, or if she and Elmer worked in conjunction. Polly didn't strike me as the mastermind type, which would make her X, but looks could be deceiving. If Elmer set up the trust, could Polly be funneling the funds out? Either way, I got the feeling Elmer was a scapegoat.

"Something's going on at that bank, Troy."

"Do you really think so?" I felt so.

"Yes, I do," I answered. "What do you know about a Polly Teasdale?"

"Never heard of her."

"Well, she's best buds with Elmer Herschel, and she works at a bank in town. It wouldn't surprise me if it's the one where the trust resides." That's all I gave him since I didn't want to spell out my feelings that Herbie had been swindled until my suspicions were confirmed.

"What do you know about a man called Grizzly?" I asked.

Troy went speechless, screeched like he sat in the front seat of a rollercoaster, and knocked an object over on his desk in a thwap. "Bad news, Jester."

Figures. It was a crying shame I planned to contact him again.

After we disconnected, I switched off the TV and wandered into the living room where Lincoln scrutinized new surveillance photographs of Mr. Thanksgiving-Dinner himself...Turkey Cardoza.

He sipped on what my discriminating nose told me was coffee just this side of the tar pit. It smelled sharp, thick, and deadly to the intestines all at the same time. Sometime earlier, he'd chewed a couple of packs of gum and carelessly dropped the silver-foiled wrappers on the tile. Evidently, his anxiety had pulled a double shift.

"Any word on Turkey?" I asked, squatting down to pick up the wrappers.

Stretching both arms high, he left them to rest behind his head. In old black sweats and a white T-shirt that had three holes under the arm, he looked like a hobo. With one eye trained on the door for Willow, he removed his glasses and patted the seat next to him.

Lincoln's anger dehydrated first, followed by Alexandra's at a close second. Colton's forgiveness was halfway there, and Susan still disciplined me with every breath. Zander hovered at euphoria while Sydney didn't seem to mind I'd broken up Rock & Republic's shoe duo. As a matter of fact, she said those shoes weren't even hers.

Dylan remained Dylan...disturbingly incapable of judging me.

"Paddy and I've been batting around your theory that there might be two Turkeys," he murmured. "We're running his photographs through a facial recognition program to see if we can catch any subtle differences. If we're lucky, Turkey will lead us to someone else."

"I thought he was the point guy," I said confused, plopping down beside him.

"One guy doesn't wield that much power, Darcy. Not someone

society would deem moderately successful, at best. We're looking for a bigger bank account."

"Who?"

"I don't know yet. Intuition tells me Turkey is up to something that my source isn't aware of. I'm beginning to wonder about the third family he's representing."

Ditto on the wondering...

Detective Battle contacted Lincoln on Monday, and evidently, the conversation got pretty hairy. Grizzly's building had basically been scrubbed clean because when a group of detectives went in to investigate, they found nothing but a spotless facility. What did they expect, the pinky finger wrapped up next to a box of Godiva chocolates? Sometimes I wondered about people, I really did. Battle also claimed that the red Porsche Turbo belonged to a man named Isaac Washington. Trouble was, Isaac Washington's license hadn't expired even though he had. He died less than a year earlier, and his nephew sold it for cash to Albert Jones. When Detective Battle contacted Albert Jones, he confessed he resold the car in a street deal—to a man—before he had a chance to re-license it. In short, an unknown man drove a dead man's car that still had a legitimate license plate. "X" hadn't been assigned as a vanity plate for who drove the car at the moment. It happened to come with the ride.

"Did you ever think X might be Grizzly?" I asked him. "Maybe Elmer's a front. Maybe he's there to make the infamous X look legitimate. The man who originally owned the car is currently six feet under, and Albert Jones said he resold it to another man. Walter Ivanhoe could be that man."

Lincoln grinned, making both of his dimples scrunch up happily. "Good girl, Darcy. It did cross my mind. He would be playing twice, which would certainly up his odds of winning."

"Will they pull the Turbo over for questioning?"

"Battle will, if he can find it. Our guess is—"

"Lola's driving it," I completed.

Lincoln chuckled, placing his arm over my shoulder. "The teacher is pleased with his student."

Once again, Lincoln longingly looked at the door. It reminded me of when I opened my last report card. You hoped it would be an occasion to celebrate, but experience told you the futile hoping

sometimes caused more pain than the reality. The hoping only verified that your prayers had been ignored.

"Is Willow due home today?" I asked quietly.

He expelled a resigned yet optimistic sigh. "I pray so. She actu-
ally returned my call today, so that's a step in the right direction."
He took a few moments to let that statement clear from his mind.
"May I ask you a question?"

Lincoln had a gift. It was like mental sodium Pentothal or truth
serum. One look, and people would confess the crap they'd been
doing or their deepest darkest feelings on anything. My gut alerted
me his question would be extremely personal. "Anything," I
answered.

"How do you and your father do it?" he murmured. "Murphy's
personality is not unlike parts of mine. How does he manage to be
your friend while still fathering you?"

Gee, I'd never really thought of our relationship in those terms.
"He doesn't expect a lot from me," I explained. Lincoln narrowed
his eyes, almost defensive. "Don't get me wrong. He expects me to
try my best," I explained, "but he knows that it's difficult at times.
Let's face it, Lincoln. I've got some things working against me, and
it hurts him. He's just happy with what he gets. He lectures, but at
the end of the day, he's a great listener and gets over things easily.
Perhaps," I whispered, "Willow has some things that make it hard
for her."

The way he handled his daughter might be the only thing
Lincoln had ever debated in his life. Most things were black and
white with him. Willow was a rainbow.

"Do you ever let her in on your life?" I asked.

"Rarely."

"Maybe if you did, then she'd feel inclined to share too. I told
Murphy once that I thought Dylan had a really cute butt."

Sweet, God Almighty...I actually said that.

He raised a brow, choking on a laugh. "How'd that go?"

"I wouldn't recommend it, but you get my point, right?"

"I get your point, dear."

"Why don't you go to *her*?"

He exhaled. "A lot of people want me dead. So when Willow got
the bright idea to drop my last name, I faded into the background

and never fought it." It had never entered my mind that his exile had been self-imposed. "In the grand scheme of things, it's worked well," he murmured. "As far as I can tell, none of my enemies know of anyone other than Colton, and my boy can fend for himself. Colton's never broadcast the fact Willow's his sister, and that wasn't only to legitimize her talent, it was mostly at my request."

"That stinks," I whispered.

"It's safe," he said. Squeezing me into a tight hug, both of us felt like we were at the mercy of someone else. I hated that feeling. Life didn't dole out mercy much. And unfortunately, when it did, it didn't always cut to the core of your pain.

A few minutes before one o'clock, Lincoln's jaw had dropped comatose, and Dylan was heavy breathing like a weirdo at a peep show. I, however, felt like someone lit a firecracker up my behind.

I needed to run.

Well, I needed to run or kill Grizzly in his sleep, and the first one sounded like the option I could live with until I bought one of those *Murder for Dummies* books.

"Up and at 'em, stud." I whistled, jostling Dylan awake.

Dylan drew in a quick gasp of breath rolling to his stomach, the sheets skimming dangerously low on his hips. I caught my bottom lip between my teeth, frowning at my own thoughts. That didn't feel like me...not with anyone...especially not with Dylan. Darcy and Dylan—best friends, nothing more. He probably looked ugly and disfigured and totally repulsive under the sheets anyway.

Riiiiight...and I had some swampland in Tallahassee that was alligator-free.

"Oh, God," he prayed.

"*Please, God*," I said giggling.

Dylan tugged the pillow over his head and mumbled, "Not again."

I lugged the pillow away, laughing. "Let's jog, Big Man," I said. Dylan palmed his eyes, leaning over to squint at the clock.

"You need to run at one a.m.?" he asked with a confused wince. I jogged in place, kicking my knees high like a marching band. I'd already inserted my contacts and switched out of my pajamas, wearing red Nike jogging clothes and sneakers. Under the erroneous assumption I'd go away, Dylan rolled to his side. I blasted the TV, switched on the lights, and drew the blinds up—allowing the moonlight to shine mercilessly in his face. "You're evil," he moaned in torment. "I swear, Darcy, you're absolutely pure evil."

I broad jumped onto his bed, continuing the jog. "I've got restless legs syndrome. They're creeping and crawling, and I need to get all of those little critters off of them."

Dylan threw back the covers and lazily swung his legs over the bed. I spun around for him to pull on the shorts he'd discarded earlier. After a few seconds, I bounced to the floor and onto his bare back. One would think that would've gone well. Dylan could strong-arm an elephant, except he was still partially asleep. Stumbling forward, he went down on one knee. My head bonked the back of his skull, his cheek grazed the tile, and before I could apologize, we tangled together like monkeys in a barrel.

Oh boy...Me likey being a monkey.

"My cheek is broken," he moaned.

"We can go slowly if you need a Band-Aid," I said, hugging him to the floor.

Dylan reached back and yanked my hair...*hard*. Shoot. Hormones bubbled like the hot springs in Arkansas. And why pick right then? I thought hormones bubbled when you were at a candlelit dinner, wearing nice clothes, saying inappropriate things to one another... not when something felt painful.

Ugh, what did I know.

"Don't insult me, Darcy," he murmured. "Whenever you beat me, it's because I let you. I need a new best friend. One who lets me sleep. One who doesn't take off in the middle of the night to jump from a window. You're not normal, sweetheart, and when I'm not afraid of the answer, maybe I'll investigate what that says about *me*."

Murphy raised me, for God's sake. He wasn't Mother Goose.

But I wouldn't allow that slam to go unanswered. "Listen, bud. You wouldn't like me if I was boring, and if I'm not normal, you're even more abnormal for being cognizant of that fact and not breaking up with me."

Oh, crap. If he broke up with me, I'd die.

Dylan burst forth a hearty laugh, unoffended. He shoved us off the tile, wiggled his jaw around, and motioned for me to jump on piggyback style. He led us down the hall into the kitchen to disarm the security system. "Are your eyes closed?" he teased. They actually were. I didn't want nor need the temptation.

"Yes, master," I replied. "They're closed." He punched in a sequence, and when the light went green, I slid down his back while he laced up his sneakers he'd left by the door. After quickly penning Lincoln a note, he grabbed his black Ranger cap off the table and flipped it around with the bill facing backward.

The moon haloed overhead as we stepped outside and took off at a record mile pace. Normally, it might be eerie and spooky, but with Dylan, it seemed normal and nice. The air smelled of a fresh sea breeze, and the only sounds distinguishable were the chirp of crickets, a warble of a bullfrog, and the song of a lonely dove.

As the leaves gently whipped in the breeze, he asked, "What's bothering you?"

Like a moron, I said, "Nothing."

"You always experience insomnia when something's bothering you, sweetheart, because it's not normal to run at this hour." Dylan and I turned the first corner, and although I wanted to divulge my suspicions about Lola, Elmer, and X, I reduced my explanation to the simplest of terms.

"I saw him, D." We jogged a couple of hundred yards before he responded.

"I believe you, Darc. I'm just trying to determine how to help you."

"Well, start thinking...because vacation's almost over."

We jogged the length of a football field when Dylan murmured, "Anything else?"

Picking up speed, I spit it out, along with whatever breath remained in my body. "Your parents...hate me," I huffed.

Dylan giggled like a little girl. "My parents love you and are trying to keep Murphy from killing you. It's purely an act of mercy." It didn't feel like mercy. It felt like pariah. Truth of the matter, I deserved to be treated like a pariah. I needed an act of contrition, but unfortunately, those sorts of acts were alien to me.

My brain operated on sin.

Sweat rolled down my face and pooled at my lower back. I needed a shower. "This was stupid," I said with a giggle.

"You seem to attract stupid," he said, chuckling with a snide undertone. That undertone held another meaning. A meaning meant for my new brothers.

"You're mad," I said, but he didn't respond. "Don't be angry with Kyd and Tricky because I know...you are." They'd both telephoned daily, and Dylan went three shades of anger when I answered. It wasn't like we were having a tête-à-tête about another date with OBT. They simply checked to ensure all my body parts were intact after our unexpected skydive.

"I'm not angry," he said smoothly. Lie, lie, lie.

Dylan's voice didn't convulse nearly as much as mine, but something unstable boiled beneath it.

"Then what...*makes* you angry?" I wheezed out.

"Nothing ever really...bothers me. The only thing that bothers me...is what is bothering you."

Liar, liar, pants on fire. "So Kyd and Tricky were *bothering* me," I pushed. Dylan's thighs beautifully bit the pavement, the sinews tightening and hinting of an extraordinary power. His landscape was ridiculously unreal. With each length of his gait, his legs rolled and dripped with sweat. For a brief second of madness, I wanted to lap it up. Good God, Almighty. I needed a chastity belt...or my lady parts removed. My thoughts went beyond weird. I usually lived for weird, but that felt too weird, even for me.

I hadn't gathered Dylan spoke until he said, "What's wrong?"

I'm a hoochie momma in the making, that's what's wrong, I thought.

"I don't get it," I muttered, trying to explain my behavior.

"Okay," Dylan said, succumbing to a sigh, "I suppose I'm somewhat angry. They put you in jeopardy."

"I asked Kyd to help *me*, D. There's no sense in getting your panties in a bunch."

"Oh, my panties are in a bunch all right. You're my guest. They knew better, and notice they aren't calling me to offer any explanation." That would be like asking someone to stay away from flesh-eating bacteria. Only a moron wouldn't heed the warning.

I said, "D, they're my brothers. I promise I'll love...your future girlfriend...so you must promise to love my brothers...I already have." I hated his girlfriend, but if I said that out loud, perhaps it would convince my brain otherwise.

"I'm not promising that," he grumbled.

"Why?"

"I have my reasons."

Dylan acted like his blood had iced-over...and for once was frugal with his words.

Chapter Twenty-Six

CATFIGHT

Guilt consumed me.

Should I even try to count up all of my offenses? If tapping into government property was frowned upon, walking into OBT would make a preacher swear. I was literally a victim of my own impulsivity, but I was fifteen years old, and I'd learned to embrace my dysfunction. Maybe that was step-one to recovery, or maybe I'd employed rationalization at its finest. Either way, the universe didn't take too kindly when you rationalized. Right when I thought it couldn't get any worse, life cut me off at the knees with another dose of how-low-can-you-go.

Yankee pranced inside the back pool entrance and was an albino-blonde. She'd either dumped a bottle of peroxide on her head or her hair aged fifty years overnight. My stomach burned and twisted, and it felt like I'd scarfed a jar of habanero peppers.

"Greetings, ladies," she said with an entitled smirk. That statement felt as fake as her hair. She slinked over the black pavers in a barely-there red bikini, worming her way directly between Sydney and me who lay totally horizontal on chaise lounges. It was convection-oven sweltering, and I'd been drinking everything in sight like a camel in the desert. I'd chugged two bottles of water, a can of Coke, and half a glass of iced tea and hadn't had the need to tinkle once. Wearing my skimpiest of white bikinis, for me that meant the string part stretched two inches instead of one. For Sydney, it meant a pink piece of thread her mother made the sign of the cross over. They argued, but Sydney laughed and hiked it up higher.

"Where's Dylan?" Yankee asked snootily.

"Out," Sydney snapped. Not true. Dylan had just swam two-dozen laps and stepped inside to watch a ballgame.

But guess what, Darcy's lips were sealed.

Yankee lifted her chin in a pout. "I'll wait."

Whatever, I thought. *And I hope you drop dead in the process.*

"We should get to know each other, Darcy," she said smugly. "We obviously will be spending a lot of time together this year."

Let's hope not. When I didn't answer and shockingly groaned, Yankee flipped the smugness into out-and-out hostility. Her head creepily snapped around like an owl, the front of her body not even moving. If it were a horror movie, I'd lay money she was the Devil... or at least, his creepy pet.

"Let me ask again," she hissed. "Do you care for him?"

"Of course, she does, Yankee," Sydney angrily answered for me. "They've been together since they were six. No one's ever going to break that bond."

Yankee smirked. "I wouldn't be so sure about that."

Sydney shoved her oversized, white sunglasses down over her eyes, symbolically blocking out the annoyance.

When Yankee continued to glare in my direction, my voice surprisingly found the appropriate sass. "I'm not going anywhere, Yankee...so deal."

Sydney laughed louder than was probably warranted. God knew I bluffed, but the girl made me say and do things totally out of character.

Yankee sat down on the edge of my seat, perused her nails, and gave my body a once-over like it was subpar. "You may think you have a chance, but he's the type that bores easily. What do you think of *that*?"

Earth-shattering, actually.

Dylan *was* the type who appeared to lose interest once he got what he wanted. He conquered something and then set out to find something else equally as challenging. We watched a commercial once where a guy sat in a recliner and bounced a ping-pong ball onto a coffee table, where it then hopped into a nearby cup. Dylan did that over and over until he could perform the feat on command. But once he'd mastered it, the ping-pong ball was history. Dylan tended to be highly driven or casually indifferent. What if he'd do that with me? Wouldn't it be more logical to hold onto the friendship than try to rebuild after a breakup? But it was *me*, for God's sake. When did I ever do logical?

"What's his type?" she pushed.

Good question. "I dunno," I said. But I knew it didn't include empty-headed.

"You're his best friend, and you don't know?" she scoffed with laughter.

Yankee's smug sarcasm struck a nerve. I knew everything about Dylan's likes and habits: his favorite ice cream, what he liked on his pizza, his secret stash of cash in his car, and even where he kept his journals that I never read. But his particular tastes in females we'd never discussed. Not because he'd rebuff the conversation—maybe because I didn't want to know the answer.

"I'll tell you," Sydney rasped out, reaching over to tweak my nose. "Tall, blonde, knock-out body, funny, a little quirky," she said and laughed, "with a face that could stop traffic."

Yankee threw her hand over her chest, gasping, "He likes Mary Cartwright?" Heck, we all knew Sydney wasn't referring to Mary Cartwright. She merely played nice trying to throw Yankee off the trail and onto me. "You almost sound like you're talking about Darcy," Yankee said, laughing even harder. "Obviously, that isn't true."

My hand begged to deck her.

"You have no class, Yankee," Sydney seethed.

"You're just mad my house is bigger than yours," she said.

Sydney tipped her head in concession. "Yours *is* bigger, but mine doesn't look like a pink fish bowl that a Christmas tree threw up on." I bit back laughter. Sydney 1, Yankee 0. The Knobleckers' home had a pinky glow with lawn ornaments of dolphins, jellyfish, and an octopus on steroids. Plus, their place seemed overly-lit. You strolled past it at night, and it might as well have been the International Space Station.

Yankee stiffened so quickly she toppled my chair. "You take that back," she fumed toward Sydney.

"I don't take back the truth. Besides," Sydney's voice rasped, "my father *paid* for his. It wasn't a lucky windfall at the state of Louisiana's expense." *Me-owch*. I laughed. Sydney 2, Yankee 0. "And if you insult my sister again, I'll pluck out both your eyes and rip out your bottled blonde hair. You look like a freaking albino wench, Yankee. And as much as you try, you're never going to morph your second-rate face into Darcy's."

Game over: Sydney 3, Yankee 0.

It all happened so fast that it felt like I'd imagined it.

We had a honest-to-goodness catfight. Yankee sprang for Sydney who already stood on both feet, lunging straight for Yankee's face. I somehow wrenched my way between the two who shoved, scratched, and shouted things so obscenely profane I needed an urban dictionary to keep up. Getting jostled around in the process, I caught the southpaw of Yankee's blood-red nails, a heavy-handed slap from Sydney, and quickly deduced the process might leave a mark.

My iced tea got knocked over, and I stumbled backward with one foot in the shallow end of the pool. I felt positive we were going to drown one another until someone wedged themselves in the middle and jerked Yankee out by her hair. She kicked and screamed she would "kill the beeyotch." As the fighting slowly stopped, I took a deep breath, feeling like I'd just climbed the pyramids in South America. I would've sworn I was in decent shape, but who would've thought all my energy would be suspended in less than two minutes of a fight? Once my breathing regulated, I glanced up into Kyd's shocked, blushing red, and totally mortified face.

"I'm sorry, ladies!" he barked. "Yankee is out of line!" Kyd wore baby blue board shorts, ready for swimming. My guess was he felt that his invitation—although he'd never had one—got permanently rescinded.

Yankee wore a sick, sadistic pleasure on her face, and frankly, the left side of her head appeared balding. "*You're* sorry?" she screamed exasperated. "Sydney insulted *us*! If anyone was out of line, it was *her!*"

Kyd gritted his teeth, swiping a hand through his sandy-blond hair. "I'm sure you provoked it, and you probably destroyed any chance you'd ever had of dating Dylan."

All three of us glanced to Sydney.

Whatever Sydney said usually flew. Sydney smiled broadly in my direction, giving me an over-my-dead-body look. But then again, she *did* love her brother. If Dylan all of a sudden decided to tango with Yankee, my guess was Sydney would provide the rubber stamp.

"Should my brother want it," she said diplomatically, "he shall have it. But let me make myself clear." She turned to me, and her black eyes softened into a deep, hypnotic shade of gray. "My brother wants that in-your-face kind of love. The kind you can't control. The kind you don't know whether to be embarrassed of or envious of. My brother wants his world to be rocked or simply," she paused, "he'd rather not." She bore a hardened gaze into Yankee. "He's not interested in you, Yankee. If he were, we'd *all* know it. In fact, he wouldn't be able to keep his hands off of you."

I couldn't help it, but I gave Yankee a below-zero stare. I didn't know if I truly looked threatening, but God knew I *felt* threatened. She glared back, and after a few seconds, she shockingly looked away blinking first. *Good for you, Darcy*, I complimented myself. *You'd better get used to her kind of girl*.

Kyd apologized again, dragging Yankee and her wenchified self back toward the fish bowl.

When they quietly slipped out the gate, Sydney dropped back down into her seat, crossing her legs like it was a bad experience all but put behind her. Me, I was a nervous wreck. I swept my tongue across my teeth, checking to see if the porcelain was still intact. God knew I didn't want to go the braces route again.

"Darcy," Sydney purred, smoothing down her suit, "I think it's best we keep this incident between the two of us. I'm not sure anyone will understand it, including my little brother."

"Fine by me," I mumbled, falling into my chair.

We both sat there drowning in the recall until Sydney broke the tension. "Do you want to get out of here? Like in twenty minutes?"

"Yeah," I said, "but first, I've got to make a phone call."

I eavesdropped on Lincoln speaking with Paddy about both Turkeys. Subtle differences, or personal peculiarities, existed between the two that didn't match up. They both were right-handed and smoked cigarettes, but they didn't smoke with the same mannerisms. Turkey Number One removed his cigarettes from their package by tapping the top of the pack three times, until one popped up. Immediately, he'd shove it in his mouth. Turkey Number Two carefully fingered the stick out, drew it to his nose for a smell, and lazily slid it in his lips. Number One looked at the door, over his right shoulder when in a hurry. Number Two narrowed his eyes, occasionally glancing at his watch. Lincoln's boys were evaluating six months' worth of videotape, so it wasn't like they were taking a stab in the dark. Their faces appeared identical, but the pupils on Number One's eyes briefly dilated if someone stood too close to him. Number Two could not give a rat's arse what anyone did and didn't have an autonomic response at all. My guess was Turkey Number Two was the badder of the duo.

Ten tootsie rolls later, Troy verified what I thought to be true. "Jester, you were right," he said exhaling. "Polly Teasdale works at Bank of America. She's a teller, but once you're inside it's reasonable to believe you have access to anything. Are you thinking what I'm thinking?"

I blew out some CO_2 as I brushed my hair, pulling it up into a high ponytail. "I do, but if something dicey is going on, that doesn't necessarily mean those funneling the money can lead us to Cisco. If it's Polly, she could merely be money hungry and taking advantage of a bad situation. Knowing that Lola gambles like she does, I'm led to believe there's another plot besides kidnapping a child. If we're lucky, when we unravel that plot, Cisco will come along with it."

After Troy and I shut down the call, I changed into a white miniskirt, navy tank top, and pulled the zebra laces out of my Chuck Taylors, exchanging them for tie-dyed red. After a brief conversation and neck massage from Zander, I stole away into the bathroom to contact Grizzly. There might be a lot of stupid running through my veins, but no one could accuse me of being an out-and-out fool. I'd memorized the number on his business card before Lincoln confiscated it earlier. Walter Ivanhoe remained the only person who could tell me if Polly Teasdale was, indeed, the point person in the disappearance of Cisco Medina. If it were Polly, however, where did the woman with the expensive shoes fit in?

"It's Legs," I said when he answered.

"Hello, Legs," he murmured, remembering me. "Nice exit, by the way."

"A bumpy one," I said giggling. "I broke a heel. If you run across Republic, tell him Rock misses him."

"I'll be sure to do that. Describe Republic for me."

"Black, strappy, size seven and four inches, but I need an eight."

His voice chuckled lowly, and suddenly my temperature spiked up to feverish. The man epitomized suave because in one beat I forgot he was old enough for an AARP card. "To what do I owe the pleasure," he murmured, "other than a new shoe?"

Be a verb, Darcy. "I'm going to shoot straight, Walter."

"Call me, Grizzly."

"Okay, Grizzly. Are you X?"

He belted out a laugh so hearty I flipped on the water faucet for fear the rest of the household would hear. "Why? Do you want to play?" he asked.

Bluff...bluff...bluff.

"If I play," which I can't, "I want to make sure two people aren't playing together. If Lola's playing for X, how do I know *you* aren't X? Let me be clear, Grizzly, I hate it when things aren't fair."

Crap, I couldn't believe my girl cojones had the gall to say that. "Ah," he murmured impressed, "you're a smart girl, Legs, but I'm not X." He sounded believable. I collapsed on the toilet seat, totally befuddled. If he didn't masquerade as X, then Polly must be the best gothic mastermind around.

"Then are you sure X is a woman?"

"If you weren't a teenager, questions like these would alarm me."

I stood back up, fiddling around in the medicine cabinet until I found a tube of sunshine-orange lip gloss on the top shelf. After I rolled on a coat, I raised my shirt and swabbed alcohol on my newly pierced navel with a cotton ball.

"I merely want to make sure I know what I'm getting into," I said. Sort of like my belly ring. I should've asked more questions because the price of fashion and vanity—not to mention good health—required a bit more energy than I'd intended to expend.

"Lynx refers to X as a—" *bleeping bleep* "That insinuates female."

Spit it out, Darcy. Pucker up and spit to your heart's desire. "Does X have her little boy?"

I heard him sigh, even though I was certain he didn't want me to hear it. "I've wondered that myself," he said quickly, a tad too relaxed. I cleared my throat once.

Then again.

And again.

Dang, could I actually be onto something? After I regained my composure, I asked, "Why does X keep someone like Elmer Hershel on her payroll? I'm going to be honest, Grizzly. He put the *mo* in moron."

Noise was heavy wherever Grizzly happened to be. Still, I detected the velvety tone of a female. "How much longer?" she whined.

"Good question," he murmured to me. "I would say X is playing more than one game."

"How does your game work anyway?"

"I get a cut off of everything that passes on my table. The people who come to me don't need money, Legs. They come merely for the thrill, and they like to win."

"Lynx?"

"She needs the money." Then that meant X liked to win...vis-à-vis Lola.

That got me to thinking. If Lola was indeed the best card counter around, those earnings were technically hers. X must hold something pretty substantial over Lola's head for Lola to continue to agree to play for nothing. And P.S., why did X need someone like Elmer Herschel to be her hired eyes?

Forty minutes later, Sydney was still tardy. In other words, I would've had time to kill and pluck a chicken. I should've expected it. Sydney's average was more than thirty, less than sixty minutes late. I lay on the bed with Zander as he recapped our night of adventure while I watched the clock tick closer and closer to six p.m. Once I'd terminated the call with Grizzly, I decided to visit Bank of America and view Polly Teasdale in action. I flipped open my iPhone to set up an appointment with Eleanor Talley too.

"Eleanor Talley," she answered. Eleanor sounded all business although I happened to phone on her personal number. From voice alone, I placed her in the forty to fifty-year-old range with the possibility of a slight North Eastern accent.

"Hi, Eleanor. I'm Darcy Walker. Herbie Knoblecker gave me your number."

Eleanor didn't even hesitate with a reply. "He did?" she said and laughed. "Why any friend of Herbie's is a friend of mine. What can I do for you, Darcy?" Oh, boy. When you talk to the bank, tell them you're going to give them more cash.

I took a deep breath, knowing it might be my last chance. "I'd like to donate money to the Trust for Cisco Medina."

Sydney cranked up the radio and tapped around until she landed on a classic station, playing a song featuring The Who. How apropos. How FREAKING apropos. We guzzled our iced Frappuccinos and turned onto I-Drive a little past five o'clock. We cruised in Willow's Audi R8, purring twenty miles above the speed limit. I thought once about telling Sydney to lose a few miles, but I wasn't in the position to stand in judgment of what I considered misdemeanors anyway.

I had one Chuck Taylor in felony.

Once in the parking lot, Sydney took another call from a dejected and down in the dumps ex-boyfriend. Man, I really needed to ask what his name was.

"I'll be back in a few," I said to her.

She put her hand over her cell with a tender smile. "Take your time," she purred breezily. I shoved my iPhone into my purse and shuffled out of the car.

I pulled open the tinted black doors and propped my sunglasses on my head. Once inside, Bank of America was your typical financial institution. Faux mahogany furniture decorated the lobby, including a navy leather couch on one wall, and four palm tree fabric covered chairs on the other. Glass end tables scattered both sides of the furniture, housing bank brochures. In the center sat a narrow island with deposit and withdrawal slips one could fill out before approaching the teller counter on the far wall.

To not look so obvious, I snagged a few and leaned up against the island making chicken scratch with an ink pen. Three people worked the reception with an empty slot for a fourth. So far, no sign of Polly Teasdale, and as far as I knew, Eleanor Talley could be gone for the day.

Right when I conceded defeat, the mahogany door opened to the middle office and out strode Polly Teasdale...surprisingly ungothic.

Words alone could've knocked me over.

If she hadn't worn a gold nametag that said "Polly," I wouldn't have recognized her. She was dressed conservatively in a navy pencil skirt and matching blazer. The jacket's buttons hung unsnapped, allowing a tailored white blouse to peek through, accessorized by two-inch navy pumps. Her black hair was pulled back into a tight bun and pearl earrings draped modestly from both ears. Polly honestly looked like someone who could tell you a heck of a lot about banking.

Like kismet drew us together, we rubbed eyeballs.

After my heart stopped and resumed a beat, I gave her some teeth. Polly dispensed a customer-friendly smile as she confidently padded forward. I didn't know whether to act surprised or admit we'd been introduced before. Frankly, I had the urge to blurt out that Elmer was a freak of nature who probably gave her fleas, but before I could do anything, she said, "Darcy?"

I considered acting blasé but knew panic was written all over my face. "Y-yyes?" I sputtered. How in the world did she know my name?

"Right this way," she said and smiled. Polly stole a glance at the brass clock on the wall right when the corner office door marked "Bank Manager" cracked wide, spitting out who I assumed was Eleanor Talley herself.

Eleanor hit the rafters at basketball center tall, and if she ever got the urge to smash me, she could do it with a thumb. I took her to be well over seventy-two inches without her black heels. Her heather-gray pants and menswear shirt were tailored to an athletic build and a nice contrast to her suntanned skin. Dark brown hair fell chin-length next to chestnut eyes, a button nose, and thin peachy-pink lips. Not exceptionally pretty but not ugly either.

She took two long strides, our eyes locking. "Hello, you must be

Darcy. I just spoke with Herbie, and I recognize you by his description."

I sort of nodded, sort of peed my pants.

Still, I had no chance to respond because directly following after her was—*holy cow!*—Gertrude Burr. Fate threw me a curveball and smacked me right in the face. Yes, I knew Gertrude recommended Livingston & Associates (Howie's employer) to help find Cisco, but shouldn't she be home mourning Howie's head? He held the title of her former boyfriend, but she was nothing but smiles...and new Botox.

My mind played the events again. Howie had the word Medina in his mouth. Had he known something he'd wanted to warn Gertrude about? Or did Gertrude have something to do with him losing his body? By the looks of things, she seemed awfully chummy with the woman holding Herbie's and her money.

Maybe that meant nothing.

Maybe that meant everything.

"H-hhello," I stammered again. My eyes bounced over to Polly who returned another smile, but something different lined the curve of her lips. Somebody help me. It felt like a setup with no backup available but Sydney, which was no backup really if it meant interrupting her during a phone call.

Eleanor swung her black leather bag over her shoulder, sweeping her hand toward her office, a paragon of customer appreciation. "Please, make yourselves comfortable. I'm on my way out. I'm boating this weekend, but Polly will take care of you."

Polly led the way and following like a well-trained dog trotted Gertrude. How in the world had I managed the VIP treatment? For all they knew, I'd give them a George Washington, not a few C-notes or bequeath all of my earthly possessions.

I slipped into one of the beige chairs in front of the mahogany desk, assessing the environment. Eleanor's office exploded with business commendations: Branch of the Year, Best Consumer Internet Bank, a few sports awards from Dartmouth, and inspirational framed prints—the biggest saying, "Let Me Help You Find Success." Beige stock paper nestled underneath a paperweight, and next to it was sage-colored stationery with "ET" in the upper left quadrant.

Polly slipped into Eleanor's chair too easily in my opinion. Like she had aspirations of taking over her job or a job of equal or greater importance.

"You look lovely," Polly gushed to Gertrude as we settled in. As usual, Gertrude was impeccably dressed: white cotton sundress, with platinum jewelry flowing like a waterfall. By the small talk, I got the feeling they knew one another outside of a professional setting. "How do you two know one another?" I asked.

On the corner of Eleanor's desk were foiled mints in a glass bowl. I tried to act nonchalant but nonetheless plunged my hand into the center and pilfered about six. Some girls couldn't eat when they were nervous. Unfortunately, I consumed enough trashy food for a fast food joint. Unwrapping one of the silver foils, I tossed the white candy in my mouth.

"Gertie and Eleanor rowed against one another in college," Polly answered. "I rowed in high school. I guess we just have that in common."

I found the whole rowing story surprising. Eleanor definitely had more testosterone than the norm, but Gertrude—in spite of her Victorian name—did not strike me as athletic. In truth, her stature was built so rail-thin, she'd snap in two during a rainstorm.

"Where'd you row?" I asked, unwrapping another mint, shoving it in the other side.

Gertrude lightly giggled. "I rowed at Yale and Eleanor rowed at Dartmouth. We had quite the rivalry. Neither of us liked to lose."

Polly lifted a brow as she pecked on the keyboard with one hand, opening a ledger with the other. "Oh, yeah?" She laughed strangely. "I've played cards with both of you, and you seem to have the corner on that market. Last time we played, you flipped over a table when you lost at gin rummy." I stifled a cough...all three enjoyed a card game...together. "My boyfriend and I are going to play again this weekend," Polly continued. "Why don't you join us?"

I coughed again, and when I didn't have any water to wash the mint down, I swallowed real hard hoping the spit would do the job.

Gertrude's face fell, genuinely disappointed. "I can't Friday. Pooky and I have something already planned, but the rest of the weekend's open."

I suddenly felt like a third wheel as their two-way conversation left me virtually unnecessary. I ran scenarios, debating what each of these variables could mean. I came here thinking Polly more than likely was X. It made the most sense—she *did* have a relationship with Elmer—but it appeared too easy. But, in contrast, why complicate what didn't need complicated? Could Eleanor be the worst boss in the world, not having a clue what went down under her own nose? Even though all three enjoyed a card game, I still couldn't catch a feel to the true identity of X. Gertrude perhaps? She donated money to the trust and recommended that Livingston & Associates be hired. All I needed was a connection to Lola because Gertrude looked guiltier than sin.

Once I pulled out my wallet, Polly broke from the conversation and took the bill I extended. Gertrude offered an authentic smile, but someone needed to remind her that she didn't work there. She had one of her Jimmy Choo shoes propped on the top of the desk, rearranging the diamond anklet around her long and slender leg.

"Looks like we might run in the negative this month," Polly said, sighing and making a few scratches in the notebook. "That breaks my heart. Your money will be well spent, Darcy." *How could that be?* I thought. Herbie gave $10K a month, and FX, Incorporated hadn't billed for sixty days. In essence, there should be $20K sitting there from Herbie alone. Gertrude, as Herbie said, was probably good for a grand, so we were basically talking plus $20K in total.

"How much *is* there?" Gertrude asked, eyes aghast, suddenly upset.

"Less than fifteen hundred dollars," Polly whispered.

They both stole worried glances at one another, eyebrows crumpled up in pain as though the end of the world neared. Trouble was, I didn't know if any of their concern was heartfelt. The longer I sat there, the more I knew something was wrong. Terribly wrong? Yeah...I just didn't know how to make it right.

Before I could weigh the repercussions, I gazed into Gertrude's big, brown eyes and leaned into her personal space. "So let's get down to business, Gertrude," I blurted out. "Did they ever find Howie's body? And what about the dead guy in your pool? That's an awful lot of dead body, girl. What's up?"

Chapter Twenty-Seven

THE FIRING SQUAD

I had a crook in my neck and was pretty sure vertebrae C4 and C5 had fallen out of alignment. I rolled off the couch, thinking the hard tile might pop them back into place. Instead, I landed on top of Dylan with an, "Ugh."

"Good morning to you too," he said and chuckled.

Talk about a meeting of the minds. His practically swished inside of mine.

Feasting my eyes on my best friend, his amber eyes blinked sleepily and tender—his naked chest cut, rippled, and harder than bedrock. Dylan looked and smelled divine. By the sticky feeling in my T-shirt, I'd shot straight to rapid decomposition.

When he kneaded his fingertips into my lower back, I blanked out and buried my head in his neck. Welcome to Stressville, people...there was no exit sign.

"Are you okay?" he murmured groggily.

Not really, and the more he touched me, the less I could construct a sentence.

Dylan leaned forward and lightly kissed my hair, still massaging away my restless night. "What's wrong, sweetheart? You crawled in at four a.m., told me you had a bad dream, and wanted *again*," he said, giggling with emphasis, "to snuggle up with me."

Funny thing was, I had no recollection whatsoever of that

conversation or what I might've done to him in the dark. I'd become a dirty girl...a dirty girl with no control whatsoever.

"Something is screwy with my pineal gland," I mumbled. "I can't sleep."

"I know something's screwy with your pineal gland," he said and chuckled, "but you can't keep sneaking into my room. The best I could offer was the floor. It might've been worth leaving my bed, Darc. Nice wake up, call. You feel *goooood*."

I had to agree. It certainly qualified as a howdy-and-a-half, but the last thing he needed was for his massive ego to balloon even more. It barely made it through the door now. I leaned forward and headbutted him, immediately wishing I hadn't...his head was as hard as a freaking coconut.

A frown ran across his temple, his black eyebrows knitting into one. "You're mean, sweetheart, and you might want to lay off the late night doughnuts."

Low blow. I wasn't fat—granted, I binged on the sweets—but the best I could tell I looked at least average...(well, close).

The conversation went from zero to neutron bomb in seconds flat. Dylan and I rolled and thrashed around on the floor, twisted together like a candy cane. My hands attempted to circle his throat. His doubled around mine as he intermittently attacked my ribs. The entire time I replayed the dream that paraded my night with Cisco.

I imagined him in the dark, hearing noises and not knowing their origin. Crippled with fear, he couldn't seek the comfort of someone's arms because those sleeping near him weren't people he could trust. As the night grew, my dreams grew even darker. Cisco happily played at the park, venturing down the slide. Segue to a warehouse, and the two of us frantically ran hand-in-hand for two doors in the distance. Choosing the door on the right, when we stumbled inside, we wound up in the "out of town business" room in Grizzly's building. No meat cleavers were in sight, but dead bodies hung from the ceiling with Howie's head suspended in the air, trying to pull one of them down.

Okay, it was horror movie league, but I should've expected it. When I asked Gertrude for the 411 on Howie's body, she straightened her back, defensively—as if I'd touched on a subject that extremely embarrassed her, and she didn't want to acknowledge it in front of Polly. Fortunately, or rather unfortunately, I wasn't in the mood to protect her feelings. As I continued with a pigheaded stare, a crack surfaced in the carefully constructed facade of gracefulness that Gertrude showed the world. She broke...saying the body washed ashore in Daytona Beach, found floating in the breakwaters. I should've been happy with that information, but I pressed on in regards to the man discovered dead in her pool. Gertrude literally stood up, said her quick "Goodbyes," and told me to mind my blankety-blank business.

At the door, she pivoted one last time and unloaded an F-bomb.

Huh, guess I struck a nerve.

I didn't understand my relentless need to unravel the mysteries in front of me. Regarding Cisco, perhaps it was because I knew firsthand that paralyzing and debilitating pain when your nuclear family went away. Most days I successfully buried the grief, but on the days it resurrected itself, I realized the term "emotionally numb" signaled progress. Pain was a funny thing. The physical you could heal from. The mental didn't always cooperate.

Dylan finally got the upper hand, flipping me over, pinning my arms to my sides. As he slowly bent down to whisper in my ear, I found myself needing air. If I thought the situation with Cisco felt dubious, the ambiguity with Dylan literally had me in a chokehold.

"I like this position of dominion, sweetheart," he murmured in a tease. "I'm the boss here, so if you get rebellious again, remember I've only been toying with you. I can have you flat on your stomach, begging me for pretty much anything at a moment's notice."

Immediately, I went still—like the atmosphere right before the train-like sounds of a tornado hit. I had two urges—to kiss him or bail like a rat on a sinking ship. If I thought Howie's head seemed bizarre, the situation with Dylan was the craziest, most disturbing thing I'd experienced in a while. In other words, I liked it. And the thought offended me to the bone. Not wanting to be bested, I looked over my shoulder to see what I dealt with—big mistake—his eyes had taken on the hue of his father's. Black, smoldering, merciless...lurid. Whenever he gave me that look, I forgot how to spell my own name.

I opened my mouth but not a doggone thing came out. *Gah!* I wanted to kick my own behind.

"That's right," he said, laughing darkly. "Chew on that for a while."

Chew on it? I'm pretty sure I wanted it to melt in my mouth.

Lincoln snored on the sofa opposite us...somehow missing the entire PG-13 episode. With a growling snort, he coiled to his side as Dylan rolled to his back and played with a strand of my hair. I wasn't sure how long we lay there—Dylan didn't seem in a hurry to move—but you could always count on my big mouth to sabotage the mood. "So how's Yankee these days, D? Is that a line you would've used on her?"

I might as well have called the Mother Mary a skanky 'ho. Dylan sucked in a big gasp of air, muttering, "Here we go," out loud.

I propped my head on my elbow, facing him with a steely expression. *Confession time*, my eyes said. I'd tell him what I'd been doing, and by goodness he'd tell me—once and for all—what lay behind Yankee's kiss and unnatural obsession. I was hard pressed to think she'd be stupid enough to make a fool of herself. In fact, she appeared to be surprised when he didn't agree for an encore.

My intentions were quickly drowned out when my iPhone buzzed.

Not wanting to wake his grandfather, Dylan quickly bolted up and retrieved it from the ottoman, shrugging at the Orlando prefixed number as he placed it in my palm.

"Hullo?" I mumbled. I had plans to murder that person. Darcy Walker finally had the nerve to ask Dylan Taylor about the not-so-secret females in his life, and that call just napalmed me.

"Jester, it's Hector," he greeted. Suddenly, I was in the forgiving mood. What could Hector, the notorious diamond stud thief, possibly want from *me*?

Placing my hand over the receiver, I mouthed, "Diamond stud thief," to Dylan.

Dylan studied me closely, the only movement on his face being one raised brow. "So do you have a thing with said diamond stud thief?" he murmured.

"It's torrid," I said grinning.

"How torrid?"

"Hot, bothered, and nothin' but skin."

There it was. That delicious, untamable look he gave me which proved once and for all I was an idiot. An idiot that shouldn't hang around a guy that tanked her self-esteem every time she looked at him.

"Sweetheart, you can't even begin to fathom hot and bothered."

I, honest to God, said, "No shiz."

"Yeah, no shiz," he grinned naughtily. "I'm making breakfast. No tattoos, no belly rings, no *nothing*, Darcy. I'm serious."

Dylan pushed off the floor and pointed a finger in my face. "Yes, Master," I muttered, sticking out my tongue sarcastically. I watched his, um...shorts, as he cockily strutted away, wondering why no one else felt the room swaying. I shook my head hard, attempting to focus. "Hey, Hector. How are you?"

"I'm good," he said, "and first off, thanks for the threads. My little girl loved them." A couple of days earlier, I got a case of the guilts for cutting down on Hector's fencing profits and had Dylan take me shopping. I bought three outfits that would fit Marjorie and dropped them off at the shop. It obviously didn't negate the fact I'd bought stolen goods and that Hector happily sold them. Still, I hoped the thought counted for some sort of absolution on Judgment Day.

"You're welcome. What's up?"

"Elmer Herschel came into the shop yesterday bragging about his high class girlfriend."

I cocked my head to the side, speculating where the conversation was headed. Elmer hadn't made my to-do list for the day. My goal was to poke away at Gertrude Burr. I had a feeling the connection with Howie and that note held the key. First thing I'd planned, however, was to tell Kyd my suspicions and have him handle the situation at the bank. Herbie would be befuddled, but Kyd was as cunning as they came. If anything, he could stop his father's donations and offer free counseling on alien abduction.

I couldn't deny the intrigue. "Was her name Polly?"

"That gothic chick?" he asked.

"Yes."

"No, but she came with him. He didn't provide a name of his

girlfriend, but he said she was really smart about managing their money and drove a nice red sports car."

My mouth went dry. I choked out, "Did he mention what kind?"

"A Porsche Turbo."

I needed a pacemaker. My heart flip-flopped all over the place. Sitting up, I tucked my knees to my chest, hugging them in place with one hand. Obviously, we could cross Polly off as the girlfriend. Who did that leave—Lola?

"Lola drives a Turbo, Hector," I coughed out in explanation. "Do you honestly think she's dating Elmer?" Maybe X didn't exist. Maybe Lola had her own little boy and cast herself off as X's bootlicker.

Hector laughed. "Lola drives a lot of cars, chicky. That girl's always running a scam. All I know is Elmer affectionately referred to his woman as Moose. You should've seen his tattoo, Jester," he cackled. "He wanted moose over his heart except he couldn't take the burn and left it at moo. So now, he has moo right above his nipple! It made me think of a milking cow!"

Normally, I would've found the humor in the situation. What real man wanted to leave "moo" over his nipple? The thought brought a whole new level of disgusting. "Anything else?" I asked.

"He went on and on about too many responsibilities and how he'd been thrown into a ready-made family. He complained about babysitting but said he did it because he loved her. And that's not all. He wore nice clothes. As in really nice designer gear."

All of the air left my body. "Crap," was all I could manage.

"Jester, are you okay?"

I coughed and breathed in and out three times. "Yeah," I finally sputtered, "then that means he's gotten into Cisco's trust. Even if Polly isn't *the* girlfriend, she still could be funding him. Plus, he's stashing the little boy somewhere."

"Exactly, but that doesn't explain the Medinas."

"He must have something on the grandparents to make them want to run."

"What better than to threaten to kill that little boy?"

I needed a paper bag. I needed a paper bag the size of Texas. When I started the gig, it was merely a pipe dream that I could make a difference. I had absolutely no freaking idea I might actually succeed.

I shut down the convo and lay there for a while, contemplating my next steps. When I got nothing but a headache, I shuffled into the kitchen, hoisting myself up on a barstool. I liked watching Dylan cook. He hummed and nothing ever burned while he'd carry on three conversations at one time. He poured me a glass of orange juice while he placed his cell phone in my hand. "Darc, your little sister is looking for you," he said with a wink. Not true. If she were looking for me, she would've dialed my number instead of his. She was going through Dylan-withdrawal.

Dylan scooped breakfast of eggs and sausage onto a white ceramic plate. "Hey, M. What's up?" I held the phone under my chin as I downed half my OJ and buttered a piece of french bread.

"I don't like my body," she said with a sigh.

Dylan rolled his eyes, taking the stool next to me. Evidently, she'd unloaded the same statement on him. "What's wrong with your body?" I asked. "You're beautiful."

"I want to be like you, Darc." God love her, she needed a different role model. I stared at my plate and took two forkfuls of each in a clockwise pattern. I needed to arrest control, even if I systematically ate my food. "And why's that?"

"I want a booty. Should I put voodoo cream on my behind?"

"Couldn't hurt," I said. After we talked about her plans for the day, I hung up and briefly wondered if she'd be sitting on hooters by morning. I thumbed in the speed dial for home. Talk about the blind leading the blind...right then was the boobless leading the buttless.

"Strike the booty?" she asked.

I shoved a piece of egg in my mouth and mumbled, "Just fire up your habaneros, M. Let's give the booty a few more years."

I didn't want to give Cisco a few more anythings. A few more anythings would make his picture on the back of a milk carton have whiskers. After we ate in silence, I cleared off the table, running both our dishes and glasses underneath the faucet, stacking them one-by-one in the dishwasher.

Dylan hopped up on the granite countertop in front of me, tucking a stray wisp of hair behind my ear. He appeared relaxed earlier: bedhead beautiful, dimples deep, looking like a million bucks when my breath was zombie-in-the-making.

Hopefully not a premonition of things to come.

"What's up with the most beautiful girl in the world?" he murmured gently.

Oh, where to begin? Could I drum up the required skills to act upon the information I had? In the grand scheme of things, I had no choice. My insecurities paled in comparison to what the potential outcome could be.

I dove right in, forgoing the preamble. "I need to tell you something," I whispered, bracing both hands on his knees. The expression on his face didn't waver or appear surprised. Instead, he offered an exhaling smile of relief, acting as if he'd been waiting for it.

———

"What's the punch line?" Lincoln grumbled.

Dylan threaded his fingers deeper into mine as we hunkered down on the white leather sofa. After I explained my dilemma, he didn't even take the time to gather his own thoughts. He grabbed my hand, pulled his father out of bed, and led us back to his still snoring grandfather. Honest to God, it felt like the firing squad. But then again, the firing squad would be easier. One pull of the trigger, and it would be over.

Dylan murmured, "There is none, Grandpa."

Lincoln paused, giving me a look of chastisement. I should've expected as much. "So you think Lola is either X or one of a combination of Gertrude and this Polly?"

I gave him a nod, recapping what Hector had said along with the suspicions I had from my bank visit. "I do. Gertrude is involved up to her Botox'd eyeballs. Howie's note said 'Medina.' Howie knew something and was trying to tell her or accuse her of something, and we already know he'd been working the case. Maybe he found out the truth and was *killed* for the truth."

Lincoln pondered that for a second, pinching the space between his eyes. "I don't like Grizzly," he finally muttered, "and not one thing Detective Battle told me about him was honorable."

"Just because you don't like him doesn't mean he's the mastermind here," I blurted out in contest. Dylan tightened his hand with a minuscule jerk, demanding submission. "Why would you think that?" I continued with more tact.

Lincoln removed his glasses, rubbing both eyes with his fingertips. Lincoln and Colton both stood in the den in their boxer briefs. Lincoln perched on the edge of the couch cushion, Colton standing next to him with his chest and legs as rigid as a fighting Gladiator's. I honestly didn't think either was aware they were half clothed in front of a female guest. First of all, they considered me family, so they were either processing too much information or didn't give a rat's rear end about social conventions. My guess would be the latter.

"You're sure about that?" Colton answered for him, raising both brows in a challenge. "You did say Gertrude had a pooky bear of a boyfriend. Bears can be grizzly."

Anyhoo...

I was sort of angry that little fact slipped by me. Could Grizzly have been the man at Gertrude's house the day the coroner pulled a body from her pool? I suppose so—their builds were the same—and so were their confident mannerisms. But Battle claimed that Grizzly liked young girls. Gertrude might be attractive, but she sure as heck didn't tip the scales at teenager. Point being, after a closer look at the bank, she looked too plastic—possibly more so than Minda Sue Knoblecker. And believe me. That was saying something.

No one uttered another word, and by the swoosh of emotion that rolled through the room, judgment day was near. My eyes slid over to Dylan's, but his were already sealed up tight.

His father boomed, "Need I remind you that you are *my ward* on vacation?!"

Yup, roast Darcy time. "I stayed in my bed, Colton," I mumbled.

"That's a loose interpretation of the law, Darcy. Your father trusts me."

Well, yeah. Whatever. No kidding. If it got me Cisco Medina alive, then it was worth the extra risk.

I offered him a genuine smile of apology. His frown said it wasn't accepted. When he expelled a disgruntled noise toward his son, Dylan sat there as the beleaguered best friend, accepting blame for not being able to predict my every move. Heck, *I* couldn't predict my every move, but being my best friend pretty much made him cannon fodder.

I glanced to Colton, tenderly squeezing Dylan's hand. "It's not his fault, Colton. Please don't be angry or punish him for what I did."

Colton opened his mouth twice, appraising Dylan's condition. His gaze next fell on Lincoln, hoping for a solution to the problem. Seriously, there was no easy fix...I'd been searching for two weeks.

Colton paced in a tight circle, head down, hands crossed behind his lower back. Crap, it reminded me of when a lion stalked its prey, basically grounding it when it grew tired of the game.

Lincoln continued to rub both eyes, causing me to doubt he'd ever see clearly again. "Felix Xavier, huh?"

I sighed. "Yes. Why?"

Colton interrupted him, eyes narrowed. "His last name begins with an X, Darcy. This whole situation reeks all the way around."

I felt like cussing...telling them all to incinerate in the land of hot lava.

Here I thought I'd done pretty well managing the information, and I'd overlooked what could be conclusive evidence. That might insinuate a level of corruption that would take me longer than a couple of days to untangle. I guess there was a possibility Felix Xavier bought the Turbo. That meant he could've billed the trust and got paid for no work. But why hire Lola to represent X? Why take her little boy? Even if it was simple blackmail—to ensure she brought in earnings each week—that still didn't wrap up the situation with Elmer Hershel. Elmer had a girlfriend with money, and he implied to Hector that Polly didn't hold that title.

"I, umm, never thought of that," I mumbled.

"Could it be that you've been tackling too many things all on your own?" Colton grumbled. I think he meant that statement rhetorically, but I answered anyway.

"Yes," I said, "but Detective Battle reported that X was the legitimate license plate of Isaac Washington, and the registration didn't change when Albert Jones bought it and resold. The coincidence is all just a fluke."

Colton set his jaw firmer. "Yes, but it's too peculiar to accept as fact, especially when kidnapping, not to mention embezzlement of funds, is on the table. This other company—Livingston & Associates—you said they went out of business. Did they file? Do you have a contact for them?"

I shook my head in the negative and felt less confident in my abilities than I did at the beginning of the conversation. Lincoln must've seen my confidence deflate. He blew out a breath. "This is why we work in teams, Darcy," he said. Well, no kidding, but we both knew they wouldn't have placed me on the roster even if I'd begged on bended knee. "Do you understand what the next move is?" he continued. "After I call Battle and introduce myself to Felix Xavier?"

I knew exactly what the next step entailed, and I swallowed down the urge to barf. I needed to get a confession and there was only one way to do that. "I'll set up a date with Elmer," I muttered.

A brave person would face it head on. A scaredy cat would calculate the odds of accidental death. A super-spy, wannabe like me would consider it their big break.

———

The sun beat down at one hundred and one degrees Fahrenheit, making breathing a distant memory. Then again, nothing took your breath away like Murphy Walker when he'd rather kill you and eat the remains. For me, it was a familiar sensation. Dylan, however, looked like he'd fallen naked into a pit of scorpions.

We were holed up in Colton's office, listening to my father on the speakerphone. Murphy was oblivious to his public disrobing, but Dylan reached over and hit the speaker mid-argument. Apparently, he wanted his family to know exactly what they were dealing with. And in practical terms, it kept me from rehashing his words anyway. Thing was, neither Colton nor Lincoln seemed especially intimidated. Both were studying a file on Colton's desk, not even listening. For the first time, it became clear to me both had a stupid streak.

Dylan and I were curled into one another on the black leather couch. Zander'd barreled in minutes earlier and had been kicked out. He stormed in seconds later only to be booted out again.

Finally, on attempt number three, Colton shoved him onto the floor, telling him to, "Shut his frigging mouth."

The language had gone ghetto.

"You are not going to go under-fricking-cover!" Murphy screamed. "I'm going to kick somebody's yellow-bellied, mother lovin', dog humping butt all the way from the Heartland of it All. They're not going to be able to sit down, kneel down, or kiss anyone else's butt but their own by the time they untwist the damage my fist is going to do."

Let me introduce Kentucky cursing at its finest—interpreted only by a mutual hillbilly. He spouted off things about gizzards and squirrels and gizzards that *liked* squirrels and what he considered the worst thing of all...cockroach, gizzard-lovin' squirrels. I mentally made a note to seek a definition but was pretty sure he'd coined it mid-phrase.

"Give me a name," he seethed.

"I get a company car," I said and giggled. "I'll probably even get my own insurance plan."

Dylan put a finger to my lips. "*No joking,*" he whispered.

Murphy never heard anyone's words other than the competing voices in his own brain. He shouted, "Shut up, Darcy! I'm going to freak somebody's hump so far up their spine it's going to be a toothpick!"

That statement frankly made no sense.

"Ouch," Zander shivered. Dylan launched his heel into his brother's back.

We'd just gotten off the telephone with Detective Battle, brainstorming on the perfect dance club. Dylan suggested Cowboys, which had that mechanical bull he'd been itching to ride. Primarily, it catered to the early twenties crowd, but older wannabe teen has-beens occasionally showed their faces. Since Dylan and I weren't eighteen, Detective Battle would supply fake IDs in case we were carded. My job was to find my inner-vixen and seduce Elmer into meeting me behind the mystery Moose's back. I needed to find my inner-idiot—that wouldn't be hard. My inner-she-devil? I had more of a chance of harvesting cheese from the moon.

Murphy belted out, "Your goddanged..."

"Omigosh," I whispered, "don't say the curse word of all curse words, Dad. Even I know you shouldn't take God's name in vain."

It was the big, number three on the list of ten.

Murphy gasped, "You just said *omigosh*! Were you praying, kid? I said *dang*! And believe me, I'm *praying*," he emphasized, "when I gosh-danged, dog-humpin' *say* it!"

Murphy was his own brand of Holy Roller. He prayed out loud, all day long, not caring who heard him. Unfortunately, he ruled with an iron fist with a propensity to eat his young. The way I saw it, I'd better count my blessings. Number one, I was going undercover—big thrill. Number two, Cisco might be home by morning—even bigger thrill. Number three, if I pulled things off, Murphy wouldn't physically eat me. Biggest thrill of all. That meant Darcy Walker would live to die another day.

"So that's a yes?" I said, giggling again.

Murphy always talked in terms of electronics when he felt people needed a rewiring. He bellowed, "Hit the pause button, kid, and shut your mouth. Now give me the name!"

Dylan was uncharacteristically quiet, looking as if he was in the beginning stages of organ failure. While I wiped away a bead of sweat rolling down his temple, he mouthed, "Answer your father."

When my lips didn't do anything more than part, Lincoln padded over and touched me on the shoulder, nodding that I should comply. But Murphy was a lit powder keg.

"Dad, you need to be rational about this," I said. "A little boy is missing. I don't want to provide a name if you're going to dismiss this opportunity without thinking it through. The cop I'm working with is a pro. You'll trust him."

Murphy's voice bottomed out to an intimidating base. "Let me set something straight, kid. I'm a pro at what I do. I'd rather kick somebody's ass than kiss it. So give me a name, and I'll make sure he witnesses *my* professional abilities."

For some reason, giving him a name felt like a behemoth blunder, but my choices were limited. I briefly met Dylan's eyes as he closed his, mumbling a prayer of desperation.

"Lincoln Taylor," I reluctantly spit out. Nothing but bone-chilling silence followed as Lincoln took the phone out of my shaking palm.

Chapter Twenty-Eight

LOCKED, LOADED & GUNNING FOR BEAR

*T*ime hung heavily, and I had a miracle to pull off. Unfortunately, I didn't feel particularly supernatural. Trouble was, the gig had an expiration date of less than thirty-six hours, and Murphy had eaten up the past two.

He'd grounded me—no shocker there—and I'd lost access to all of my Apple products for the foreseeable future as soon as I returned home. Plus, Murphy demanded that I give him ten percent of every one of my paychecks for the next twenty-five years. Things could be worse. All I knew was the day started out stellar and then snowballed into a crap-load of crap as soon as Murphy got involved.

The usual.

As I tried to regain a semblance of who I was hours earlier, Dylan maneuvered us back to sit on the corner of his father's desk, pulling me between his legs. Dylan always let me break free from our hugs first, and it wasn't abnormal for the embrace to last anywhere from five seconds to five minutes. Calling Elmer was the next part of the plan, but my finger couldn't do the walking, and frankly, the hug caressed me like warm water, sluicing down my skin.

"Make the call, sweetheart," he whispered in my ear. "I'll be right beside you, yeah?"

When hysterical laughter burst from my body, Dylan pried my cell phone out of my hand and scrolled through my contact list, still holding me to his side.

"Herschel, right?" he asked. I gave him a kill-me-now look. He thumbed his way down the docket and hit the call button, launching the speakerphone. My mind fumbled through the possibilities. Would he even remember me? Could I seduce him into going? Did I even understand seduction? It consisted of batting your eyelashes and breathy giggling, right?

Elmer answered on the third ring. "Elmer," he muttered gruffly.

"Hi, Elmer. It's—" Dylan reminded me what his grandfather said with icy, merciless eyes and a possessive tug on my lower back. *Not your real name*, Lincoln had warned. Not a problem. I'd never given him my real name in the first place.

"It's, umm...Buffy."

Dylan snickered, catching a laugh in his throat.

Elmer said, "What can I do you for, Buffy?"

"I was hoping you remembered me. I accidentally found myself in your office the other day."

His breathing grew thick and heavy, like some warthog burrowing in the dirt. "The girl with the long legs who I'd like to do things to?"

Dylan hissed through his teeth. *Dear God*, I thought, *please don't provide a definition*.

"Does the offer still stand to take me dancing?" I quickly asked.

"I, uh, might have to maneuver some things around, but I couldn't turn down an attractive, little dumpling like you. You want me, doncha?" First off, the word dumpling wouldn't make anyone feel attractive, and secondly, I'd rather have an abscessed tooth. But the verb in me had a job to do.

Dylan pulled me even closer, coaxing me to answer. "Midnight tomorrow? Cowboys?" I asked.

Elmer's breathing did triple time. "Yeah, midnight works for me. Dress nice. I like my women leggy, showing tons of skin."

———

"No, Paddy!" Lincoln roared. "We can't let her *do* that!"

I couldn't pretend to possess selective hearing because when Lincoln bellowed, it sounded like an attack by coyote-munching mountain lions.

I didn't know the time...only that it ticked past midnight, Thursday morning. I'd swum by the moonlight, and when I opted against a shower, a quick sniff of my armpits reminded me I still smelled like yesterday. Lincoln and I had been the dynamic duo for the past thirty minutes in a dark house illuminated only by our insomnia and two floor lamps. Crime scene and surveillance photographs were strung out on the ottoman in front of us, along with meat and potato leftovers for him, homemade cookies the size of the solar system for me. In between my normal eavesdropping, I heard the word—plain as day—Giuseppe. Giuseppe, I reminded myself, happened to be one of the names on the backs of the photographs in Lincoln's Cardoza file. The photographs were so heinous, whoever committed the murders ranked as one of the biggest sociopaths to ever breathe air.

Lincoln had reached his limit with the case—add my shenanigans—and he'd probably apply for early retirement. Smelling cigar smoke earlier, I located tiny flecks of gray and white ash peppering the floor underneath his feet. Lincoln didn't smoke (i.e., the official story). It was safe to say if he picked up the habit as a stress reliever —hypothetically speaking, of course—Alexandra would force-feed an industrial-strength cleaning agent and hold him down until he choked. When his back was turned, I cleaned it up, not mentioning a word. I owed him.

The house blew iceberg cold, and I snuggled deeper under my covers with a chocolate chip cookie in my cheek, reading *Atlas of the Stars*. Answers with my situation weren't coming in a rush, and the night felt like another snoozefest.

Until Alexandra bounded down the hall...

Bringing holy hell along with her.

Her black hair swung nimbly around her shoulders, her red silk robe moving like she'd been propelled by the wind. But nothing— not even a runaway car—moved faster than her mouth.

All I understood was, "Lincoln...blah, blah, blah, Greek stuff. Children...blah, blah, blah, more Greek." And a wagging finger with what I knew definitively as, "Blah, blah, blah, Greek profanity." Funny how my mind could pick out the swear words, even though I barely understood anything else.

I was dirty, so what.

Lincoln mumbled a curse as the ripples on his naked chest tensed, anticipating an argument he sensed he'd already lost. He had three distinct scars on his torso from bullet holes. One on the right breast had traveled straight through, and the other two were abdominal wounds—the bullets dug out during surgery. It's as if all the blood gushed to them at once, reminding him he had a job that might not always be worth it.

Although he placed his hand over the receiver, I heard Paddy laughing in the background. "I don't understand what you're *saying*, Alexandra!" Lincoln yelled back. "Slow down!"

I couldn't help but stir the pot. "You go, girl!" I said and then giggled.

Funny, they both ignored me.

Lincoln haphazardly tossed his cell phone onto the cushion next to him, pushing off the couch. "*Slow down!*" he screamed again.

His command only gave Alexandra's temper a shot of adrenaline. It was common knowledge, Grandma had a low boiling point when she was younger, but the woman had chilled and depicted the epitome of manners. But if her feathers ever got ruffled, life as you knew it would come to an abrupt and painful end.

Lincoln motioned frantically to take the discussion to the kitchen, and Alexandra followed like a spitting cobra hissing at his heels. He switched on the chandelier hanging over the bar area, like he figuratively tried to shed light on what he didn't understand. Funny thing was, one light flickered not quite able to embrace the current. For a split second, he focused on the bulb, willing it to work, but when Alexandra angrily grabbed his wrist, he jumped like he'd just dodged a landmine.

I picked up his discarded cell phone, drawing my knees to my chest. "Hey, Paddy," I explained. "We're in the throes of another World War."

Paddy chuckled while the argument ratcheted to an even nastier decibel. "I'd rather use sandpaper as toilet tissue than go toe-to-toe with Alexandra Taylor." Paddy then said, "Hold on, doll." What the heck, I didn't have anything else to do.

Paddy began speaking with someone else, and something told me—barring brownies falling from the sky—to block out the entire world except for him. "What?" I heard him ask a person with him. I plugged my left ear with my finger, while gluing my right ear even tighter to the receiver.

The guy Paddy conversed with screeched, "Tell Lincoln the problem has traveled east!"

Paddy's voice went raw. "Blessed Mother," he whispered in prayer. "Lincoln has to call me, doll. Like now, like yesterday. Oh, Jesus," he prayed again. "This is bad. Bad, bad, *bad*." The man said something else incomprehensible, and Paddy's breathing careened erratic. "I've changed my mind, Darcy," he said nervously. "I'm going to hang on."

I yawned, feigning sleep...hoping beyond hope he'd continue to unwittingly dispense information. All at once, both conversations took a turn for the worse, and more questions than answers filled the air.

"I don't know how to deep-six this thing!" Paddy screamed exasperated.

"It's too late to deep-six *anything*, Paddy! He needs to sleep with one eye open!" the other man bellowed.

"Oh, God," Paddy whispered again. "Darcy, put him on...*now*. Pull him away from her, tackle him to the ground, do it, doll. This is beyond the pale. *Beyond*," he emphasized.

The moment I opened my mouth, Alexandra let loose the biggest string of Grecian obscenities imaginable, and Lincoln cursed, "Damn."

Paddy recited part of the Rosary. "Ummm," I sputtered.

"Not possible?" he completed in a sigh. That certainly was one way to term divorce court.

Glancing over at Lincoln and Alexandra, interrupting them would be the equivalent of running into a burning building. My brain literally flipped, and what little enjoyment I had earlier was snuffed out by the mind-blowing conversation of Paddy and the other male. They gave a quick rundown of two other cases they were working besides Turkey Cardoza, and they didn't sing, "For he's a jolly, good fella," about either of them. My ears transfixed on each detail—drugs, murder, burglary—and I speculated whether Paddy's behind-the-scenes saga had anything to do with Lincoln and Alexandra's argument.

For some reason, I knew the answer was yes.

The only name I could make out time and again was "Pixie." God only knew what or whom he referred to because when I dumbly asked, "Who's Pixie," Paddy recognized I'd been eavesdropping and shut that portion of the convo down. Really, sometime soon I needed to convince my foot to stay out of my mouth.

Paddy asked the man again, "So you're sure the problem's moving?"

"It's already moved!" he barked agitated. "That's what the note said, and they want Lincoln. The person that squealed is scared beyond comprehension, and the verbiage actually sounded like a little kid."

Who wanted Lincoln? The "problem" or the "person" writing the note? I thought. I prayed the person made it to see another sunrise, but honestly, I wondered if Lincoln would. I found myself muttering, "Please, God. Let them both live" over and over again. What circumstance set Lincoln off in the first place? Paddy wanted a female to do something Lincoln objected to. What on God's green, unholy Earth could it be? Could she be the female informant in the Cardoza case?

My eyes bounced back to Lincoln and Alexandra as a barstool screeched across the tile, careened by Lincoln's PO'd foot. Alexandra clutched her long, red robe tightly to her chest, as if attempting to shield herself from what they were debating. Lincoln had both hands on her shoulders, his posture hunched over and in jeopardy by a back that looked like it couldn't carry one more thing.

Then it was like the lights went out on their conversation altogether. They were in a vacuum. I read his lips, "I'll take care of it, Lex. I love you, and I promise I'll take care of it."

When Alexandra's voice rose to an even mightier volume, Lincoln's agitation returned like a stubborn cold. "I have absolutely *no idea*, Alexandra!" he bellowed.

Alexandra spouted more Greek mumbo-jumbo, and Lincoln threw up both of his hands, rambling he needed Jackal to decode. He marched swiftly past me down the two hundred yard trek to his son's bedroom, stopped to shake his head, glanced at the cell phone in my hand, and turned on his heels to battle with Alexandra once more.

The aberrant nature of their argument alone was disconcerting.

Since I'd known them, they'd always been loving and a hot-chocolate-by-the-fire kind of cozy. Right then, she acted like she wanted to take his LA-issued gun and bullet-hole his butt. The word that came out of her mouth next left Lincoln's blood pumping at hyper speed—a word that brought a cold brush of dread with it. "P-PPixe," she stuttered. "PP-Pixie."

After one long blink to register the word, Lincoln's pallor faded to a ghostly white. He took off in a dead run for his son's room, leaving a sobbing Alexandra in his wake.

—————

"Hey, it's me."

Oh, boy, Kyd's timing resembled a hemorrhoidectomy. The time would never be right even though circumstances told you the process was inevitable.

"Hey, Kyd," I mumbled.

"Listen, I've missed you, and I need to speak with Dylan. We need to clear the air. I don't like the way we left things."

Wow. Wow. Wow. That insinuated they'd already had a conversation. "Have you already spoken with him," I asked, "and furthermore, you're still living?"

Kyd choked on a laugh. "No. He sort of throws off anger even from across the street. And frankly, I deserve it. I've already apologized to Mister Taylor, and the fact Dylan didn't contact me lets me know he's doing that for you. But the way I know him, he has to be dying inside."

I unzipped my cosmetics bag and tripled the eyeliner, swiped my lashes with kohl-black mascara, rolling on a healthy coat of Don't Tell Mom. I suspicioned Kyd had spoken with Colton, which honestly piled on the guilt. I shouldn't have placed him in that situation, but when I went after big game (and you had a gun), you were either hunting with me or I'd take your weapon.

I groaned, "Can we do this tomorrow?"

Kyd went bullheaded. "I'd rather do it today."

Some dead space filled the air as I made another circle around my eyes, making them raccoon and smoky dark. If I didn't turn our conversation off, there was a good chance he'd walk across the street. "Now's not a good time," I exhaled.

"I don't care. I really need to apologize to him. It's bothering me."

"Would you like me to quote that verbatim or paraphrase in a way which doesn't make you sound like you have boobs?" I smirked.

I actually stopped to stare at myself in the mirror...that was pretty darn funny. I was officially the funniest person I knew. I preened like a freaking peacock.

"My God, Darcy, quit joking," he said sighing. Silence. "For someone that's easy going and perpetually happy, Dylan can flip very quickly into dark, brooding, and unbearably tormented. Why would you say that is?" When I didn't respond, he added quietly, "I think whatever you are sets his world in motion."

I burst into giggles. "What are you, the love doctor?"

Kyd sounded tired, or perhaps tired of me. "Exactly what are you to one another, Legs? And if I legitimately take you on a date, will he and I still be able to be friends?"

I stopped dead in my tracks. I didn't know what we were. Lincoln and Alexandra's argument bothered me so much I snuck into Dylan's room at five a.m., asking for his take on the tension. I even mentioned my suspicions about the person named Pixie. He'd murmured, *It's probably something to do with Willow, sweetheart*. He then ran his fingers through my hair, said *Mmmm, you smell good*, and kissed me on the mouth. Kissed. Me. *Kissed me*, I said. And it didn't qualify as a peck either. We're talking a good sixty seconds of Holy. Crap. That's Awesome. I even moved my lips a few times and lightly touched his cheeks, crossing my fingers my technique wasn't repulsive. Right at the moment it started to get interesting, he moaned into my mouth and rolled back over. I sat there massaging my lips... toes curling...dumbstruck. In fact, I had to crawl out of the room on all fours because my legs wouldn't work.

Dylan had never full on kissed me before, and I honest to God think he was dreaming. He'd come close to my lips one other time when he kissed me on his return spring break trip from Maui. I'd concluded something strange blew in the air that day, or maybe he'd been hungry.

"You act like it would bother you if the two of you weren't

friends," I said. "I'm not trying to be confrontational, but you goad him, Kyd. And honestly, that bothers me. I love him and am loyal to him. One nation, under God, indivisible, and all of that other Pledge of Allegiance stuff. Don't ever forget that."

I'd needed to say that for some time, and frankly, you could only make peace for so long before you had to draw the battle lines. Dylan and I would *always* be on the same side no matter what fate or circumstances lined up against us.

Kyd slowly exhaled. "I'm very aware of your relationship, and not all of our conversations have been contentious. Dylan's extremely easy to talk to with very little, if any, judgment." He went silent for a beat. "What's going to happen when you date someone?"

Nothing good, I guess. Dylan had always been take-no-prisoners where I was concerned. Me dating? Kyd's legs would be stumped at the knees with his ribcage as bookends. Did I hold that against Dylan? Not in the slightest. I'd already planned to gut his girlfriend. Regardless, should I even take Kyd seriously? He gave me the impression he over-thought things, possibly dealt with anal retention, and misplaced altruistic love. Then again, call me a happy verb. I didn't pause to think about anything more than if dessert came before my meal or afterward.

I lined my lips once more. "Umm, our relationship is what it's always been." Confusing. "And dating is a gray area we're working out as we go."

Kyd and I disconnected after I swore that I'd call as soon as the sun woke up. A minute later, I thumbed in Troy's digits and left a message for him to be at Cowboys at midnight. Right when I shimmied into a white sundress, Sydney entered the restroom waving a black lace push-up bra along with a red and black plaid cropped top...and when I say cropped, I mean right below the habaneros. It felt like someone took a baseball bat to my forehead. The length fell roughly six inches but frankly wasn't as eye widening as the accompanying twelve-inch frayed jean skirt. First impression? Hoochie momma in the making.

After she excused herself, I dressed and shoved my feet inside red cowboy boots that hit me lower calf, giving my hair another squirt of freeze spray for a retro style of big hair. When I clomped into the den, Sydney stopped chomping her gum, instantly overcome with the brilliance of her creation. Tweaking my appearance, she unbuttoned the top two buttons to where the lace peeked through—like come and get my Barely-Bs.

Zander sauntered by, earbuds blasting a tune, crunching down a bag of Cheetos that littered across his bare chest. "Sweet," he said grinning.

"Slut," Sydney purred.

"Shiii-," Dylan mumbled.

Colton delivered a well-made slap to the back of his son's head.

Lincoln barked out a warning for Dylan to get with the program. A muscle ticced in Dylan's cheek. From top-to-bottom I looked easy. Dylan aimed for hard-to-get. I cradled his face in my hands, almost as if a precursor to some major lip action. He clasped his hands over mine, holding them tightly in place. "I should be the least of your worries, Grandpa. Vamp it up, Buffy," he said and winked. "Play the part."

Frankly, I didn't know what a Buffy entailed, but my guess was it included that lights-are-on, but-no-one's-home thing going on in my eyes.

On the couch in front of us sat my houndstooth bucket hat and a black suede Stetson. Dylan chose my lucky hat, dusting off imaginary dust, placing it on my head like I'd break if he shoved too hard. His mother and grandmother stood ramrod straight in the kitchen by the doorway. Alexandra looked guilty of killing something. Susan gave a tight smile like she'd skinned it.

Not one of my smarter moves, I dispensed a pinky wave and hotfooted it to Colton's Bentley.

Lincoln and Colton were loading an arsenal for a foxhole of soldiers into his car. Lincoln carried his GLOCK, Jackal, in the left side of his pants. While he handed a GLOCK 23 to Colton (who had a concealed carry in several states), he hiked up his khakis and strapped a .38 Smith & Wesson to his right ankle as Colton placed a .223 rifle next to a 12-gauge shotgun, slamming the trunk lid shut.

"Locked, loaded, and gunning for bear," he told his father. Colton appeared different than I'd ever seen him. Over the years, I'd called him "Door Number Three" because a sales job was the last thing he'd wanted to do. Other than keeping tabs on his sister, he basically chose the career because he couldn't stomach sitting behind a desk all day. "Door Number Two"—a police officer—obviously still ignited a passion in his blood.

"Which one's mine?" I asked giggling.

"Ha-ha," he said humorless.

When I named the gun brands, he raised a smirking brow. "And you know that how?" he murmured.

"I'm a Walker...Kentucky DNA...trust me, I know."

"Oh, God," Dylan prayed again, running both hands through his hair. His father cast a downturned look in his direction, debated a thought, and let it slide.

"I need to make another call to your father," Colton said to me. Colton and Lincoln both made several calls to Murphy, reminding him he had veto-power at any time. Murphy contemplated it a few hours earlier but spent most of the conversation apologizing that I was...well, Darcy.

Dylan bent over and cracked his back, stood aright, and rolled his neck. He'd dressed in typical Florida fashion with a white golf shirt and khaki shorts, sporting light gray Under Armour sneakers I'd never seen before. He should be happy-go-lucky at his age. Instead, he looked like he'd rather share a meal with maggots.

Lincoln let his eyes roam up and down his grandson's body with a grin. "I'll take care of her, son."

Dylan gave a somber nod as Lincoln dispatched details he'd hammered out with Detective Battle. Since it was Battle's home turf, he'd be calling the shots from a van in the parking lot after he planted a receiver underneath my blouse, inserting an earpiece in my right ear. Several plainclothes officers would be rocking away with us on the floor. Dylan would accompany me in—his father and grandfather? Didn't have a clue what they were doing.

I didn't ask...they sure as heck didn't tell.

Lincoln retrieved Jackal out from under his loose fitting white oxford, checking the magazine before slipping it back inside his gun with a click. "Get close to him, dear," he murmured. "Find a weak spot and push. Do you understand?" The gist of the assignment pretty much meant body-to-body. I got it, and the goal was to not gack all over him.

Chapter Twenty-Nine

WHAT'S IN A NAME?

Thursday night brought out the serious dancers at Cowboys. It was Ladies' Night, and patrons were bumping and grinding and doing things so obscenely animalistic it looked like something straight off the Discovery Channel. As we pushed through the crowd, whatever apprehension Dylan felt earlier dissipated with each blare of the dance mix. His shoulders bobbed, which in turn helped me to soak up the party mood. As he reached for my hand, I squeezed his last three fingers, and for some insane reason leaned forward to feel what all the fuss was about.

The moment I molded myself to his body...all bets were off.

I forgot my name, my address, even what I'd had for breakfast. I couldn't form a complete coherent thought. Dylan was jaw-dropping man candy...a cruel punctuation mark to a girl who felt nothing but average (or close).

I could do one of two things: back off to a respectable distance or hold on for dear life. Without another thought, I inched myself so close that one step more would've practically had me in front.

Dylan immediately sensed my mood had changed. He murmured, "Are you okay, sweetheart?"

All I thought was, *Mother may I*. "She'd say no," I mumbled. "No matter how much I'd beg, I can assure you she'd say 'no, you're a bad girl, and lay off the shama lama, ding-dong.'"

"...What?"

"I now understand," I croaked with despair. Burying the side of my face into his shoulders, I swallowed down the realization.

Our relationship was doomed.

He angled his right ear toward me. "I didn't hear you, sweetheart."

"N-*n-nothing*."

"Just a little further, Darc," he encouraged, squeezing my hand reassuringly. "Almost there."

A quick scan of the crowd netted a few hundred people in attendance, ranging from high school age to early twenties, with a good number of middle-aged has-beens intermixed throughout the several thousand square foot space. The ceiling stood high, and the dark ambiance painted a seriously sexy atmosphere that burned even brighter on the shiny hardwood floor. Pub tables were scattered all over the joint with short skirts and high heel and cowboy boot legs, ripe for the taking.

Then there was me: the hoochie momma.

I certainly got some looks, but I imagined myself as Buffy and tried to look even dumber than normal. I did your basic bar stuff. I checked out the DJ, the servers, the patrons—trying to act nonchalant—yet the universe had the unspoken rule that a girl's eyes fell on the best looking guy around...no matter what the distractions. An invisible spotlight bounced off a group of attractive females, canoodling around one lucky guy during the "Harlem Shake." When the crowd parted, it showed—big gasp!—a smiling Kyd Knoblecker.

Well, well, well, I said to myself. *No Mary...probably why he's smiling.*

I nervously tugged on Dylan's hand. "Do you see—"

Dylan inhaled, exhaling deeper. "Yes, go on with the evening as planned. I'll intercept if need be."

In khaki shorts, designer loafers, and a white shirt unbuttoned to his chest, Kyd schmoozed and gesticulated wildly. He had that captain of the sport's team persona in every pronounced movement. Unless my best friend stepped onto the scene, then Dylan Taylor outranked him.

Like piranhas on thrashing legs, the quartet of girls shifted their attention to Dylan as soon as we hit the dance floor. Once they shoved their eyes back in their heads, they narrowed their stare, perusing me—homing in on my hair, my boots, and my clothing to detect a weakness. They only stopped when Dylan strutted around, placing both hands on my hips with a territorial grin. "Harlem Shake" didn't call for him to be in my personal space, but Dylan decided to improvise...his "Harlem" right up against mine.

Devastated...all four were devastated with his actions. I couldn't blame them. Right then, I sported slutitude. Even *I* knew slutitude would always win.

"Show me what you've got," he flirted, pulling me closer.

I could dance. Okay, really dance. We line-danced for a while. Then I bumped hips with someone in a yellow chicken suit, while passing a naked blow-up doll over my head that was crowd surfing. Once the song ended, the music transitioned into Blake Shelton's "Footloose." Throwing both arms around Dylan's neck, I foxed one knee between his and pitched a taunting smile in Kyd's direction.

Kyd ran a hand through his thick hair, took one look at my lack of clothing, blinked hard twice, and then mouthed, "We need to talk."

"Later," I mouthed back. He twisted the white shell choker around his neck, seconds from snapping it in two. I didn't plan on giving Kyd anything, but I couldn't deny the head rush for someone to find me attractive. Or, in that case—easy.

After three more tunes, the groove wound down and Dylan drew me into his arms during Hunter Hayes's "Wanted." Still no sign of Elmer, and the clock ticked at twelve-thirty.

"He's going to stand me up," I whispered in Dylan's ear, my tongue licking off the rest of my lipstick.

"Shhh, it's a good sign. Something must be going down."

Dylan splayed his large hand across my bare lower back—and all rational thought went into Code Blue. It practically waylaid me into forgetting why we came. I loved Dylan, and being close to him—in that setting—didn't do anything good for my overactive hormonal imagination. It happened to be a prime example of all of those confusing feelings between us. Dylan was the best friend. I was supposed to think he had cooties. But for some reason, the first thought to materialize in my mind was our kiss.

Real or not real, that kiss packed some major G-force...and I wanted a repeat.

I boldly looked up, staring into his lips. "I can't think when you do that," I whispered. "It actually feels good."

"Sweetheart, do you want to kiss me?" he flirted in a giggle.

"No!" *Maybe*, I thought. My eyes went wide, issuing a firm (I think) denial.

"Well, you're standing extremely close to someone that's only your best friend."

Dylan's chuckle reverberated so low my insides turned into mush. Against my better wishes, I sidled even closer, moving my hands slowly down the planes of his shoulders, resting on the hard curves of his deltoid muscles...gripping them. It hit me then that my body said one thing while my mouth said another. I growled through bared teeth, "I'm on the job. Aren't you supposed to stand close when you're slow dancing on the job? I can't help it that I have a standard of excellence."

"Mmm," he murmured in my ear. "I'm all about excellence."

We were clustered together like sardines, swaying and gyrating in synchronicity. Whoever said you could have too much of a good thing, obviously hadn't danced with Dylan. As I played the part, it became crystal clear I wasn't actually playing. Being intimate with him came as easy as breathing. I didn't ever want to share him but had a sick feeling the day would come too soon.

Dylan dropped a soft kiss on my forehead and moved around behind me, one arm circled around my waist. After some really dirty dancing, I thread my arms back to lock around his head...except it wasn't Dylan...I felt a permed mullet. A quick and panicked pivot to my right showed me boogieing down with Elmer Herschel.

God. Help. Me. Not. To. Laugh.

Elmer had dressed in a tuxedo shirt, black bow tie, wearing too short tuxedo pants and patent leather shoes with white tube socks. Totally fitting, since watching him dance was like seeing a crippled penguin do the jitterbug. He bounced and flapped all over the place. I didn't know whether to laugh or take a drug for motion sickness.

"What's shakin', Buffy?" he said. A whole lot of penguin.

"You can really bust a move, Elmer," I bragged. I didn't want to bumble through things. Still, I almost tossed my cookies and evacuated my bowels. Elmer's aftershave mixed with his body odor suggested he was way past the sell-by-date.

Take a deep breath, Darcy, I told myself. *Take a deep breath and act like you've been here before.*

I gave him a relieved smile, mixed with a little bit of a pout. "I was afraid you'd forgotten about me," I pouted.

"Nah," he said. "Elmer had something come up."

So far, so good, I heard Detective Battle say.

———

Cowboys had a big, black mechanical bull—a new attraction Dylan had heard about through his Orlando-based grapevine. Guys and girls took turns bucking to and fro like fools. It didn't look particularly scary. In truth, it seemed rather fun until Elmer decided, "Buffy needs to take a ride."

Holy. Bull. Gods.

I had no idea how to ride a freaking bull.

If you asked me how I'd come to sit on the bull, I'd say it was Divine Intervention because next thing I knew, I was sitting in a pit as a man in jeans and a cowboy hat flipped the start button. My hands sweat like a greasy pig as I gripped the reins and tentatively slid my boots inside the leather stirrups. At first, it was a piece of cake. The bull rocked slowly back and forth, but the moment I adjusted to the movement, the vibration began sending shock waves to my face. Vibrate. Pitch forward. Pulsate again. Pitch backward. I flopped around like a fish out of water, but when the crowd erupted into cheers, my inner-attention-getter threw her left arm in the air and YOLO'd it up.

Right on cue, "Save a Horse, Ride a Cowboy" hit the airwaves, and the group grew even rowdier. I bucked. Rolled. Whipped my hair back and forth in a 360-degree circle. I looked like a freaking superstar. When I erroneously grinned at the operator, he took it as confirmation to give me the full rodeo treatment. Before I could scream, "No," he activated the buck-and-spin speed, and the shaking intensified. Starting at my butt bone, it traveled the length of my spine and stopped at the base of my chin, then unexpectedly dropped down to my girl parts. I moaned like a porn star—well, what I thought a porn star might sound like—but my guess was it was more like a wildebeest. My jean skirt rode up to the hoochie zone, and my Barely-Bs practically bounced up and hit me in the face.

Somewhere in the crowd, my eyes found Elmer who was jumping up and down like a kid at the candy store. I wondered if I broke a record for staying on the longest, but the moment I got cocky, the bull bucked me into the air, and I landed facedown onto the padded flooring.

My skirt was above my waist.

My panties were...exposed.

I didn't sign on for that.

And I really didn't sign on to watch Dylan receive a lap dance from head-over-high-heels-in-lust Yankee Knoblecker. The moment Elmer pulled me back to the dance floor, I spotted Dylan about forty feet away dirty dancing—no, let me clarify, *filthy* dancing—with Yankee. Wearing a skin-tight, white stretchy dress, her hands snaked deep down into his back pockets, his arms resting on her shoulders. Yankee stood vastly shorter than Dylan, and her batting blue eyes stared up into his face like he held the answers to all of life's problems.

Best case scenario? He was vying for a Golden Globe. Worst case? I'd perform hip and groin removal surgery later.

Trying to regulate my breathing, I recalled Elmer's and my last exchange before he forced the mechanical bull on me. He claimed he'd been late because something came up...what was the something?

I blurted, "Elmer, was the 'something' that came up your girlfriend?"

Elmer ignored the question, doing a full-spin. "I like to dance, Buffy." Even though the tempo had slowed, Elmer square danced. He hooked his arm in mine, and I morphed into his robotic version. Luckily, I'd been trained in the genre. Although, my father had a radically conservative bent, on the days the stress became too much, he'd blast the stereo and dance until exhausted. Thing was, Murphy had complete body control and could go boneless on command. Elmer was in full-blown rigor mortis and needed a coffin.

The giggles and guffaws verified we looked like idiots.

Three songs later, my creativity suddenly went AWOL. I twined my fingers through his hairy stubs and took the party to a vacant two-seat bistro. After we were situated, Elmer dunked his stubby fingers in the wooden nut bowl and proceeded to shove peanuts one-by-one inside my closed mouth. I didn't consider myself a germaphobe, but everyone knew you shouldn't eat nuts in a bar. I smiled, reluctantly gulping them down. Picking up another, he left his finger resting on my lower lip.

Find a weakness and push, I told myself. Once I thought about it, my tactic wasn't complex. Elmer was a lunkhead. His involvement—whether with Gertrude, Polly, or even Lola—no doubt, meant errand boy.

Choking it down, I leaned over and gently placed my hand on his knee. "You're a catch, Elmer."

"You understand me," he grumbled.

Tell him you do, Detective Battle coached in my ear.

"Yes," I swore, and as much as I hated to do it, I let my fingers swim in the bowl of nuts, grabbing a fingerful to feed him. "Doesn't your girlfriend?"

"She don't get me," he muttered.

"I'm sorry. Well, how's your social life? Do you get out much?"

"The world doesn't see enough of Elmer Herschel."

"Why's that?"

He grunted loud, "I babysit my woman's kid."

The verb in me started itching as I dumped the nuts onto the table, lining them up from biggest to smallest. "Boy or girl? I have a six-year-old little sister."

Elmer crossed his leg over his knee, repositioning his tube socks. "Boy," he answered in a frown. "He's a five-year-old little brat."

"My sister can be a handful too," I said.

Elmer flashed an impressive bucktoothed grin. "You look good tonight. My woman always looks good."

"Your girlfriend? What does she look like?"

"Good," he repeated.

"What's her name?" I asked, hoping he'd let it slip.

"We have nicknames."

"Oh, yeah? What are they?"

"That's a secret, Buffy. Elmer wants to hold you." I didn't want to sit on Elmer's lap, but a sting meant I'd pretty much signed on for anything.

When I'd halfway scooted onto his lap, he surprised me by turning the tables and crawling onto mine. My lap collapsed in protest but surprisingly held up the weight. "What does her little boy look like?" I choked out.

"Your normal little boy except this one's too smart."

The conversation felt like an exercise in futility. I glanced around for Dylan, merely to get a nod of encouragement, but he appeared too busy dipping Yankee to the ground amidst a quintet of girls waiting their turns. I frowned to myself. Wow, we needed to have a talk, but that was so totally on the backburner.

Keep it rolling, I heard in my ear. "Comfy?" I asked.

"Are you going to tell Elmer why you came to the Saturday night game? We saw you there. And why were you at our apartment building?"

If I was crossing the street, let's just say a cab nailed me.

I would've sworn he hadn't recognized me. With my heart beating louder than the music, I decided to be *unbelievably* and perhaps *stupidly* blunt.

"What's the name of the little boy, Elmer?" I whispered.

He hesitated, as his body grew stiffer. "I don't know what you're talking about."

"Yes, you do," I said. "Somebody's making you keep him. You took him. You framed the grandparents by putting that dye in their home and scared them into thinking you'd throw their daughter in jail. Here's what I think happened. I think the woman at The Gap told you about someone seeing Cisco. That made you scared, so in case a cop produced a search warrant to scour the Medinas' place, you thought you'd be one step ahead with the hair dye." *Be careful*, I heard Battle growl.

"Why would I do that?"

"You knew about Lola's identity as Lynx, and for some reason, you wanted to keep her services as a card counter. What better way to do that than to threaten her little boy?"

"If the grandparents were innocent, why would they run?" Elmer asked slyly.

"Perhaps they were more afraid of standing still."

In one blink, Elmer morphed from boneheaded errand boy, to cold, calculating, and not-to-be-messed with felon. "Buffy has a very active imagination," he warned.

Somehow, I kept my voice even-keel. "If it isn't true, then why did you agree to meet me?"

"Elmer was curious. Plus, Elmer's an exceptional dancer."

I didn't know what to do next. I practically had a confession, but to close the book on the case, I needed a name. "Is Cisco okay?"

"That's not his name no more," he muttered. "We changed it."

Sweet mercy. Whoa. Wow. Sonovagun.

Detective Battle gasped in my ear. *We've got him!* he shouted. *Get his location, and give me her name.*

"Who does Lola play for, Elmer?" I pushed. "Who's X?"

Elmer buried his face in my neck, tightening his arms like a child not wanting to let go. "Elmer doesn't want to answer that."

"Does your girlfriend hold you?" I asked, trying another angle.

"Not a lot. I think she's using Elmer."

"But you love her?" I whispered. Elmer nodded. I honestly think I was conversing with multiple people the way he eased in and out of first and third person speech. "You're in love with a woman who makes you do things you don't necessarily want to do."

He jumped to another personality, his voice dripping with cynicism. "Nah, Elmer doesn't care to do them. We just wanted to know what Buffy knows."

Even though he was a flaming fruitcake, I was guardedly optimistic I could close the deal. My gut said to keep up the surrogate mommy routine. As Elmer nestled in tighter, a tentative yet determined hand latched onto my shoulder. I glanced back into the eyes of a confused, agitated, and totally abhorred Kyd. By the expression on his face, he was one sentence away from blowing the lid off of everything.

Bloody hell...

"Hey," he murmured, frowning and jerking his head toward Elmer. "Who's the date?" Kyd yanked Elmer off of my lap, holding him down in his seat, one hand angrily glued to his shoulder.

"This is Elmer," I explained. *Keep Elmer talking*, Detective Battle warned in my ear.

"Elmer," Kyd repeated, suspiciously eyeing him. "Does Taylor know about Elmer?"

We both immediately scanned the dance floor and spotted Dylan savagely fighting his way through a crowd that was within inches of fire code violation. He didn't just fight the crowd. It was like Moses parting the Red Sea and then smiling when the bad guys drowned. A glance behind him, leaning up against the bar, unveiled a smiling Grizzly chatting up a brunette. *Say what??* I might as well have seen a geyser in the Sahara Desert. I didn't do anything for a beat. No breaths in. No breaths out. Just stood there and realized I was totally out of my league. The girl accompanying him was string bean skinny and model-tall. Bubbly. Trendy. Wearing a smile that promised dumber-than-dirt. Detective Battle was dead-on. The girl looked right around my age. If Gertrude still held the title of Grizzly's significant other, trouble definitely brewed in Botox paradise.

Right then, a man eased out of the shadows, tapping Grizzly on the shoulder. Like Grizzly, his build was stalwart, and he'd dressed in lightweight khaki pants and a short-sleeved silk shirt. His white hair was shorn short, everything tailored to perfection, but a voice in my head warned "too perfect." When Grizzly turned to face him, the man angled his face backward, briefly glancing in my direction. He wore mirrored sunglasses, so it was virtually impossible to get a read on him, but what features I could distinguish sucked me under. It's as though my body had knowledge of something my mind hadn't quite registered.

"I-I'm busy, Kyd," I stammered, my throat constricting.

Kyd pulled me out of my seat, sandwiching me between him and a profusely sweating Elmer. "I would've brought you tonight," he said tightly. "What's up?"

Insert nervous laughter. "Wh-where's Mary?" I sputtered.

"We're on a break," he answered, eyes narrowing.

Elmer stood up, his nose crammed into Kyd's chin. "Elmer's going to break your face. Get away from my woman."

Kyd laughed loudly. "Darcy's not your woman."

"Darcy?" Elmer asked confused.

She's been made! Detective Battle screamed in my ear.

If I'd had a sword, I would've fallen on it. It would've been less painful than what came next. In one heartbeat, Elmer's eyes became violent, and his voice spluttered and yowled things unidentifiable to the human ear. Next thing I knew, he went kung-fu fighter and smacked me twice in the face. My jaw stung with the force, and my vision went on whiteout, rolling like the smoke of a rapidly growing fire. I took a deep breath to fill my lungs but still felt like I'd hit a brick wall.

Kyd's eyes flashed angrily—his temper gaining speed like a tropical storm in the Gulf. He crumpled Elmer's collar in his angry fist. "You idiot! Now you've really pissed me off!"

It went downhill fast from there.

I considered myself a lover, not a fighter, but when it came to little kids, I always thought of Marjorie. Granted, she'd probably be a stripper someday, but Cisco might find the cure for the common cold or even be a televangelist. So as I swung on their behalf, Kyd cursed and punched, embracing his bad boy side. Elmer wasn't exactly what I'd call a seasoned brawler. In fact, his shortcomings were more pronounced than mine. After a bloodcurdling, girly scream, he took a swipe at Kyd but accidentally jacked the jaw of a bystander. Bystander went berserk and came at all three of us like a mixed martial arts champion. His arms and legs performed roundhouse kicks accompanied by a hand thrust under the jaw. Thankfully, Elmer received the brunt of it, but amidst the flailing arms and legs, I received a bloody lip, nuts down my bra, and a few bottles whizzed by my head.

After I mentally rewired my jaw, I watched Dylan scale two bar tables and dive into the middle of the brawl, acting on pure instinct. The unknown bystander took a swing at him, and when Dylan ducked and delivered a heavy punch to his gut, the man coughed deeply and thought better of any future altercations. He kicked at Elmer two more times, dusted off his clothes, and backed away cursing. Still itching for a fight, Dylan then tossed Kyd to the side, apparently wanting the honors of silencing Elmer himself. But I wasn't positive whom we were talking to. Elmer screamed things that sounded as though they came from multiple sources.

Dylan threw a left-handed jab, swiveled his fist around, cocking Elmer with his elbow. He landed another blow with his right hand, as Kyd warded off a bouncer who'd joined the fray. For a fraction of a dumb-butt second, I made another disastrous attempt to kick the ever lovin' crap out of Elmer. I'd like to think I looked like a prized fighter, but I was pretty sure I hit a lot of air. Elmer somehow got ahold of my ankle, and I fell backward and cracked my head on the hardwood floor.

My brain sloshed around...I actually heard it.

Somehow, I managed to stand, and out of nowhere two men broke through the group that had circled us. One yelled, "Orlando police," while the other waved a silver badge. But you know how the hecklers can be. As soon as someone lost prime viewing, they linked arms and circled in tighter. For each foot of progress they made, the good guys lost two feet of ground.

Elmer lay supine on the floor. Dylan had a knee in his chest, his massive fingers wound tightly around his throat. "My mother taught me to use my manners, Herschel, so I'm going to give you two options," he snarled. "Would you like me to crush your windpipe or snap your neck? I assure you, I can do both successfully."

Arrogance unleashed. I almost laughed. You never knew what would come out of Dylan's mouth.

Elmer jerked around as though he'd just been electrocuted. "Just exactly what did Elmer do?"

"Let him go!" one of the undercovers demanded.

We could've been attacked by a legion of blood-sucking vampires, and Dylan would've ignored the command. He squeezed tighter, and Elmer's face turned the color of ripe cranberries.

From bleary eyes, I spied Detective Battle and Dylan's father muscle through the opposite side. Detective Battle waved his badge, saying calmly, "Dylan, let him go."

"Squeeze it tighter," Kyd coaxed, turning my head around to palm the goose egg.

"Did I land any shots?" I asked excitedly. Kyd didn't answer. Instead, he looked at me like I'd listed the ingredients on a pipe bomb.

Battle laid a gentle hand on Dylan's shoulder. "Dylan," he eased even calmer.

Colton pushed past Detective Battle, horrified. "Unhand him, son! That's an order from your father!" As sophisticated as Dylan comported himself, there was a hint of savagery, unchained. He briskly shook his head, trying to resurrect the good side he'd just buried. In a one-handed jerk, Colton yanked him by the scruff of his shirt to his feet.

I gave Dylan an enthusiastic, two thumbs up.

I was a moron...

Detective Battle dragged Elmer off the floor while Dylan and Kyd destroyed him with their eyes. Let's put it this way. If looks could kill, he'd be wearing his Sunday best, lying in a pine box.

"Just exactly what did Elmer do?" he repeated to Detective Battle.

"Don't play coy with me," Detective Battle growled. "You kidnapped Cisco Medina, and now you're going to show me where he is. You have the right to remain silent..."

———————

"Troy," he said again excitedly, "Troy Brown."

Troy had a baby face with a strawberry-blond soul patch on his chin. About my height and weight, he wore khaki pants, a light blue short-sleeved button down shirt, and leather topsiders. Sort of nerdy. His face alone could've passed for a fourteen-year-old, and he struck me as the type who was one way in-person and totally opposite behind the anonymous comfort of his keyboard.

Not the normal fastard I would've guessed.

"Exactly *why* are you here again?" Detective Battle asked again. Detective Battle pulled a three-by-five spiral pad from the back pocket of his jeans. His crumpled navy T-shirt stood in stark contrast to the relief lining his face. He appeared at peace...or at least partially.

Troy likewise jotted notes in his reporter's notebook. "My source," he explained. "Her name's Jester. She called and said there'd be a big story going down. I'm new, and she wanted me to land on the front page."

Detective Battle played with the corners of his graying mustache while he raised an inquisitive brow in my direction. I gave him a dumb blonde look, mixed with a little bit of righteous indignation. Crap, he might've figured it out. "Who exactly *is* Jester?" he asked Troy. "We'd like to get her statement."

Troy shrugged an answer, deflated. "I wish I knew. I owe her a date."

As Troy scribbled down a few statements from Detective Battle, I shoved Kyd and made him second in line, stealing away to the restroom before anyone could interview me. Why I wanted to remain anonymous wasn't readily clear, but suddenly anonymity and obscurity appealed to me. Things weren't finished yet, and in my opinion, it was too early for a celebration. Cisco hadn't been reunited with his family, and in the back of my mind, I doubted if Elmer was truly capable of producing him. Plus, Elmer hadn't provided the name of X.

The identity of X was crucial.

For some reason, I thought of the line in *Romeo and Juliet* "What's in a Name?" So what meaning lay in the tattoo "moose?" And who masqueraded as the mysterious X anyway? Was she Elmer's girlfriend? And where in God's holy name did Grizzly go? Lincoln and Colton watched him enter the building and combed the area, but the fracas had slowed things down.

I popped all of my knuckles and washed my hands, staring in the mirror. Things felt anti-climactic. Too neat. Sure they could shine a light in Elmer's eyes and torture him into confession, but that seemed too easy—and likely wouldn't unearth all the answers—especially for a man who probably held more secrets than his IQ could juggle.

My cell phone belted out Milli Vanilli, and the picture that materialized was of Zander. "Is it over?" he asked as I answered.

"Sort of," I said glumly. "Zander, what makes people pick certain tattoos?" When I previously placed the tramp stamp of angel wings on my lower back, I chose it not only because it looked cool but because I liked the concept of an angel watching over me.

"Well, I assume it's because that item means something special," Zander answered, "but my guess is it means something more to the person that *sees* it than *wears* it."

Maybe a better question would've been, *Why would someone's nickname be Moose?*

I shut down the convo and pondered the thought. Ripping a paper towel from the dispenser, I wiped my hands, throwing it into the wastebasket by the door. I clicked on my iPhone and scrolled through the photos I took of Elmer's desk: utility bills and a sage-colored stationery with a visible "O-S-E." I cleared my throat, stopping dead in the thought. Oh, boy, that "O-S-E" probably represented the latter part of Moose. Why couldn't I have snagged that letter? More than likely, it held the answers. Had Lola sent it? Gertrude? Polly? Someone else altogether? The answer sat on the tip of my tongue.

What am I missing? I asked myself.

"Your head in a few minutes...just like Howie."

Chapter Thirty
SURVIVAL 101

$\mathcal{I}$ understood that I said that out loud, only after someone answered.

The lock activated on the restroom door, and I stared helplessly into the reflection of Eleanor Talley. Eleanor foamed at the mouth like a mad dog. For a woman dressed impeccably as a bank manager, her black tracksuit and running shoes were brand mismatched, and her thick brown hair looked like a porcupine's. If I were a betting girl, I'd say she was one step from the insane asylum or getting a poison dart from animal control.

Ab-SOLUTE-ly fabulous, I thought. I might've just hammered the last nail in my coffin.

"You twit!" she screamed, pointing in my face. "I'm not going to let you ruin this for me!"

"Ruin what?" I asked, feigning ignorance, because frankly I still felt ignorant. I would've laid money on Polly and practically bet my life on Gertrude. And Lola? Even though I felt semi-sorry for her, she'd never be on my Christmas card list.

On instinct, I scrambled backed toward the sink, but Eleanor took three angry steps forward, circling one hand around my neck. My hands darted up defensively, covering her wrist, but the woman's grip was like a Sasquatch. I got nowhere, and when I tried to wriggle away, she tightened all five fingers and began to squeeze. "You're Elmer's...girlfriend?" I spit out.

"Yes," she seethed. "I'm—"

"Moo?" I said, stupidly giggling. Someone needed to cut out my tongue.

"Moose!" she shouted offended. "That money is mine each week, and Elmer and Lynx help me *get* it!"

"You're X?" I verified in a cough.

"I'm your executioner." Eleanor's features went as hard as granite, her blackened eyes meaning every treacherous word. Immediately, that piece of the puzzle edged into place. Elmer must've been the man who Albert Jones sold the Porsche Turbo to, who purchased it in Eleanor's stead. And the word moose? I should've known. Dartmouth's unofficial mascot was a moose—that bit of trivia complements of Zander.

"Are you blackmailing Lola...for her services?" I wheezed.

"I call it business," she squeezed harder. "That little boy is my security deposit. Elmer found him playing by himself, and when he called me, I got an idea that was a godsend."

My guess was it didn't come from God.

Relax, Darcy, I told myself. *Stay calm. Think your way out of this*. Her squeezing my neck, however, made my eyes bug out like ping pong balls. A high heat filled my vision, and I knew my capillaries were seconds from rupturing. Cold fear gripped my heart. I was running out of time. "You were involved...before?"

Eleanor's eyes shockingly turned misty. My word, she actually cared for him. I didn't know if too many inhabitants likewise occupied her brain, or if she had one foot in cuckoo. "My tastes vary."

No dispute there. "Polly?" I asked.

"Doesn't ask many questions. Do you know how easy this happened to be?" she bragged. "People rarely check their statements with automatic withdrawal. And when you blow through the amount of money that Herbie and Gertie do monthly, one more line item means nothing. And lucky for me, neither have accountants who pay their bills."

"Plus, the trust was set up by Elmer," I gasped. "So since he was the executor, you didn't have to worry about him asking questions."

"Yes, Herbie and Gertie should've asked for monthly itemized expenditures, but they didn't." And she'd obviously capitalized on their big hearts and unequivocal faith.

Anger churned in my chest. Besides the fact she tried to make my head a PEZ dispenser, I was beginning to hate the woman. I didn't like the way hate made me feel, but Eleanor might've been worth the icky feeling. "Are you in debt? Is that why?" I said. "Or are you merely a money-grubbing skank?"

If I hadn't heard the funeral march before, I sure as heck did then. She narrowed her eyes, pressing her thumb into my larynx. "Yes," she answered to what I assumed was both.

"Where are the grandparents?" I asked, breathing roughly.

"Your guess is as good as mine."

"Cisco?"

Eleanor gave me a grin like the Joker gave young Bruce Wayne after he killed his parents in *Batman*. In that moment, I realized she wouldn't give me anything more regarding Cisco, and my only hope was that Detective Battle could find him. Eleanor squeezed tighter, and what oxygen I had left knocked on my brain, reminding me of one other unanswered question: Howie Cantrell. When the woman manhandling your neck might also be a murderer, trust me, you don't want to ask if she's a fan of decapitation. But the verb in me couldn't leave it uncovered. Only one answer made sense, and I needed to get her to say it.

"Howie found out, didn't he?" I gasped. "He found out...and planned to tell Gertrude that one of her oldest friends needed the nuthouse."

Eleanor spaced out for a second, just totally went to some other place, and if I thought I understood insanity before, I witnessed the actual flipping of the switch. Her blackened eyes went totally dead, not one glimmer of light showed in her pupils. With another squeeze, my throat constricted even more.

"Howie and I took a boat ride," she confessed emotionless. "The propeller might've gotten a little out of hand."

Of course...

As horrific as the admission sounded, I experienced an unexpected peace. I got a confession—a partial one, unfortunately—but I wasn't sure anyone would benefit from it. We were alone. In general, females went to the restroom in pairs for some girlfriend kiss-and-tell or basically to get the job done. I didn't seem to be in either phase. Plus in a place like Cowboys, idle time lessened your chances on the meat market. That left more fighting. I hoped that fortune favored the brave because Eleanor acted like one of us wouldn't leave alive.

Before I went completely out cold, I dug deep and headbutted her with the force of a mule's hind leg. She staggered backward—her arms and legs going in all directions at one time—and then she fumbled around behind her, attempting to unlock the door. Did she plan to run? I heard a loud click twice but didn't know if that signaled success or was self-deception on my part. While I sucked in as much air as I could, I still didn't have enough time to regroup before she came at me again. Lunging for my hair, she latched ahold and yanked me toward her, causing me to fall flat-backed onto the floor.

My lucky hat tumbled out to the side, landing bucket-side up. "Your hair," Eleanor said, laughing with a menace, standing overtop me. "It's green, just like Elmer said. I think we should *wash it*."

If I was fearful before, I did a complete-180 into fight-for-your-life rage. Talk about adding insult to injury. She and Elmer were giving me an inferiority complex—well, larger than I already had—but at least, I wasn't as grossly dysfunctional as they were. Elmer obviously had told her about me. Did he also tell her he'd asked me out on a date?

"You're..." I paused, "you're...mean, you're ugly, and you're an effing female dog!"

Oh, God. That was my first attempt at cursing, and it sounded like the fifth grade playground.

Eleanor pulled and bounced me along as I crab-walked backward on the floor. She kicked open a stall, full intentions of instituting a swirly. Dear, Lord. Prayers didn't come easy for me, but I didn't want my head in the toilet. Overall, the room smelled like citrus, perfume, and rainwater, but it didn't overshadow the fact that it was still a toilet that God only knew whom had relieved themselves in.

Blood pumped furiously in my veins as I kicked and pawed, making note to take a self-defense class. I shouted the word, "Ergonomics!" which totally sailed over Eleanor's head, and why wouldn't it? Who in their right mind said the word ergonomics? I never cursed, but once I typed the abbreviation WTF on a text to my friend Justice, and my autocorrect changed it to the word ergonomics. As a result, if I was pushed beyond my limit, I shouted out the word.

Clearly, a testament that I'd slipped over the edge.

Inches from the toilet, I made one last-ditch effort for freedom and lodged a heel into the corner of the metal door. Gaining some leverage, I crashed my shoulder into her knee, and the moment she staggered, I jammed backward again until she landed butt-first in the bowl. Eleanor pierced the air with a horrified scream, water splashing as she thrashed like an alligator in the death roll. Prying my heel lose, I stumbled up and curled the fingers on my right hand into a fist—knowing I should pound her face, not knowing if I had the required nerve.

Eleanor's chin looked pretty hard, manly even, and when she pushed a few inches out of the bowl, I closed my eyes and swung like a heavyweight. On impact, the flesh of my knuckles split, road-rashed like it had been scraped along the highway. Unfortunately, my punch didn't seem to faze her for more than a few seconds.

"That money and Elmer are m-*mmine!*" she stuttered, trying to stand.

Shaking out my right hand, I then hauled off and smacked her with my left. Bloody spittle flew from her mouth and drip-dropped to her chin. Before she could suck in another breath, I whacked her again, even harder.

"That's for scaring that little boy!" I screamed, launching my boot into her shin. "And that's," I said, kicking again, "for telling me I had bad hair."

She ugged a curse, sinking lower in the bowl. I had not one bit of remorse. Not one. In fact, she should count herself lucky I didn't have a gun. I slammed the door shut and eyed a padded bench sitting flush against the wall. Quickly scooting it over, I jammed it up against the door, trapping her inside. I stood there, trying to gain some perspective on what had just happened.

As Eleanor continued to founder like a beached whale, I took two cautious steps over a pool of water slowly oozing across the floor. Shaking the water from my feet, not one thing inhabited my mind other than getting the heck out of Dodge and placing Eleanor in handcuffs. Hopping over a wet roll of toilet paper, out of nowhere it felt like an asteroid knocked me over. My teeth rattled in my head. Couldn't breathe. Saw stars. Bit my tongue. Once I regained my bearings, I stooped down and picked up the sunglasses of the person I'd collided with.

My hands got sweaty.

Then turned ice-cold.

Cautiously tilting my chin upward, I stared into eyes as crystal blue as the translucent waters in Tahiti. Reality came fast and hard. I traveled back to the first day of vacation when I sat across from Lincoln, looking at a five-by-seven black and white photo of Turkey Cardoza, his trophy wife, and two envoys representing different mob families. Turkey wasn't the man in my presence though. It was one of the others. In that particular photograph, the man's profile had been highlighted, and the file clerk in my head reminded me it wasn't our first face-to-face encounter. In actuality, it was our second. He'd just spoken with Grizzly minutes earlier but was also the man who'd threatened me when I busted up the amputation-in-progress in Grizzly's building. And biggest gulp of all, the man just might be "the problem" that "traveled east," according to Paddy.

Geographically, Orlando lay to the east of Los Angeles.

That could only mean one thing: the Taylor clan had been marked.

No doubt, the situation was what Paddy tried to warn Lincoln about, but I didn't want to calculate the odds of both of these cases being related. I didn't think they were, even though circumstances suggested otherwise. Funny thing was, it seemed the death wish Dylan feared I had might be receiving a little help from evil forces. I didn't ask for things like that to happen. Somehow, they just always did.

The man appeared bigger, meaner, and more "mobby" in person. In his large right hand, he gripped my lucky hat. Slowly replacing it on my head, he forcefully poked the barrel of his pistol in my ribs, giving a quick jerk over his shoulder toward the door. Call me a genius, but I'd interpreted that as I needed to move, or I'd get real friendly with a bullet.

Eleanor barked out a line of expletives as she pushed herself out of the bowl, screaming I wasn't going to take the kid and her man. Swinging the door wide, the bench screeched across the floor as she shoved her way out. Eleanor's face blanched. Terror-stricken when she registered someone held a gun at my chest. She glanced at Blue Eyes and then to me—then back at the bathroom stall she wished she'd never exited.

Palming both hands high, her chin quivered, and she surprisingly cowered like a whipped dog. You'd think she'd sic all that crazy onto him, but she stumbled behind me, making me her human shield. Funny what fear could do. You'd find yourself hanging onto the person less threatening. Survival 101, I guess. Here Eleanor huddled next to me like we were girlfriends when moments earlier she'd had plans to drown the life out of me.

I remembered the tagline from the 1956 version of *Invasion of the Body Snatchers*..."*There was nothing to hold onto...except each other*." Wow, my options in life were a decapitation devotee or someone who rubberstamped an amputation. Neither sounded appealing, but if it was my day to die, I at least wanted to connect the dots.

"Turkey Cardoza sent you," I whispered to him. Nothing. "Are you going to kill us?"

Even more nothing. I might be stupid, but I wasn't an idiot. Situations like that didn't occur out of the blue, inside a vacuum. Wise guys liked to send messages. They weren't the ransom type. They could give a flying flip about money when they were laundering it elsewhere. If they wanted Lincoln to back off the Turkey hunt, what better way than to take something he cared about??

And the man believed I was a blood relative.

Even though I had no affinity for Eleanor, I didn't want him to shoot her. If Eleanor died, we might never get the answer to where she'd been stashing Cisco. But how could I convince him to only take *me*? Eleanor remained a witness, and I'd watched enough movies to know that an extra set of eyes weren't what criminals deemed the perfect crime. *Appeal to his sense of decency*, I told myself. It might be hard to find because the man was holding a gun to my gut.

I gazed into his eyes, trying my best to shift into a hostage negotiator. "She kidnapped a little boy and hasn't told anyone where he is yet," I said. "Don't kill her now. Let her tell the authorities where he is. You can have someone...umm...shiv her in prison."

Darcy, Darcy, Darcy, you might as well have put the weapon in his hand. The good angel sighed. *Aw, it's for a good cause,* the devil said, bursting into laughter.

No kidding, those words weren't something fifteen-year-old girls used in real life situations. Heck, your average adult didn't, but my goal was to buy the both of us some time. Granted, I'd thrown Eleanor under the bus, but if my plan worked, then at least she'd live and Cisco might be home by daybreak.

Blue Eyes lifted his gun, and for a split second, I waited for my life to flash before my eyes...it didn't. Heck, I didn't know what that meant. Maybe it meant I hadn't lived long enough, or maybe I wasn't smart enough to go to the light. After a second to debate, with an angry grimace Blue Eyes reared back and struck a shrieking Eleanor on the side of the head with the butt of his gun. She grunted twice, her tongue shot out to the side, and she sunk down my back to the floor in a broken heap.

If that represented a harbinger of things to come, I'd be on the floor next or in the trunk of his car. Blue Eyes bore his gaze into mine like a laser beam. "You make a sound," he threatened, "and I'll shoot the first person we see." The situation was so bad it seemed almost incomprehensible. I had enough bad things on my conscience. A dead body wasn't one I wanted to add to the list.

We left Eleanor lying in a pool of water as he pushed me in front of him, left hand clutching my shoulder, the other ramming his pistol into my kidney. Giving the assumption I was onboard with the plan, I knew enough to not let anyone take me away from a venue.

It empowered them and weakened you.

"Open the door," he ordered.

I wasn't positive I had the proper enthusiasm, but I hoped my inner-idiot seized the opportunity to prove me different. My hand slid through the handle, and my only line of defense was to do what I did best.

Chapter Thirty-One

2-FOR-1 SPECIAL

---

*T*alk and bargain.

Immediately, uncontrollable chatter spewed from my mouth, rolling like a tsunami in the South Pacific.

"So do you have any kids? Who do you think is going to win the World Series? Honest to God," I paused, looking over my shoulder, "do you think we'll ever go back to the moon?"

I had no forethought on my verbiage. Only that I pulled things out of my own rear end. The cords in his neck bulged, and clearly, I'd become an irritation. His voice demanded no refusal. "Shut up, and keep walking," he barked.

I didn't.

"Turkey sent you, right?" He remained tight-lipped. "Then you must be the errand boy."

"I've never been an errand boy," he said, snorting angrily.

"Oh, I'm sorry. The lapdog then."

My word, I practically begged for a bullet to the back of my head. He couldn't care less about his and Turkey's interpersonal relationship, and he answered my question with another menacing shove forward. Stepping both feet outside, the party atmosphere had been reborn, but the tension between psycho killer and me turned radioactive. When my body stiffened, he went scarecrow and stiffened even more.

Music piped loud, and what my periphery could make out, Kyd

still talked to Troy, Elmer was no doubt in the back of a squad car, and I found the thick, black crown of Dylan's head about twenty feet away. My body instantly ached, my heart yearning to yell out to him, but if Dylan chose to get medieval—you know, rip him to shreds and desecrate the body—there was a good chance his body would be swiss cheese.

I didn't want my best friend to be swiss cheese.

Blue Eyes tilted his gun toward a rear exit, as the aficionado in me smelled coffee. I drew in a deep whiff and slowed my gait. "Can I have a cup of coffee for the road?" Once again, he shoved the barrel tighter into my lower back. "I'll be in a better mood," I rationalized.

My boots shuffled three more feet ahead.

People huddled together, moving in groups like a gaggle of geese. One girl danced nervously, trying to fit in. A guy sitting at the bar next to her slouched over his drink, checking out a pair of women dancing close by. Neither appeared particularly happy, but they were alive...with plans for tomorrow. An ice-cold thought sliced through me. Dreams would be shattered if I didn't go along with his wishes.

I was here...no going back...my only choice was to let it play itself out.

My mind wandered back to the spring when the psycho student chased me with a loaded gun. In that situation, I made myself bait to save those around me, but how horrifying and mentally traumatizing it felt during the process. In retrospect, I had operated on complete and utter shock. Frozen. Moving erratically. Not even slowing down to breathe. At the moment, I knew what I'd be in for, but even if I tried things differently and yelled for assistance, Blue Eyes undoubtedly would still take me or someone else hostage.

Someone else with the potential to not make it out alive.

Ten more steps brought us to the exit sign. My eyes locked with a large, imposing man who stood only a few feet from the door. Dressed in a dark jeans and a black T-shirt with Cowboys stitched over his heart, his short, brown hair rounded out a face almost devoid of features. His upper frame looked immense, his arms barely crossing comfortably above his chest because of the bulge. If he was the bouncer, he definitely didn't possess the gift of intuition.

I shook like a leaf, but he merely glanced down at me from his more-than-six-foot frame and stepped out of the way.

My hand circled the knob as I led us out into the cool, midnight air. The temperature felt Baltic by Florida standards, and my body immediately wrinkled like a prune. The sounds of cruising cars and honking horns blared along the street. The ambience was dark and lonely and shockingly not a soul was to be found in the parking lot.

Figures.

Just Blue Eyes and me.

All alone.

I meandered through two parked cars that had pulled in haphazardly and bravely (or stupidly) spun around. "Could you at least tell me your name?" I asked.

His crystal-blue eyes spoke words I didn't know the definitions for. They blinked old, weary, and the thug quality I'd recognized earlier had surprisingly faded from view. Blue Eyes suddenly appeared as if he despised the assignment. Not the response I would've expected from a career criminal.

His shoulders sagged a fraction, even though his gun was firmly planted dead center in my abdomen. Blinking his eyes slowly, he replied, "I'm Bats Giuseppe."

"Bats Giuseppe," I repeated.

Oh, my word.

Not only was the man pictured in the surveillance photographs with Turkey Cardoza, but Giuseppe (along with Bonnano and Carlotto) happened to be written on the backs of the photographs in Lincoln's Cardoza file. Did Giuseppe shove a bomb in that man's mouth, bludgeon the other, or hang someone in a warehouse like Paddy's video documented? If he was responsible for just one of those murders, then the best I could hope for was a quick death.

I took a shaky breath. "Were you the man responsible for sending that video to Lincoln's partner two weeks ago? The video where a man had been torched and hanged, then...um...well, his head fell off?"

"Cardoza," was the emotionless answer.

"Cardoza sent it, or Cardoza was the perpetrator?"

His answer would reveal a lot. "Cardoza is sick," he muttered.

So Bats stole it, and Turkey Cardoza had a deranged and demented pastime. That video was leverage for Bats...had to be.

"Bats, I suppose you don't want anyone to know your real name either, huh?" Bats gave a slow, steady inhale and exhale. "I have a little sister," I whispered, trying to make a plea. "I always wanted a brother, but when you're raised by a single dad, that dream died years ago. I'm fifteen, almost sixteen, and I'm from Cincinnati. I've never had a boyfriend or even gone on a date. I suck at school, and I know that's probably considered a bad word, but at times it's merely the best description. I honestly have a hard time sitting still. Like I'm trying to outrun the reality that's in front of me. It hurts me that very few understand me, but it's just," I paused, "...it's just that I'd rather be doing other things, you know? Like tonight, I helped the police find a little boy...I hope so, at least. I try to..." I stopped, the tears threatening to fall. "I try to right some wrongs, I guess, because no one righted them for me. It haunts me, sir, not having a mother live with me, and I've never been good at anything except attracting trouble. I'm sure you understand that, but I'm going to give you a piece of advice. If you have plans to kill me, my father will hunt you down. And he won't be quick or humane about the way he disposes of you. So you might want to leave the country or buy a one-way ticket to Saturn, but even that might not be far enough away from his temper."

Bats stared at me as if he knew the ending to my story without even turning the next page. For what seemed like an eternity, he breathed and I breathed. A vertical line deepened between his eyes, and his lips painted into a hard, steely line. He contemplated his next move, but it was a foregone conclusion I was merely stalling.

He looked to the sky, finally saying, "I'm called Bats because I'm a loner and prefer to operate in the dark."

Okay...progress. "My real name's Darcy, and it means dark. My parents were idiots because I'm blonde. We're sort of like family." I offered a sheepish smile and said, "Would you be my honorary brother?"

I moronically demonstrated the initiation.

Just flapped my chicken wings like a dumb-butt bird.

That proposal sounded a little differently in my brain. You know, he responded, "OMG! Really?! That's awesome!" and then kicked the gravel in bashful embarrassment, and we skipped away hand-in-hand.

Bats lifted his gun to his temple, metaphorically scratching his head in question. His expression saying he thought me the stupidest human being he'd ever run across. Honestly, I agreed. My actions definitely wouldn't make my list of *Top Ten Ways To Negotiate Your Way Out of Getting Murdered* but would definitely make the gag reel.

After a few seconds of disbelief, his voice lowered once again. "Walk."

"Could you at least do me a favor?" I begged. Long pause, and it hit me like a ton of bricks I'd asked a murderer to do the right thing and follow my dying wishes. I fisted my hands at my sides and baited him, lifting a defiant chin. If he thought I'd back down, then he'd be waiting for the Devil to build a snowman in Hell. But should I even take his word? What other recourse did I have? My request meant too much to ignore without giving it a try. "Could you get word to my best friend that I love him?" I choked out. "He's Lincoln's grandson, and I just...love him."

My dying thoughts I always knew would be of my best friend. Even if we led separate lives, my heart would never cease to yearn for him and how he made me feel like the most special human being in his world. We promised one another to go through everything together, whatever that would bring. Right then, I was faced with an overwhelming guilt of leaving him in the lurch of a thing called life.

"You're brave," he muttered astonished.

Open to interpretation. "Please," I begged in a whisper, "tell my best friend. His name is Dylan."

Bats must've seen the determination in my eyes because his breath caught in his chest, and he nodded. He'd given me more than expected but less than conducive to additional conversation. Bats was definitely as dark and twisty as me, and no doubt something happened to fundamentally change who he was...or wanted to be. But the reality was, he happened to be a mean SOB with a history of killing people.

He nudged his pistol firmly into my gut. "Turn back around, Darcy, and walk to the black Benz in the second row of cars."

Inwardly, I sighed and quickly glanced around. No makeshift

weapon lay anywhere that I could attack him with. The way I saw it, this particular moment could be my final six-by-eight plot of land if I didn't do something fast. There was only one option—at least one I could think of. I briefly closed my eyes, knowing it was now or never. *Don't ever get into a car with a stranger*, I heard my father say. *Nothing good will ever come from it.*

Fudge...

My eyeballs popped out, while my sense of survival screamed, *Run for your life!* I knew enough from Murphy that if anyone ever had a gun to my back, then I needed to zigzag while running. A moving target was too hard to hit. How he knew that I wasn't sure, but he said it with such conviction, I filed it away for future use. Another lesson: If I get hit, play dead. I aimed for not getting hit, period.

Be a verb, Darcy, I told myself. *Be a verb and run your arse straight to Georgia.*

I took off for the last row of cars, running like a drunk thoroughbred.

"Stop!" he shouted.

I staggered and went down on a knee but found my balance and kept moving in a zigzag.

He bellowed another, "Stop!" while the night air suddenly rang with footfalls.

Ducking down in row four, I monkey crawled into row five and took out sideways for row six. "Don't make me shoot!" he screamed in exasperation.

"Aaah, *you* shoot, and *I'm* going to shoot," a deep and familiar voice boomed from behind.

Time stood still.

I stayed crouched, heart beating loudly in my chest, waiting for a big bang to split the atmosphere in two. When nothing but quiet stretched between us, I slowly crept my way up the back of a green Honda Accord—one hand after the other—to see who'd joined the party. Sweat dripped down my back as I peered through the rear window and guardedly stood up.

Lincoln.

Looking like a gunfighter.

Standing underneath a security light, the beam haloed over him and cast a long shadow, making him appear larger than anyone else. He held his gun tightly in his left hand, his right cupping it for steady aim.

"Well, well, well," Lincoln deadpanned, eyes narrowed on the target. "Looks like I've bagged the 2-for-1 special."

Bats immediately stopped running, casting a look of apology in my direction, pivoting around practically looking euphoric. Say what?? Lincoln likewise sported a face of satisfaction. Where his face was hardened before—scrutinizing Bats's actions—now it appeared more receptive, curious to see what Bats had to offer.

"You got my message, I presume," Lincoln murmured.

Right when I almost suggested we just hug it out, a man appeared from thin air, weapon drawn, and pointed at Giuseppe's temple. He stood around six feet tall with orangey-red hair, ruddy features, dressed in commando black. "Look what the divil delivered," he grunted in an Irish brogue...*Paddy*? "Hawareya, Bats? I'd extend my hand, but you can see the pickle we're in."

Two more men materialized from behind rows one and two: dark clothing, black ballcaps, and hulking frames, with faces expressionless to the point of being robotic. Knowing Lincoln, these guys probably weren't even Florida's finest. They either took the red-eye from out West or were men who did a job and were in-and-out, no questions asked.

Both crouched low to the ground, forming a tight square around Bats. We stood in an isolated perimeter, but my intuition told me more backup existed outside its boundaries.

"I know you're out there," Lincoln murmured, and by the gentle tone in his voice, I knew he was addressing me. "Battle found him, dear. Cisco was at her house. He's fine, but I need you to allow me to take care of business."

The words took awhile to sink in. It's as though they smacked me right in the ears and refused to do anything until I understood the depths of their meaning. The "fat lady" just sang. Cisco's alive. *Alive!* I rejoiced. The insomnia, nightmares, lectures, and near brushes with death were all suddenly worth it. The instances where people told me to conform—prayed I'd conform—didn't sting quite as much anymore. My ADHD mind locked onto a target and proved to the world it had been a blessing and not a curse. I wanted a day. Five days. Weeks to celebrate and do the I-told-you-so, but I had to deal with Bats Giuseppe. If that added twist went into the death spiral, then at least I'd die with a smile on my face.

I stayed put as Lincoln suggested and knew enough to not add another variable to the mix.

Darcy Walker, beacon of discretion.

Paddy removed the gun from Bats's hand, kicking it toward Lincoln. "Circle on in here, boys," he said, chuckling sarcastically. "Now we're just one big happy family."

Lincoln picked up the gun and stalked forward, one deliberate step at a time, smooth and calculating as a cougar ready to strike. "This wasn't exactly the terms of our meeting, Giuseppe."

Terms of their meeting? What the...?

"Well, they weren't exactly my terms either," Bats protested. "If you're going to offer me protection, I had to make sure you weren't selling me out. You were talking to Grizzly not thirty minutes earlier, and that man would sell out his own mother. What business do you have with him? That's what threw me, man."

Piecing that conversation together, Bats must be the man Paddy had been talking to who wouldn't take the deal they'd offered—the man Paddy claimed had made all kinds of weird demands. As for Bats wondering why Grizzly was in attendance? The obvious conclusion was simple: the right hand didn't know what the left was doing. And as far as Grizzly even being at Cowboys? The explanation could be mere coincidence, or more than likely Grizzly got word of the shakedown of Eleanor. Would Battle have told him? Maybe. Or maybe Eleanor ran her mouth that the proverbial walls were closing in. All I knew was Grizzly was a man with a very broad reach since Bats Giuseppe had been in his OBT building in the first place. Question was, was that little amputation done on Grizzly's behalf? I was inclined to believe that it had been. And it wouldn't surprise me if Grizzly had been harboring Bats until Bats had the perfect opportunity to take Lincoln out. A favor Grizzly owed the LA mob, perhaps? Whatever the case, it was obvious that Bats had worked a deal with Lincoln behind everyone's back.

Lincoln's face went cold, bordering heartless, and I knew he contemplated blasting him on the term sell-out.

"My business with Grizzly was a different kind of business that involved another leech on society's ass. Paddy, however, was here solely to help me find *you*, Bats. So imagine my surprise when he calls me that he's tailing you, and you then wind up here. Then you go and kidnap someone who belongs to me, and now I've got to pay the redhead overtime. You were sent here to take me out by order of Turkey, right?" Bats didn't dispute it. "God, I love it when I'm one step ahead," Lincoln murmured, laughing hollowly.

"Why contact me and not Weasel?" Bats asked.

More than likely Weasel was the other man seated with Turkey in that surveillance photograph.

"I refuse to do business with Weasel Bonnano," Paddy said, snorting loudly. "Anyone with a forename of Weasel doesn't exactly give me the warm fuzzies. Besides, he smells like he made love to a tobacco plant."

"Give me her name," Lincoln demanded.

Bats said nothing. Paddy must've delivered unexpected pain because Bats released a sharp yelp that I felt in my bones. "You know, Bats," Paddy muttered, "my daddy said to beware of the anger of a patient man, and now I'm angry. I flew out here and lost three hours that I'd planned to spend with Mickey Mouse. You'd better answer, or I'm going to show you on a scale of one-to-eat-some-lead how angry I am."

"Give me her name," Lincoln ordered again.

Immediately, I knew he referred to Pixie. Pixie (who I'd bet my sorry big, white arse) had somehow contacted Alexandra Taylor. Bats's voice shook like a glass of water during an earthquake. "Nn-o one knows," he promised. "I swear it. I don't hurt females anyway."

"Another reason we picked you," Paddy said, snorting sarcastically. "Who woulda thought this Irishman would find a wise guy with some scruples?"

Lincoln rolled his neck, once again with a command. "Turn around."

Why?

Was an execution next?

Paddy and the others escorted Bats into a darkened portion of the property, past all cars, around a group of swaying trees. As soon as traffic sounds picked up, Lincoln steadily raised his gun and took aim. Before I could swallow, three *psss-psss-psss* sounds ricocheted the night air, followed by a loud whelp as Bats staggered to the pavement. Bats immediately slammed a palm over the wound, trying not to writhe. Lincoln had popped a cap in his left buttocks while a continuous hiss deflated the back tires of a nearby Aston Martin.

Sweet God in Heaven, he'd just sent Grizzly a message.

Lincoln shoved his gun into the back of his pants as Paddy and the two men grabbed Bats by the shoulders, dragging him to a black SUV. Although he'd been momentarily incapacitated, I didn't feel Bats would've objected if he could've gone on his own accord. Bats wanted what they'd offered—I saw it in his face—more than the pay-off of pain.

Once Lincoln told them to, "Make things look believable," they shoved him inside.

"The girl," Bats moaned loudly. "Darcy...is she all right?"

Employing an unnatural speed, Lincoln lunged through the open door so fast it was barely visible to the naked eye. Next thing I knew, Bats screamed in raw agony, futilely thrashing around until his mouth was muzzled. Maybe it was one of those ignorance-is-bliss situations.

I tasted the coffee I never had, turned, and promptly threw up.

Chapter Thirty-Two

OUT OF SIGHT, OUT OF MIND

I placed both hands on Colton's shoulders and steered him back toward his room.

I'd met him in the hallway, dressed from the waist down, with his briefcase in his hand and a ballcap on his head. He said he was batting cleanup while constructing a memo on counterterrorism to the State Department. Heaven knew what that meant, but I wished him good luck and smacked him in the rear.

Stupid...I was STOOPID.

The man's mind floated off to the great beyond after two weeks of chaos with me. I'd say I was sorry, but I knew he'd never remember, and I'd always felt those after-the-fact sorrys didn't mean a whole lot anyway. Sorrys were for accidents, not things so premeditated even a temporary insanity defense was useless.

After I lied to myself that there were no lasting effects of the trauma, I slowly tiptoed down the darkened hall to my own personal heater. Wearing boxer shorts, Dylan's discarded shirt, and tube socks in honor of Elmer, I hoisted myself onto the bottom of the bed, crawling up the silk sheets to the free pillow. Dylan smelled extra yummy, like a cream puff bar that'd made a baby with a marshmallow.

"Psst," I whispered, "you smell good. Normally, you smell like dirt, but tonight you're lip-smacking league."

"Why thank you," he said. Okay, that voice didn't belong to Dylan. It sounded too feathery and...*feminine*.

"Willow?" I asked and giggled.

Willow rose up, switching on the glass lamp by the side of Dylan's bed. "The one and only," she said, lightly laughing. I stood there bewitched by her presence, looking at a legend in the making. No one, and I mean *no one*, had ever been created more beautifully than Willow Taylor. She gracefully threw back the covers, and I slid under the sheets next to her. For once, I'd worn my glasses. Willow had on a tiny black T-shirt with a human skull silk-screened on the front. It looked creepy and marvelous at the same time. Wow, I wanted it and would somehow make it mine before I hitched a ride back to the Midwest.

I rolled onto my side to face her. "When did you get in?"

"A couple of hours ago," she answered. "Dylan was writing in his journal as I tiptoed by. I always enjoy talking to my nephew." She unleashed a sly smile, as if it meant something else. "It appears you can't get enough of him either."

The thought embarrassed me. Talking to her was like looking at his dead ringer. Dylan and Willow were both photocopies of Colton. The resemblance was freakishly bizarre, only the contours of Willow's features were softer. "Where is he?" I asked.

Willow and I both looked around all four corners, seeing only a neat room, not an item out of place. "Last I remember, we were deep in conversation," she said, admitting she'd fallen asleep. "You missed him?"

I always missed Dylan. "He relaxes me, so when I can't sleep, I seem to seek him out instinctively. It's hard to explain." And frankly, he probably couldn't explain it either.

Willow unveiled a warm, lazy smile. She gazed around his room once more, like she hadn't been in here for ages and tried to remember the design. I had a feeling things were easier for her that way. Sometimes walking in someone else's belongings didn't resurrect the warmth you had for them. All it did was make you miss them more.

"You don't need to explain love," she said, sighing wistfully. "I hear you've had quite a bit of excitement this week. Most of it in the last few hours."

That certainly was one way to spin a date with death. Let's face it, folks. My sense of survival was a late bloomer. If it didn't mature soon, I wouldn't even be here next year. "I was due."

Willow sighed heavily. "Me too. It's been a tough week."

"What's wrong? You don't sound so good."

Willow suddenly appeared to have aged a decade, her black eyes sorrowful and sallow. "Henry and I broke up," she said with an exhausted exhale. "Although I know it's the right thing, I don't like hurting anyone, you know?"

No one should ever come to me to dispense relationship advice. The relationships in my life were with my dead fish and mutilated hermit crabs. I was pretty sure those were an exercise on what *not* to do.

"I'm sorry, Willow. I've never even kissed anyone. I'm not sure I'm qualified to comment."

Wow, how embarrassing, but I had a feeling my virginal status was something invisibly tattooed to my forehead. Dylan and I might've kissed, but the fact he acted one hundred percent the same caused me to believe that my hormonal imagination manufactured the whole darn thing.

Willow reached out and tucked my hair behind my ear. "Why do you suppose that is?"

Good question. I actually didn't have a legitimate answer even I'd believe. I guess it boiled down to the fact that I was: one, chicken and two, well...there *was* no two. Chicken trumped everything. Still, there'd been opportunity—mainly by way of her next-door neighbor.

"Kyd still is..."

"*Kyd*," she interrupted with a laugh.

I giggled. "Yeah, a proposition per breath, but I don't want to split my time between Dylan and someone else. There are a couple of girls who texted him this week, and it—"

"Bothers you?" she interrupted softly.

My groan was a dead giveaway. "I hate them already," I admitted. Well, hate seemed like a minor word—I wanted them quartered and puked out into the universe, knocked around by a few meteors, never to be seen again. Yeah, that sounded good.

"Give me the scoop," she encouraged with a dancing smile. "I love to gossip."

Rolling over, I picked up Dylan's cell phone from the nightstand, scrolling to the photographs of whom I referred to as Exhibit A—blonde, and Exhibit B—redhead. Both had two unanswered texts from the day before, and a quick thumb-through showed he'd responded back to a couple a few days before. Rather benignly, but still...an answer was an answer. All I knew was that blonde and redhead, et al., needed to G-O.

Taking it from my hand, Willow narrowed her eyes and looked at them with a snort. "There's no comparison. The blonde looks like an airhead, and the redhead's attributes aren't God-given. They're plastic."

"Do guys care about that?" I asked, because I already struggled with the airhead quality...and God knew I HAD NO BOOBS.

Willow remained noncommittal. My interpretation was it depended on the guy. "My nephew thinks you're perfect," she replied diplomatically, "and I have to agree. Still," she digressed, "sometimes you have to help things along."

Before I could object, with her long, graceful fingers, Willow typed a text to Exhibit A that said: *Sorry, red is my favorite color.* Exhibit B got: *Blonde is sorta my thing.*

"Willow, he's gonna die!" I shrieked with a giggle.

Once again a snort. "*He,*" she emphasized, "isn't going to know unless you tell him." Willow deleted their contact information, messages, and sent box replies before returning it to his nightstand. "Having your father as a cop taught me a few things. Remove the evidence of your crime."

That might be a temporary fix, but it sure as heck wouldn't be permanent. "It still isn't going to remove his in-demand status," I grumbled.

"One day and one girl at a time, but he tells me you're in-demand, too, and I can assure you that might upset him more than it does you. Dylan said you were unbelievably beautiful, but he underesti-mated his adjective. Frankly, you're breathtaking." She leaned over and touched my deltoid muscle. "Do you work out? Yoga? Pilates?"

"I curl a lot of cookies."

Willow laughed so loudly it echoed off the tile. "Well, it's paying off. I could have you working by noon. Maybe even in a spread with me."

Cue the dropped jaw. "You're kidding."

Willow donned the business demeanor of her big brother. Eyes narrowed, jaw lifted, like she'd bury anything or anyone who threatened her cash flow. "I don't joke about those sorts of things, and I certainly wouldn't take a picture with anyone who'd ruin my reputation."

Let's be real. Unless we were shooting the *Farmer's Almanac,* I'd ruin the shot.

When I gave her a polite, "No thanks," Willow frowned, talked some more about Henry, and rebounded the conversation back on Dylan and me.

"I envy the easiness of your relationship." She sighed. "I've had to be an adult for so long, I'd love to find the right man to help *me* relax. You need to hang onto that, Darcy."

I didn't like to put people on the spot, but here we were, the dead of night, dissecting my non-existent love life and soon-to-be-over best friendship. After all Lincoln had done for me, I felt obligated to lob a few words on his behalf.

"Your parents missed you," I whispered.

Willow glanced out toward the lighted hallway. My guess was Lincoln left the lamp on, hoping she'd miraculously appear. "Aunt Susan told me," she said quietly. "She and Dylan are a lot alike. They're—"

"Zen," I answered.

She threw her head back, once again giggling. "I'm *never* zen."

That made two of us. Her definition of zen included beluga caviar with fifty pulsating jets of a Jacuzzi. Mine involved passing junior year without Saturday school and a prescription for an antidepressant.

"It's hard to look Daddy in the face sometimes, you know?" she continued. "Daddy's made a career of what *should* be. Sometimes my *is* would hurt him."

Well, I guess I got the *is* part. At times I caused the *is*. Others, it was thrust upon me with no time for negotiations or restitution of all those things I put off until tomorrow. But at least she had two parents in the picture.

"I've spent many nights with Lincoln this week," I told her. "I stuck my nose in his business, accidentally attracted a mobster, and he had my back when I didn't even know he was looking. I think you should trust him with the truth. He and Grandma were the first to forgive me when I should've been boxed up and airmailed back home."

Willow's face appeared drawn, aged, and pained once more. She didn't say yes, she didn't say no. So I took it as a maybe.

———

I slammed the paper shut while I threw a drink of overly sugared coffee down my throat. Darky Walton. Who in the heckity heck was Darky Walton? Obviously, it was a less-than-stellar ending to an otherwise perfect caper. But one would at least think—*at least*—they'd spell my freaking name right.

Dumb-butt newspaper.

Somebody needed to be fired.

As I dropped down at the kitchen table, I contemplated calling Troy for a reprint. But I knew that meant he'd unmask Jester as Darcy Walker, and for some reason, I still chose to live in the wind. My iPhone had five missed calls, but I didn't want to acknowledge my true identity. Not yet, at least, and as far as I could tell, no one knew about Jester except Hector and Bats Giuseppe. Both of them, I assumed, understood confidentiality more than most.

Still, it stunk to be Darky Walton. Darky Walton sounded like varnish remover or one of those super antibiotics.

"Good morning, Darky," Lincoln said and chuckled. Lincoln'd crawled into bed the same time as I had. One would think he'd likewise look like crap. Instead, his demeanor said he could've climbed the Matterhorn in Geneva. My brain functioned at baked bananas.

He deposited a FedEx overnight package on the table addressed to Legs. "I figured this was you," he murmured, rolling his eyes.

Oh, boy, I couldn't venture a guess who'd sent it. Kyd was more the in-person type, and Federal Express didn't seem like Tricky's modus operandi.

While he was preoccupied pulling bottled water out of the refrigerator and answering a text, I quickly ripped the perforated zipper off the white carton and opened a shoebox stamped Rock & Republic, size eight. I laughed loudly as I read the note.

> *Legs,*
>
> It was a pleasure meeting such a talented, beautiful girl as you. The search for your missing shoe wasn't successful, but please accept this replacement gift from me.
>
> *Grizzly*
>
> *P.S. I actually prefer Jester.*

The laugh evolved into a snorting hiccup when it registered Grizzly had sent them. I wadded the note up in a fist, stymied. How in the heck did he compute that I was Jester, where I'd been residing, and have something delivered in the course of a few hours—in the right size?

And let me ask again...JESTER??

The Taylors could never know, or it would be a poop storm of epic proportions. Overwhelmed, I sank down in my seat, clonked my head on the wrought-iron frame, and slid down the black fabric like a sticky slug. I met the floor with an explosive thwack, and the chair whapped twice on the tile. When I told myself that incident only existed in my mind, it screeched again reminding me I was a moron.

I let out a big heavy sigh.

Some things never changed...

Lincoln twisted the top off his water, eyes immediately darting to the open box of shoes as he helped me up. "Are you okay, dear?"

"My butt feels like I sat in acid."

He chuckled while he slid into the seat next to me. "So you're upset about Darky?"

I chose to stick with the obvious. "Yeah."

He released a moan of condolence. "That's what happens when

you refuse to be interviewed and sneak out the backdoor with a mobster."

I rolled my eyes glumly, shoving over an untouched plate of hummus and pita chips, opting for a lunch of three glazed dough-nuts. "So umm, Bats is...umm...you know," I stumbled, "Turkey's guy—"

"Bats is proving useful," was his politically correct let's-keep-Darcy-in-the-dark statement. His jaw clamped down like a clam, and I realized Lincoln would never give me information again for the rest of my not-so-long life. Well, you know what, I figured that'd be his response. So before I fell asleep, I located his cell phone and copied down two numbers that made several calls to him a week that he never dialed as return calls. One or both had to be his contact. When I dialed, both numbers rang nonstop. Those on the other end either weren't home, didn't have an answering machine, or the caller had used a payphone or burner phone. In my humble interpretation of an informant, my thoughts were they'd used the latter.

I tried not to act too overly triumphant, and although a payphone or burner phone would prove difficult to stake out, I didn't give up easily. Even from an opposite coastline.

Pixie's tush was mine...even if it took awhile.

Willow inched onto Lincoln's lap, carrying a container of straw-berry cheesecake yogurt. Obviously, Lincoln and Alexandra were beyond ecstatic. My feelings were once Willow flashed her pearly whites, Lincoln would find a way to wrap up loose ends with Detec-tive Battle...*indefinitely*.

She was barefoot, meticulously coiffed in a casual black sundress, and only one hundred and thirty-five pounds at six foot one. It didn't matter if you weighed a buck thirty-five when you had that much height on you. It only meant you were one skinny step closer to Heaven.

Willow lifted the lid on the box. "Cute shoes," she said. "Who are they from?"

First impulse had been to cover my big, white, booty...but Grizzly knew where I'd been staying, and if he kept sniffing around, he'd eventually unearth Willow. I needed to fess up because her days of anonymity went the way of the wooly mammoth. Not to mention, she might have a target on her back.

I nervously unfolded the crumpled note, slowly sliding it over.

Lincoln's eyes zoomed in on Grizzly, his breath caught twice, and he winced like his gut burst into an inferno. He never mentioned Jester, and frankly, I didn't think he even registered the word. It was all he could do to keep from aiming his gun. The vice cop was gone, replaced by a frantic father who gripped his daughter's wrist so hard it looked in danger of snapping.

Willow burst into laughter. "You know Walter?" she asked. I almost upchucked. Lincoln swallowed his down. Willow registered his discomfort, touching his arm. "Grizzly can be lecherous and inappropriate, Dad, but he'd never hurt our family. He's gotten me out of a few scrapes with no strings attached."

From what I'd seen of Grizzly, his world was that outer circle of Dante's Inferno. The place where nothing but crap happens amongst the baddest of the bad. No doubt, Lincoln pondered what circles his daughter ran in. He believed there were strings attached to everything. After last night, I had to agree.

His voice sounded breathy, like he'd gone into anaphylactic shock. "Did he know of our connection before last night?" he gasped agitated. Willow shook her head no. "Does he know of your mother? Has he ever been at this home? Threatened you? Blackmailed you?"

Lincoln's rage ticked like a thermonuclear device one second away from decimating civilization. Tears rolled down his cheeks, and he wasn't even aware Willow had begun to wipe them away. No wonder she never told her father anything. Lincoln was eons worse than Murphy.

Willow responded with a tender, "No to all of your questions, Daddy. I've always done what you've taught me. The less you give people, the less they can use against you. Photographs of you and Momma are only in my room."

I inched my fingers over to the note and quickly slid it inside my tube sock. Out of sight, out of mind...I hoped.

Willow hugged Lincoln deeply as he took one big breath. Next on his agenda (just my guess) would be to contract private surveillance for his daughter. Possibly from FX, Incorporated. Lincoln divulged that the two men accompanying him and Paddy were Felix Xavier and one of his hired guns. They weren't too pleased to know they'd been had and volunteered front and center for the party Lincoln had expected. I was sure they'd gotten paid rather handsomely, but then again, guys like that had odd hobbies. The thrill was probably worth a pro bono gig.

Once Lincoln broke free, Willow picked up a shoe, twirling it around, trying to divert his attentions. "I'd ask to borrow," she said with a smile, "but I wear a nine."

Huh, who in the world was the owner of the shoes I'd demolished? Another model? Gift from a designer? *What-evvvs.* I shrugged. Looked like Darcy had a new pair of shoes.

Willow ran a well-manicured nail down the front page, scanning the lead story with a frown. "Darky?" she said, trying not to laugh. I raised my hand. "One would think the *Orlando Sentinel* would get it right. They win a lot of awards. I dated the sports editor over there for a while until I discovered he was married." The muscles ticced in Lincoln's neck. I kicked him under the table.

"Are you sure it wasn't the copy editor?" I mumbled. "That guy's flubbed up two vital pieces of information. FX, Incorporated and my God-given name."

Lincoln managed a laugh. "She's got a point, Will. If he couldn't get Darky's name right," I raised my hand again, "then no wonder he forgot he took a vow."

Willow gave her father the twinkled-eye look, which landed her on the cover of *Vogue* when she was only sixteen. Normally, that conversation would be the death knell for Lincoln, but he was still on this side of the dirt.

Half a baloney sandwich later, I finished explaining to Herbie how Eleanor siphoned off his money. Kyd had me break it down earlier, but then I concluded Kyd only wanted to talk. Talk about Mary... talk about me...talk about the differences between Mary and me. Kyd confused me, but I didn't think it wise to tamper with a four-year relationship simply because of a girl he saw for two weeks in the summer. What I *did* know was when I finally picked a boyfriend it wouldn't be a guy already taken. I had a low enough self-esteem. Why put myself in a competitive situation where no one emerged the winner?

Besides, can you just say...skeevy.

Tricky had finished saying goodbye, escorting Herbie back to the Escalade they'd been washing in their circle drive. His exact words, "Eleanor's not an alien, Herbie. She was just stealing your money." *Good luck with that conversation,* I thought. No matter how he spun it, Herbie would never be playing with a full deck.

Kyd whispered out a sigh, leaning up against the basketball goal. "I now understand why Taylor finds you so fascinating."

"Fascinating, no," I said and laughed. "Obligated, yes. He keeps my hyperactivity and compulsive tendencies in check."

"I can see that," he said quietly. "Come here." I didn't want to 'come here.' Kyd had a faraway look in his eyes that spoke of joint checking accounts and tag-teaming the nightly baby feedings. The wind came in relentless waves, rocking me back and forth. I couldn't tell if it tried to blow me back home...or closer to Kyd.

Quickly hammering myself in reverse, I stepped one sneaker inside the soapy bucket they'd used to wash the SUV, the other sliding in a pool of water. It felt like I'd hit an oil slick. I slipped backward onto the grass, backward rolled into a palm frond, and then bounced butt-first into a bed of begonias. Instinct told me it wasn't over. Perhaps the hysterical laughing of Tricky clued me in or the dumbfounded disbelief of Kyd who'd been struck motionless. The bucket slow mo'd in the air and landed with a ting in the middle of my lap. My shorts and white tank were soaked down to my frothy underwear.

Immediately my tongue poised to say every sacrilege and cuss word I could think of, but all that came out was, "Wow."

After everyone took a moment to let that crap jell, Kyd pulled me up into his arms. "Come here, Miss Wow," he said, chuckling in one of those deep manly sounds. At that point, I succumbed to the situation. You hoped no one witnessed your stupidity. Unfortunately, mine had been laid out for public consumption.

Kyd held out two towels, and I was in dire need of three. As we blotted my arms and legs dry, the punch in my gut alerted me Kyd wanted to get personal.

"Thanks," I mumbled as we finished. Kyd threw them to the ground beneath our feet, taking both my hands tenderly in his.

"You've hijacked my heart, Darcy," he murmured. When I responded with a blush, he sighed in explanation. "Yes, Mary and I have our problems, but she's always been...Mary," he said wistfully. "*My* Mary. Now she'll always be second best."

I nibbled my bottom lip. "I'm sorry," I whispered.

He appeared thoughtful. "*I'm* not. Is it easy for you to talk to me?" *Yup*, I said to myself. "Does that bother you?" *Yup*, I admitted again. "Does it confuse your nice, little compartmentalized world?" *Yuppers*. "Think about what it does to mine."

"Kyd, I..."

He shook his head, signaling there was no more need for words. "At least, tell me you'll take care of yourself. I worry about the situations you get yourself into and the varying reasons why." Okay, so I had self-destructive tendencies, but that was pretty much common knowledge. Unfortunately, no amount of self-talk in the world made me safe to turn loose without a chaperone. "Call me?" he choked out in request.

I made a promise I intended to keep. "Every week," I vowed.

Chapter Thirty-Three

THE DOG DAYS OF SUMMER

*R*eformed bad boy or not, my father had one quality he'd never lost. He was a fighter, especially on another's behalf. Murphy Walker could break your heart but also had a fist swinging on your behalf if he felt someone hurt you or anyone else down on their luck. My father was the most complicated human being ever engineered.

"So she took a spin in the toilet?" he cackled.

"It was a self-flusher, Murphy. At last count, she spun in the middle of three." Thankfully, my wire hadn't stopped transmitting. The technician in the van scored the whole confession on audiotape, found Lincoln when Bats materialized, and then placed Cowboys on lockdown once we'd exited the building. Evidently, Grizzly coughed up his suspicion that Eleanor was X once Jackal convinced him the wise thing would be to talk. It wasn't readily apparent which Jackal Lincoln referred to—the GLOCK model or his human counterpart. All I knew was Colton wore a frown bigger than the wrinkles on a prune. In retrospect, my conversation with Bats lasted about twenty minutes of pure terror, but I was dying to know what went down when I'd been bargaining to breathe again.

"And this Polly?" he continued.

"Going back to Washington, I suppose." Polly worked undercover for the Securities and Exchange Commission. Apparently, Eleanor had been on their radar for some time. Polly discovered the connection with Elmer and walked in his world for a while... although she hadn't pieced together one single thing about Cisco.

Polly, I'm guessing, had some stupid in her.

Murphy's voice lowered. "And this...*other man?*"

Lincoln had explained the entire history with Bats Giuseppe, not once...but three times. Evidently, Murphy needed a fourth.

"My feelings are he's getting a new life, blah, blah, blah after he's useful."

"Are you at least getting the Turbo as a consolation prize?" he asked chuckling.

I wish. It had been impounded, having been confiscated from Eleanor's garage. "No," I groaned, "but the woman in the expensive shoes was an actress they'd hired."

"Her career's short-lived, kid. Everyone knows that high heels don't go with sweatpants." I heard and felt a sigh coming. "I'm proud of you, Darc. Angry, but still proud. So about the Apple people..."

It wasn't the time for a joke. I'd only seen my father cry once, but his voice had cracked half a dozen times in our conversation. I needed to receive whatever he wanted to say and just shut up. "I'm back on fruit?" I asked.

Murphy backpedaled on the discipline. "You do need to balance out your diet, kid. Apples are no longer forbidden."

I ended the call with my father. Throwing the last of my clothes into my luggage, I closed up *Atlas of the Stars* after I read the paragraph on Sirius again. Sirius meant scorcher, responsible for the phrase the "Dog Days of Summer" or the hottest time of the year. People were supposed to be so exhausted and famished by heat that nothing of any worth ever happened.

We might've just proven that statement wrong.

It was Friday evening, and vacation was all but over. Cisco had been returned to Hank, Lola was turning state's evidence, and the Medinas weren't hiding out in nearby Ocala anymore. I got to see Cisco for a few moments earlier in the afternoon, and what the heck, I added another brother to my clan. He was a brainy little man and said he held onto what he knew was true...his family loved him, and they'd find him.

Lola was allowed to speak with him once during his captivity, but it had been so disturbing, Eleanor cut the call short—unfortunately, it never grew into another occurrence. Lola was always told she had one last game, but Eleanor's greed for the win couldn't be sated, and Lola, unfortunately, trusted no one enough to confide in them.

Cisco ended our meeting by interviewing me on my likes and dislikes, bound and determined to tell me how he'd survived. A dark, eerie feeling descended on me while he'd spoke, as if someone skipped across my premature grave, and I'd one day need his words to survive. I shook off the thought, convincing myself that my imagination—once again—operated in the Grimms Fairytale world.

Needing to find my other half, I rolled my luggage to the front door, peeking in each room along the way. The bulk of the family partied poolside, along with Paddy and some other badges who were friends of Lincoln's. No Dylan was in sight. I felt a nagging pang of imbalance and loneliness. If I had to think about it, he was the one element in my universe that remained as essential as air and water. He made my life easier. He made me feel blessed. And he made me feel special when there really wasn't anything to feel special about.

Thank God, I thought, that occasionally Dylan was just downright dumb.

Migrating toward his room, I found the french doors wide open with Dylan sitting in the grass, relaxing back on his elbows, watching and drinking in the sunset.

Dylan looked like...*magic*. I inwardly sighed. He sported a plain gray T-shirt, red athletic shorts, long muscular legs, and barefoot. As a cool breeze blew through his raven-black hair, he closed his eyes—like he drank in the last bit of daylight in what had been a record high one hundred and three degrees.

I rested against the doors, reflecting on our relationship. The last thing I'd ever want would be to jeopardize what we had together—even if it sometimes seemed unidentifiable. Would a relationship with Kyd—or a relationship with anyone—jeopardize or place a strain on it?

It would...by God, it would.

"Come sit with me, Darc," he murmured, not turning around or opening his eyes.

"How'd you know?" I said and laughed. Dylan rose up, still not turning, tapping the space next to him.

"I'll never need anything or anyone to point me in your direction. I always...*feel you*."

Walking outside, I let the grass swim and plunge deeply between my toes. Inching up behind him, I dropped down, molded myself to his back, my arms and legs wrapping around his waist. "I love you," I whispered into his neck.

Dylan leaned into me and reached back, sliding the fingers of his left hand through my hair. "Always," he murmured. "I swear, sweetheart, it will forever be *always*, and I'm so, *so*," he paused, breathing deep, "proud of you."

Dylan's voice pulsed about an octave deeper than everyone else's, but when he spoke, it always rang soft and soothing. For a brief moment, it almost lulled me to sleep. I'd never truly felt proud of myself. Not really. My mother—how do I phrase things, "went away"—when I was nine. Working through that grief was like cutting your fingernails too short. Nothing would feel better until you sucked it up or applied nail lengthener. Trouble was, it had been six years, and I was still working with nubs. Things happened to me then...things no one should have to endure...at least not publicly. My self-esteem plummeted to the lowest depths imaginable as a result. And Dylan? He never left me...he held out his hand and pulled me back.

I whispered, "I miss her, D. Do you think she'd be proud? Did I do the right thing?"

The air went quiet for a few breaths as Dylan collected his thoughts...and probably emotions. Bad memories did that to a person, and frankly, he probably tried to gauge whether it would be a good conversation or an A-Bomb of tears. Sometimes, the emotions of my mother struck hard and merciless, and he was left putting the wreckage back together. Others, I could focus on one recollection and smile for days.

"Yes," he finally said quietly. "Your mother would be unbelievably proud of you. What you did is more than I'll ever accomplish, Darc. Mothers across the world are thankful for you. You were smart, fearless, and convicted. You can't teach that. You're either born with it or granted it by God. So yes," he paused confidently, "you did the right thing."

That answer alone was the hallmark of Dylantopia—good always won in the end. Trouble was, many people met their end before they ever saw their happy ending. Those were the situations I couldn't reconcile. At times, God seemed far, far away in some distant land and the innocent were left unguarded. Or at least, it seemed like they were, and in my experience, feeling abandoned was as bad as *being* abandoned.

The larger my doubts grew, the more I found myself hanging tighter to him. As usual, his touch brought a beautiful energy, and it reminded me how dead I felt when he wasn't around. I'd already begun to feel the dull pain of an overwhelming numbness encase my body. The problem with all of my escapades was that the buzz seemed short-lived. Heaven help me, my latest buzz hadn't even lasted twenty-four hours.

I kept the laugh to myself.

"You scared me," he murmured. How did I feel about vacation? Fan-*freaking*-tastic stuff. Dylan, however, would need to be institutionalized by the time we graduated.

I turned his face to meet mine, but his eyes were misty, unsettled, and raw with fear. Three short gasps escaped his lips as he looked to the sky, blinking away tears before they fell.

I couldn't find the words to respond, so I tenderly kissed the back of his neck. *I'm sorry*. I kissed. *I'm sorry, I'm sorry, I'm sorry*, I finished three more times. Nothing was suggestive or compromising or outside our normal boundaries. I merely wanted to love on him and kiss away his worries.

After a dozen more heartbeats, Dylan murmured, "It's never enough, is it?" speaking of our time together.

Nope. Not by a long shot. "One day you're not going to want me around, D, and it's going to break my heart," I whispered. Ironically, the wind kicked up a notch, sending blue-green, feather-veined leaves to weep and float to the lake before us. A storm was brewing, just as in my heart.

"Shh," he said, reassuring me, "that will never happen."

"But what if it *does*?" I protested. "I'll always be Darcy Walker who looks at the sunset and remembers this might be her favorite vacation with the best friend she's ever had."

My God, my idea of fun wasn't normal...I needed to figure out what that meant.

Dylan's back tensed in hesitation, as though his body decided not to voice what his mind had dictated. "What?" I asked, tightening my grip. "You seem like there's something you want to say, but you don't. Full disclosure, right?" A grim nod was all I received. "D? Ripping off the Band-Aid is usually your department."

He sighed...long and hard.

"I'm aware of the irony, Darcy," he murmured. "I'm usually the open one, but I don't know how to talk to you about the changes between us. And when I muster the courage, I fail miserably at every turn. My personality is not to allow feelings to lie dormant, and when I force them to, I literally feel sick inside."

I wanted to crawl inside his soul and have him promise that things would never change, but parts of our lives were off-limits, even to one another. I couldn't find any anger. Look at me. I'd never divulged what I'd been doing right under his own nose—things that included Kyd. Even though I had no plans to take things further with Kyd, in all honesty, Dylan didn't know that.

"He's nothing to me," I blurted out, "and neither was Liam Woods." Dylan briefly stiffened but didn't add anything of worth to the conversation. The longer the stillness spread, it felt like I'd been skinned and boiled alive. My eyes closed briefly. Opened. Winced at the subject matter. I couldn't take the obscurity anymore, and if he wouldn't do anything to paint our black and white picture in color, then I would. "Did you ever go out with Yankee?"

Dylan inhaled sharply, stiffening even more. "Yes," he said on an exhale.

"Did you like it?"

"No," he answered quickly.

"Did you ever go out with Brynn Hathaway?" Silence. A raw and painful silence. And that silence spoke for itself. "Answer me, D. I've answered the biggest questions that I know have been on your mind. Turnabout is fair play."

Dylan expelled what not only sounded like the last breath in his body, but the weight of the fact he'd been keeping something hidden he wished he would've shared. Jeez, guess it was out-with-secrets night. "Yes," he murmured, gently stroking my hands with his thumbs. "I did recently go out with her, and I do like her, Darc... just not enough."

My heart began to hurt, like someone ripped it out of my chest and left it to shrivel up and die. Oh, crap. Oh, crap, oh, crap, oh crap. "Not enough for what?" I whispered.

"To take me away from you."

Keeping the tears from falling proved futile. So Dylan wasn't the kiss-and-tell type...how quaint. Pain hit me at my very core. It struck me in the center of my chest and kept growing...until every part of me ached, even my hair. "That hurts me," I whispered.

"Hurts you because I did it, or hurts you because you didn't know?"

"Does it matter?" I sniffed quietly.

Dylan responded, even quieter. "It matters...it matters to me."

"Then yes," I whispered, pain catching in my throat. "Yes to both."

Dylan tenderly squeezed my hands in his, and I knew that was an apology. "I've done a lot of things on this vacation," he murmured, "*allowed* a lot of things to happen, but they've all been to get your attention. I apologize that I wasn't more direct. Our relationship has never been about mind games...and I don't ever wish it to become that."

On that we were in agreement. "What are we to one another, D?"

It felt like weeks had passed. Months. Just the two of us together, dissecting what had always been simple. "Aw, sweetheart," he finally answered softly, "it's more than I am with anyone else. You'll always be the girl...I can't live without."

Those words used to be enough, but seasons changed. And people changed. "You're going to college," I said panicked. "My guess is some place far away. Perhaps even here. You'll meet girls," I choked out, "you'll like them, you'll love them," I whispered, "and you'll want to spend time with them. I don't know, D, maybe even me too."

Noooooooooooo. No, no, noooo. I only said that because my ego poked me in the ribs to not sound so desperate.

We both sat there absorbing what we knew was the next logical step in our relationship. Our lives were changing and neither of us felt comfortable with the change.

"Why do you think that circumstances leave you the only one feeling vulnerable?" he asked, an emotion tickling his voice I couldn't quite put my finger on. "My love for you is bigger than any circumstance, Darcy, but that doesn't mean you're the only one who battles the uneasiness."

But you're you, I thought, *and I'm me*. He'd enjoy the college life. I'd flip burgers in a fast food joint. Great things would be written about him in the paper. I'd do my best to dodge the obituaries and prison roundup. That didn't add up to the HEA, or happily-ever-after. It seemed more like inequality and reason for revolution.

"Things change," I kept insisting.

His breathing intensified, like he was one synapse away from a panic attack. "They'll change only if you desire it," he murmured. "I'm not going to get star struck by some unknown girl or some girl who I already know. I've got the brightest star in the universe hugging me, and I don't want anyone else's arms to take her place. Trust me, honey, there is no Dylan without Darcy, and no one will *ever* fill my heart like you do. But promise me," he murmured seriously. "Promise me, you'll just think about...us together...consider it, sweetheart...please...it's what I want..."

I had brain damage. Maybe when I fell off that barstool at Cowboys, my brainstem disconnected because Dylan almost sounded like he was asking me to consider dating him. While I sat there speechless, he murmured more comforting words in Greek. Oftentimes I asked for an interpretation. Others, I merely liked the way Darcy resonated from his lips. He said it differently, thicker and deeper—like we both were someone different within the confines of somewhere else. I listened to it over and over, knowing it held a meaning I probably should inquire about, but the deepest part of my soul told me it promised always.

EPILOGUE: JUST WHEN YOU THINK IT'S SAFE

$\mathcal{M}$y iPhone crooned Brenda Lee's "Break It to Me Gently." That ringtone was a tad morose, but dude, that day was comin' soon.

"Morning, Vinnie," I greeted, giggling and punching the speaker.

"Morning, Dolce. I need to see you tonight. I've got a lead on the yellow Dodge Charger."

"What do you mean you've got a lead?"

"Christ, Dolce. Don't you know what 'I've got a lead' means?"

"Yes, nimrod, but you don't need to bring Christ into the picture." My God, Vinnie Vecchione was basically begging for a lightning bolt to incinerate us both. "Besides, how can you be back in town tonight?" I asked confused. "You *are* still at college, right?"

"Um, yeah," he answered evasively, "but the Bug lost a few eyelashes, and I need to get them fixed."

Well, God forbid, the Bug couldn't see...

Vinnie drove a Pepto-Bismol pink Volkswagen Bug—with black plastic eyelashes. He won it when he plastered his hand to its hood all night in a Breast Cancer Awareness Marathon. He also picked up two dates that evening and a bad case of jock itch...I didn't ask questions.

"It's really important, Dolce. Just call me after school."

Vinnie hung up without further ado. He'd earned a football scholarship at Ohio State University and was the only person I'd told about the man in the yellow Dodge Charger—the man who'd slammed me in the trunk of his car, only to take me out, and abandon me in the middle of nowhere. Vinnie had made it his mission to find him because the man gave me the impression that he knew me. And it wasn't just that Dodge Charger Man saved me from a psycho student one evening, unbeknownst to me. He'd said things that made me believe he knew my past...and my parents' past. So far, Vinnie had come up empty-handed. Vinnie either wasn't as good as I thought he was, or simply put, the other guy was better.

I shoved my toothbrush back in my mouth when my phone immediately rang again. I broke into a smile when I saw the Orlando prefix. "Hey, buddy," I greeted Cisco. "You're going back to school today too?"

"Yes," he replied happily. "Thanks for the new ant farm."

I spit out the toothpaste, swished a Dixie cup's worth of water in my mouth, and then wiped dry on a faded hand towel. It was Monday, day-one of junior year. Murphy made fried chicken and waffles for breakfast, trying to get me in the mood. Good eating, but I'd flossed my teeth twice trying to remove "the deep South" from my smile.

"I'm glad you like it," I said, walking downstairs, but I couldn't help but wonder if it ticked off the ants.

It reminded me of my neighborhood. People didn't move into BTCC to retire. Most moved in counting the days until they crawled out. My father couldn't bring himself to leave the home he and my mother built, ergo I was the oldest kid on the block. School, at best, provided me with camaraderie, but the one thing I despised was the throng of girls who flocked to Dylan daily. Obviously, I woke a little more than bitter, but I had an edgy feeling Brynn Hathaway would cause me problems...*big* problems...of the shama lama, ding-dong kind.

Not to mention I was B-O-R-E-D.

I was victim to my own self.

Murphy glanced outside chuckling, as I disconnected with Cisco and glumly rolled on clear lip gloss. "It appears your limousine has arrived. Your boy's driving his father's Suburban."

"D's here?" I asked surprised. And that car seemed a little large for the occasion.

Shoving my lucky hat on my head, I grabbed my copper Jansport backpack and slung it over my right shoulder, opening the door. Dylan had Jon Bradshaw and Finn Lively—brothers one and two—with him as they idled in the driveway. Last night, he'd hosted his annual all-boys slumber party before school started. Sort of like a goodbye-to-summer, hello-to-hell sort of celebration. Times like these it stunk to be born with ovaries. Parents automatically assumed it would be an orgy.

"This is your year to shine," Marjorie said. She tugged on my skirt, standing partially nude behind me. Let's hope it was her year to figure out the laws of public decency called for an invention called clothing.

I swatted her pink panties, giggling. "Thanks, M."

I jogged outside, throwing a goodbye kiss toward the bus stop along the way.

The clouds in the sky looked like cotton balls, and the air felt desert arid. Just thinking about it made my underarms sweat, but nothing instilled white-knuckled panic in me more than school-work. Maybe that's why Murphy made soul food, trying to fill me with love. Unfortunately, we'd both learned the hard way, love didn't always conquer all. The best you could hope for was peace. Peace happened to be foreign to my brain.

Heaven knew I'd need help. My day was planned out with seven subjects, knowing a good chance existed I'd only get a legitimate A—without extra credit and blood sacrifices—in one of them. In general, the attention-challenged like me either found their life's calling or were doomed to fail when someone asked your square-peg mind to fit through society's round hole. You could eventually get it through, but some sort of irreparable damage would be endured in the process.

After school, my outlook wasn't much better. I was off to work at Belinski's Bookstore. I hadn't clocked any time for weeks and needed to knuckle down and get back into a routine, even if it included mindless activity. Thing was, Belinski's wasn't a bookstore. It was a mausoleum. An average night consisted of more than four, less than ten customers.

When I neared the newly washed black SUV, I caught the whiff of testosterone and didn't know whether to run for cover or fall prostrate and beg, *Please, Santa, please.* Jon Bradshaw (nicknamed Grumpy), swung the passenger door wide while Dylan let out a wolf whistle.

"To what do I owe the pleasure?" I asked, deeply frowning. "Penance? Guilt?? Bring a leper to school day???"

"Bring a leper to school day," Grumpy said and chuckled. I smacked him on the forehead as he mumbled something about Dylan losing his ever-lovin' mind.

"Good morning, sweetheart," Dylan murmured. "You look *loooovely.*" It depended on how you defined lovely. Even I knew I needed to make an effort to show I'd aged gracefully over the summer. Showcasing my lucky hat, I'd slinked on Willow's black T-shirt and paired it with a black miniskirt and my Nike Classic Cortez sneakers. Plus, I applied an extra dose of voodoo cream, hoping to look centerfold-ready by first period.

As of six a.m., I smelled like motor oil.

"Why didn't you bring your car?" I asked.

Dylan turned the volume down on the radio, all smiles. "Lively," he said, his head pitching to Finn sitting in the back, "brought four pieces of luggage for one outfit this morning. I needed a bigger car."

"I see," I said. "Grumpy needs to take some fashion cues. He looks like he schlepped out of the sewer."

"Shut up, Walker," Grumpy grumbled. He hoisted himself out of the front seat in a holey white T, old sneakers, and khaki cargo shorts. His wavy brown hair looked weeks late on a cut, lying over deep-set, hard-as-nails eyes. He maneuvered around to whisper in my ear, "Brynn called."

Well, helloooooo, Benedict Arnold.

I was slapped with a cold knot of dread. I'd never particularly liked the girl, but I had a feeling there might be some good in her. Good that I needed to discredit. I longed to publicly embarrass her, make her cry, and dye her perfectly brown waves peach. Problem was, she looked like a Botticelli angel—all sweet, spotless, and pristine pure.

My name didn't make that particular Rolodex.

I should have expected as much. I'd left Dylan hanging...just hanging. After his confession that he felt something—or *maybe* felt something (okay, he was pretty adamant)—I stared at him like a deer-in-the-headlights. Let's just say I'd morphine'd the mood, and whatever else he'd planned to say was swiftly stalled.

Ugh, I stunk at relationships...evidently, Brynn didn't.

I climbed into the seat and threw my backpack in the rear, aiming for Grumpy's head. "Whhhaaaaatttt the what, Walker?!" he gasped, rubbing his crown when my backpack met its mark.

"The Devil made me," was my excuse.

A smile played at Dylan's lips. "You're naughty today, Darc. You're cute when you're naughty, but that's not usually a good sign."

"I'm in a bad mood," I grumbled. *Other than Brynn*, I omitted, I said, "My invitation to the party got lost in the mail."

Clothed in an Abercrombie red and white vintage polo, no doubt about it Brynn would appreciate the view. Dylan's black hair was shorn short, classically styled, and meticulously irresistible. I fought off the urge to rearrange his face with my calculator.

Dylan sighed as if he expected our conversation, gently stroking my cheek with the backs of his knuckles. "Darc, we've already gone over this. You're a beautiful girl, and we're three teenage guys. Trust me, it doesn't work that way." Well, how *did* it work because he sure as heck let me snuggle with him in O-Town. "Come over here, and show me some love," he said, adding a flirty wink.

"I'd rather suck face with a mole."

"That's not very nice, sweetheart," he said, activating his little girl giggle.

"Nice isn't in my particular skillset, Lover Boy."

"Lover Boy?" he echoed.

"Lover Boy."

"That's what you said," he murmured with a grin.

"That's what I said. One day I'm going to kill your mockingbird mouth, D." I snorted. "You're the most infuriating person I've ever met."

"That's passion," he murmured flirtatiously, "and I haven't forgotten where we left things. It's all I've been thinking about, and I do intend on resurrecting that conversation. You know," he paused, "the one where we were outside my room...looking at the lake...your legs were around my waist...and it felt good."

I heard moaning and groaning from the backseat. "You're going to do this in front of *them*?" I gasped, eyes widening.

"I'm going to do it in front of whomever I please."

Pound. Pound. Pound went my heart. Oh, God, oh, God, oh, God. "That doesn't shock me," I said, trying to change the subject. "You like them better than me. In fact, you like *everyone* better than me." (cough, Brynn, cough) "You might as well say it because my heart sure as heck feels it."

Dylan threw his chin back, like I'd cold-cocked him. "Where'd that come from?" he groaned.

"Don't sugarcoat your little all-males slumber party, D. I was bored out of my mind last night doing big, fat, *zero*!"

Not totally true. I texted anyone who would chat up until midnight.

"Whoa, *min vän* is in a foul mood," Finn said, laughing from the backseat. All three of us spun around simultaneously for clarification. "Swedish for 'my friend,'" he interpreted. Finn Lively had sky-blue eyes with tousled blond hair to his chin. He tried on a different accent each day—all the elements of a ladies' man—combined with a face that screamed flat-out beautiful. "Smile, *min vän*," he coaxed.

Smile? I wanted to push all of them in front of a subway.

"Nice shirt," he said, grinning at me.

I glanced down at the white skull on my chest, falling in love all over again. "Willow," was my explanation.

He and Grumpy sighed a naughty sound as their mugs went goo-goo eyed. Actually, it proved to be an easy transaction. I manufactured some puppy-dog eyes and simply said, *Please*.

"Willow's going to have my child one day," Finn murmured on an exhale.

Dylan danced around, having an eeeuw moment since Willow was his aunt. "Button up your shirt, Lively," he groaned. Both of Finn's arms were straddled across the bench seat, his chiseled chest peeking through a blue and white fitted plaid shirt, unsnapped to his navel. You know, a roundhouse kick to your libido.

I gulped...then gulped again.

"Nah," Finn said, grinning smugly, "I saved the view for Darcy."

Dylan's eyes shot up in the rearview mirror, like two missiles looking for a target. "Shut up, Finn, before my foot's up your..." *bleeping bleep*.

"He's in love," Finn mouthed.

Yeah, whatever, I grumbled to myself. My fist had a little sumpthin' sumpthin' for his face once we got out of the car.

I grasped the coffee he waved in front of me as a peace offering: (A) because I was thirsty; and (B) because I operated in codependent idiot mode. He must've experienced a major case of the guilts, because he'd bought it at United Dairy Farmers, my favorite. By no means was it a specialty store. It was gas station coffee. But it had the right combo of coffee, caffeine, and sugar to punch my taste-buds in the face each morning.

Buckling myself in, I wiggled down in the seat as he backed out of the driveway and made our way to Valley High. Traffic flow was heavy, bumper to bumper. At times, we moved at a crawl. Others, Dylan slammed on the brakes because a vehicle unexpectedly stopped in front of him. Horns blared loud at each intersection, and the one-fingered salute was the norm.

Yup...your typical first day back to school.

While Finn named off two senior girls he'd date before week's end, and Grumpy grunted it was the year Clementine Miriam Rabinowitz would date a Gentile, I thought my head would blow right off my shoulders. Especially when Grumpy chuckled that he'd like to double date with Dylan and Brynn. I wanted to kill him. I wanted to rip his eyeballs out and make him swallow those suckers down.

Unbuckling myself, I climbed halfway between the seats and started smacking the living daylights out of him. My head on the floor, my butt up in the air like the hump on a camel.

"Walker," he said, chuckling and dodging my hands, "I was joking." Well, it didn't sound like joking, and it sure as heck didn't feel like it to my churning gut. Especially when Grumpy unsnapped himself and attempted to pull me onto the floorboard of the backseat.

I grabbed the curly hair on his legs and started twisting. "You're as hairy as freaking Big Foot!" I said and giggled.

"Ow!" He laughed.

My lucky hat fell to Finn's feet. He picked it up and shoved it on his head as he flipped open the latest edition of '68 *Zombie Comics* and started reading. "Now, now, kiddies," he purred. "Let's all love one another."

"Hey," Dylan said, half giggling and half threatening, tugging me toward him by my right shoe. "You're going to hurt her, Bradshaw. Let her go, or I'm going to—"

I heard the sounds of metal slicing and crumpling as the Suburban suddenly skidded to the left into the middle of the inter-section. An image tumbled through my mind of Dylan's right arm darting out in front of me, while power like a tidal wave rolled through my body. It lifted me up—viciously moving my body without consent—and I suddenly launched forward with glass splin-tering around me like a freezing rain. I was flying through the wind-shield when I heard another crunch and glimpsed Grumpy sailing through the side window at the precise same time. *No airbag*, I thought calmly. They didn't arm because we weren't buckled, or something else had kept them from deploying. My flight felt like it took a lifetime as my ragdoll body twisted sideways before coming to rest on my back on the highway in front of us. The last thing audible was Dylan's horrified scream and then suddenly nothing except a horn stuck on beep.

The pavement didn't seem hard, even though I felt gravel prickle the back of my wet and sticky head. Were my brains spilled on the pavement? I couldn't move—but nothing hurt—and I briefly wondered if I'd been paralyzed. My chest didn't feel right, but Grumpy's guttural groan soon drowned out the hissing and crack-ling in my lungs. No strength to lift my head, my eyes slid over to the left where he lay facedown, arms down to his sides, about twenty meters away. My Nike shoe lay next to him, untied. Strug-gling to make sense of what'd happened, I saw that the Suburban looked like an accordion, trapped between two cars. A Lincoln Town Car had struck the passenger side and a blue mini-van had hammered the driver's side door. Where was Finn? Was Dylan okay?

I love you, I should've said. I needed to check on him...I needed to check on him.

Fighting through the haze of smoke pouring from the hood, I glimpsed a man with overly gelled hair push open the driver's side door of his crumpled Lincoln. Once outside, he walked behind it, and calmly past Grumpy. Just stepped right over him, not even caring if he was living or breathing. The man had just T-boned us. He should be groggy or as motionless as me. Maybe I'd laid here longer than I thought I had. Wearing expensive wingtip shoes, he squatted down and pushed my hair off my head with a hand so mottled it appeared he'd stuck it in a burning blast furnace. His face was hard when his lips moved, but as much as I tried, I couldn't make out his words past the thick smell of cigar breath. My brain snapped to attention.

Weasel Bonnano, I thought, and I saw the message in his eyes.

"Tell Lincoln Turkey's coming."

NOTE FROM THE AUTHOR

Thank you so much for reading No Brainer! If you read this book and enjoyed it, I'd be honored if you'd recommend it to other friends or readers' groups and leave a star rating at the retailer in which you purchased the book. Your words mean so much to authors and help other readers discover new worlds.

ABOUT THE AUTHOR

A.J. lives in Cincinnati with her husband, two daughters, an ADD dog, and a spoiled hamster burial site in her backyard. When she's not writing, she's reading, binge-watching the heck out of some show or eavesdropping-slash-creeping on those around her. And maybe searching the skies for aliens whenever the mood hits.

For more books and updates, connect with her on social media and at:
https://www.ajlape.com

ACKNOWLEDGMENTS

A special thank you to my husband, Dean, and daughters, Zoe and Mackie, for welcoming Darcy Walker into our family; my parents for drilling in my head that anything is possible; my beta readers—Heather Mcguire, Sandra Ruiter, Joyce Stevens, Mom & Dad, and Brianne Whitmire for helping me polish things up; my critique partner, Debbie Brooks, for the many phone calls and plot "what if" conversations; LaDonna Haddock Thompson for giving me the scoop on detective life; CR Everett, Heather Mcguire, Dodie Miracle, and Kellie Mounce for proofreading; Mary-Nancy Smith, for being a joy and crutch to lean on through every phase of the process; Jeri Conner, Brooke Freiberger, and Justin Strasser for giving me the scoop on O-Town. Kim Shaw for being my author Valentine (I hope you like your character Spike); my sweet Justine Littleton for keeping Darcy alive on FB, the best-dressed fictional character ever, and for organizing my first blog tour; the A. J. Lape Street Team, YA Ninjas, and Secret Sisters for the shares and support; and finally to my fans, FB friends, bloggers, reviewers, and Twitter-verse who have supported me, words can't express how you've made Darcyville feel welcome.